THEY WERE BOUND BY *ok*
A CENTURIES-OLD CONSPIRACY
OF SECRECY AND SCANDAL . . .
NOW ONE VALIANT WOMAN SEEKS
THE TRUTH OF HER HERITAGE—
AND THREATENS TO DESTROY THEM ALL

LILI—Her talent and ambition masked a vulnerability born of childhood grief and love betrayed, but until she determined to face the past she could not defeat it.

ANDY—Descended from a dynasty he despised, he swore to separate himself from the evil done by his forebears . . . even if it cost him the woman he loved.

LOY—Her exquisite beauty concealed tragedy and heart-wrenching loss . . . a legacy that threatened all she cherished.

DIEGO—Brilliant and ruthless, was he a heartless monster or only a man who could never forgive?

IRENE—After half a century she no longer knew truth from lies . . . but she was haunted by the echoes of anguish.

All of them must learn that the sins of the past can be buried, but they can never be forgotten. . . .

Bantam Books by Beverly Byrne

THE FIREBIRDS
THE FLAMES OF VENGEANCE
A LASTING FIRE
THE MORGAN WOMEN

The Firebirds

BEVERLY BYRNE

BANTAM BOOKS
NEW YORK · TORONTO · LONDON · SYDNEY · AUCKLAND

THE FIREBIRDS

A Bantam Fanfare Book/ May 1992

FANFARE and the portrayal of a boxed "ff" are trademarks of Bantam
Books, a division of Bantam Doubleday Dell Publishing Group, Inc.

ISBN 0-553-29613-2

Published simultaneously in the United States and Canada

Bantam Books are published by Bantam Books, a division of Bantam Doubleday Dell Publishing Group, Inc. Its trademark, consisting
of the words "Bantam Books" and the portrayal of a rooster, is Registered in U.S. Patent and Trademark Office and in other countries.
Marca Registrada. Bantam Books, 666 Fifth Avenue, New York, New
York 10103.

PRINTED IN THE UNITED STATES OF AMERICA

RAD   0 9 8 7 6 5 4 3 2 1

Acknowledgments

In the course of researching the Mendoza trilogy I called on the specialized knowledge of many people. My grateful thanks to Dorothea Goode, Lansing Holden, Ursula Minch, Charles Stewart Owens, Judith Trezies Owens, John Southam, and Nuria Tubau Suedes—and to the numerous authors of books written yesterday and years ago whose labors made mine possible. Thanks, too, to the gay and wise and *cariñosa* people of Córdoba, whose foresight has preserved so much of the past in their exquisite city; to my tireless editor, Carolyn Nichols; to my agent, Henry Morrison, whose unwavering support sustained this effort through a long and particularly fraught birthing—and first, last, and in between, to my husband, who bears the silence.

Author's Note

All the settings in this story are real except for Fielding, Massachusetts, which I made up. Those who hail from the place of the sacred cod, as I do, will know where it's supposed to be located, and that it isn't there.

And a final word—the tale of the Mendozas is informed by history, but it is a novelized view of both past and present. Nonetheless, I hope it is not untrue.

Piensa que el suspiro tierno
y el grito, desaparecen
en la corriente del viento . . .

Think that the tender sigh
and the scream, disappear
in the rushing of the wind . . .

—FEDERICO GARCÍA LORCA

❧ Prologue ❧

England: 1939

At a few minutes past two P.M. on the seventh of April, a single ray of sunlight glimmered on the sodden earth of a rainswept garden in Sussex. Lady Swanning tipped her extremely pretty young face upward and felt the welcome warmth. At that moment she heard the first cuckoo of spring.

The bird's distinctive call echoed in the stillness of the garden. It was Good Friday, and most of the staff of the great house had been released from their duties for the afternoon. Lady Swanning and the bird had the far-flung lawns and the beds of tender spring flowers entirely to themselves.

She thought about the cuckoo. Somewhere it would find the nest of another bird and deposit one of its eggs. When the hatchlings emerged, the cuckoo baby would destroy the rightful children, either by pecking them to death or pushing them to the ground. The conscripted foster parents, unaware of how they'd been duped, would nurture the changeling. Lady Swanning believed the cuckoo was a marvelously clever creature.

The sunlight faded and another bank of clouds rolled across the Sussex downs. Lady Swanning glanced at her elegant gold watch. Two-thirty, almost time. Casting a last look at the garden, she began walking toward the great stone house built centuries before.

How sad that she must leave all this. She had loved her life since marriage, adored the excitement of race meetings and dinner parties and balls, thrived on being the feted and admired young wife of Emery Preston-Wilde, the thirteenth Viscount Swanning.

Regret did not alter her decision.

As she had anticipated, the servants had left for church and the house was hushed and still. Lady Swanning and her husband were also expected to attend the service. Emery was to read one of the lessons, as his forebears had done for generations. This year would be different, for reasons which only Lady Swanning understood.

In the gun room she quickly found what she wanted, a Mauser that Emery had appropriated from a German officer in the Great War. Like all her husband's guns, the pistol was oiled and ready. To become a lethal weapon it had only to be loaded with the cartridges kept in a locked drawer in the sixteenth-century Jacobean cabinet. The night before, while Emery slept, she'd taken the key. It had been quite simple.

Loaded now, the small snub-nosed pistol fit easily into the pocket of her tweed jacket. Lady Swanning returned to the long corridor, her footsteps making no sound on the Oriental carpet. Moments later she stood before the study door and looked again at her watch. It was two forty-five.

"I'll be in my study," her husband had said at lunch. "Meet me there and we'll go on to church. Say, quarter to three?" He'd looked up from his poached salmon. "Do try for once to be on time, my dear."

She was exactly on time. Lady Swanning smiled, then went in. Emery stood with his back to her, staring out the tall French doors that led to a walled rose garden. He was a big man. His form blotted out much of the gray light. "Damned rain's starting again," he said without looking around.

"Yes." She took the pistol from her pocket and thumbed off the safety catch. It made only the tiniest sound.

"Well, nothing for it, we have to go."

"No," she said quietly. "I don't think so. Not today."

"Don't be silly. There's no way we can—" He turned, an expression of annoyance on his face. Then he saw the gun. "What are you doing with that?"

She didn't answer. It seemed to her unnecessary since her intention must be obvious.

The cook, the parlor maid, the chauffeur, and her ladyship's social secretary were the skeleton staff in the house that afternoon. At five minutes to three the cook and the maid heard two explosive noises and ran to the study. They found Lord Swanning lying facedown in a pool of blood. Their first impression was that he'd fallen and injured himself. The cook struggled to roll the viscount over. That's when she saw his staring eyes and the gaping, bloody wound in his chest and began to scream.

The chauffeur and the secretary arrived within moments, summoned by the screams, though both subsequently denied hearing the shots.

Lady Swanning was nowhere to be found. The police looked long and hard—until a few months later when war broke out and diverted them—but she seemed to have vanished from the earth.

PART ONE

Lili and Loy

❧ 1 ❧

New York: 1980

On an evening in late April the illustrious Gatzinger Gallery of Modern Art was closed to the public but crammed full of people. No effort had been spared for this show by an artist who happened to be the latest darling of the fickle critics. His single name, Markoff, was repeated dozens of times on a series of sequin-embroidered silk banners suspended from the ceiling. The vivid primary colors of his paintings were spotlighted on black-draped walls.

Lili Cramer stood a few feet from the door and surveyed the throng. The gallery's publicists had done their job. The glitterati were out in force. Within twenty seconds she'd identified Jerry Hall and Robert DeNiro, each the center of a small universe of admirers. Andy Warhol was there. So was Shirley MacLaine. And in the spaces between the major luminaries were slightly less famous faces. Like hers.

"Great show last week, Lili," a man called.

She had no idea who he was, which intensified her frisson of pleasure. Lili grinned and blew a kiss. Then, as if cued by a reprimanding guardian angel, Barbara Walters moved across her line of vision. Lili chuckled. She could forget her delusions of grandeur. Fame was doing your thing in prime time on one of the networks, not half an hour a week on cable. And she'd better stop playing name that celebrity or she'd never find the old friend she'd come to meet.

Barely five feet four in heels, Lili had to stand on tiptoe and crane her neck to begin a systematic search of the crowd. She couldn't hold the position. She gave up trying to spot Peter Fowler from a distance and began working her way toward a familiar-looking head of curly brown hair. Wrong choice, she realized when she got a little closer. Peter was pushing fifty and the man she was stalking was considerably younger. Besides, he didn't have Peter's trademark bushy mustache.

She hesitated, unsure which direction to take. Yet another woman's face came into focus. This time Lili caught her breath in genuine awe. In a room full of beautiful people, this lady shone. She shimmered. She was exquisite. The woman was talking to someone. She tilted her head and laughed. Then, perhaps drawn by the magnetic force of Lili's stare, she turned and their eyes met. For a fleeting second Lili basked in the radiance of the woman's smile. When she looked away, it was as if the lights had gone out. Lili felt . . . deprived. Crazy.

She gave herself a mental shake and resumed her search, allowing the ebb and flow of the crowd to nudge her forward. Moments later she was standing behind Peter Fowler. He was studying a painting with total concentration, unaware of her approach.

Lili moved up and linked her arm through his. "Hi. And before you say anything, I'm not late. I've been here at least fifteen minutes. I couldn't find you in this mad scene."

"Hi. Pretty wild, isn't it? What's your opinion of this guy's stuff?"

"I haven't really looked at it yet. I'm more interested in you. The penguin suit is very becoming." Peter's well-cut dinner jacket sat easily on his broad shoulders. The formality of the starched white shirt and black bow tie somehow accentuated the twinkle of fun in his blue eyes. "Five bucks says the suit's Armani," Lili added.

"You win. Put it on my tab. Listen, I can't believe how long it is since I've seen you." He looked deep into her large hazel eyes, stroked her shiny burnished-mahogany hair, then moved his hand to her forehead as if he were checking for a fever. "Blazing. I'm glad to see that the old Lili Cramer sizzle is still working. Seriously, you look great. Except maybe a touch too thin."

"This side of anorexia, there's no such thing as too thin. And you're supposed to say only nice things on my birthday."

"Okay. How about your special table at Pepe's. Vintage champagne. Lobster bisque. Your all-time-favorite duck with green peppercorns."

"Those are the right words. But I warn you, if the duck's not on tonight, you're history."

"It's on," Peter promised. "I arranged everything with Pepe."

"You really are an angel." She leaned forward and kissed his cheek. "I can't wait. Let's go."

"In a minute. First, tell me what you think of this picture."

The painting he'd been examining was a wash of enamel-shiny pink bisected with two jagged-edged stripes of dark red that seemed to drip blood. Lili gave the canvas her full attention for something less than five seconds. Then she shook her head. "I don't like it. As a matter of fact, I hate it."

Peter shrugged. "So do I. Which is odd, because I very much like Loyola Perez."

"Who's she?"

"The lady who owns this dubious masterpiece that's worth maybe a million. She lent it for the show. I met her last night at the little party before the big party. They're giving Markoff the full treatment."

"And you, apparently. I didn't know that importing arty magazines got you on the A list in these rarified circles."

"Sometimes it does." Peter took her arm. "Come on, let's get out of here. I'm starved."

They worked their way through the crowd to the foyer. Lili kept trying to spot the woman whose looks had so stunned her earlier. No luck. She felt oddly let down. She wanted to see her again, confirm that extraordinary first impression, ask Peter for his. Apparently, the woman had left, and though it was ridiculous, that made Lili sad. Then, while they were waiting to reclaim their coats from the checkroom, she suddenly appeared—alone, which seemed incredible—and came straight toward them. "Peter," Lili began eagerly, "do you by any chance—"

Before she could finish the question, Peter had left her side. Lili watched him stride forward and stretch out his hand. The woman took it and Lili saw again that luminous smile. She hadn't been mistaken. This was undoubtedly the most beautiful female she'd ever seen.

It was impossible to guess her age, her looks were timeless. She had a full-lipped, plummy mouth set below prominent cheekbones and a classic straight nose. The shape of her head was breathtakingly lovely, perfectly sculpted. The effect was enhanced by black hair drawn sleekly into a luxuriantly thick chignon at the nape of her long neck. She was wearing an austere black gown, her only accessory a pair of sparkling earrings that Lili was certain were real rubies.

Peter and the woman moved closer. Lili heard Peter say, "I saw your painting. It's certainly interesting." Then they'd reached Lili's side. "Señora Perez," Peter said. "I'd like you to meet my old and very dear friend Lili Cramer. You've probably seen her on television telling you what and where to eat. Lili, this is Loyola Perez."

Silence. Neither woman spoke. Lili knew she was staring, but she couldn't help herself. Inexplicably, Loyola Perez totally unnerved her. Most remarkable of all, she seemed equally taken aback.

It was Señora Perez who spoke first. "So this is Lili Cramer," she said softly. "How extraordinary . . . Lili Cramer." This time her smile was different: softer and somehow more personal. "I'm absolutely delighted to meet you, my dear. I have seen you on television—many times—and I love your show."

"Thank you," Lili murmured.

A man appeared, nodded to Peter and Lili, and whisked Loyola Perez away. For a moment they stared after her. Lili summed it up. "Wow."

"Yeah," Peter said. "That's what I think too."

Pepe's was a little restaurant in Greenwich Village that Lili had discovered the previous year and helped to make famous. So it wasn't surprising that Pepe himself greeted them enthusiastically.

"Welcome, Lili. Happy birthday. Tonight we cook for you a symphony. Mr. Fowler and me, we've arranged everything."

They had the same table in the rear where Lili had sat when she put the restaurant on television. That was one of the things that made her show so popular. On *Dining Out, Eating In* Lili took her camera crews into actual restaurants and talked about the food as it was served. Then she went into the kitchen and discussed its equipment and layout and the special features of the design.

Two years earlier few people had believed the program would have nationwide appeal, but Lili had proved them wrong. At heart everyone was a voyeur, even in Peoria and Kansas City. When you weren't salivating over *Dallas* or *Falcon Crest*, what better to spy on than glitzy New York?

"First a little pastry with a bit of cheese," Pepe said and snapped his fingers. Two waiters materialized. One opened a bottle of Dom Pérignon, the other produced a plate of hot morsels of buttery crust spiraled with pungent Gorgonzola.

Peter and Lili sampled the food and the wine and pronounced both wonderful. After that they were left alone.

"Happy birthday." Peter lifted his champagne in a toast. "Thank you for spending it with me."

"Thank you for remembering and suggesting it."

"Do I detect a hint of poor-me?"

"Maybe a little around the edges. Peter, do you realize I'm thirty today?"

"Welcome to adulthood. From my ancient vantage point thirty is barely past being a little kid."

"I looked close in the mirror this morning. Lines."

He chuckled. "Change your night cream. Maybe you'll grow up to look like Loyola Perez."

"Fat chance," Lili said glumly. "Peter, she knocks me out, blows me away. I don't know why she has such an effect on me, but . . ." Lili let the words trail away. It was hard for her to understand her reactions to Loyola Perez, much less explain them. And there was also the question of Señora Perez's reactions to her. "Listen, was it my imagination, or was she examining me like a bug under a microscope?"

"I saw some evidence of more than a passing interest," Peter admitted. "I was going to ask you about it."

Lili shrugged. "I don't have any explanation. Unless—Peter, is she perhaps a new item in your social calendar?"

He threw back his head and guffawed. "I should be so lucky. I met her only last night. I'm told she's horrendously wealthy but doesn't do the society rounds. Apparently, this event was an exception because she was one of Markoff's first buyers."

She knew he was telling the truth; nonetheless, Lili had a familiar feeling of injured proprietorship. She always reacted this way to the women in Peter's life. She knew it was absurd—they'd been nothing but friends for over five years.

If Peter were aware of her thoughts, he didn't let on. "Tell me everything you've been doing," he said. "I haven't seen you in almost two months."

"I will, but first you tell me how you remembered my birthday. I was astounded when you called last week."

"No mystery." He grinned at her. "It's been marked in my calendar since 1974 in London. Every year I transfer the notation."

She sipped her champagne and leaned back. "London, 1974. It seems like another lifetime."

"Stop being maudlin. Six years isn't such a long time. Things don't change that much. By the way, that's a great sweater."

It was white, hand-knit, and had a black sequined butterfly on the front. Lili had paired it with black silk trousers. "The outfit's a birthday present from me to me," she said. "I'm glad you like it."

"I do. But I can remember when you never bought anything except jeans. Is this a new Lili?"

"Not exactly. I have to dress well for the show. Besides, I can afford more than jeans now."

"I've been meaning to ask you about that. Why don't you buy a condo? You must be making a fortune."

"Peter, I'm on cable. With the exercise freaks and the sex doctors and the phony wrestlers and the late-night blue movies. It's not network, lover. Rich I'm not."

"All the same, you're the one who once told me that buying was cheaper in the long run."

She'd made the comment when they were both Americans abroad, making their way in London. Lili had bought a house, but Peter had always lived in a rented apartment.

"Of course buying is better," Lili agreed. "But you need some capital for a down payment. Mine is otherwise engaged." For four years she'd been plowing every penny she could spare into a go-go mutual fund. Lili was saving for a purpose she nurtured in her heart—and never discussed.

"But you pay rent," Peter insisted. "That's pouring money down the drain."

"Not really. I have a ten-year lease and my outlay is less than the maintenance on a condo would be. How did we get into this boring conversation?"

"I don't know. From your sweater I think. You were going to tell me what you've been doing."

"So I was. The show once a week, of course. That takes about fifteen hours of preparation. And a few remodeling jobs. I'm doing a restaurant kitchen near Lincoln Center at the moment. And Dan Kerry, my agent, is trying to sell a book based on the television series. And I've been talking to a cookware company that's hoping to move up-market. They want to use me in their ad campaign. We might make a deal."

"Don't sign anything without a smart lawyer," Peter admonished.

Lili nodded. "Don't worry, Dan Kerry looks after me."

A waiter arrived with the lobster bisque Peter and Pepe had decided on. The soup was surprisingly delicate, thin scallops of lobster and light-as-air circles of salmon mousse in a tarragon-scented cream. A spray of fresh tarragon decorated the shallow bowls, and within minutes it was all that was left. "Exquisite," Lili proclaimed.

Pepe himself brought the juicy rare duck breast to their table. He carved it with careful concentration and set the succulent pink slices atop a sauce fragrant with brandy and green peppercorns. Later there was a birthday cake made of almond meringue layers and mocha butter cream. "Heaven is here and now," Lili told Pepe and Peter as she finished the last bite. "I can't thank you guys enough."

"Me you thank only for the champagne," the restaurateur admitted. "For the rest Mr. Fowler pays."

Peter and Lili giggled and Pepe left them alone with a bottle of superb Armagnac.

An hour later they were in a taxi heading uptown to her apartment on East Eighty-first Street. Lili leaned over and kissed Peter's cheek. "You're wonderful. It was a spectacular birthday dinner."

He hugged her quickly. "I enjoyed it too. And you deserve the best, Lili." He turned serious. "Don't settle for less."

"I don't plan to."

The taxi stopped in front of her building. Lili got out and waited while Peter paid the fare. "Come up for coffee," she said.

"Love to, only I mustn't stay late. I have a breakfast appointment tomorrow. It's one of New York's more insane habits, but easy to fall into."

Lili's apartment was lovely; she couldn't live anywhere without making it so. None of the furniture was particularly expensive. There were no antiques or designer originals. Instead, everything was intensely personal. Rather than a sofa, Lili had outsize chairs upholstered in a vibrant teal blue and dusty rose chintz. The floor was covered with diminutive old Oriental carpets she'd picked up for a song. They were faded and worn, and somehow because of that they worked brilliantly in the room.

There were a number of house plants, but books were the most important feature of the decor. Lili continually added to the eclectic collection she'd brought from England. Many of the shelves were filled with cookbooks, some old and rare and valuable. They were her special passion.

The kitchen was Mexican in feeling, blue and white tiles and a terra-cotta floor. Peter stood in the doorway and watched her grind fresh beans and add a cardamom seed to the brewing coffee. "A lady who practices what she preaches. But what would your public think of this kitchen? It's pretty, but you don't have all the high-tech built-ins."

"Of course not. I don't own this place, as you were reminding me earlier."

"I suppose we'd better not start that again."

"No."

Lili poured the aromatic coffee into small pristine white cups, put them on a slick electric-blue tray, and carried them into the living room. They sat across from each other in her oversize chairs, toes almost touching on the large hassock between them. She'd put some Bach on the stereo, the Juilliard String Quartet playing the fourth Brandenburg concerto. They sipped and listened.

Tonight the elegant precision of the music didn't work its usual magic for Lili, and the coffee tasted bitter and unsatisfying. Thirty years old. Fighting all the time to get ahead and stay ahead.

She glanced at Peter. His eyes were closed, his pleasant face appealing in repose. He still wore his hair slightly long, and neither it nor his mustache betrayed any hint of gray. Steady, kind, reliable, unchanging Peter. No man she'd ever known had the power to hold on to her affection so well. Lili felt a surge of warmth and gratitude for his friendship. Maybe she was a fool, maybe she should try again to feel something more than sisterly warmth for this thoroughly nice man.

The Bach finished with a series of elegant violin intricacies that drew all the themes together, then ended with a deeply satisfying chord. The silence quivered.

"There is order in the universe," Peter said softly.

He took a deep breath, put down his cup, crossed to her, and lay his hand on her head. Lili leaned against him. Neither of them said anything for long seconds. Then Peter gently pushed her away. "No. Not the right reasons, sweetheart. I'm sorry, but I'd know I'm only a substitute for the real thing. You're still pining over—"

Lili held up her hand. "Please, don't say his name. I can't stand it."

"You've proved my point."

She smiled a rueful sort of smile. "I suppose I have. And you're probably right about tonight. So good night, and thanks for a special evening."

Loyola Perez called Peter Fowler a week after the museum party. "You probably don't remember me. We met—"

"Of course I remember you." Her voice conjured her image—extraordinary beauty enhanced by an aura of power and mystery. "I'm delighted to hear from you, Señora Perez, but to what do I owe the pleasure?"

"I think I'm being silly, but I want to locate a magazine I knew in Spain years ago. A sort of gossipy weekly. I'm wondering if it's still published and it occurred to me that you might know."

He pulled a pad and pencil from the corner of the desk. "If you give me the name, I can probably find out."

She did and he said he'd check and get back to her.

A few days later he telephoned. "*Semana* is still in business, but not distributed over here. I managed to get my hands on a few copies for you."

"That's marvelous! How very kind. You must come for a drink, Mr. Fowler. Please."

When he hung up Peter was grinning.

He'd imagined Loyola Perez in some super East Side apartment, maybe in one of the fabulous buildings on Fifth Avenue overlooking Central Park, but she lived in the Village on West Tenth Street. It was a good address, not a great one. When he got inside he understood. The house had been built around the turn of the century and never chopped into apartments. It boasted high ceilings, wonderful parquet floors, at least one fireplace, and lovely old paneling.

"What a fabulous home," he enthused.

"I'm lucky. In Manhattan a whole house is a rarity. What do you drink, Mr. Fowler?"

"Scotch and water, and please call me Peter."

"If you will call me Loy."

"Your name's a rarity too. Can I ask its origins?"

She poured whiskey into his glass and paused before adding ice or water. "Do you really want me to dilute this?"

Peter glanced toward the ebony Chinese table where she was fixing drinks and saw the bottle of pale single malt. "Definitely not. I didn't realize you were going to produce such a treasure."

The long green dress she wore swished lightly on the thick rug when she crossed the room to bring him his drink. It was the most sensuous of sounds. Peter took the glass but didn't manage to touch her fingers. He wanted to. He felt like a kid at the movies, fantasizing about a glamorous star on the screen.

"Getting back to your question, my name is Spanish," Loy said. "For St. Ignatius of Loyola. It's a town in northern Spain."

"Do you come from Spain? You speak perfect American English."

She laughed the vibrant, throaty laugh that delighted him. "I should. I was born and raised in New England, of Spanish descent as it happens. I married a man from Madrid when I was very young. He took me to Spain and I stayed there until a few years ago."

Peter wondered if she was widowed or divorced. It was not the sort of question he felt he could ask. Warm and friendly as she was, Loy had a way of holding intimacy at bay. "Did you like Spain?" he asked instead.

"Very much. But I like New York too."

He sipped the smoky-tasting whiskey and couldn't think of a single thing to say. This woman tied his tongue, made him feel callow and awkward. Nonetheless, he adored being in the same room with her.

She was the perfect hostess, quick to fill any lull in the conversation. "Of course since Franco's death and the coming of what they call *democracia,* everything has changed."

"For the better?"

Loy hesitated. "For the young people and the future, yes, certainly. For those of us who had grown comfortable with the old ways, it's not so clear-cut."

"But Franco was a tyrant, a dictator."

She shrugged and the green hostess gown moved with a sighing rustle. "Yes, but even dictators have their uses."

"I suppose so." He finished his drink and refused another. "I'd love it, but I have a dinner engagement."

Loy smiled. "I hope she's young and beautiful."

"*He* is old and ugly," Peter said. "In this town they do

business at all three meals. It's crazy, but I've learned you have to run with the pack or get left behind."

"Surely you don't spend all your time doing business, Peter?"

He chuckled. "I try not to. And before I forget, here are your magazines." He took three copies of the gaudy weekly from his briefcase. "I hope this is what you wanted."

She thumbed through them with a look of pleasure. "Oh, yes, exactly. You must think me very crude. But I so miss the gossip, the everyday things. After all those years . . ." She let the explanation trail away and smiled a small, slightly guilty smile.

He caught himself wondering how old she was. Fifty maybe, possibly a year or two more. It was immaterial. Loyola Perez was a woman beyond any glib categorization by age. "I understand perfectly," he said. "I'll try to get some more copies and see if they'll accept a foreign subscription."

It was as he was leaving that Loy said he must come to dinner sometime. "Sometime soon," she added. "May I call you to arrange things?"

"I would like that very much." She had put out her hand and he'd taken it; now he was reluctant to let it go. "Look, I'd like to suggest something more definite. I'm going abroad on business in a couple of days, but perhaps—"

Loy extracted her hand from his, but she favored him with another of her spectacular smiles. "Call me when you get back. We'll arrange something."

She sounded absolutely sincere. It wasn't one of those comments like "Let's have lunch sometime." She meant it. She wanted to see him again.

Peter walked down Tenth Street feeling as exhilarated as he'd ever felt in his life. What was it Lili had said? Wow! Yeah, wow and double wow.

❧ 2 ❧

New York and Florida: 1980

Peter Fowler had developed the concept behind his business while he was in London. In those days he'd been editor of the British edition of an up-market American design magazine. When changes at the top cost him his job, he'd rejected the idea of staying in publishing, but magazines were the only thing he knew. Which led to his idea.

The notion of importing foreign publications wasn't unique, but Peter had combed Europe and ferreted out journals that were small, specialized, and largely unknown. What they had in common was a concentration on art and exclusivity. After he put the list together he forged an efficient distribution network based on supplying private subscribers and the various stopping and shopping places of the international set.

It was a small business and the market was so limited it was destined to remain so. Peter and a secretary did it all. In early May he had to leave her in charge while he took a long-scheduled business trip to Europe.

As soon as he got back to New York he phoned Loy. He'd been counting the minutes until he could do so. "This is Peter Fowler. How are you?"

"Very well, thanks. How nice to hear from you. Are you enjoying our tardy spring?"

Outside his office Manhattan was basking in newly arrived warmth and sun. "Loving it, but from a distance. All the year's the same in my climate-controlled cell."

"What a shame."

"Yes, it is. Listen, I'm calling because I was in Madrid last week, and I picked up some reading material for you."

"Peter, you are a treasure, a kind and thoughtful man." Her voice was both gay and sincere. There was nothing brittle in Loyola Perez's charm.

"I could send them over by messenger, or better yet we could meet for lunch."

"We could, but I have a nicer idea. Will you come to dinner on Friday?"

"I'd love to."

"Wonderful. We'll be ten I think, maybe twelve. Perhaps you'll bring that charming Miss Cramer. I'm a great fan, I'd love to see her again."

When they hung up he called Lili. "You've been invited to dinner with Loyola Perez. Friday night. How about it, will you come?"

"Why should I? You'll moon over her all evening."

"Probably," he agreed. "But you should come anyway, because she's special. Like you."

"Well, you wiggled out of that one," Lili said. "Okay, I'm free as it happens. What time?"

"Eight-thirty. Pick you up at eight."

The evening was lovely, with only the slightest hint of a chill. Lili wore an emerald green velvet hacking jacket over an ice-blue satin jump suit, with lots of gold chains and small opal studs in her ears. Peter said she looked great.

"What about the earrings?" she demanded anxiously.

He had to push back her chin-length hair and peer closely to see them. "They're fine. What about them?"

"They're the first pair I've ever worn in my life. I had my ears pierced a couple of weeks ago."

He chuckled. "Lili, you're a case of arrested development. C'mon, we don't want to be late."

He hadn't warned her, and the block and the outside of the house were no preparation. Lili caught her breath when a white-jacketed butler opened the door to a candlelit entry foyer hung with impressive paintings in heavy gilt frames.

They were shown into the living room and Loy came to them at once. She wore a long red silk skirt and matching jacket with a white lace blouse and a jeweled comb in her black hair. Instantly Lili felt awkward and badly dressed.

The warmth of Loyola Perez's greeting dispelled the feeling. It wasn't what she said but the way she said it. "I'm so pleased you could come, Miss Cramer." She took Lili's hand. "Let me introduce you to the others."

"Please call me Lili."

"I'd like that very much."

There were nine other guests. Two couples who looked fortyish and seemed to have something to do with auctions and antiques, a young woman reporter for the *Times* with a man whose occupation was unclear, and an elderly Venezuelan poet named Santiago, who was apparently in the role of host.

When they went in to dinner Lili found herself on the Venezuelan's left. He had a silvery goatee and mustache and twinkling eyes, and he wore a rusty-black satin jacket and a string tie. "You are on television?" he asked Lili.

"Yes. I have a weekly program on cable."

He leaned over and twinkled even more. "And what do you do weekly on cable?"

"I talk about restaurants and kitchens and food."

Santiago seemed to find this enormously amusing. He laughed heartily. "But that's wonderful. Only in America."

"And what are you doing here?"

"Reading poetry in Spanish in drafty dark halls where very few people come."

After dinner the butler served coffee and brandy in the living room, while clever talk and tinkling laughter made a mellow accompaniment to the elegant surroundings. Lili sipped from a fragile porcelain cup and kept sneaking looks at her hostess. Maybe Loy Perez wouldn't look so beautiful in the cold light of day, but right now she was spectacular.

A few moments later Loy came and sat beside her. "I've been longing to talk to you, Lili. I must confess I'm addicted to your show. I never miss it. It isn't very sophisticated of me to admit that when you're a guest in my house, is it?"

Lili laughed heartily. "I think it's great. Thank you, you've made my evening."

Loy laughed with her, the gray eyes danced and sparkled and there was a hint of conspiracy in her smile. "The rest of them are pretty dull, aren't they?" she said very softly. "Let's ignore them. Tell me how you learned so much about food and kitchens."

Before long Lili, usually so guarded about the things closest to her heart, was chatting eagerly with this extraordinary woman. After twenty minutes she realized she'd been speaking nonstop. "God! I'm sorry. You seem to have uncorked me and it all fizzed over."

"Like champagne," Loy said. "I enjoyed it." She sounded as if she meant it. "Now I have to play hostess. Can we meet again and talk some more, Lili?"

"I'd like that," Lili said.

After a few days Lili's thoughts about Loyola Perez dimmed in the press of work. Dan Kerry had an idea for a new twist on her show, kitchens in history. He wanted to make a pilot and tout it to the networks. Getting picked up by CBS or NBC or ABC was the ultimate goal in Lili's world. It represented prestige, a seal of approval no cable station could convey, and a good deal more money for her to stash away for her special project.

Lili put in hours on the pilot while continuing all her other commitments. There was no time to think of anything but business until a night in June when she came home after eleven and found a message from Loyola Perez on her answering machine. Would Lili please return the call—any time up to one A.M?

"You did really mean for me to call this late, didn't you?" Lili asked when Loy answered the phone.

"Oh, yes, I don't go to sleep until the small hours of the morning. A terrible Spanish habit, but I can't break it."

"Do you siesta too?"

Loy giggled. "My secret vice. Yes, I do sometimes. Listen, my dear, I called to ask if you ever take private customers. I'm longing to do something with my kitchen."

Lili said that she did, and the following week she was again in Loy's house.

This time there were no servants visible and everything was much less formal. Loy wore a navy cotton skirt and a green blouse, and her legs were bare and her feet in green leather thongs. The living room was bright with sun. Maybe Loy wasn't as young as she first seemed, Lili realized, but she was equally gorgeous without the candlelight. Some women had all the luck. She wanted to dislike Loyola Perez, but it was impossible not to respond to her charm.

Lili fought its lure. She made an effort to assert her own personality, her professionalism. "Okay, let's get down to business. Show me the kitchen."

Loy led her through the dining room and the butler's pantry into a large room with avocado-green appliances and white cabinets. To Lili's experienced eye it was obviously an old kitchen that had been updated sometime in the sixties.

"The first thing to think about is how you use it," Lili said. "How much cooking do you do?"

Loy looked chagrined. "I don't. I never learned how. I employ a couple, the wife cooks. Today's their day off," she added. "Look."

She opened the refrigerator. There was a covered casserole with a note on the lid that gave heating instructions, and a plastic-wrapped sandwich garnished with parsley and carrot curls.

"Got it," Lili said. "You want to do the kitchen over so the cook will love you so much she'll never leave. That's the problem with servants, I'm told."

Loy cocked her head. "Are you rubbing my nose in the uselessness of belonging to the privileged class?"

"Did it sound like that? I'm sorry. It's none of my business. And anybody who looks as decorative as you do certainly isn't useless."

"Decorative," Loy said softly. "Yes, I suppose that's mostly been my function. Don't blame me for it, Lili, I really never had any choice. Now, what about this pedestrian room? Can you make it wonderful?"

"Yes, I can. But I can't suggest anything specific without talking to your cook. A kitchen is very personal."

Loy shook her head. "She won't cooperate. She hates the idea of all the remodeling mess."

"Then why do it?"

Loy shrugged and perched on a stool drawn up by the counter. "Maybe I'm simply bored. Maybe it's not a good idea."

"No, I don't think it is."

Loy brightened. "But you're here and that's nice. Let's go around the corner for lunch. There's a new Japanese place on Sixth Avenue. Do you like sushi?"

"Love it," Lili admitted.

Within an hour she also had to admit to herself that she also loved Loyola Perez. Apart from her phenomenal looks, Loy was easy to be with, and she had a marvelous sense of humor. They laughed a lot and by the time Lili left they'd made a lunch date for the following week.

In July Peter called and invited Lili to a Mets game to be followed by an early supper. From the start of the afternoon she knew something was bothering him. The fact that the Mets lost didn't help.

After the game she suggested pizza, but he was set on barbecue at some new place he'd heard of in the wilds of Queens. The cabbie didn't know where it was and they got lost. It was after seven and they were starving by the time they arrived at the restaurant.

Peter's expression was positively grim. Lili fumbled around the edges of his mood, but she couldn't find the right moment to flatly ask him what was wrong.

Eventually a small mountain of ribs and two mighty steins of beer were delivered to their booth. The ribs were fantastic. Peter gave her a look that said "I told you so," but they ate in silence until he finally asked, "You've been seeing a lot of Loy Perez, haven't you?"

At first Lili didn't realize it was more than a casual question. She put down a bone she'd chewed clean and wiped her fingers on one of a stack of thick paper napkins. "Mmm, yes. Have you?"

"I try to. Only I don't seem to have your appeal."

His tone told her more than the words. Lili hesitated. "Peter, she's a lot older than you are."

"I don't think so. I'm forty-eight. Four, maybe five years."

"I don't know for sure, but I think she could be older."

"Nuts. No way."

"Okay. It's not important, is it?"

He shrugged. "You're the one who brought up age. More to the point, do you know if she's widowed or divorced? I keep wondering if she's holding me off because there's a Señor Perez alive and well and living God knows where? Maybe she's still married."

Lili looked pensive. "Loy's never mentioned it."

"Not to me either. Okay, answer an easier one, does she ever talk about me?"

He was like a teenager having a first crush. Any little crumb would do. Lili reached over and touched his hand. "Quite a bit, as a matter of fact."

Loy did mention Peter's name frequently. But Lili had the impression Loy was matchmaking, encouraging Lili to think romantically of Peter. She decided she'd better not explain.

"What does she say?" he demanded.

"That she likes you a lot." That was true.

"That's all? She likes me?"

Lili hesitated again. There was no point in misleading him, it wasn't fair. "That's all I'm aware of." She searched for something to dispel his gloom. "Tell you what, Loy's coming to my place for dinner Tuesday night. It was going to be the two of us and girl talk. You come too. It will be fun."

"I'm not much on girl talk," Peter said.

"For God's sake, don't be difficult, Peter. What about it, will you come?"

He nodded and even managed to smile.

"It will be fun," Lili said again.

It was, and that started a pattern.

Usually it was Loy who suggested arrangements. She was always saying things like "Peter, come and listen to music with Lili and me. I have a new recording of Placido Domingo doing *Don Giovanni* at Covent Garden." Or "I found this wonderful new Mexican restaurant, let's you and me and Lili go."

Much as he was besotted by Loy, and he admitted to Lili that he was, the trio made Peter uncomfortable. The friendship between the two women seemed to him a wholly female thing, slightly exclusive and exotic.

"You're crazy," Lili said when he mentioned it. "It's 1980, friends don't come by gender. Anyway, I never exclude you and neither does Loy."

No, far from it—but neither would Loy exclude Lili. A couple of times Lili deliberately begged off because she knew how Peter felt. But Loy didn't suggest that she and Peter go ahead anyway. She merely changed the date or the time and the threesome continued.

Inevitably, there were occasions when Lili saw Loy without Peter. A shopping trip, for instance, like the one in September when Lili wanted to buy a raincoat at a sale in Bloomingdale's. It wouldn't occur to her to involve Peter, but it was perfectly natural to ask Loy to come along and advise.

"Nothing here is right," Loy said after they pawed through the racks of special-purchase coats.

Lili sighed. "No. Too bad. I really need a raincoat."

"You give up too easily," Loy said, and insisted they look in the Calvin Klein boutique. "He's just right for you, Lili. The right line and the right feeling. Casual elegance."

It was an attitude Lili had never developed. Her closet was full of things she didn't like after she got them home, and nothing ever seemed to go with anything else. Lili was sure about taste and design in many areas, but when it came to clothes, she lacked the confidence to say that any designer's style was "right" for her.

Loy's touch, on the other hand, was sure. She had what all women want and few possess—flair. She went directly to a rack containing three coats and selected one. "This is it, try it on."

Lili did and it was perfect. It had a great cut and was a dark but lively gray-blue that suited her coloring. She pulled out her charge card and they found a salesgirl. Then they waited for the interminable numbers to be tapped into the computer.

Lili glanced at her watch. "I've got an appointment in forty-five minutes, but we have time for a sandwich if you're hungry."

"Starved," Loy admitted.

They went downstairs to the store's Espresso Bar because that was faster than going out and looking for a restaurant. Both women resisted croissants stuffed with ham and melted cheese and ordered salads. It was while they were eating that Loy announced she was going to Palm Beach for the month of October.

"That's early for Florida," Lili said. "Why don't you wait until it gets colder?"

"I'm perverse, I love New York in the winter. Anyway, I'm not going for a vacation. I have a house in Palm Beach. The problem is I hate the place."

"Don't let the chamber of commerce hear that. They'll burn a cross on your lawn, or tar and feather you or something."

Loy sighed. "I know. I admitted to being perverse."

"Why did you buy the house if you hate Palm Beach?"

"It seemed like a good idea at the time. All that sun, it felt a little like Spain. But it's not my sort of place. I gave the house to an agent to rent because the real estate market was depressed. Now it's better, so I think I should go down and make arrangements to sell."

They finished their salads and Lili succumbed to the lure of blackberry sherbet. Loy settled for coffee. "Is Palm Beach near Stuart?" Lili asked.

Loy was stirring a low calorie sugar substitute into her cup. She didn't look up. "About forty miles south. Why do you ask?"

"My mother lives in Stuart."

Loy was still staring at her coffee. "Oh, does she? You never mention your mother."

That was true. Lili never spoke of the past and neither did Loy. Their friendship was based on enjoying the moment. "There's nothing much to mention," she said. "We keep in touch, but we're not close."

"But Lili, that's awful. Surely—"

Lili held up her hand. "Don't lecture me. My mother is unique. Not your average loving parent. I got fed up and something that happened years and years ago finally stuck in my throat and I exploded."

"When was this?"

"The explosion almost five years ago, the other thing a few years before that."

"That's a long time to carry a grudge. Are you sure you're still angry, or is it simply a habit?"

"Oh, I'm still angry all right. But it's not an outright split. We talk on the phone about once a month."

Loy shook her beautifully groomed head. "That's not good enough. You should try to see things from her point of view. She probably feels terrible that she doesn't see more of you."

"You don't know Irene Petworth Cramer," Lili said. Then she added impulsively, "Loy, do you have any children?" It was strange that they'd become really close friends and she didn't know that. Strange, too, that after she asked the question Lili was embarrassed. She had a sense of invading forbidden territory.

Loy didn't meet Lili's eyes. "No," she murmured.

Lili realized she'd intruded on an old sadness. She felt rotten. "Oh, well, sometimes the mother-daughter thing isn't so great. Me and Irene for instance."

"I think you may regret your attitude. Why not come to Florida for a few days while I'm there? You could stay with me and visit your mother."

A waiter appeared with the check and Lili grabbed it. "No, it's my turn," she replied to Loy's protest. That sort of gesture was important to her; she wasn't trading on Loy's fortune. "As for the visit, thanks for asking, but I can't get away at the moment. We're still working on the pilot. Dan thinks there's a good chance one of the networks will bite."

When they parted, Lili wasn't thinking of the all-important pilot. She was thinking of old wounds that had never healed.

As Loy had told Lili, the town of Stuart was only forty miles from Palm Beach. It was an easy drive over excellent roads. Loy was there in half an hour.

The complex she was seeking was set back from the highway and despite its size had only one well-guarded entrance. Security was a high value in these parts, originality was not. The development, called Casas del Sol, consisted of a grid of look-alike streets that a builder had plunked down on a stretch of flat Florida real estate.

Loy easily found the corner of Bella Vista Road and Conquistador Drive. She parked the car beside a duplex apartment with a small pergola-shaded terrace and a lawn so perfectly manicured it looked like plastic. The grounds were tended by the management. Casas del Sol promised carefree living.

There was no need to ring. Irene Cramer had been standing by the window, watching. She opened the door instantly. "Come in." Her voice had a thickened quality, as if she'd been crying.

"How are you? You look well."

"I am well." Irene took the paisley shawl Loy wore over a white linen dress and laid it carefully across the back of a cushioned wicker chair. "I've made tea. Would you like to be inside or out?"

"Inside," Loy said. "The sun's terribly hot."

Irene poured spiced orange-scented tea into simple white cups. "Constant Comment," she said softly. "You used to love it."

"I still do." Loy sipped the tea delicately, then set the cup on the saucer. "Irene, don't be angry with me. It happened quite naturally. I had to do only the smallest amount of manipulating. There's this man she's friendly with. His name's Peter Fowler, he's very nice. I met him by chance, and through him I met her. It really was an accident of fate. Lili doesn't suspect a thing. How could she?"

"I don't know. But Lili's very smart, very quick. Don't underestimate her."

"I'm not going to. You mustn't worry." Loy looked across the wicker table that separated them. Irene was staring at her clenched hands. The knuckles were white. "It will be all right," Loy said. "I promise. She finally mentioned the trouble between you. I'm sure I can smooth it over. You'd like that, wouldn't you?"

Irene shrugged. "Yes, I would. But you won't change her mind. Not even you. Lili is . . . tenacious. Once she gets an idea, that's it."

"We'll see," Loy said. Irene's misery seemed to exude an aura and Loy felt her pain. Looking away from Irene's rigid figure, Loy surveyed the room. "I didn't realize you still had that." She pointed to a painting of an English country scene.

"Yes," Irene said. "I kept it after I sold everything else. I intended to give it to Lili as a memento, but the way she feels now, I don't dare mention it."

Loy nodded. "Keep it until things are better between you. I'm sure they will be eventually." She cocked her dark head and looked more closely at the painting. "Odd to think that's the only thing left."

Irene twisted a handkerchief between her white fingers. "You sound like Lili. I didn't do anything wrong. I told you years ago, I was being sensible. I didn't want to burden you."

"Of course. I understand. Besides, I think you've done everything right from the moment she was born."

"Thank you, that's important to me." Irene's cheeks flushed with pleasure, but she still didn't smile.

"Irene, please, you mustn't be angry with me."

"I'm not, at least not about Lili. Why shouldn't you get to know her? When she first went abroad, I suggested Spain. I thought I'd put her in your path, so to speak. But she insisted on England. What I'm upset about is that you haven't come here in such a long time. Palm Beach and Stuart are close, that's what we said. But you rented the house to strangers, and now you're selling. Anyway, you spend all your time in Manhattan."

"I have to be careful," Loy said.

"I know." Irene sighed. "We won't talk about the past anymore." She leaned forward and took Loy's hand and for the first time that afternoon she smiled.

That night Irene followed her long-established ritual. She stood naked in front of a full-length mirror and carefully examined her reflection. She ran her palms along her thighs and over her belly and up her midriff, and finally cupped her small breasts in her hands. Then she leaned forward and examined her face, tracing her features with quick, exploratory fingers—as if she needed to be reassured of her existence.

Somewhere beyond the window an owl hooted. Irene thought of other birds in other places, of the cuckoos of England and the ravens of France and the hoopoes of Spain. She half turned and glanced back over her shoulder at her buttocks. They were still firm and tight, though she wasn't young anymore. She half closed her eyes and she thought she saw a whip rise and fall. The image was so vivid she flinched. And began to sob.

A few moments later she was calm. She reminded herself that everything was different now. She was safe. Irene dried her eyes and put on a white batiste nightgown embroidered with rosebuds and crawled into her narrow bed. She slept soundly and chastely and without regrets.

❧ 3 ❧

Fielding, Massachusetts: 1955–63

Most folks in the small town of Fielding felt sorry for little Lili Cramer, who lived in the big house on Woods Road and had only one parent.

It was the child's mother, Irene Petworth Cramer, who made the townspeople uneasy and stirred their sympathy for Lili. Irene was one of their own, born and raised in Fielding, but they'd always had doubts about her. She had left home years before, and they would have forgotten her entirely if she hadn't come back in '51 as a widow with a baby daughter. Since then the vaguely negative reactions had grown more pronounced.

For one thing, Irene never permitted Lili to call her Mom or Mommy. The little girl always had to say "Mother." For another, according to Rose Carmichael, who cleaned for the Cramers, the child was made to be unnaturally careful with her toys. " 'It was expensive, Lili,' that's what Irene always says," Rose reported.

Each time Rose left the house on Woods Road she went to the grocery store on Fielding's main street to gossip. "I don't know what's going to become of Lili," she said on one of these visits. "It's not right, the way she's being brought up."

The other women nodded their heads and made disapproving noises. "Call her Irene Petworth or Irene Cramer," one of them said. "Marriage didn't change her a bit. And now she's giving herself airs because she's living in the big house."

"Nothing new in that," another added. "Irene always gave herself airs. Grew up an iceberg and she still is. And she's freezing that poor little girl to death." -

What they didn't know was that the child had found something to love. Long before she understood what made the house she lived in unique and beautiful, Lili fastened all her affection and trust on it. In her mind the house became a substitute for the father she'd never known.

"He died when you were born," Irene explained each time Lili asked. "Then we came home."

By the time she was five and the women in the grocery store were talking about her, Lili had drawn two conclusions from Irene's terse explanation. Her father's death was somehow connected with her birth, her fault in some way, and home was where people didn't die and you were safe. "You used to live here when you were a little girl, right?" she pressed her mother.

"Yes, I lived in Fielding. All the Petworths did."

Lili understood that Irene had been named Petworth before she married the man who died. What she never realized was that in those days the Petworths hadn't lived in the house on Woods Road.

She found out about that the following year when she turned six and started first grade in the Abraham Lincoln School. As well as getting used to hearing Miss White call her Liliane—no one else ever used her full formal name— Lili had to accept certain other realities of growing up.

Irene was unaware of what was happening until a rainy November afternoon when she decided to pick up her daughter after school. Lili was trembling and trying not to cry as she ran from the playground. The accusing words burst out as soon as she clambered into the old Chevrolét. "Is it true our house isn't really ours?"

"Lili, what nonsense, of course it's ours."

"Miss White says it's somebody else's. Their name is Kent."

Irene stiffened and didn't respond.

The little girl's story tumbled out in a rush. "Miss White

read us the sign in the hall across from the principal's office. It says a man named Samuel Kent gave the money to build the school and named it after Abraham Lincoln."

Irene nodded agreement. "I know that, Lili. I went to the same school when I was a little girl. I told you so."

By now Lili was sobbing inconsolably. "Yes, but Miss White said Mr. Kent built our house too. And everybody who lived there was always named Kent. She says it's the Kent house."

Irene took a deep breath. "Stop crying, Lili. The Kents used to own our house and it was called the Kent place. But it's not theirs now, it's ours."

Despite that simple explanation, the pain of the teacher's revelations did not go away. Lili felt threatened in her very soul. All the emotion Irene never allowed her to display was vested in the big shingled house with its slate roof, oak floors, and screened porch hung with vining wisteria. Even though she didn't have a father, she was safe because of the square rooms, the two big fireplaces, and the dining room full of sparkling colored glass. Now Miss White had made Lili's haven feel less safe, less inviolable. Now she must cling to the house with all her strength, or the Kents would come back and take it away.

There were a great many Kents in Fielding. By the time she was seven, Lili could read the signs that said KENT'S PHARMACY and KENT INSURANCE COMPANY. It helped that neither of those places was as big as Petworth's Department Store. "There are lots of people named Petworth in Fielding, aren't there?" she anxiously asked her mother.

"Yes," Irene agreed, her attention on something she was sewing. "Why?"

"I was wondering if there were more Petworths or more Kents."

"The things you think of, Lili. I haven't the faintest idea. You have a great many Petworth cousins, in any case."

Christmas was the only time Lili ever saw these distant relatives. Each year on the holiday Irene took her to a house across town where lots of Petworths lived. They gave one another presents and ate a lot and seemed quite friendly, but none of them ever came to the house on Woods Road. Lili was nine and in the fourth grade before she learned anything of their past.

The teacher was a local-history enthusiast. She explained about twenty settlers arriving from England in 1650 and choosing the site fourteen miles southwest of Boston and naming it Fielding.

"A man named Josiah Kent came to Fielding in 1652 and dammed a section of Willock's stream to make a millpond. Josiah built a mill and there have been Kents here ever since." The teacher's eyes lighted on Lili. "Of course the Petworths are our other 'first family.' Lili, your ancestors were mostly farmers until Tom Petworth became a miller and took over the Kent mill. That was in 1756."

Lili listened intently. Here was another instance of Petworths replacing Kents, the way she and her mother had done on Woods Road. That was some comfort, but she longed to learn more about her house. Who had built it? When? She asked her mother, but Irene said she didn't remember any of the details, and she got that look on her face that meant it was better to drop the subject. Lili knew the look well and she usually backed off when it appeared, but she always went on thinking about whatever it was that had roused her curiosity. And sooner or later she'd ask again.

Lili's questions about her dead father, for instance, always made Irene's eyes go blank and her mouth tighten. But when Lili was twelve she decided to bring up the subject once more.

Irene was working on a set of needlepoint covers for the dining room chairs. The pattern was of pink roses on an ecru background. It was slow, infinitely painstaking work, but when Irene stitched she was placid and composed. "I'm restoring the covers that used to be on the chairs long ago," she'd explained. They were upholstered in dull brown velvet now, and Irene said she wouldn't change them until she had embroidered seats and backs for all eight. Lili sometimes thought that might take a lifetime.

On the afternoon that Lili posed her question, her mother's blond head was bent over the frame that held the fabric, and she didn't look up when Lili asked, "Can't you tell me anything about my father? I know he died when I was born, but what else?"

Irene went on stitching. "He was English. I lived in England until you were born and he died and I brought you home."

"Then I'm half English?"

"Yes, that's right."

"Why did he die?"

"Nobody knows why people die, Lili." Irene always insisted on correct speech. "What you want to ask is how did he die? An automobile accident."

Lili's hazel eyes took on the color of her surroundings or what she was wearing. When she was concentrating hard, as she was then, they seemed to become darker, more greenish-blue. "Was I in the car?"

"Not exactly. You hadn't been born. I was expecting."

Here was new information, more clarity. Lili plunged ahead, eager to take advantage of Irene's unusual willingness to supply a few details. "What was his first name?"

"Whose?"

"My father's, of course."

"Don't take that tone with me, please," Irene said softly. She never shouted, even when she was annoyed. "His name was Harry Cramer."

"Do I look like him? Are there any pictures?"

"No, you don't look particularly like Harry Cramer."

"Who, then?" Lili demanded. "I don't look like you."

"I think you do, a little. Anyway, there are hundreds of ancestors you could look like, generations of marrying and intermarrying. That's particularly true in a town like Fielding."

"But—"

"If you don't mind," Irene interrupted, "I don't find this a pleasant topic of conversation. I really don't care to discuss it further."

End of inquiry. And confirmation of what Lili had begun to suspect. Her mother wasn't sorry when her husband died. Probably if he hadn't, they'd have divorced. Lili wondered if English people did that. That same afternoon she took her bike and went to the public library. Lili had devoured books since she'd discovered how many questions they could answer.

The library didn't disappoint her; there was plenty of information about England. "Try this, Lili," Miss Demel, the librarian, urged. "You like Dickens." The book she offered was *A Child's History of England.*

Lili shook her head. Her hair was the color of dark mahogany, absolutely straight, very thick, and always shining clean. She wore it short, with bangs, and it bobbed when she moved her head. Irene always said, "You're not pretty, Lili, but your hair is very nice." Lili often despaired of her small turned-up nose, what she thought of as her funny-color eyes, and the little crease in her chin, but she'd learned to like her hair.

Now she pushed the heavy bangs aside in an unconscious gesture and refused the book Miss Demel was suggesting. "I like Dickens' stories, but I want to know about England now."

"Oh?" Miss Demel sounded surprised. "Why England?"

"Because my father was English."

"Oh, yes," the librarian agreed. "I knew that, but I forgot." Of course she knew; in Fielding people always knew all about their neighbors. What mattered to Lili was that Miss Demel didn't try to stifle her curiosity. "Let's see what we can find," the librarian said.

At the end of her investigation Lili decided that most things in England today were a lot like they were in America, not strange and old-fashioned like they were in *Oliver Twist* or *Great Expectations.* So Irene must have been going to divorce Harry Cramer, that's why she never talked about him. Especially since then he'd died and it was sad and tragic, and probably she felt awful about what she'd planned.

Soon after Lili's thirteenth birthday Mrs. Carmichael announced her retirement. Irene said they couldn't afford to hire a new cleaning woman now that Lili was growing up and needed more clothes. They would have to do all the cleaning themselves. Lili might have complained, except that she still loved the house so passionately.

Every Saturday morning Irene washed the flow-blue dishes

and the cranberry· glass in the dining room while Lili did the dusting and vacuuming. Lili never grumbled, she loved making the golden grain of the oak staircase glow until she could see her face in it. And when all her chores were done she always gave herself a secret treat. She opened the cedar-lined drawers and cupboards in the upstairs hall and inhaled the rich woodsy scent, and looked at the old table and bed linens that were carefully wrapped in tissue and stored away.

The contents of the drawers raised all the old questions anew. Irene had bought the property fully furnished, but who had chosen all these things? When? What was the story of the house? One Saturday morning when she helped with the cleaning it seemed to Lili that the very walls were encouraging her to learn the secrets and share the mystery. So she went to the library.

"Of course, dear," Miss Demel said. "The old Kent place has quite a story attached. I'm surprised your mother hasn't told it to you."

Lili shrugged and the librarian said no more, but gave her a small book published by the local Historical Society, *Fielding in the Nineteenth Century*. "It's all in here," she promised.

Lili took the book eagerly. She was dying to read it, but she didn't go straight home. Instead, she left her bike behind some bushes on the road and cut through the woods to the far end of her property. There was a ruined old chicken coop where she wasn't supposed to go because it was dangerous. That made it a great place to be alone for long stretches. Lili settled herself with the precious book, hugging it to her a moment before she opened it.

She found what she wanted almost immediately. "The old Kent mansion on Woods Road" was the caption beneath a sepia-tinted photograph taken in 1890. Except that the maple trees lining the front drive were smaller, and there was a horse and buggy standing near the porch that led to the dutch door, it might have been taken yesterday.

Lili breathed a sigh of pure joy. Her house was as it had always been, as it always would be. Except it didn't belong to the Kents now, it belonged to her mother and to her.

On the page following the picture there were two paragraphs of text. "The biggest and most important house in Fielding was built by Dutch carpenters in 1870 at the behest of Samuel Kent. The Kent house has fourteen rooms, is built to a European floor plan, and was one of the earliest houses in these parts to boast indoor plumbing. It's first occupants were Samuel Kent and the bride he brought home from New York, Amanda Manning.

"Apart from its charming design, the Kent house has another distinction, it is the only place in Fielding where a genuine masterpiece can be found. A painting by Constable hangs in the front parlor, a wedding gift to Amanda from her parents. At present Thomas Kent, the son of Amanda and Samuel, is the owner of the house and lives there with his wife, the former Jane Shilton of Dedham, and their daughter, who was named Amanda after her grandmother."

Lili flipped back to the beginning of the book. Miss Demel had taught her about publication dates. This one said 1921. That explained why the book didn't say that the Kent house was now the Cramer house, but she imagined it must be accurate about the rest.

Lili turned a few more pages and found photographs of Amanda Manning Kent and her husband, Samuel. Amanda was very pretty in her old-fashioned hairstyle and dress. Sam looked as if he wanted to laugh but had to be serious because his picture was being taken. Lili found it easy to imagine them living in the big house on Woods Road.

When she finally went home, Irene was waiting for her and looking anxious. "Lili, where have you been? I've been expecting you for hours."

"I went to the library. Miss Demel gave me a copy of an old book about Fielding. Our house is in it. Look."

Irene hesitated a moment, then took the book. She looked at the picture of the house and read the brief description of its origin. Then, without saying anything, she handed the book back to Lili.

"Did you know them?" Lili demanded. "You must have known Amanda."

Irene turned away and started for the kitchen. "Of course, I didn't know her. I wasn't born until after she was dead."

"Not the grandmother," Lili insisted, following her mother down the hall. "The other Amanda. The one who the book says lived here and was Jane and Thomas Kent's daughter."

Irene was at the sink now, busily scrubbing carrots. "Yes, I suppose I did. At least by sight."

Lili was disappointed. "I thought maybe you were friends, but I guess she was younger than you."

"Yes," Irene agreed. "A little. Listen, Lili—" Irene paused, her fingers tightly gripping a paring knife. "You mustn't ever mention Amanda to anyone in town."

"Why not?" Lili's hazel eyes opened wide. "That sounds weird."

"She moved away and there was a scandal. No one likes to talk about it. After all, lots of Kents still live here."

There wasn't any point in more questions. Irene had that closed look on her face. Anyway, Lili wasn't really interested in the young Amanda. The couple who had been the first occupants of the house were much more romantic.

After reading the book, Lili daydreamed about Samuel and Amanda every time she opened the cedar drawers and fondled the delicate linens. Sometimes it was almost as if she could hear the music and laughter that must have filled the rooms in those days. Lili promised herself that when she grew up and the house was hers she'd have big parties so the sound would return.

Lili had not thought much about the picture hanging over the fireplace in the front parlor until she read about it in the book published by the Historical Society. She and her mother seldom used that room. They preferred the sitting room because it had thickly upholstered sofas and chairs. The parlor wasn't comfortable. It had stiff Victorian furniture with carved wooden frames and unyielding cushions covered in dusky red velvet. But according to the book, the picture was important.

Lili went back to the library. "Constable, John, 1776–1837," she read in a reference work on famous artists. "With Turner, J.M.W., England's most famous landscapist." She wanted more information, but she didn't know where to look. Miss Demel was home with the flu and the temporary librarian wasn't anyone Lili knew. She had to wait.

That night Lili couldn't fall asleep. When she heard the clock in the hall chime one, she got up and went downstairs to the front parlor.

Lili stood in the dark for a moment or two, loving the house, feeling somehow that it was loving her back. Finally she switched on the tiny lamp on one of the marble-topped tables and immediately pulled the cord that closed the heavy velvet drapes, so if her mother happened to be awake she wouldn't chance to see a reflection on the driveway. Then she turned and looked at the painting.

Lili knew nothing about art. Why this picture was supposed to be so special was a mystery. It was a painting of a field with a haystack and some big trees and a few people. It didn't excite her because of its beauty, but its associations. The Constable had been given to Sam and Amanda. It had hung right there over the fireplace since they moved in. It belonged to the house—and to her.

Lili started to switch off the light. The small bulb highlighted a section of one wall while leaving the rest in darkness. That made her really notice the wallpaper for the first time in years. The design was wreaths of tiny dark rosebuds on a beige background. One of the marvels of the house was that the paper in the front parlor was the original, unchanged in nearly a century. "Because the room's used so seldom" was Irene's explanation. True, but Lili realized it must also be true that the paper had faded.

She turned to the painting once more. It had been hanging there almost since the paper was put up. So behind it the wallpaper would be absolutely fresh and new. . . . Lili couldn't resist; she had to look.

She pulled one of the red velvet chairs close to the fireplace and climbed up on it, then moved the painting a bit, but it didn't reveal what she wanted to see. The light was behind her, shielded by her body. She bit her lip and hesitated. What if there was an accident? What if she damaged the precious Constable in some way? But she wouldn't; she'd be very careful.

The picture was heavier than she expected. Lili braced herself for a real effort and lifted it off its hook. Then she lowered the painting, propped it against the back of the chair, and climbed down. She stepped back a few paces, looked up at the portion of wall she'd revealed, and caught her breath.

The newly exposed rectangle of wallpaper was a revelation. The rosebuds were vivid red, their twined stems a vibrant green. The background color was rich yellow-white cream, not the insipid beige she'd looked at all her life. Sam and Amanda had chosen a bright, gay paper. Their front parlor had been planned for parties and good times and happy people.

"I'll find some way to have it made new again," she whispered. "When I'm rich and famous I'll have parties here too, and the paper will be like it was in Sam and Amanda's day." It was a promise to their ghosts.

Lili looked down at the Constable. The picture wasn't much different now than it was at eye level, and it still didn't seem particularly special. Beyond the closed door she heard the clock strike two, time to go back to bed.

Lili climbed on the chair, gripped the gilt frame of the painting, and glanced down to see the exact position of the hanging wire. What she saw was a little wad of paper shoved between the frame and the canvas backing. Without a moment's hesitation she reached down and gently worked the screw of paper loose.

When she'd rehung the painting and climbed down from the chair, she carried her find nearer to the lamplight. Very carefully she undid the numerous folds, and found that she was holding a small envelope. She could feel that there was something inside, and see that there was nothing written on the front. She turned the envelope over. It was sealed, and there were a few words in faded ink below the flap. The creases made the writing difficult to decipher, but not impossible. "Córdoba, Spain. The house of . . ." It was M something, but she couldn't read the last bit. The ink was smudged, as if it hadn't been quite dry before the envelope was folded over and over.

Lili resisted the urge to rip it open. If she was going to do it without tearing through the writing, she needed a tool. Her nail file should be perfect.

It never occurred to her that perhaps she was disturbing her beloved ghosts, that perhaps Sam and Amanda would disapprove.

❧ 4 ❧

London: 1970

So what did she expect, Lili asked herself, horse-drawn carriages and chimney sweeps? It's 1970, Dickens is dead, long live Mary Quant and Ringo Starr.

Lili Cramer had come to England because she couldn't draw. Her dream of becoming an architect, her despair when she thought Irene couldn't afford to send her to college, her elation when she discovered that money had been put aside for the purpose—Irene wouldn't say by whom, but Lili was convinced it had been her dead father—all that emotion had come to nothing. At the end of her sophomore year at Boston University Lili had a C-minus average, because she was flunking all the required art courses.

"I have wonderful ideas," she'd told her mother, "but an architect has to put them on paper so other people can see them and builders can make them happen. I can't do that."

"And you're getting fat," Irene had replied.

Lili knew what she meant. When she was unhappy, Lili nibbled constantly. She was putting on weight, so her mother knew she was miserable.

Irene had suggested that Lili change her major. Lili had decided instead to change her life.

"I want to go to Europe," she announced.

It was summer and they were having dinner in the dining

room on Woods Road while shafts of rosy evening sunlight fired the display of cranberry glass in the bay window. "Europe," Irene repeated. She said it slowly as if the idea was beyond imagining.

"Yes, to England."

Irene's head shot up. "No!" She almost spat out the word. "England has a terrible climate," she added more gently.

"That's hardly the point," Lili said. "You're forgetting Harry Cramer. I'm half English." She leaned forward, speaking urgently. "Look, you've never said much, but I know it wasn't happy for you. Which doesn't mean—"

"That's not entirely true," Irene interrupted. "There was a time when I was wildly happy there," she whispered.

There was an extraordinary, almost mystic quality to Irene's words. In all Lili's twenty years she had never heard her mother speak in such a tone. She stared at Irene and understood that something momentous had happened over the tuna-fish casserole.

Briefly, Irene's gray eyes met Lili's and it seemed she might explain. Instead, she got up from the table and began clearing . . . and Lili thought she might have imagined the whole thing.

"What will it accomplish if you take this trip?" Irene asked when she brought in the dessert.

"Not a trip exactly. I want to live somewhere else for a while. I've been thinking of . . . of finding some Cramer relatives."

"No," Irene said again, less vehemently this time. "That won't be possible. They're all dead."

"That doesn't make sense. There has to be someone."

"No one. Get that idea out of your head, Lili. I don't want you to be disappointed."

Lili lay down her spoon and pushed away her half-eaten ice cream. "I definitely intend to go," she said firmly. "It will make it a lot easier if you'll let me use the rest of my education money to finance the trip."

Irene went to the window and adjusted the position of one of the blue-red vases. "The money . . . Oh, yes, of course."

That had been the biggest stumbling block in Lili's mind, and her mother had dismissed it as the least important consideration. "Thanks." She had stared at Irene's rigid back and not known what else to say.

"Lili, how about Spain?"

Lili was nonplussed. She'd expected arguments about going away, not that her mother would suggest alternative destinations. "Why would I go to Spain? What would I do there? I don't speak Spanish."

"You could learn."

Lili had declined to take a crash course in Spanish. England was where she wanted to go, for reasons she did not entirely explain, and in the end Irene shrugged and agreed. She'd been very cooperative after that, and helped Lili with all the arrangements. It had been Irene who discovered that fares were cheaper in the autumn. So Lili had waited until October. Now she was at last in England—and scared to death.

Three days after she arrived in London, Lili went to Carnaby Street. According to everything she'd read, Carnaby Street and the Kings Road had become the most exciting streets in London. She wore brown slacks and a beige sweater, a plaid scarf over her hair, and sneakers—and found she was a dull little wren surrounded by birds of extraordinary plumage.

Most of the men sported lots of gold jewelry and velvet jackets. The girls wore leather skirts that barely covered their buttocks, with scarlet stockings and thigh-high boots. After two hours Lili hurried back to the small hotel in Paddington that Irene had recommended.

"I suspect the Crescent Gardens Hotel hasn't changed much since your time," she wrote to her mother. "It's still clean and respectable and cheap, as you remembered. . . ."

The hotel was mostly occupied by residents, elderly people who sat in a room called the lounge and watched television endlessly, never seeming to move. But for less than forty dollars a week Lili got a tiny room and a big breakfast, so she stayed.

She'd been sure coming to England was the right thing to do. After Carnaby Street and the Crescent Gardens Hotel she wasn't so certain. Stop worrying, Lili told herself at the end of the first week. Do what you came here to do.

She would put her secret plan in action. She'd find a school that would teach her about English domestic architecture. She didn't want to study for a degree but to take individual courses.

Lili sat down with the Yellow Pages, made a list, and began visiting a number of colleges and universities. All the interviews were the same.

"Exactly what is it you wish to study, Miss Cramer?"

"Houses."

"Mmm, I see. The history of houses?"

"Well, yes. But more than that. How they're made."

"Ah, I see, architecture. That's fine. Now, Miss Cramer, do you have a portfolio we can see? Architecture is part of the Fine Arts Department . . ."

Inevitably, Lili fled.

Since she hadn't discussed her plans with Irene, at least she didn't need to report another failure.

The days dragged on and her disappointment escalated into near panic. What was she going to do? Where could she go? What, if anything, was her place in the world and how was she going to earn a living? Toward the end of October she happened on a bit of balm for her soul.

What Lili discovered was the decorative arts wing of the Victoria and Albert Museum. She'd wandered in by chance, and found ecstasy. Naturally, she returned. Each morning she walked through Hyde Park to the museum and spent hours among its treasures. She loved them all, whether it was the exquisite detail of a tiny figurine, or the glorious gilt and satin draperies of a recreated Regency bedroom.

After three weeks the excursions to the V&A had calmed her and buoyed her spirits. Lili decided to try the other thing she'd come to London to do. She began calling the Cramers listed in the telephone book.

"Hello, my name is Lili Cramer. I'm an American but my father was English. Harry Cramer. I was wondering if . . ." She said it all in a rush, before they could decide she was a crank or a saleswoman and hang up. Mostly people were polite and kind, but no one claimed her as a long-lost relative.

One lady did mention an uncle named Harry, but she added a question. "You don't happen to be a black gal, do you?" Lili said no, she wasn't. "Then you're not related to us," the woman said, chuckling.

At the end of three hours Lili had to admit that maybe her mother had been right and Harry Cramer didn't have any family to find. One more failure. Thank God for the V&A; it would keep her sane until she could make another plan.

She continued to visit the museum every morning and finally someone spoke to her. He was a tall, skinny guy with shaggy blond hair and horn-rimmed glasses, dressed with surprising formality in a dark suit and a tie, though he didn't seem much older than she. "You come here every day, don't you?" he asked without preamble.

Lili was immediately on the defensive. "I'm studying."

"I see. What?"

"Houses." That lame definition which never seemed to say what she meant.

He accepted it without question. "You're American. I made a bet with myself that you were. I've been watching you all week."

"Is that why you come here, to watch me?" After she said it, Lili realized it sounded horribly conceited. "I mean—"

He laughed. "I know what you mean. I'm writing a novel and I need to know what sixteenth-century clothes and furniture looked like. And before you ask, I'm not a real novelist yet. This is my first book, and no publisher's beating down my door."

She started to say something, but a group of noisy kids in school uniforms appeared, led by a harried-looking woman who kept repeating, "This is your heritage, children. Please pay attention."

The young man took her arm and led her to the door. "Have lunch with me. Please. I know we don't know each other, but I'm relatively harmless. And I have the impression that no one has yet properly welcomed you to Britain."

Lili knew Irene would be appalled. A pickup was a pickup, even in a museum. But she had to talk to someone beside the geriatrics in the hotel. "Thanks, I'd love to."

It was November 20, cold, gray, and damp. They paused on the museum steps while he helped her into her navy coat and put on his own of rather shabby tweed. Then he offered his hand. "By the way, I'm Andy Mendoza."

"Lili Cramer," she said, taking his hand and finding his grip firm and pleasant.

"Okay, Lili, are you already bored with our national dish or can I entice you to roast beef and Yorkshire pudding?"

The thought of red meat made her salivate. She'd been living on sandwiches and trying for days to scare up enough courage to go into a real restaurant and order a decent meal. "That sounds wonderful."

"Smashing. I know a great place that's walking distance."

The restaurant was on busy Brompton Road. It had paneled walls, sparkling white tablecloths, and clients who looked like businessmen. Not one of them appeared to be under fifty. While they waited for a table, Lili shot a surreptitious glance at her escort. No, she wasn't mistaken. He was young. But his choosing this restaurant seemed peculiar.

He caught her looking at him and grinned. "Last night I tried to decide if it should be a pub or this place. This seemed like a better idea for the first time."

"Last night?"

"Yes. That's when I made up my mind that if you were in the museum again, I'd introduce myself and ask you to lunch."

"But why?"

He chuckled, but before he could answer, the maître d' appeared. "Mr. Mendoza, nice to see you, sir. A table for two?"

"Yes, please."

The maître d' turned to help Lili with her coat, and she was suddenly painfully aware of her black slacks and faded blue sweater. The few other women in the dining room all wore dresses or suits and looked like her mother.

At least Lili had enough brains not to make excuses. She

consciously lifted her head as they were led to a table in the corner.

"May I order for you?" Andy asked. "Since it's supposed to be a welcome-to-London lunch?"

She nodded and he conferred with the waiter for a moment, then spoke to her. "In keeping with the occasion, it's all straightforward English food. So we should skip wine and drink beer. Okay?" Lili agreed and Andy finished ordering.

When the waiter left, Lili cocked her head and studied the strange man across the table. "You're very sure of yourself, Andy Mendoza. Who are you?"

"A struggling young writer, as I said."

"Maybe, but I don't think that's all of it."

"Enough for now. What are you doing here, and for how long?"

"I'm not sure, and a year. There, I can specialize in cryptic answers too."

"Touché." The beers came and he lifted his and toasted her. "Welcome. And you should always wear blue, it shows off your fantastic eyes."

Her efforts at cool sophistication were undone. No one had ever told her she had fantastic eyes. Lili felt her cheeks redden, and she sipped her beer in silence.

They ate oxtail soup, and roast beef with a kind of crusty popover called Yorkshire pudding, and cabbage and carrots and roast potatoes, and finished with apple pie and custard sauce. It was delicious.

"I may never eat again," Lili said when the last empty plate had been cleared and they were waiting for coffee.

He leaned forward. "Now, tell me the secret. Who are you really? An heiress escaping the society scene, a Hollywood star running from your studio, an art spy staking out the V&A . . ."

Lili exploded with laughter. "None of the above. Why should I be?"

"Because there's something about you that makes me imagine all sorts of exotic and wonderful things. I think it's the way you move. As if you're bottling up a whole lot of energy and any minute it's going to burst free." He saw her look of incredulity. "I'm sorry, I can't help it. I make up stories about everyone I see. I suppose it's why I want to be a novelist."

Lili shook her head. "I hate to disappoint you, but the only thing I am is"—she groped for an explanation—"at loose ends."

"Okay," Andy Mendoza said. "We'll tie up a few."

"Why are you rushing me?"

Andy slowed his pace along the broad boulevard beside the ocean. The water was December-fierce, slathered with foam and crashing on the beach, but there was sun. "Sorry, I didn't realize I was walking too fast."

"That's not what I meant." The east wind was cutting. Lili shoved her hands deeper into the pockets of her quilted nylon parka and drew it closer to her body. She realized she'd dredged the expression from Irene's vocabulary. "I mean a rush as in calling all the time, seeing so much of me, taking me places."

He spun around so his back was to the wind and he faced her, but he kept walking. "Where the hell was that little town you grew up in, on the moon? Why do you think?"

"I don't know. That's why I'm asking."

"You've never had a boyfriend, have you?"

"Of course I have. Lots."

"You're lying." He faced forward again and they walked on.

He'd phoned her at six this Wednesday morning. "Let's go for a drive. I want a day out of London." By seven-thirty they were on the road, Andy quiet and preoccupied, Lili happy to enjoy the scenery flashing by the window. Andy's car was not the Jag she'd imagined, but a Morris Oxford, the British equivalent of her mother's Chevy, but he drove it as if it were a sports car, with great skill and confidence, and very fast.

In two hours he'd turned off at an exit marked Brighton. "It's a summer-holiday place. Probably deserted now. We'll be intrepid pioneers exploring a ghost town." Andy parked the Morris in a lot behind the train station. "Let's walk a bit. Brighton is very Victorian, you'll like the archtecture."

She did. They'd worked their way slowly along the residential streets, down to the wide avenue fronting the ocean where she asked about rushing and he accused her of lying about boyfriends. Straight ahead of them was Brighton Pier, a summer diversion erected in Edwardian times.

The long wooden structure stretched fingerlike into the sea. It housed a dance hall, an arcade, and shops that sold "souvenirs of your holiday at the seaside." They were all boarded over now.

"Come out to the edge," Andy said. He strode ahead of her and hunched over a rickety wooden railing. The wind whipped his sandy hair back from his high forehead, seemed to hone the planes of his angular face. "I came here a few times when I was a kid. We fished off the pier one day."

"Well, I hope it was warmer than this," Lili muttered.

"You're cold," he said with some surprise.

"Ah, you noticed."

"C'mon, we'll find somewhere warm."

Nothing was open on the seafront. They climbed a steep hill and in the back streets discovered a small bakery that also served hot drinks. Andy ordered coffee and a plate of cakes stuffed with whipped cream. When he offered them to her, Lili shook her head.

"Go on. You need some sustenance after I nearly froze you to death. Besides, with your shiny hair and turned-up nose, it sort of suits you to be plump." She didn't reply, but he saw her expression. "I'm sorry. That was thoughtless. Like when kids called me four-eyes at school."

"You look terrific in glasses. They balance your face."

"I don't mind them now, but it took most of my twenty-seven years and Michael Caine to convince me."

"Why Michael Caine?"

"There was this film where he was a big, tough hero and he wore glasses. He made them look sexy."

"When you were little, is that what you wanted to be, a big, tough, sexy hero?"

"I guess so." He seldom talked about his childhood, only elliptical references, given and then snatched back. Like now. "We were discussing you, not me."

"I'm not usually as overweight as this, only a little pudgy normally. But I eat when I'm unhappy, and last year at Boston University I was miserable." She'd told him about the shattered dream of being an architect.

He looked hard at her, the glasses magnifying his yellow-brown tiger eyes. "Are you still miserable?"

"No," she admitted. "But since I came to England I seem to eat all the wrong things." She gestured at the cakes. "Stuff like that."

"We're big on stodge and starch. It's the bloody climate. But as I said, it wouldn't suit you to be Twiggy."

The bakery was very warm. Lili shrugged out of her parka. "There's a long way between skinny and this."

"Do you think your breasts would be as marvelous if you lost weight?"

She was speechless.

"Don't look like that. They are. Especially when you wear that light green blouse with the flowers. I have dreams about them."

"Andy, I don't—"

"Sleep with men. I know. One of your charms is that you're somehow not a modern girl. More like an exotic anachronism suddenly come to life. Anyway, I'm not about to rape you. This is a scientific discussion. Purely objective. Can you lose weight and still keep those luscious mammary glands? It's a simple question, deserves an answer."

She couldn't help it. She started to giggle. He had an amazing facility of startling her into laughter. "I think so."

"Okay. Then we'll put you on a diet. So you'll feel better about yourself. But only—" He paused and leaned back and studied her. "Half a stone, seven pounds to you." He got up. "Let's go, there's a chemist across the road."

Outside what she still thought of as a drugstore, he peered through the window, then fished a penny out of his pocket. "They've got a scale. You go in alone. I won't ask what you weigh, but you've got to tell me about every ounce you lose. The absolute truth. Agreed?"

They shook hands solemnly and she went inside.

Lili came out looking horrified. The little card in her pocket said she weighed nine and a half stone, one hundred and thirty-three pounds. "Seven pounds won't be nearly enough."

"We'll see."

They drove back slowly, taking byways and stopping for a late lunch at a village pub called the Swanning Arms. Andy insisted she must have only mineral water and a salad. He drank two pints of beer and ate steak and kidney pie followed by ice cream. "I'm not on the diet, you are," he said by way of apology.

"Too bad I can't give you my seven pounds."

"I was born noodle-shaped. Nothing seems to change it. My nanny stuffed me full of vitamins and calories, but it didn't help."

Another of the quick references that indicated he was a child of privilege who had grown up in a world she'd only read about. Lili ventured a question. "Did you live around here? You seem to know the area well."

"Not exactly. An aunt lived nearby. If you like, I'll show you the house after lunch. Speaking of past times"—he didn't look at her but concentrated on his food—"what did you say was the name of that town? You know, the one on the moon. Field-something?"

"Fielding. And definitely not on the moon. Fourteen miles southwest of Boston. What made you think of that?"

"I don't know." He didn't meet her eyes when he said it. Lili had a strange momentary suspicion. He was lying. Seconds later she dismissed it as absurd.

Andy was leaning back in his seat now, eyeing her speculatively. "They produce remarkable women in Fielding."

"A judgment based on insufficient evidence," she said, grinning. "I'm the only woman from Fielding you've ever met."

"Yes, but . . ."

"But what?"

"Nothing. You're remarkable enough to convince me."

Lili flushed with pleasure and went back to her salad. When they'd finished the meal and left the pub she told herself she wasn't still starving, it was all in her head.

They drove through the tiny village onto a road bordered with tall elms. A few leaves yet clung to the branches and danced in the wind. Occasionally one drifted to the ground in a winter ballet of incredible grace. "It's beautiful here," Lili said.

"I agree. Sometimes I think Sussex is my favorite county in England." Andy gestured to a knoll on their right. "That's Swanning Park up there." He stopped by a huge gate with pineapple finials.

"Pineapples are a Chinese symbol for welcome," Lili told him.

"Maybe, but we can't go in. I don't know the family who lives there now."

It wasn't possible to see much of the house from the road. Lili had a blurred impression of something massive in honeyed stone, obscured by yet more trees. "Couldn't we walk around it a bit?"

Andy slammed the car into gear. "No. As a matter of fact, I hate the bloody place." He drove off with his face set in grim, hard lines and Lili didn't ask any more questions.

It was five when he pulled up in front of the Crescent Gardens Hotel. "Do you mind being left so early? I think maybe I can work a bit."

She smiled at him. "No, I don't mind. It's been a wonderful day."

He'd kissed her a few times and often he held her hand. Now he leaned over and took her face between his palms. "You're wonderful," he said. And he kissed her hard, his mouth fastened on hers and open, so she could taste the beer and the pipe he sometimes smoked.

Andy broke the kiss, not her. He pulled back and got out of the car and came around and opened her door. He was the first young man she'd ever met who made the polite gesture seem absolutely natural.

"Good night," he murmured, and returned to the car and drove away before she could answer.

Lili really didn't mind his dropping her off early. She understood how important his writing was to him. She knew, too, that he earned nothing from it. What he lived on was a mystery, though he always seemed to have enough money.

Andy had what he referred to as a bed-sit, a studio apartment, the other side of town in Hackney. To which, somewhat surprisingly, she thought, she'd never been invited.

Upstairs in her hotel room Lili could still taste his mouth, feel his kiss. She took off her jacket and her blouse and her bra and stared at her breasts in the wavy mirror over the small dressing table.

"Half a pound in ten days isn't much," she said disconsolately.

"I agree. Have you been cheating?"

They were in a pub off Leicester Square. The Beatles were singing about Strawberry Fields Forever and a huge crowd was talking and laughing, particularly loud perhaps because it was four days to Christmas. "What did you say? I can't hear you."

Andy leaned forward and whispered directly into her ear. "Have you been cheating, little fatty with the delicious tits?"

She turned beet-red. "Maybe a little," she admitted. She never commented on his outrageous remarks because she never knew what to say.

He laughed at her obvious discomfort and tweaked her nose. "It's wicked of me to make you blush, but I enjoy it. Drink up your mineral water or we'll be late for the film."

She had no idea what the movie was about; she kept thinking about Andy and imagining him touching her breasts.

Lili was a virgin by default. In sixties Fielding there were good girls and bad girls and Lili Cramer was clearly marked as good. God knew her mother had never lectured about the perils or pleasures of sex. It was one more topic Irene did not discuss. At school Lili was taught the basics of reproduction and that she shouldn't have a baby unless she was married. As for a self-driven imperative, a need, until now she had successfully tamped any incipient fires. But Andy was kindling a blaze.

His fingers were long and thin like the rest of him. She wanted to stroke each one, to press them to her flesh. In the darkened theater she felt her nipples swell and rub against her bra. Andy didn't so much as hold her hand.

He did, however, link her arm through his when they came out onto the street. Leicester Square was lit by neon and an enormous moon. A crowd had gathered and someone was strumming a guitar. They were singing carols. "I have to go away for Christmas," Andy said.

Lili's stomach flipped and she swallowed a sudden lump in her throat. She'd assumed they would spend the holiday together.

"I'll be back soon after New Year's," he said when he left her in Paddington. "Call you then."

The period from December 22 to January 3 was so awful, Lili hated ever afterward to remember it. She felt isolated, and utterly alone in a new and frightening way.

Lili spent Christmas Day in bed reading magazines and eating candy. She didn't have a telephone in her room, so at four in the afternoon she went down to the hotel lobby to call her mother. It was eleven A.M. in Fielding, Irene would not yet have left for the annual gathering of the Petworths.

"Are you well, Lili?" Irene asked immediately.

"Oh, yes. Very well. You?"

"I'm fine. Will you have a nice Christmas?"

"Had. It's late, already dark here. I had lunch with friends."

"Yes, of course, I forgot the time difference. I'm so glad you had a good time. Nice of you to call, dear. We mustn't speak longer, it's very expensive. I'll give your love to everyone."

"Yes, do that. Merry Christmas, Mother."

"Merry Christmas, Lili."

She went upstairs and stood for a moment staring at the framed snapshot of her beautiful house in Fielding. Then she lay on the narrow bed and wept. Eventually, she slept, and dreamed not of home but of Andy Mendoza.

It was late morning on January 3 when the lady who ran the hotel tapped on her door and informed Lili that Mr. Mendoza was downstairs. God! She hadn't expected him, wasn't dressed, and hadn't washed her hair for a week. "Tell him I'll be down in a few minutes," Lili said.

In twenty minutes she appeared in the lobby with her head wrapped turban-style in a paisley print scarf. It didn't look bad with her burgundy winter coat and black boots. In fact, Andy said she looked terrific. "Have you been busy? Sorry I arrived without phoning. Got back late last night."

"It's okay. Sorry you had to wait." She avoided the question about being busy. Lili was determined to be cool and sophisticated. Andy mustn't know she'd been depressed and angry and pining.

"I have your Christmas present," he said, tugging her toward the door, "but I can't bring it to you. Has to be the other way around."

She had nothing for him. Since he'd left she had been convinced she would never see him again. "I didn't do any Christmas shopping. I've had the flu," Lili lied.

By this time they were in Andy's car and he was heading south on Edgware Road. "It's not far," he said as he threaded his Morris through the traffic. He was humming under his breath, and every once in a while he glanced at Lili and grinned. Lili knew he was happy to be with her, and her spirits soared.

"We're here," Andy announced as he turned into a tree-lined cul-de-sac called Prince's Mews. The short street was lined with Georgian houses. "Converted from stables," he explained. "Super, aren't they?"

"Beautiful," Lili agreed. She was almost overcome with the loveliness of the houses and with her own happiness. What she was experiencing was the sudden, exquisitely intense sensation of being resurrected from the grave.

"We're looking for number eight. Here it is." Andy had a key in his hand.

"Andy! Have you bought one of these places?"

He laughed. "No. Come along, love, I'll explain inside."

The door he unlocked was painted black and flanked by terra-cotta urns planted with small fir trees. He led her into a small square foyer with open doors on either side. Lili had a quick impression of wonderful dark woodwork against pastel paint and wallpaper—and nothing else. There wasn't a stick of furniture.

"Dining room and drawing room as will be," Andy said. "Kitchen's straight ahead." He gestured to a closed door. "Upstairs there's supposed to be two bedrooms and a bath. Let's go see."

They climbed a straight flight of stairs without a railing, hewn out of some heavy black wood, to a room with a view of the tiny backyard. There was a single bed covered with a calico-clad feather quilt, a small pine chest with four drawers, and a mound of assorted cushions on the floor. There was also a fireplace that had recently been used and not cleaned.

"Somebody's living here." Lili said in surprise. "I thought it was vacant."

"Not exactly. The house belongs to my cousin Charles. He bought the place last month and camped out for a few days. Now he's off to Nairobi for a year."

"And you're going to move in. Oh, Andy, how marvelous! It's great."

"You don't listen very well, pretty Lili." He came over and took both her hands in his. Each of them still wore gloves, but Lili could feel the warmth of his flesh. "I said it was your Christmas present. *You're* going to move in."

"Me? I can't, Andy. I could never afford to rent a place like this."

"No rent. It's free. Charles only wants someone reliable to look after it while he's away. He's rich as Croesus and preoccupied with taking pictures of flora and fauna, that's why he's gone to Kenya. Handed me the key and asked would I, as an act of cousinly charity, make whatever arrangements needed making. You're the best arrangement I can imagine. You bloody well need to get out of that mausoleum you're living in, and you're reliable. You are, aren't you?"

Shades of her mother. *Do be sensible, Lili.* Reliable was the same thing. "Yes, I guess I am. Listen, are you telling me the truth?" She tipped back her head and looked at him. "It sounds like something out of that book you're writing."

"I'm writing about the sixteenth century. And there's no character like my cousin Charles. He's too unreal for a book. But yes, it's the God's honest truth."

Suddenly she asked the question that had been lurking in the back of her mind since the moment she saw him. "Andy, where have you been?"

He took off his gloves and didn't look at her. "With my family for Christmas. I told you I was going."

"Yes, you did. Where is your family?"

"Up north. A part of the country called the Lake District, Grasmere in Westmoreland to be precise. Does that do?"

"It should," she admitted. "But I have the feeling I'm being . . . duped." Her joy of half an hour ago was fading, replaced by a feeling of panic, and the sense that she was driving him away. But she couldn't stop herself.

"Duped. It's an odd word to choose. By whom, me?" He still wasn't looking at her.

"No," she said slowly. "Myself perhaps. I keep thinking you're nice Andy Mendoza whom I know and . . . care about. But on another level I think you're somebody I don't know at all."

He didn't answer.

"Andy, are you very rich? You said your cousin Charles was rich as Croesus. Are all the Mendozas wealthy?"

"Some of them. Not me." He was staring out the window at the garden below and his voice was flat and without emotion. "I have the income from a trust. Five thousand a year. Which is far from a fortune these days, but it's enough to keep me, and means I can try my hand at doing a novel." He turned back to face her. "There's nothing sinister about it, Lili." The tiger eyes had clouded over.

"Oh, God, I've really loused things up, haven't I? First of all, it's none of my damned business. Second, you had a special surprise and I ruined it. I'm sorry. Please don't be too angry with me."

His expression was grave when he crossed the room and put his fingers on the top button of her coat. "Let's start this scene over, shall we? We've just come in. Miss Cramer, may I take your coat?"

"Yes, thank you, Mr. Mendoza." She managed a light tone, but her arms hung leaden at her sides.

Andy unbuttoned the coat, slipped it from her shoulders, and threw it on the bed. She wore a brown tweed skirt and a chunky white fisherman's-knit sweater. He studied her for a moment, then raised his hands to her head. "I want to see your beautiful hair."

Lili remembered the scarf. She moaned. "It's going to look awful. It was soaking wet when I tied it up. I washed it as soon as I heard you were downstairs, but I didn't have time to dry it."

He smiled and pushed the scarf off without undoing it. Her dark hair tumbled free. She'd been letting it grow since she left home, and now it was shoulder-length. Andy lifted the heavy mane in his hands. "Still damp. You'll get pneumonia." His eyes lit up. "Let's make a fire. There's some coal in that scuttle."

He was quick and expert and soon the coals were glowing. "Sit over here on these cushions. Close to the fire."

He sat beside her, running his fingers through her hair and pulling out the tangles. "What did you do while I was away?"

"Oh, the usual things." She was trembling and her voice sounded distant in her own ears.

"And what are they? When we first met you said you were studying. But are you?"

"I don't know. I told you about my architecture abortion. I don't really want to talk about all that." She didn't want to talk at all, she wanted him to kiss her. They were so close, she could see the pores of his skin, the faint shadow of beard developing anew.

He leaned forward slightly and put his lips on hers. It was a light, fleeting touch rather than a kiss, and over almost at once. Andy stretched out full-length and poked at the fire, then he stroked her hair again. "It's dry. Let's go downstairs and take another look around. We haven't inspected the kitchen."

They had to put their coats back on because the central heating had been disconnected. "It's fired by gas, according to Charles. Economical. And you can have a phone installed. That's not very dear. Seems to me, even after paying for the utilities you'll live for less than at that grim hotel. Especially since you won't have to eat out."

Lili was still trembling inside, still achingly conscious of his physical nearness, but she was also slowly assimilating the idea that if she wished, she could live in this little jewel of a house. "Even empty it's gorgeous. And yes, it will certainly be cheaper."

"Okay, then that's settled. We'll go to the markets this weekend, Portobello on Saturday and Petticoat Lane on Sunday. You can pick up a few sticks of furniture for next to nothing if we're lucky." He hesitated. "Will your budget stretch to that? You can probably sell whatever you buy when you leave England."

"Yes, I guess so. With what I'll save on the hotel I can afford to spend a little extra." All that really registered in Lili's mind was his casual mention of her going away. He thought of her as a temporary phenomenon, a passing phase. Certainly no one who might ever be a permanent part of his life. She shivered.

"You're cold again. Let's take a quick look at the kitchen, then push on. I'll ring the Gas Board tomorrow and have them reconnect the heating."

They opened the door to the kitchen—and stopped dead in amazement. The whole house represented a loving and careful restoration by the owner who had preceded Andy's cousin Charles, but that hadn't prepared them for this. The kitchen was fully equipped, not empty like the other rooms, and it looked as if it had been lifted whole from some coffee-table book on how the best people do things.

"Blimey," Andy murmured. "Charles didn't say a thing about this. Maybe he never came in here."

Lili was struck dumb by the sheer perfection of it all. The floor was made of polished bricks that glowed with dark red fire. The walls were tiled in a blue-and-white pattern reminiscent of Delft. They were interrupted by open shelves and an overhanging pot rack, all crammed with copper utensils.

"Charles must have bought the pots and pans with the house," Andy said. "I can't imagine them being here otherwise."

One side of the room had two sinks, a large gas range, a stainless steel refrigerator, and a free-standing butcher block. The other side, separated from the work area by a pine counter, was dominated by French doors leading to the garden and a round table with four chairs in the same pale wood as the counter.

Lili started to cry.

"Hey, what's the matter? You silly little fool, what are you crying for?" Andy reached out and shook her, half in exasperation, half in humor.

"Because it's perfect," Lili said between sniffles. "When I say I want to make beautiful houses, this is what I mean. But I can't get anybody to understand. And there's something else."

He was hugging her now, and laughing. "What else?"

"What am I going to do in here? I've never cooked anything in my whole damned life."

❦ 5 ❧

London and Fielding: 1971

"I brought you a few books." Andy put a plastic bag on the rickety mahogany table in the living room of the house in Prince's Mews. Lili had moved in ten days earlier. The table and a lumpy blue-velvet sofa were the only pieces of furniture she had so far acquired.

"What have you been up to?" he asked, eyeing the black smudge on her cheek.

Lili knew it was there. She rubbed at it ineffectually. "I'm a mess, aren't I? I've been polishing the copper in the kitchen. Wait a minute and I'll run up and change."

"Hold on, love. Aren't you even going to look at these?" He gestured to the books.

They were all paperbacks. Lili picked up the top one in the pile. It was a cookbook, so were the rest. She looked at them solemnly, one by one, then at Andy. "These wouldn't have anything to do with that burned omelette I fed you last night, would they?"

"No, I think they're related to the raw spaghetti on Monday. I now realize there's a difference between al dente and tooth-cracking hard."

"I have to agree." She gathered the books into a neat stack. "Don't worry, I bought frozen chicken pies for tonight. I don't have to do anything but heat them up."

The pies weren't bad. "I considered getting Chinese food,"

Lili said when they'd finished, "but I didn't know if you liked it."

"I do. Have to if you're English, part of our colonial past. Second sons couldn't inherit, so they were sent out to bash a few natives and they developed a taste for the local grub."

"Are you a second son?"

"Yes and no."

"How can that be?"

He laughed. "My mother was my father's second wife. I'm her one and only, but his second. Elementary, my dear Watson."

She made a face. "Once they're explained, most things are, Sherlock."

"Lili, why did you decide to come to London for your year abroad? Why not someplace romantic like Paris?"

She smiled. "You think London isn't romantic because it's your home. To a foreigner it's our friend Sherlock Holmes, and the Tower and Westminster Abbey. All very romantic."

"Mmm. I wondered if there was something else."

"Yes, there was. My father was English."

Andy was clearing the table, his back to her. "He died when you were born, you said. Had he been in America long before that?"

"Not in America at all, as far as I know. My mother met and married him over here." She paused a moment. "I don't think they were happy together. Mother's never said, but I've always thought she was going to get a divorce. Then he was killed in an automobile accident and that tied things up neatly, so she went home. Irene likes things to be neat."

Andy came back to the table and put his hands on her shoulders. "So you came to London to look for your roots, at least half of them."

"Not exactly, but I did think I might find some relatives. I spent hours calling every Cramer in the phone book. The only ones that had a Harry were black. Besides, their Harry is alive. Mother said all my father's relatives were dead. I guess she was right."

"Maybe," Andy said, sitting down beside her. "Or maybe the family's not from London."

She stared at him wide-eyed. "That's so obvious, I can't believe I didn't think of it. But where would I get phone books for all of England? How could I call all those people?"

"Let me help. I know a bit about that kind of research."

"Could you really take on such an enormous job and come up with something?"

"I could try, if you want me to."

"Yes," she said instantly. "If it's not too much trouble."

"No trouble at all." He took a notebook from his pocket and a ball-point pen. "Let's see, you were born in 1950. When were your folks married?"

Lili had the distinct impression he'd planned this, knew exactly what his questions should be. But that was silly. Moreover, she wasn't going to be much help.

"I don't know when they were married. I don't know anything except that his name was Harry Cramer and he was killed in an automobile accident before I was born. When my mother was pregnant. So the accident has to have happened sometime in the nine months before March of 1950. Oh, and one other thing, she said she wasn't in the car. He must have been alone."

Andy shrugged. "You can't jump to that conclusion; it's prejudicial to research. First, you don't know they weren't happy. You've assumed it. Second, there's no way to guess anything about who was or wasn't in the car with Harry Cramer. We'll have to try to find out."

He made a few more notes, then flipped the pad closed and glanced out the window. "It's a nice evening, let's take a walk."

They went as far as Marble Arch, not touching but moving in unison, content with each other's company, feeling no need to talk. The bright lights of Oxford Street were ahead of them, and they could see the subdued glow of the expensive hotels of Park Lane. "Which land is dreamier," Lili sang softly. "Acadia or Bohemia?"

"Who'll give the answer, the Gypsy or the dancer?" Andy joined in.

"I used to sing that all the time when I was a kid, but I didn't think everybody knew it."

He took her hand. "Not everybody, me. Let's go back."

Somehow a sense of urgency crept into their movement, a sense of rushing toward something. The house was warm and welcoming because Lili clung to her American habits and never turned the heat off when she went out. "It feels great," Andy said. "Hooray for the decadent Americans."

"I'm not decadent," Lili protested. "I'm sensible and reliable and at least half of me is good Puritan New England stock."

He leaned forward and put his hands on either side of her, trapping her against the wall. "Are you truly a Puritan?"

"I don't think so," Lili said softly.

He kissed her. This time she sensed that he wasn't going to pull away. Lili pressed close to him, and Andy put his arms around her, and they clung to each other for a long time. When at last they inched apart, he pressed his cheek to her hair. "You smell like sunshine, you always do," he whispered. "I promised myself this wasn't going to happen, but . . . I want to stay with you tonight. I want to so damn much."

"I want you to." She spoke in a small, tremulous voice, but without hesitation.

"I'm glad. Let's go upstairs, then, shall we?"

They made love in the single narrow bed beneath the calico quilt, because for some reason there was no radiator in this room and they hadn't taken the time to make a fire. The moon shone through the window and lit the pile of clothes they'd dropped on the cushions.

Their limbs intertwined in the enveloping dark. Lili's were short and meaty and fair, Andy's long and sinewed and surprisingly tanned. She saw the golden hue of his skin when the quilt slid almost to the floor. His head was on her belly, kissing the flesh round her navel, one leg beneath her buttocks, one hand caressing with the lightest possible touch the hard, erect nipples of her breasts. He moved and his tongue traveled slowly up her midriff until his mouth was where his hand had been. Lili moaned softly.

Time passed and they did not hurry. Once Andy raised his

head and said, "You're as beautiful as I knew you'd be," and he stroked her all over with something that communicated itself as wonder. Later still he asked, "Is it the first time for you?"

"Yes," she whispered.

"I'll be gentle. Don't be frightened."

"I'm not frightened."

And she wasn't.

Lili lay with her head on Andy's chest, feeling for the first time in her life as if everything in her world was absolutely perfect. "Why did you promise yourself this wasn't going to happen?" she asked.

He took a few seconds to answer. "Because I want to concentrate on my work. I want to give no hostages to fortune."

"Am I a hostage?"

"Probably, but I'm past caring."

"I have another question."

"What is it?" he murmured sleepily.

"Am I a modern girl now?"

He laughed so hard, his whole frame shook and he hugged her and kissed her all the while.

Lili thought she might die from happiness.

When she woke he wasn't there. But the fire was lit and before she could panic she heard his foot on the stairs.

Andy came in wearing only a towel wrapped round his waist and carrying a tray with two boiled eggs, buttered toast, and a pot of tea. They pulled the cushions close to the glowing coals and ate and talked about nothing in particular and laughed a lot.

The terrible part didn't happen until an hour later, when they were downstairs in the gorgeous kitchen washing the dishes.

"Lili, I have to say this because I care a great deal about you. You mustn't fall in love with me."

She didn't answer. How could she when she was already so totally and completely in love with him, and surely he must know?

• • •

"I don't believe you made this." Andy helped himself to another serving of a provençal vegetable ragout.

Lili was teaching herself to cook, using the books Andy had brought her and others she'd recently acquired. She was getting quite good in the kitchen.

"Look," he said between bites. "I seem to be eating here all the time, so I should contribute to the housekeeping."

"Don't be silly, you're busy with your writing. I like cleaning and I'm beginning to love cooking."

He chuckled. "I mean the money for groceries. It's a nice workingclass expression, ' 'ere's the 'ouskeeping, love,' he says as he comes up from the pit and hands the careworn woman a few coppers with which to feed her brood of ten."

"Oh, I see." She was about to refuse, but she thought better of it. It was another link, a tie, a sign that they were a couple. "If you like."

"It's fair," he said, reaching for a third helping of the ragout.

"Don't stuff yourself, we have crème caramel for dessert." Lili's diet had been forgotten with the advent of the cookbooks.

The custards were perfect golden mounds shimmering on small white plates, quivering slightly beneath their amber coating. Andy made enthusiastic noises. "What converted you? When I bought you the cookery books, you didn't seem all that impressed."

She'd thought of the old expression about the way to a man's heart, but she wasn't going to tell him that. "This kitchen. How could you see this every day and not want to use it?"

"I wouldn't know. My bed-sit has a single gas ring and a fridge that's crowded if you try to keep butter and milk at the same time."

She did not meet his gaze. "Andy, why haven't you ever shown me your apartment?"

"Why bother? It's nothing like this." He waved his hand, dismissing any serious overtones to her question.

That night, after they'd loved and he'd left as he usually did because he wanted to be able to start writing early in the morning, she dreamed she went to his apartment and there was a woman there.

In Lili's dream the woman was old and ugly and terrifying. "I'm Mrs. Andy Mendoza," the dream woman said, cackling cruel laughter.

A week later Andy reported on the results of his search for Harry Cramer. "Absolutely nothing."

"What do you mean?"

"Exactly that. Nothing, *nada, nicht*. There's no trace of any Harry Cramer killed in an automobile accident in the second half of 1949 or the first quarter of 1950."

Lili stared at him. "Are you sure?"

"Reasonably so. I checked all the newspaper files. Something like that is always reported in some paper."

"Maybe you missed it."

He shook his head. "No, I don't make that kind of mistake."

She started to say he couldn't be certain, but something about the expression on his face forestalled her. He *was* certain.

"Look," he asked, "could you be wrong about the accident happening in England? Maybe they were somewhere else."

"No," Lili said slowly. "I don't think so. Mother's always said very little about it, as I told you. But those few facts are clear. She said that Harry Cramer was killed in a car crash in England before I was born."

He looked angry. "Then we've come up empty, dammit."

They were sitting on the blue sofa. Lili reached over and stroked his forehead. "Don't look so glum. It doesn't really matter."

"It doesn't make sense. I don't like things that don't make sense."

It was his disappointment, not hers, that provoked her suggestion. "I'll write to my mother and ask for more details. She must figure I'm going to look for some Cramer relatives even though she said there were none."

He brightened instantly. "Yes, do that. All I need is his date of birth. Then I can start from the other end, at Somerset House with the birth records."

Lili wrote to Irene that night and mailed the letter the next morning; after that they could only wait.

Toward the end of February there was a knock on Lili's door at ten in the morning. She knew it wasn't Andy. He was working; besides, he had his own key.

The caller was a petite young woman swaddled in a white woolen hat, a yards-long candy-cane-striped scarf, and a bright-red belted coat. The coat ended at mid-thigh and beneath it she wore white stockings and white leather boots. "Oh, I say, I'm sorry! I expected to find Charles Mendoza. I must have the wrong address."

"You're in the right place, but Charles is away in Africa. I'm staying in his house."

"Africa! And he didn't tell me."

The wind was from the north, cuttingly cold, and it was blowing straight into the hall. "Come in for a minute," Lili said.

The woman stepped across the threshold and slammed the door firmly behind her. "That's better. When did Sir Charles leave for the wilds?"

Sir Charles? Lili thought she must be joking. "Right after Christmas. I've been looking after the house since January tenth."

"Lucky you. It's a super house, isn't it? And you're an American."

It wasn't clear if the two statements were meant to be related. "I agree about the house, and yes, I am an American. Lili Cramer from Boston." She'd learned that was easier than trying to explain the whereabouts of Fielding.

The other woman extended her hand. "Ruth Owens. I work with Sir Charles on some of his projects."

It was not a joke. Apparently her landlord, Andy's cousin, had a title. Lili had no chance to react. Ruth Owens was still chattering. "I've been in Scotland since early December, right up in the Orkneys. The end of the world, so I've been out of touch. But Charles and I were scheduled to do Galanthus and Eranthis starting the first of March. Sorry to burst in on you like this."

Lili had no idea what she was talking about. But Ruth Owens knew things about Charles Mendoza, so she probably knew something about Andy as well. "Would you like a cup of coffee? It's no trouble."

"Thanks, I don't drink coffee or tea, but I'd love some hot water. It's freezing out there. The Orkneys were warmer."

Lili led the way into the kitchen. "This is the nicest room in the house. The rest isn't furnished except with some old things I've picked up. I'm afraid I don't know where the Orkneys are. Or what you and Charles Mendoza do together. He's a photographer, isn't he?"

"Yes. He specializes in natural subjects and does commissions for museums and zoos and geographical societies. I'm his sketcher. I go out in the field with him and do the technical drawings that accompany the photos. At least I *was* Charles's sketcher. Apparently, he's taken someone else to Africa."

Ruth had removed her coat and hat. Underneath she wore a white knit dress that was simply an elongated turtleneck sweater. She was wonderfully thin, had very short red curly hair, blue eyes, and freckles. Lili had on brown wool slacks and her fisherman's sweater, and felt outclassed.

"The Orkneys are the northernmost Scottish isles," the redhead continued. "I was with a team surveying Ericaceae, that's heaths and heathers. They're native to Scotland and lots of them bloom in autumn and winter."

Lili brought the coffeepot to the table. "You're sure you won't have some of this?"

"No thanks. I eat only natural foods. Plain hot water will be fine. A bit of lemon would be nice if you have it."

Lili got the lemon and sliced it. "Sugar?"

"Not unless it's raw."

"No, sorry."

"Not to worry. Where did you meet Charles?"

"I never have." Lili chose her words carefully. "He asked his cousin Andy to find someone to stay in the house."

"Ah! Uptight Andrew with the social conscience. The family black sheep. Is Andy a friend of yours?"

"Yes, we're . . . close friends."

"Oh, I see. I haven't said anything to offend, have I?"

"No. I'm fascinated. Why is Andy the black sheep?"

"His mother, for one thing. I mean, here's this ancient clan with their pedigrees all sorted out and any flaws nicely papered over, then Lord Westlake, whose been a widower for ages, suddenly marries a workingclass Yorkshire lass twenty-four years younger than he is." Ruth rolled her eyes upward. "*Quel* scandal!"

"Wait a minute," Lili said quickly. "Andy's name isn't Westlake, it's Mendoza."

Ruth giggled. "Your American is showing. Westlake is a title, titles and surnames are often not the same."

"Surname is last name, right?"

"Right. Andy's father was Ian Charles Mendoza, His Lordship, the fourth Baron Westlake. Westlake is also a place, the family seat. It's a huge Tudor house in the Lake District with acres and acres attached."

"What happened after Andy's father married his mother?" Lili asked.

"That's the juiciest part. She had the nerve to produce a son, our Andy. I think old Westlake was fifty when Andy was born, and he already had an heir. Then Andy turned out . . . different."

"How do you mean different?"

"All that uptight correctness. Among themselves the peerage are prone to kicking up their heels and emptying a sherry bottle before lunch. Andy isn't like that. When he wrote a series of articles for the Manchester *Guardian* about the nasty results of some of their pernicious inbreeding, the rest of the Mendozas practically disowned him."

"He's not disowned. He goes home for the holidays. Does Andy have a title? He's never said."

"I said almost disowned. Usually the nobs close ranks when the occasion demands. Certainly the Mendozas do. And Andy can't have the title, he's the second son. His cousin Charles got a K.C.B. a few years back, Knight Commander to you, that's why he's 'sir.' Knighthoods are an honor for something you yourself have done, in Charles's case take remarkable pictures. They're not hereditary and they don't make you a member of the peerage. The present Lord Westlake is Andy's elder half brother, Mark. Moreover, as peers go, barons are the bottom of the heap. Their kids don't have courtesy titles. Andy gets to be addressed as 'the honorable' on an envelope. That's it."

Lili was remembering what Andy had said about second sons. "And nowadays there aren't any colonies for him to run off to."

"Exactly," Ruth said, as if she'd been party to the conversation. "So he gets a little jealous and eccentric. Most of them do."

"Ah, yes," Andy said the next day when he heard about Lili's visitor. "Little Ruthie Owens. No tits and a big mouth. How did you get on?"

"I like her," Lili admitted. "She invited me to lunch next Saturday."

He cocked his head, took off his glasses, and studied her. "Are you sure that's the set you want to run with?"

"What set? What run? I'm having lunch with one woman. You don't approve?"

He twirled his glasses by the earpiece between thumb and forefinger. "It's none of my business, is it? But if you'll forgive the crudeness, la Owens is a ballbreaker."

"That's hardly going to bother me, since I don't have any."

"No, you don't, do you. Lili, are we quarreling? About Ruth Owens, for God's sake?"

"I'm not quarreling."

"You're edgy as hell, and when you get that tight look around the mouth, something's wrong."

He was on cushions on the floor; she was lying on the blue couch. Lili flipped onto her belly and rested her chin in her hands. "Andy, why didn't you tell me you've had work published? You always make it seem that you're struggling to begin as a writer. Ruth said you did a series of articles for a newspaper. And lots of other things."

"A big mouth, as I said. That was nonfiction. Reporting, not writing. A novel is different."

"Okay, but you're always so mysterious about everything. I mean, you never explained about being the son of a lord and—"

"Losing out to my elder half brother," he interrupted. "Jesus! She really puked it all out, didn't she? How long was she here, a week?"

"An hour. She talks fast." Lili chuckled. She couldn't help it.

A few seconds later Andy was chuckling too. "I like people who laugh at their own jokes," he said.

He came over and pushed her to one side of the couch. "Move that fulsome arse and let me have some room. Listen, love, one of the best things about you is that you're free of a lot of English prejudices. You don't care about who's going to inherit what, or parties where everyone's named Fiona or Nigel. I haven't wanted to sully your American innocence because I enjoy it."

She put her head in his lap and sighed. "You always have an explanation that makes me feel stupid and petty and childish."

"You're alone too much; you imagine sinister motives where none exist. I wish you'd try again to enroll in some course."

"They won't let me study what interests me, so I can't. And you mustn't disapprove of my seeing Ruth. She's fascinating and she'll teach me a lot."

"All the wrong things."

"I don't think so.

At five the next morning Andy crept out of her bed. "Don't tiptoe," Lili murmured. "I'm awake."

"Vas is! Dr. Mendoza's sleeping potion did not work? Ve must administer ze dose number two, or is it three?" He knelt beside her and kissed her softly, then stopped. "I don't think I'd be much good. I'm a bit on edge."

"Why?" She took her arms from around his neck and sat up.

"I'm having lunch with my agent today. After he has a meeting with a publisher who may be interested in my novel."

"Andy, you didn't tell me you'd finished it!"

"I haven't. But Barry, my agent, says the first several chapters are so good, he may be able to land a contract for the novel. I'm not sure he's right."

Until that moment she hadn't known he had an agent. Another misconception corrected. Andy was not quite the struggling unknown she'd imagined. "Will you be devastated if the publisher says no?"

"Sure. Then I'll get over it and go on working and wait for Barry to find another publisher. Can I make myself a boiled egg before I go? I'm starved. It must be nerves."

"I'll come down and make us both an early breakfast."

He protested, but not too strongly. They went to the kitchen in the predawn dark and Lili made scrambled eggs and bacon and toast and coffee and he wolfed down everything.

"Call me after the lunch date, will you?"

"Yes. To celebrate or to moan."

Instead, her phone rang at eleven. "Barry called to say the publishers are preparing a contract," Andy announced gleefully. "I don't know the terms yet, but I don't really care."

"Darling, that's terrific. I'm so happy for you!" The *darling* slipped out because his excitement was contagious. Andy never used any term of endearment other than the ubiquitous "love," which she'd learned early on meant nothing; even the grocer called her love. Instinctively, she'd followed his lead.

But being darling for once didn't seem to bother him. "I'm happy for me too. And I want you there for the celebration. Come to lunch with us. Barry's been longing to meet you."

The thought that he discussed her with the other man was startling, and very nice. "I'd love to, but are you sure it's all right?"

"Of course it is. It's the Grill Room at the Dorchester, no less. If the publisher had turned us down, it would have been fish and chips. Wear something wonderful."

"I don't have anything wonderful." She hadn't bought new clothes in London; she couldn't afford to. Lili thought of Ruth Owens in her chic red and white. "I'll embarrass you, I'd better not come."

"That's absurd. Wear the knit dress I like, the bluish one."

"It's too tight."

He laughed. "That's why I like it. Barry will too. Twelve forty-five in the lobby of the Dorchester Hotel. Don't let me down."

After she hung up, Lili thought for a moment, then dialed Ruth Owens's number. "This is Lili Cramer. I'm sorry to be a nuisance, but I need help."

"Hello, Lili. You're not a nuisance. I'm still in bed. I was lying here being bored. What kind of help?"

"What's appropriate to wear to a mostly business lunch at the Dorchester?"

"Restaurant or Grill Room?"

"Grill Room." Lili hadn't realized the different rooms were significant.

"That's good. You can wear anything that looks great on you to the Grill Room. Even trousers are okay."

Lili didn't answer. She knew Ruth meant a pants suit, not slacks and a sweater. She didn't own a pants suit.

"That doesn't seem to help much," Ruth said when the silence had lasted for some seconds. "I take it you don't have anything you think is great enough. And it's important."

"Right on both counts."

"Mmm . . . listen, tell you what, I'll drop by and see if I can help you decide. Be at your place in half an hour. What time's your lunch?"

"Quarter to one."

"Okay, that's enough time. Anyway, you can be fashionably late."

Ruth arrived in jeans, boots, and a big sweater. She wore no makeup, her short hair was tousled, and she was carrying a suitcase. Lili had washed her hair and was wielding her hair dryer.

"Your hair's fabulous, you know," Ruth said.

"Yes, I do know. But that's it. Sum total of the assets: one."

Ruth stepped back and eyed her. "Not true. Great eyes and those pudgy cheeks suit you."

"The rest of the pudge doesn't."

"I'm not sure. It isn't fashionable, but you're rounded, not lumpy. Andy Mendoza likes it, doesn't he? Is your lunch with him?"

"Yes, and his agent. It's a celebration. Andy's sold his novel."

"Really! I wonder how the family will take that."

Lili was immediately sorry she'd spoken. "Oh, God, it's probably a secret. He'll be furious with me. Don't tell, please."

Ruth shrugged. "I don't spend my time discussing the doings of the Mendozas. C'mon, show me your clothes and let's see what we can do. I brought a few accessories that might help."

She agreed with Andy. "This aquamarine knit is good. Let's see it on you. Oh, yes, definitely. It's a little long, but they say the mini's going to be out this spring. Something called maxi will be in. I'll need a whole new wardrobe. Anyway, the color does great things for your eyes. Do you have boots?"

"Only black ones." Lili took them from the closet. "My coat's burgundy. Seems like a lot of colors."

Ruth eyed the coat. "No good. I've got something better." She opened the suitcase. "Most of my things would be too small for you, but this boxy jacket shouldn't be."

It was black fox fur, hip-length. "It's beautiful, but really, I didn't mean to—"

"Stop talking and put it on."

"I can't, Ruth. It's awfully nice of you, but it's fur and it must be expensive."

"You're not going to abscond with it, are you? Or drink too much and throw up all over it? What's the difference? You can bring it back when you come for lunch on Saturday. There, I knew it would look great."

It did. The snug knit dress, the knee-length boots, the fluffy fur that framed her face and her long, straight, dark hair were marvelous together. Lili looked in the mirror and smiled.

"We've gone backward," Ruth said. "You need some makeup. Take off that jacket for the nonce and let's get to it." She vetoed the turquoise eye shadow Lili was going to use. "Has to be gray. You must have some." She pawed through the makeup in the bathroom medicine chest and located an eye shadow she liked and applied it with cool, deft fingers.

"Now a light lipstick and some blusher. Your skin's great, you don't need foundation." She worked quickly and finished with a flourish. "A dab of blusher in that cleft in your chin. To emphasize it. Great, gives you character. There, you're gorgeous."

Lili looked in the mirror. Maybe not gorgeous, but good. Very good. The gray eye shadow made her hazel eyes more blue; they reflected the dress. And for once she didn't see the creased chin as a deformity.

"You look fabulous," Ruth pronounced as she helped Lili into the black fur. "And it's twenty to one. Off you go."

Irene kept Lili's letter a long time. Days stretched into weeks and she read it and reread it, and did nothing. Each time the hastily written words chilled her anew: "Probably you won't be surprised to hear that I'm trying to see if maybe you were mistaken and someone from my father's family is still alive, but so far no luck. I know you hate to talk about it, but won't you tell me what part of England Harry Cramer came from? And when he was born? And, if you can bear it, when and where the accident happened? So I can look in the right place . . ."

Each night while she stared into the mirror reliving the past—reassuring herself that it was past—Irene laughed a small, bitter laugh. She'd brought it on herself. She let Lili go abroad and even financed the trip. But she'd been so disturbed by the child's pain, and so certain that whatever she said, Lili would go anyway. And after all these years, surely it was safe?

You're a fool, Irene told herself. Now the chickens are coming home to roost. Now the sins of the fathers will be visited upon the children. But she did nothing.

On a snowy February day a second letter arrived from London. "Did you get mine about my father?" Lili wrote. "Won't you please answer my questions? A close friend is helping me investigate. I've been meaning to tell you about him. . . ."

Irene read it through once, disbelieving, then a second time. The words were like snakes on the page. They slithered toward her through a shimmer of tears. This wasn't simply a shattering coincidence, it was heaven's judgment.

Early the next morning she sat in bed after a sleepless night, and admitted that she could not deal with this alone. She'd have to break the rules. This was the emergency they'd always known might happen someday.

Irene rose and went into the bathroom and washed and brushed her teeth and made up and got dressed. Carefully, as if she were about to keep a very important appointment. Finally, when she was completely ready, she sat on the corner of her bed and picked up the telephone and dialed the international operator and gave her a number in Madrid.

Seconds later she heard, *"Sí, buenas tardes. Dígame."*

The Spanish greeting unnerved her. Irene stumbled out a name, tried to recall the few Spanish phrases she'd once known. Her stutterings were swiftly interrupted.

"It's you, darling, isn't it? Yes, of course it's me. What is it? What's wrong?"

Irene sighed. "Thank God. I hoped you'd answer yourself. If it was him, I didn't know—"

"No, he isn't here at the moment. Tell me what's happened." The woman who was halfway across the world spoke slowly, patiently, with a concerted effort to soothe.

Irene blurted out the terrible words. "Lili's looking for Harry Cramer in England."

A long pause, then, "Well, I suppose we should have expected she'd do that."

"She keeps writing me questions. Wants to know where he was from, when he died, things like that."

"Yes," the woman said again. "I'm not surprised."

Irene took a deep breath. "That's not all," she hesitated. "She has a friend, a boyfriend I think, though she doesn't say that exactly."

"Yes?" The woman in Spain was still patient.

"He's Lord Westlake's son. His name is Andy Mendoza."

A sharp intake of breath was audible over the wires. "Oh, my God."

"It's unbelievable, isn't it? What do I do?"

"There's not much you can do, is there? There's nothing you dare tell her about Harry Cramer. Or about the Mendozas."

"No, of course not. But I'm terrified. She won't give up. Lili can be terribly stubborn. She'll keep looking, and she'll keep hounding me. God knows what I'll blurt out if I get desperate."

The woman in Spain understood that part of Irene's character. She never had been any good in a crisis. That was almost how the whole thing had started. "Let me think," she said. And a few seconds later: "I'll have to see if I can do something from here."

"Oh, yes," Irene almost sobbed with gratitude. "That would be so much better. If you could—"

"Yes," the woman said firmly. "Stop worrying. I can, I will. Put it out of your mind."

"You always make everything better," Irene said. "Always. I'm so grateful."

A small laugh traveled the long distance between Madrid and Fielding. "I'm the one who should be grateful. Put it out of your mind," she said again. "All my love, pet," she added gently. "Good-bye."

The connection was broken. Irene sat silent for a moment, deep in thought. Then she stood up and straightened the skirt of her tailored woolen dress. She glanced into the mirror as she left the bedroom. She looked fine. Cracks had started to appear in a façade created long before. The genie had almost escaped the bottle—but she'd put it back. She was cool, self-possessed Irene Petworth Cramer again.

❧ 6 ❧

London and Madrid: 1971

Ruth Owens lived in a welter of short streets surrounding a small park known as Ennismore Gardens, in a flat quixotically carved out of a former single-family home. "Three floors, but only one room on each," she explained as she showed Lili in. "And two of them aren't big enough to turn around in."

"It's very nice," Lili said politely.

"It's a bloody shambles," Ruth corrected her. "I'm hoping to buy a super two-bedroom flat in a new block, but I've got to sell this first. No takers so far."

Lili was not surprised. The middle floor, which was ninety percent of the living space, could have been nice, but the fine period details of the room were hidden by inappropriate modern furniture in shades of purple and orange.

Ruth disappeared up a flight of stairs and returned carrying a tray with two glasses. Apparently the stairs led to the kitchen. The apartment was inconvenient as well as unattractive.

"Carrot juice," Ruth said, offering Lili a glass. "I want my friends to be healthy as well as wealthy and wise. How was your lunch at the Dorchester? Did Andy like the fur jacket?"

"I think so. He didn't say much, but he looked appreciative."

Ruth giggled. "I'll bet. I've always suspected that fires smolder beneath that stern and scholarly exterior. Where did you two meet?"

"The Victoria and Albert Museum." Lili said it softly, a little embarrassed because it still sounded like a pickup to her.

"My God, where else!" Ruth lifted her glass. "Cheers."

Lili sipped the carrot juice. It wasn't bad.

"Is Andy's book going to be a smash hit and set everybody talking?" Ruth asked.

"No, apparently it's rather serious. His agent told Andy he should concentrate on writing exposés about the landed gentry. Andy wasn't happy to hear it. Or that his novel will be over most people's heads."

"Andy's over the heads of most people, at least most of the time." Ruth went upstairs again and returned with another tray. "Let's eat. It's all raw and natural. Wonderful for you."

Ruth served large helpings of salad from a big wooden bowl and cut thick slices of rough dark bread. Lili helped herself to butter. "Have you known Andy long?" she asked.

Ruth smiled. "Seven or eight years." Then, "Lili, how old are you?"

"Twenty-one next month."

"What date?"

"March twenty-second."

"Ah, Aries."

"Yes. Andy's Scorpio."

Ruth served more salad. "Andy's what, twenty-eight?"

"Twenty-seven."

The redhead stopped eating and looked at her guest. "You know everything about him, don't you? Down to what kind of scissors he uses to cut his toenails. Because you're besotted with him."

Lili didn't answer right away, but when she did she didn't look at Ruth. "I don't think I know everything. Ruth, is Andy married?"

"Married? No. What gave you that idea? Did he say he was married?"

"No. It occurred to me, that's all."

"I can assure you that unless he's hidden a bride away in the darkest hinterlands, Andy Mendoza remains on the list of eligible bachelors. And between us, though you won't thank me for saying so, I think he intends to remain that way. I don't think our Andy is catchable."

Having made this devastating pronouncement, Ruth rose and fetched dessert. "Fresh casaba melon. The only place you can get it this time of year is in Harrods' Food Halls. One nice thing about this place, it's convenient to Harrods and Harvey Nichols *and* the Kings Road. The best of the old world and the new."

"But you still want to sell it?" Lili was glad to be able to say something unconcerned with Andy.

"Desperately. You're not in the market, are you?"

"No, I'm afraid I can't afford to buy an apartment. Have many people been to look?"

"Oh, scads. But much good does it do me. They all go away and buy something else."

"Show me the kitchen and the bath." Lili pushed her chair away from the table and stood up.

Ruth led her up the stairs. The kitchen was fitted into what had obviously been a landing before the house was butchered. The bathroom was two flights down, off the tiny entrance foyer. It had purple tile and fittings that dated from the same period as the kitchen.

"It's all thirties modern," Ruth said. "There's nothing worse, is there?"

"Hard to think of anything," Lili admitted. "In my view, that was a desperately bad period for design and architecture."

Ruth produced cups of camomile tea and carob cookies. "Why are you looking so pensive?" she asked.

"Because this place has potential," Lili said. "But it needs a lot of redoing and it would be expensive."

The redhead narrowed her eyes. "How expensive?"

"I don't know. I have no idea of prices in London."

"Could you find out?"

Lili thought for a moment. "I suppose I could."

It took three weeks for the two women to come to a business arrangement, but at the end of that time Lili took on the remodeling of Ruth Owens's flat. Sometimes she couldn't believe she'd had the nerve to actually accept such a responsibility, then she remembered why she'd done it. The truth had come to her with dramatic force the evening she and Andy celebrated her twenty-first birthday. It was March, and the year in England that Irene had agreed to finance was half over. Unless she found work and began supporting herself, in six months time she would have to leave Andy. That was unthinkable.

At first she was almost paralyzed by nerves, but gradually her confidence grew. Ruth had established a budget for the job based on Lili's estimates, but in a short time it was apparent that the work could be done for less. Lili found independent craftsmen who would do a job cheaply if they were paid in cash. She located sources of used building materials. She combed London for special offers on paint and fabric—and she changed. As the work progressed, Lili came alive. She glowed with happiness and satisfaction.

"You're having a good time, aren't you?" Andy asked one evening while they were eating Lili's perfect spinach soufflé.

"Marvelous," she admitted. "I never realized it could be so much fun to spend somebody else's money."

"At last, a use for la Owens." He grinned at her. "I suppose you've been too busy to think about the fact that we haven't had any answers from your mother."

"About my father, you mean?"

"Yes. Will the real Harry Cramer please stand up."

"He can't, he's dead."

Andy didn't look at her. "Maybe. Listen, love, have you ever thought that perhaps he isn't? Could be that's why your mother is so reluctant to let it all hang out, as you Americans say. Could be he's alive."

Lili considered the enormity of this notion. "No," she said after a few seconds. "I can't tell you why I'm sure. You'd have to know my mother. Irene is painfully honest. Always correct. If I had a father alive somewhere, she wouldn't keep it from me. I can't imagine anything that would make her do that."

"Then why won't she answer your letters?"

"She does, but she doesn't answer my questions."

He was getting impatient. "So what are you going to do about it?"

Lili rose and began clearing the table. "Nothing. Not the way you mean. Confrontations between me and my mother are always the same; we're both equally stubborn."

"Do you want me simply to drop the whole inquiry?"

She paused with her hands full of dirty dishes. "You don't want to, do you? Andy, do you have some hidden agenda I don't know about?"

He didn't look at her. "Don't be silly. I think you have a right to know."

"Okay, so do I. We'll have to try another approach. What do you suggest?"

He brought the coffeepot and two mugs to the table. "I'll have to think about it. Let you know when I have an idea. God knows when that might be." He noticed her expression of despair. "Look, I'm sorry, I didn't mean to upset you. Pretend I didn't mention it. I don't want to spoil the fun you're having with Ruth's place. I like seeing you so animated."

And she liked being that way.

Lili had been working on Ruth's apartment for a month when she came home one evening and found an envelope shoved under the door. Her fingers trembled when she picked it up.

That was stupid. She was being ridiculous. But who beside Andy would push an envelope under her door? Okay, why was that something to be nervous about?

She didn't open it right away. She carried it into the living room and sat on the blue sofa and took off her sneakers and socks and rubbed her feet. She'd been standing all day, and they ached. Her neck and her shoulders ached too. Getting workmen cheap usually meant they didn't bring helpers. Lili did most of the fetching and carrying. That was the only thing wrong with her, she was tired.

She knew she was kidding herself. The envelope with her name on it lay on the cushion beside her, but she couldn't bring herself to open it. Why was she so frightened? Why this chill in the pit of her stomach? Lili made herself face the truth. What was terrifying her was that lately she had sensed a distancing in Andy.

He was there most of the time; they ate together, lay together, loved, laughed, did all the things they'd done for five months, but it wasn't the same. Andy was preoccupied, pulling away. And in the last few weeks she'd been so wrapped up in Ruth's project she'd let her guard down.

Maybe she hadn't worked quite so hard to please him. Maybe she was tired and irritable sometimes. Andy had finished his novel and he was worried about how the publishers would handle it. "They can kill a book before it's out by not making a real commitment," he'd said. She should have picked up on that, been sympathetic, got him to talk more about it, shared his anxiety. But that day she'd been bone-tired and she hadn't responded.

Lili picked up the envelope with shaking hands. If it was a farewell letter, if he was saying that he didn't want her anymore, what would she do then? "I'll die," she whispered. "I love him so much." The words echoed in the emptiness.

The letter wasn't sealed, the flap of the envelope was tucked in. Taking a deep breath, she pulled it open and removed a single sheet of folded paper. Dear God, please don't let him leave me, she prayed silently. Like when she was a kid, dear God, don't let me fail the history test . . .

Lili unfolded the note. It was four lines. "Dearest little love, something's come up and I have to go to Spain for a bit. Probably not longer than three weeks. I'll send a postcard and ring when I get back. Take care and sleep warm."

She crumpled the note in her hands and wept with a mixture of relief because it wasn't over, and misery at the thought of not seeing him for so long.

That night she lit the bedroom fire to comfort her loneliness. The coals glowed and washed the room pink. Spain, she mused as she drifted into sleep in the narrow bed. Why Spain? Funny she'd never thought of it before, but wasn't Mendoza a Spanish name?

Mark Mendoza, the fifth Baron Westlake, did not like Spain. Forget that it was the land of his ancestors, he was generations removed from those roots. He looked out the windows of the black Mercedes with the prejudiced eyes of a true Englishman. Abroad was "foreign," uncomfortable, not to be trusted. He had the grace to smile at his reaction.

The chauffeured car was moving through the outskirts of Madrid, along quiet residential streets lined with the dwellings of the comfortable middle class. The apartment houses were perfectly ordinary. The odd thing was that his cousin, Diego Parilles Mendoza, chose to live in one of them.

The Mercedes slid smoothly to curbside in front of a building little different from its neighbors. The Englishman waited until the driver opened his door. *"Esperaté aquí, Don Marco."*

Mark accepted the chauffeur's promise to wait with a brusque nod, and glanced at the unpretentious neighborhood where one of the world's richest men lived. The Mendozas were not normally given to ostentation, but Diego was a monk. At least in most things.

A maid let him in and showed him to the drawing room. It was high-ceilinged, shuttered against the sun, and furnished in heavy woods and dark colors. The somber interior was relieved only by a formal bouquet of dark red roses. He was glad not to be kept waiting long.

"Ah, Mark, thank you for coming." Diego's linguistic skills had been the basis of his control of vast amounts of the Mendoza wealth. His English was flawless and almost without accent.

Diego took both the hands of his cousin in his own. His greeting to another Spaniard would have involved a hug and kisses on both cheeks, but he understood the English. He'd had a long time to learn. Diego was sixty but looked younger. Tall, spare, and dark, he was a man who exuded a kind of determined vitality, a man definitely not done with living.

Mark Mendoza was some ten years younger and twice as broad, but this meeting was not about physical power, and he knew that where it mattered, Diego outclassed him. The Spaniard had been playing the game longer. Mark wasn't sure why he'd been summoned. He waited patiently for the older man to explain.

"Please, sit down. Some wine before we talk." Diego poured it while he spoke. "Are you hungry? My wife is away, but I can arrange for some food."

"No, the wine is fine, thank you."

"You're wondering why I asked you to come here, when we could have talked at the office."

"Yes," the Englishman agreed, "I am."

"It's a matter of some delicacy. A family matter."

Mark smiled. "Everything we talk about is 'a family matter.' And has been since the time of the Phoenicians, if the grandiose legends are to be believed."

Diego sipped his wine and nodded. "Yes, that's what they say, that the first Mendoza came to Spain from Judea with the Phoenician traders, that he settled in Córdoba and became a moneylender. You look doubtful."

Mark smiled. "I always have been a bit. It's really impossible to know, isn't it?"

Diego shrugged. "Yes, impossible."

"Anyway," Mark said. "What does it prove? However our forefathers came, whenever they arrived, they prospered and we're the result."

"Prospered," Diego repeated quietly. "That's the strange part. Jews, but they prospered through everything that's happened in Spain over the past two thousand years. Virulent anti-Semitism, even banishment, didn't drive them out."

"Because when it was inconvenient to be Jews they managed to be something else," Mark said. "We've a genius for compromise, Diego."

"Indeed, we have. That's the key to understanding us. Thankfully, our competitors have never really grasped the fact." The Spaniard smiled as he refilled their glasses. "Now, to the matter at hand. It's got nothing to do with history. I would appreciate it if you'd send for your young brother. He's with the family in Córdoba at the moment."

"Andy? Yes, I believe he is. You want him in Madrid?"

"For a day or two, yes."

Mark shrugged. The protocol of the situation demanded that he let Diego explain in his own way. "I'll send for him, of course. If you wish it."

"He'll come without any difficulty?" Diego asked.

So Diego knew of Andy's rebellious ways. Mark shrugged. "I think so. If I ask him, if I put it on a family basis. He can be difficult, but basically Andy's as much a Mendoza as you and I. Only he hates to admit it."

The ways of modern youth puzzled Diego. "Why does he hate to admit it?"

"Because he doesn't like what you and I stand for," Mark said frankly. "He doesn't approve of wealth and power."

"Then he's a fool." Diego was disappointed. There was no enlightenment here, no new insights. "I think his generation are perhaps all fools. I don't understand them."

"They can be annoying, but they're not all fools. Andy, for one, is very intelligent, make no mistake about that. Why do you want to see him?"

"I don't," Diego said mildly. "If I did, I'd simply have gone to Córdoba or invited him here. I want you to see him. Since you're in Madrid, it's convenient to settle this now."

Mark was patient with the ambiguities; he was accustomed to them. "Settle what?"

"Young Andrew has been investigating something in England. That activity troubles a lady, a close friend."

Ah, of course. Diego's mistress, it had to be. The woman was apparently his cousin's only self-indulgence in an abstemious life. Mark had known about her for years, the whole family did. But Diego was discreet and no one minded, not even his wife. "And you want me to tell Andy to stop investigating whatever it is that disturbs your close friend?" he asked.

"Yes."

"That may not work. He'll probably tell me to mind my own business. In choice Anglo-Saxon words."

"I'm sure he will. So you must be very firm, put it on the basis that you're the elder brother."

Mark chuckled. "As you pointed out, you don't understand today's youth. I can't promise to make Andy heel."

Diego found that puzzling. "But you said he has some family feeling."

"He does. Only he sees such things differently from you and me."

The older man frowned. "Very well. But you'll try?"

"Of course, since you've asked me to."

Diego nodded with satisfaction. That, at least, was the Mendoza way.

Which was what Andy said when the two brothers met a few days later in Mark's suite at the Hotel Ritz in Madrid. "It's the bloody Mendoza way, isn't it? Anybody steps on your toes, you twist their arm, or something worse. Nothing matters except that you get what you want."

"You're making a meal of it, lad," Mark said casually. "It's not a major issue. I accept that you want to spend your time writing what seems to me drivel, that's your choice. But this time you've touched a nerve close to home. So find some other cupboard to poke around in. Asking questions about this chap Cramer bothers Diego."

"Why? What's Harry Cramer to do with the family?"

Andy was on a fishing expedition. He hadn't been sure that there was a connection between Lili's father and the family. It was the link to Fielding that intrigued him. Now he waited for Mark's answer, studying his elder brother, hoping to be able to tell if he offered truth or a lie.

"I haven't any idea," Mark said. It was obvious that he meant it. "Never heard of him."

"Then why are you taking orders from Diego?"

"Not orders, I'm responding to a request from my cousin and business partner. That's common good manners, Andy. I'd appreciate you're showing some."

"And if I don't?"

Mark shrugged. "I'll be disappointed."

"That's all? You'll be disappointed. Is Diego prepared to leave it at that?"

The older brother seemed genuinely surprised. "Of course he will. He'll have to. We're not gangsters, Andy, whatever you imagine. We're decent men. Admittedly, we're accustomed to getting our own way, but there are no thugs, no bodies dropped into a river with cement overshoes. The Mendoza Group is a business concern, it's not the Mafia."

"Jesus Christ," Andy breathed softly. "You really believe that, don't you? You think you're different from ordinary criminals because you have titles and proper pedigrees and the right connections. You're not, you know, you're all bastards.

Maybe you can close your eyes to what's been done to get the Mendozas where they are. I can't. I don't intend to."

"I think this conversation has gone on long enough," Mark said. "I was asked to convey a personal request to you, I've done so. I can only add that I'll be extremely upset if you choose to ignore it."

For a moment the two men eyed each other in silence. Standoff. Andy got up and walked out.

The Madrid streets were deserted, it was late afternoon, time for the siesta that all Spaniards regarded as their God-given right. The isolation suited Andy, it allowed him to think without distractions. First he had to get his anger under control, then he needed to organize his thoughts.

That there was an indirect link he'd suspected for some time; it was part of something he'd been looking into for years. Now it seemed it could be more real than he'd guessed, a straight line from Harry Cramer to Swanning Park. And given his view of the way the Mendozas did things, that could be dangerous. That's what he'd have to bear in mind from now on. Lili could be in danger.

A few miles away, in yet another Madrid apartment, Diego Parilles Mendoza was appraising his mistress with narrowed eyes. "I have done as you asked, *querida*. Now you must tell me why."

"I can't do that," she said.

"That is . . . not polite. I thought there were no secrets between us."

The woman smiled. She was even lovelier when she smiled. "There are nothing but secrets between us."

"Yes, I know what you mean. But Harry Cramer? Who is he? Why do you care about him?"

She shook her head and reached for a cigarette from the jade box on the coffee table. She was proud of the fact that her fingers did not tremble. "You promised, Diego. I asked if you'd help without asking for an explanation, and you said you would. You're not being fair."

Diego laughed. "Fair. Do you think fairness is one of my virtues?"

"No. But it has always been your way with me."

"True." He nodded. "And have you repaid me in kind, *querida*?"

Her eyes were incredible, large and dark gray, like quicksilver. They looked into his with absolute sincerity. "Yes. Always."

"Now too?"

"Now too."

He sighed. "Very well. We will forget about this Mr. Cramer. For the moment. Does that satisfy you?"

She nodded. It was all she would get, so it had to be enough. For the moment, as Diego said.

The Sunday after Andy returned from Spain he spent the entire night with Lili, not leaving before dawn the way he usually did. They slept late. At eleven in the morning he went out and bought the *Observer* and the Sunday *Times* and a plastic-wrapped package of gooey things which Lili called Danish pastries and Andy said were sticky buns.

Lili made coffee and sliced some oranges and sprinkled them with powdered sugar, then remembered there was mint growing in the garden and dashed out the French doors and picked a handful to chop up and sprinkle on the oranges.

"A feast for royalty," Andy said.

Lili dropped a curtsy. "At your service, sire."

He stopped pouring coffee. "I wish I were king of a magic kingdom."

"Why?"

"I'd make everything perfect. No evil, no ugliness. Above all, no irony or coincidence."

"What's wrong with irony and coincidence?"

He didn't reply, and Lili let it go. She felt closer to him than she had in weeks. There was no gap yawning between them now, no sense of his withdrawing. A spring of happiness bubbled inside Lili and she drank deep and reveled in it.

After breakfast they sprawled on cushions on the floor in the living room and read the papers. Andy went at once to the book reviews; Lili thumbed idly through the other sections until she came across a special supplement in the

Times. The full-color cover showed a fabulous Elizabethan manor set in a green parkland with red-coated huntsman in the distance. It was titled "Stately Homes Open for the Season," and underneath, "It may not feel like spring, but their lordships have unlocked the gates . . ."

She read it avidly and with a growing excitement. "Andy, it says here you can visit lots of the great English houses."

"Yes, you can. It's a national mania."

"I thought all aristocrats despised the masses. Except you."

"Since the advent of death duties, they've had to learn to tolerate them."

"I don't understand."

"Death duties are a whopping inheritance tax that can wipe out a fortune with one nasty stroke," he explained. "And there's the cost of keeping serfs these days. They want at least a pound an hour to tug their forelocks. It all adds up to making the maintenance of one of those drafty old mansions shockingly expensive. So a few years back somebody hit on the scheme of letting the lumpenproletariat come in and rubberneck for half a crown."

"How much is that?"

"In our disgusting and debased new currency, twenty-five pence."

"That's all? You mean for about seventy-five cents I can actually go inside all these houses they list here?"

"Yes, but you'll need a strong stomach as well as a lot of pence. If you mean to do them all, you'll o.d. on stateliness."

"Oh, no, I won't," Lili said. She was carefully clipping the article.

Later, after they'd made love and were deciding where to go for a meal, Lili asked, "Andy, does your brother open his home for twenty-five pence?"

"No. The Mendozas are different. Not just a title and land—they're stinking rich, dabble in business. Shocking but true, the continental influence."

"What business? And what continental influence?"

"The Mendozas own a private bank. Not the sort where your ordinary yob goes to open a checking account, only businesses and governments need apply. In other words, a license to print money."

"And is there no place for you in this family firm?"

"Yes, there is if I wanted it. I didn't. I don't."

"You didn't answer my second question," Lili said.

"About the continental influence? We're a Spanish family originally. Still lots of ties."

"Is that why you went to Spain, family business?"

"No," Andy said sharply. "I don't run errands for big brother. I was following a lead for a possible new book. But please don't ask questions. I can't talk about it. It's pretty amorphous right now. If I discuss it, I'll lose it entirely. And that brings me to something else—you haven't heard from your mother, have you? I mean with any new details about the mysterious Harry Cramer."

Lili frowned. "No, not a word about him."

"Okay. Would you mind if we drop the whole thing for a bit? Because I'm thinking about a new book. It might get in my way."

"No, I don't mind. It seems pointless anyway, since we keep bumping up against a brick wall."

"Good, that's settled, then."

"For the time being," Lili said. It wasn't settled in her mind; she meant to find her father someday. But there was too much to think about right now. There was Andy, and he filled her world. She leaned over and kissed him, and she didn't mention his trip again.

ⳤ 7 ⳤ

London: 1971

Andy's novel, *A Passion to Deceive,* was published in June 1971. He hated the black and red jacket. "The lettering looks like it's dripping blood. It's not a whodunit."

He'd given Lili an autographed advance copy and she was trying to read it, but it wasn't easy. For one thing, she was deeply involved in a new project of her own; for another, the story kept getting lost in long, rambling dissertations about sixteenth-century politics and morals.

Andy knew about Lili's venture. She and Ruth Owens had gone into business doing small domestic remodeling jobs. Ruth's excellent connections enabled her to find clients, Lili decided what was to be done and how, and Ruth made drawings from Lili's verbal descriptions. It seemed to be working. They had two jobs under way, and Lili was wildly excited. Andy said he thought it was great, but he was obviously too wrapped up in his own career to think much about hers.

The day his novel was officially published Lili went with him on a tour of half a dozen bookstores between Edgware Road and Charing Cross. They found the book in three of them. "Fifty percent isn't bad," Lili said. "In America we'd say you're batting five hundred, that's a terrific average."

"This isn't America," Andy said glumly. "And three out of six is terrible. Bloody reps."

"What are reps?"

"Not what, who. They're the pimps the publisher hires to go around and peddle his wares. Bloody idiots, all of them. Illiterate probably. Haven't read a book since they left school."

Lili didn't comment. She glanced at her watch. She was supposed to be in Brixton at four to see a carpenter. It was three-thirty, but when she looked at Andy's grim face she knew she couldn't leave him. "Wait for me here a minute. I've got to make a telephone call."

He resented even that. When she returned he said, "I suppose that was about your important work."

"Yes. Andy, it's not my fault there aren't more books out. Don't make me feel rotten about the one thing I hope I can do."

They were walking up Charing Cross Road on the way to Piccadilly and yet another bookstore. He stopped and let the crowd move around him. "I'm acting like a spoiled child, aren't I? Lili, darling, I'm sorry."

It was the very first time he'd ever called her darling. She couldn't say anything. She just took his arm and squeezed.

After a few seconds they moved on, but they never got to the bookstore. They came to a wine bar called the Grapes of Rathman. "Let's go in here and drown my troubles," Andy said.

"I wonder who Rathman is?" Lili mused.

"A smart Jew." Andy looked around. "Doing well from the look of it."

She found the remark a little disturbing, a little out of kilter with what she thought of as acceptable. "Don't you like Jews?"

Andy seemed to think that was extremely funny. He laughed a long time and finally he took both her hands across the table. "My sweet Lili. You're still not a modern girl. You must be the only person in England who doesn't know that the Mendozas are Jews."

"Really? But you're not. I mean you eat pork and you don't wear one of those little round caps. Besides, you've never said you were a Jew."

"I'm not, in any religious sense. My Yorkshire mother for one thing. Orthodox Judaism says that you're a Jew only if your mother was. For another, most of the Mendozas aren't practicing Jews. Some of them are nothing and others are Church of England Protestants. But the fact remains, we're descended from an old Jewish family and everybody knows it. Suggesting I'm anti-Semitic is like calling the queen anti-monarchist."

"Okay, forget I mentioned it." She raised her glass. "Here's to *A Passion to Deceive*."

"I'll drink to that," Andy said. "Please God the critics will be kind."

They were not. There were three reviews in the Sunday papers; the *Guardian* was lukewarm, the *Observer* bad, and the most important, the *Times,* savage. Andy's agent had said the reviewers would like the book and the public wouldn't. He was apparently wrong.

"It won't matter when it sells thousands of copies," Lili said loyally.

Andy didn't bother to reply. They were in her living room and he got up and walked out without a word and she didn't say anything. She let him go because she knew he felt terrible and needed to be alone.

Lili wouldn't have been surprised if he'd not come back at all that day, but he did, a little after noon. "Sorry about the disappearing act. I was feeling sorry for myself."

"It's okay."

"No, it isn't. I keep taking my bad temper and bad luck and general lack of talent out on you."

"You don't lack talent."

"Maybe not, but I am a selfish bastard." He picked up the *Times,* which was still lying where he'd dropped it, and thumbed through the pages. "I saw something interesting while I was looking for the not-to-be-mentioned-again review. Here it is. Open garden today at Swanning Park in Sussex. Do you remember?"

"The house near Brighton. Yes."

"They're inviting the world to come and pay twenty-five pence to see the garden, in aid of some deserving charity. Would you like to drive down there?"

"Today? It's after twelve."

"I know, but it has to be today. This is a once-a-year event. Besides, we can be there by teatime. And it won't be dark for hours after that."

He was right. One of the most delightful things about June in England, Lili had discovered, was the length of the days. It didn't get dark until after ten. "I'd love to go."

"Right, get a coat and we're off."

It was a peace offering, a truly generous apology for treating her badly. Lili hadn't forgotten his last words that December day in Sussex. "I hate the bloody place," he'd said. Well, maybe he'd changed his mind. Andy was sometimes very unpredictable.

It was nearing four when they arrived at Swanning Park. The crowd milling in the gardens was extraordinarily diverse. They were young and old and middle-aged, dressed in jeans and tailored linen dresses and long ethnic skirts with peasant blouses, in tweeds and jackets and ties and no ties and yet more jeans—a complete cross-section of the British public. But the crowd had more than nationality in common, they were knowledgeable. This was no haphazard gathering of sight-seers out to spy on how the other half lives, this was a meeting of *gardeners*. Lili thought the word a title of honor.

Next to them an old woman wearing a hat and gloves was talking to a bearded boy in a tattered sweater about the merits of Euphorbia robbiae and whether it would "winter over" in Scotland.

"They all know so much," Lili murmured.

"Seem to," Andy agreed. He was quiet again, preoccupied. She wasn't sure if it was the effect of Swanning Park, or if he was still thinking about the awful reviews.

Lili looked up at the house. It was a jewel in a perfect setting. The honey-colored stone harmonized with the lush green lawns, the mansard slate roofs reflected the sun and the colors of the flowers. "God, it's gorgeous," she murmured. "Who built it? Who lives here now?"

"Built in 1603, the year Elizabeth I died, the final year of the Tudors. One of Bess's last acts was to make a chap called William Preston the first Viscount Swanning. He gave enough of his fortune to the crown to find favor. The rest he used to build this."

"It's one hell of a monument. He couldn't have done much better, could he?"

Andy shrugged. "Depends on your point of view."

"You're saying that only because you're so anti-aristocrat. Who's the viscount now?"

"There isn't one. The title was retired in 1939 when the last Lord Swanning died without an heir. No males to inherit, not even a cousin in the direct line of succession. Poof, no more viscounts. The house has had a series of owners since. Not a happy place, Swanning Park, apparently. They all sell up sooner rather than later."

"How do you know so much about it?"

Instead of answering, he said, "Let's walk a bit."

Nearby was a hand-lettered sign with arrows directing them to the iris court, the rock garden, the fernery. Andy studied it. "I seem to remember a duck pond behind the rock garden. Maybe this horde of horticulturists isn't interested in ducks."

Because of the crowd, progress was difficult and conversation impossible, but finally they reached the entrance to the rock garden. Andy steered her past it on to a narrow, half-hidden path. All at once they were alone.

"You really know your way around," Lili said.

"I told you, the last Viscount Swanning was a relative of sorts. His first wife was my father's younger sister, my aunt Phillipa. She died very young, before I was born."

Lili cocked her head and studied him. "If the viscount died in 'thirty-nine, that was before you were born too."

"Yes, but the house was entailed, legally tied up in a forest of red tape. It couldn't be sold until the entailment was revoked. My father looked after the place until 1952. He used to bring me down here sometimes."

He turned on to another path. "This way I think." In a few minutes they were out of the trees, standing on a broad grassy bank looking over a pond.

"Lovely," Lili said. Then, "Did you have to learn the history of all your relatives dead and alive? Is that how you soaked up all the details?"

"No. The articles I used to write required research. Swanning Park has always seemed a natural peg for a story. The thirteenth viscount, the one who died in 'thirty-nine, was murdered by his second wife."

"Aha! The skeletons in the closet are rattling."

He didn't join in her laughter. "Lili, do you believe in coincidence?"

She remembered the remark he'd once made. "I thought you wanted to outlaw coincidence."

"It seems like a good idea, but I don't think I can manage it. You didn't answer the question."

"Naturally, I believe in it. It happens all the time."

"Okay, I'm glad that's settled. I've got a beauty." He didn't look at her. "Does the name Amanda Kent mean anything to you?"

"Amanda . . . Jesus! Where did you dig that up? Have you been probing my unconscious? Do I talk in my sleep?" Her tone was still light and bantering.

"I'm serious, Lili. You know the name, don't you?"

"Of course. A family named Kent were among the first settlers in Fielding. They built my house, as a matter of fact. Two of the Kent women have been named Amanda."

"And the most recent one?"

She had to think for a moment. "That would be Thomas and Jane's daughter."

"What do you know about her?"

Lili frowned. "Nothing really. I asked my mother about her once. They were around the same age, but it seems they barely knew each other. Later there was some kind of scandal. Nobody in Fielding ever talks about the last Amanda Kent."

Andy didn't look at her. "I can tell you about her. She came to England. In 'thirty-six she married Emery Preston-Wilde and became his second Lady Swanning. In 'thirty-nine she put two bullets in his chest and walked out of the house and has never been seen since. The police hunted high and low, but she'd disappeared. The general belief is that she also killed herself."

Lili stared at him. The implications of his story chilled her heart. They made her feel sick. Her head started to pound.

She wasn't suffering over the probably long dead Amanda Kent. It was her life and his that Andy's words had turned into a lie.

She didn't say anything until they were in the car heading back to London. Finally the accusatory question came out as a hoarse whisper. "Andy, how long have you known about the Fielding connection with Swanning Park?"

"I started researching the Swanning murder three years ago. I intended to write an article about it."

"So when you met me, when I said I came from Fielding, you knew about Amanda Kent. Why didn't you ever say anything?"

He stared straight ahead at the road. "I had the idea that I was a novelist. I wanted to put everything to do with journalism out of my mind."

Okay, she told herself, that was an explanation. It made a crazy kind of sense. "The day you talked to me at the V&A, you couldn't possibly know I lived in Amanda Kent's old house, could you?" Her voice was weak; she sounded like a child asking for reassurance.

"Damm it! That's exactly what I was afraid you'd think. That's why I said I hated the bloody place when we saw it the first time. Of course I didn't, how could I?"

"I don't know."

"Well, I didn't," he repeated.

"You only felt sorry for me."

He banged the steering wheel with his fist and the car swerved for a moment before he regained control. "Bloody hell, Lili! I didn't feel sorry for you. I was attracted to you. I came to . . . I care a lot for you. I'm not some Fleet Street piranha out to get a story and the devil take the hindmost. It's a bloody fucking coincidence and nothing else."

"You're shouting, Andy. And you don't usually use words like that."

"I'm not usually this angry."

"At me?"

"At the whole fucking world."

It was a few minutes past ten and getting dark when he pulled up at the Prince's Mews house. The street lamps came on as she got out of the car. "Are you coming in?"

"No, not tonight, if you don't mind." He drove off without waiting to hear if she minded.

Lili cried a lot during the night. At seven she phoned him. When he answered he said, "Lili?"

"Yes, it's me. How did you know?"

"I don't know," he said gruffly. "Are you all right?"

"Not really. You?" she asked.

"Bloody marvelous. I come from a long line of survivors. We don't roll over and play dead when our girlfriends believe the worst or the critics say we have no talent."

"I don't believe the worst. Only why did you wait so long to say anything?"

"I told you why. Are we going to start all that over again?"

"No. But can I ask one more question?"

"You're going to, whatever I say."

"I think you planned all that yesterday. You took me to Swanning Park so you'd have an opportunity to talk about Amanda Kent. The fact that it was a garden open day was dumb luck. Is that right?"

"Yes."

"Okay, why did you want to tell me about it now, since you haven't all along?"

"You said one question, that's two."

"It's important, Andy. Please tell me."

He sighed and his voice sounded old and tired. "It isn't very mysterious, love. Barry Clark, my agent, has been at me for months to do a nonfiction book. The Swanning affair is high on his list of probables. Because of the Mendoza connection. That's why I went to Spain, to quiz my relatives in Córdoba."

"I see."

"I hope you do. Considering the way my novel's been received . . . Well, maybe I'll do it."

Lili felt enormously relieved. It was completely logical. "That's okay. I understand that."

"Good." His tone softened. "Can I come over tonight?"

"Definitely. I'd say come over right now, only I have to go to Brixton and see a carpenter."

"And I have to see Barry. Until about six, then. Cook me something marvelous to soothe my wounded spirit."

That evening Lili poached salmon steaks and served them with dill butter and tiny new potatoes and the season's first peas. "Traditional New England food," she told him.

"There's something to be said for New England."

"It has its points."

"Not, apparently, freedom of information." He finished the last bite of salmon and studied her. "How is it you didn't know that Amanda Kent murdered her husband? There was a worldwide search for her. They must have looked in Fielding."

"Maybe, but that was before I was born. Nobody ever told me. The Historical Society and the D.A.R. are selective about the facts they put in their little books and pamphlets. And as I said, the one time I asked my mother about her I was told never to talk about it because there had been a scandal."

He didn't look at her. "I think your mother knows a great deal."

"Why assume that?" Lili was clearing the table. She had her back to him when he answered.

"She came to England too, you said so."

"Yes, but England's not that small. And Amanda was younger than my mother. And Irene was in London, not Sussex. Besides, the Kents move in a different circle from the Petworths. Always have."

Andy frowned, went into the hall where he'd left his things, and came back with an envelope. "Have a look at these."

What he handed her were four newspaper clippings carefully wrapped in plastic. They were all many years old and all about the Swanning murder. The headlines were equally lurid. "Peeress Disappears After Murder." "Bloody Death in a Sussex Village." "Is This Woman a Murderer?" "Have You Seen Lady Swanning?"

"That's Amanda Preston-Wilde née Kent." Andy pointed to the grainy gray pictures that accompanied each article.

"There were literally reams of stories in the press, but these are special because of the pictures."

Lili skimmed the stories and stared at the photos.

"Well," he asked. "Have you seen Lady Swanning?"

"Never in my whole life."

"I thought as much." He took the clippings from her and put them away.

"Aren't there any other pictures, clearer ones?" Lili asked.

"Nope. Curious, isn't it? In that whole two-hundred-room pile down there in Sussex, they never found a picture of her ladyship. When the police were looking for her, they had to go to newspaper morgues and find these and reproduce them."

"Curiouser and curiouser. Were they strange, she and her husband? Hermits or something like that?"

"Not a bit of it. Cream of society, seen in all the best places. And there were pictures of every ancestor since the year one in the house. But none of Amanda."

Lili cocked her head. "It sounds deliberate to me. Maybe she destroyed them all before she did it. Part of her plan."

"Too bloody right, it was deliberate. But whether *she* did it or someone else, I don't know. I'll tell you another funny thing. Remember I said the house wasn't sold for years? Before it finally was in 1952, my father went down for a last look round. I was nine and he took me with him. Do you know what a muniments room is?"

"Yes, I think so. Where records are kept, right?"

"I forgot, you're a student of stately homes. That's it. The muniments are the deeds and the various royal grants and warrants, and the official rubbish given by the College of Heralds. Anyway, when we got to Swanning, my father went straight to the muniments room. As if he knew exactly what he was looking for. He took out a huge old tome and paged through it. And I'd swear he ripped something out."

"It's like a fairy story, or an old romance," Lili said in wonder. "What did he take?"

"I can't be sure, but I think it was a picture of Amanda. Out of the wedding registry. I think he'd just remembered it might be there, that everyone had overlooked that possibility. The murder story wasn't on my mind when I was nine, but later when I started working on this I remembered and made my guess. The old boy was still alive and I asked him. It was like questioning a stone wall. He denied the whole thing, said I was mixing up a number of childhood memories the way kids do."

"But why should he deny it if it was true?"

"That's what I think you call the sixty-four-dollar question. According to me, because the Mendozas are up to their necks in the murder and Lady Swanning's vanishing act."

She shivered. "You make your family sound not very nice."

"They aren't. And there's something else I haven't wanted to tell you but I think I'd better. While I was in Spain, in Córdoba in the south, I was summoned to Madrid. A conference with Mark, my half brother. Lord Westlake when he's being formal."

That was supposed to be funny, but Lili didn't laugh. She suspected she didn't want to hear what he had to say, but it was too late for that. "Go on."

"Mark told me in no uncertain terms that I was to stop trying to identify Harry Cramer."

"What?" The single word came out in a shocked, high-pitched yell. "What the hell does my father have to do with your brother?" Lili demanded.

"That's the right question," Andy said quietly. "But the answer is, I don't know. Mark was playing messenger for our cousin, Diego. Diego's a tough old buzzard, but not the official head of the family, that's another cousin named Manuel. We all call him Tío Manuel, Spanish for uncle, only in our case it denotes the head of the clan. All the same, Diego's the spider at the center of the Mendoza web. He told Mark that my poking around the Cramer thing bothered him. Diego asked my brother to warn me off."

"But why?"

"I don't know."

"That's why you said we should stop looking," Lili said slowly.

Andy had been staring at his clasped hands. Now his head jerked up. "Hang on a minute. I wasn't running scared. I'm one of them, love. That gives me a certain limited immunity. It's you I was worried about."

She couldn't hide her incredulity. "You were worried about me? In God's name, why?"

"Because the Mendozas play rough." He leaned over and fixed her with an earnest gaze. "Look, love, I know it sounds silly and melodramatic, but it's true."

"What are you suggesting?" Lili asked. "Acid in my face, pushed out a window, dropped off Tower Bridge? That kind of thing?"

"Yes."

She'd been standing, now she sat down with a thump. "You're crazy. You must be. This doesn't make any sense. Even if they're as bad as you say they are, what possible threat to them can I be? I never even heard of them until I met you." Suddenly she stopped speaking, never heard of them unless . . .

"What have you thought of?" Andy demanded.

She shook her head. "I'll tell you in a minute. First, does your family disapprove of you and me? Could that be what all this is about?"

"Now you're being silly. Affairs of the heart aren't important in their world. And they couldn't care less who I see or what I do in my private life. They've even managed to accept my writing. It's what I told you before, you're Harry Cramer's daughter. And he's some kind of link."

"Link to what?"

"The Swanning murder. He and your mother."

Lili banged her fist on the table. "No, you're wrong about that. At least about Irene. You don't know her. If you did, you'd know how absurd it is to connect her with any kind of crime, let alone murder."

Andy shrugged. "Okay, so you say. And you may well be right. All I've got is a hunch. But I don't think we know enough to simply go blundering on. Not now that we've been noticed by Diego. Please, will you take my word for that? Messing with the Mendozas can be very risky."

"The Mendozas of Córdoba? That's who they are, isn't it?"

"Yes. The Spanish branch, at least. Diego happens to live in Madrid, but that's simply a personal convenience, the heart of it all is Córdoba."

Lili folded her hands and studied the laced fingers. "And are they sometimes known as the House of Mendoza?"

"Yes again. The family dates back many hundreds of years, so that feudal-type usage isn't surprising."

"Wait here," Lili said.

She went upstairs and returned carrying an envelope. "I found this when I was thirteen. Behind a painting in my house."

She put it on the kitchen table and withdrew the old envelope from the newer one she'd put it in. "All the creases are because it was folded up very small, so it could be wedged beneath the frame of the picture. And the ink is smudged so badly, I couldn't read the last word. What do you think it is?"

Andy peered over her shoulder. "The first part's clear enough. 'Córdoba, Spain. The House of . . .' Looks like an M."

"Yes, M-E something, I always thought. The House of Mendoza?"

"Could be," Andy said. "Probably is." He was obviously trying to control his excitement, and not succeeding very well. "What's inside?"

"This." Lili withdrew the triangular fragment of engraved gold and gave it to him.

"It's part of something," he said. "Looks as if it's been cut out of a larger piece."

Lili nodded. "That's my guess."

"And these strange markings, are they by chance Hebrew letters?"

"Yes. The librarian in Fielding had it checked for me. According to her, the characters are Hebrew and the words say 'forget thee.' Don't ask me what that refers to, because I have no idea."

"And what was your mother's explanation for this little bit of memorabilia?"

"I never showed it to her."

His head snapped up and he studied her face. "Lili, doesn't that seem strange? After you've been telling me she couldn't be involved in the Amanda Kent affair?" He spoke gently, aware of the enormity of what he was suggesting.

"My mother has her oddities," Lili said. "I've never denied that. I wanted to imagine wonderful romantic things about this . . . whatever it is. I didn't want her to disillusion me, that's mostly why I never told her. But that doesn't change the fact that she couldn't be involved in anything like a murder. Besides, this had been behind the painting for over ninety years."

"How do you know that?"

"The wallpaper." She explained about the fading and the one preserved section behind the picture.

"Doesn't follow," Andy said. "You're jumping to conclusions again. Even if the painting had been in place for that long, somebody could have put this there later."

Lili frowned. "I suppose you're right. But if it had been my mother, surely sometime in the last seven years she'd have discovered it was gone and asked me about it?"

"Perhaps." He was still studying the piece of gold, turning it over in his fingers. Almost idly he asked, "What's the painting, some Victorian horror?"

"No, it's a Constable, as a matter of fact."

Andy whistled. "Incredible! Are you sure?"

"So says the family lore. And it's signed."

"Very impressive. Which one?"

"I don't know the title. It's a farm scene, a hayfield and a few people in the foreground."

"It must be worth a fortune, you do realize that?"

"Oh, yes," she said softly. "I do indeed."

Andy fondled the token. "Could I borrow this?"

"I'd rather not. I'm very superstitious about it. I think I should always have it with me."

"Okay, do you mind if I discreetly try to find out what it is?"

"No, I don't mind that."

"Good. And I'm still going to poke around on the Swanning thing, only I'll leave Cramer out of it for a while. If I find a thread that leads directly to him, I'll proceed with caution. So the hounds don't come baying again. Agreed?"

"Agreed. But whatever you find out, you have to tell me. This is my—" She almost said *fight,* then thought better of it. "I have more than a passing interest."

"Yes, you do. Now, what's for dessert?"

"Nothing special. I didn't have time. I'm spoiling you, Andy Mendoza. You're getting to sound like a male chauvinist pig. There's some ice cream in the freezer if you want it. And you can do the dishes."

❧ 8 ❧

London and Córdoba: 1971

Andy arrived at Prince's Mews a little after seven on a golden August evening. His first words were, "Sorry, love, I'm the bearer of evil tidings."

"Oh, God, what now?" Lili asked.

"My cousin Charles. I had a letter from him today. He's finished the Kenya project and he's coming home earlier than scheduled. September fifteenth. He rather hopes his house will be vacant."

Lili sat down hard on the nearest chair. "Damn. Your family seems to have it in for me. But I suppose I can't blame him. I'm not a regular tenant with a lease or anything."

"No," Andy said mournfully, "you're not. What do you want to do?"

"Find another place to live, of course. An apartment or something."

"Is it worth it for only a few months? Maybe you should return to the hotel in Paddington."

Lili stared at him. Suddenly she had a pain in her chest, where her heart was. "I'm not thinking about going back to America yet, and if I'm in a hotel, where will we . . . I mean . . ."

"I thought you had to go back after a year," he said.

"I don't have to do anything." Her voice was dull, damaged. It didn't sound like her.

"No, I suppose you don't. But I assumed . . ."

They didn't say more. In silence she served the chicken salad she'd prepared with such loving care. Andy picked up his fork, then put it down. "To hell with this. Come with me, I want to show you something."

"What?"

"Don't ask questions, come."

She followed him out to the car and they drove for about fifteen minutes, still not talking. Then they were in a neighborhood Lili had never seen, looking at red brick tenement houses linked together down narrow streets, a newspaper shop, and a small grocery. "This is Hackney," Andy said. "I'm taking you to my bed-sit."

He parked in front of one of the ubiquitous tenements and led her inside, up three flights of stairs that sliced through a grimy hall smelling of urine and fried fish. When he unlocked the door to his room, Lili saw a threadbare gray carpet, a corner occupied by a sink and a gas ring, a sofa that obviously doubled as a bed, and a desk under a window that looked out on chimneys and roofs and a narrow wedge of sky. "Toilet and bath down the hall," Andy said.

"Okay, it's awful," Lili said. "Is that what you wanted me to see?"

"Yes. Can you imagine yourself living like this? Do you wonder why I've never brought you here?"

"No. But why do you live here?"

"Because my income of five thousand pounds a year isn't enough to buy a place of my own. The pool of rental properties in London is small and very muddy. Good housing is for sale, not for let."

"You could get a mortgage on a place of your own."

"Not without trading on my name."

Lili rounded on him. "Oh, yes, don't forget to remind me how noble you are, how above using the Mendoza millions. What about me, Andy? Are you above using me?"

As soon as she said it she wanted to die, but she couldn't get the words back. They were spent, gone. They'd taken on a life of their own in the sordid little room.

Andy turned white, then flushed. "Is that what you think I've done?" He didn't raise his voice.

Lili sank down on the sofa because her legs had turned to water. "No, that's not what I meant."

"What then?"

"Andy, what are we all about? Don't you even want me to stay in England? Are you simply counting the days until it's time to put me on a plane?"

He ran his fingers through his hair. "Oh, my God, of course not. How can you say that? But I have nothing to offer that's really my own. My much-vaunted writing career is in shambles. I have no hopes of selling another novel after the last fiasco. Worse, I can't seem to write one. If I'm going to make a living, either I have to go back to journalism or find some kind of a job."

"That's all practical stuff," she whispered. "I'm asking about you and me." Only she didn't want to ask. She'd never intended this conversation. It had sneaked up and happened without her consent.

"You and me," Andy repeated. "I ask myself about that too."

He didn't say anything else, and she made the worst mistake of all. She started to cry. She hated herself for it, but she couldn't stop. He came and sat beside her and took a handkerchief from his pocket and gave it to her.

"Wipe your eyes and blow your nose. There's nothing to cry about. We'll find somewhere for you to live. Something better than this."

Later, back at Prince's Mews, they made love that was different. Perhaps because she still felt so awful, perhaps because he knew it and felt guilty. Lili clung to him and sobbed with a mixture of passion and grief, and he held her and licked the tears from her cheeks. She wanted to press ever closer, to melt her flesh into his. Their passion blended, found a common rhythm, moved the earth in a way that was new.

"It was good for you tonight, wasn't it?" he asked softly afterward.

"Yes." Lili pressed her face to his chest, still shaking, still crying a little—but now only inside.

"Me too," Andy whispered. "It's always good, but this was special. I'm sorry it took that awful scene to make it perfect. Don't be sad, little love. It will all work out."

The next day Lili decided it was up to her to make it work out. She had to do definite things, make Andy stop thinking she was a temporary phenomenon. She wrote to her mother and admitted that she was working in London—she'd been vague about that before—and that she intended to stay. Irene could stop forwarding money. Lili was earning enough to pay her way.

Her first week of apartment hunting confirmed Andy's appraisal of the rental market. Then Lili got lucky. She happened to be in an agent's office when a new listing came in. It sounded perfect, a place in an area known as Bankside, on the south side of the Thames. "I'll go over there right away," Lili said, snatching the little white card from the agent's hand.

Bankside was mostly decrepit unused docks under a pall of stench from the polluted river, but the address Lili was seeking was in a tiny oasis of charm. In the shadow of London Bridge there was one short street where a few old warehouses had been restored and tiny gardens planted. She glanced again at the card. The one-bedroom flat was being offered at thirty pounds a week. Lili rang the bell.

"Above me is a couple with two small kids," the owner of the two ground-floor rooms explained. "They're not noisy," he added quickly.

Lili wouldn't have cared if a troop of circus performers lived upstairs. Not after she saw the large open space with its polished plank floor and big windows looking out to the river, and the pleasant, comfortable furniture.

"The top two floors are occupied by the building's owners," her would-be landlord went on. "They're architects involved in the restoration of the area."

He'd already explained that he was looking for a tenant because he was taking a job in Bahrain. "How long will you be gone?" Lili asked.

"A year. But I'll want it back straightaway when I return."

"That's understood. I'll sign something to that effect if you like."

He grunted agreement.

"And the rent is—?"

"Thirty pounds a week."

She heaved a sigh of relief. She'd been terrified he was going to say three hundred, that someone had mistakenly left out a zero. Lili grinned. "Okay, I'll take it."

On the same mid-September day that she moved into the flat on Bankside, Lili passed a fish market and spotted live lobsters in the window. They were real ones with two claws, not the tail-only rock lobsters from South Africa. These came out of the cold waters around Scotland, the fishmonger explained. Impulsively, Lili bought two small ones and phoned Andy to announce that their first meal in her new home would be a celebration supper.

He arrived bearing flowers and a bottle of Taittinger. He put the champagne in the freezer to chill while she found a vase for his dark red chrysanthemums. They chatted and laughed a lot and made silly jokes, and tied big napkins around their necks so they could dip the lobster in melted butter and eat with their fingers. Nothing prepared her for his announcement.

"Lili, I'm going back to Spain."

She was pouring the last of the champagne and by sheer force of will she didn't let her hand falter. "Oh, when? For how long?"

"Tomorrow."

She took a sip of the wine. "I see. Rather sudden, isn't it? Or have you known for some time?"

"Well, yes, as a matter of fact. I'm still trying to get enough data together to do the Swanning book. I didn't mention it because you had enough on your plate, what with moving and your work." He didn't meet her gaze.

"When will you be back?"

"I'm not really sure." His voice lowered. "A few months maybe."

"I see," Lili said softly.

How was she doing this? How was she sitting here calmly drinking champagne, acting as if his words weren't cutting her apart? Why didn't she scream and rave and swear and tell him he was a bloody bastard and did he love her or not and what in hell had he been playing at for almost a year? "I see," she said again.

"I hope so. Lili, it's not only the book. I'm not sure. This is a bad time for me. I need a little breathing space."

As if she'd been suffocating him. "Okay." She rose and began running water into the sink to do the dishes, and when she turned around he had his coat on and was standing by the door.

"I think I'd better go. I'll be in touch."

She stared at him and couldn't say anything. Andy started to open the door, then he closed it and crossed to her. He put both his hands on her shoulders and leaned down and kissed her. "I've never cared so much for anyone before," he whispered. "I hope you can believe that. In a way that's what's frightening me. Give me a little time, Lili. Please."

"Andy," she whispered. "Don't leave—"

He pressed his finger to her lips. "Shh, don't say anything. It's better. I have to do what I'm doing, Lili. There's no other way. I'll call you as soon as I get back from Spain."

Lili felt the tears prickle behind her eyelids. No! Damn him, she wouldn't let him see her cry. She nodded because she didn't trust herself to speak. Then he was gone.

The echo of the door he'd closed behind him hung on in the large, pleasant living room. It hummed in the stillness, a sinister invasive buzz that bounced off the white walls and the polished wood floor and filled her head. The sound crackled in her eardrums, made a choking lump in her throat. She couldn't breathe.

Lili pressed her palms to the sides of her head, trying to close out the noise. But there wasn't any noise. It was her imagination. She was going crazy. Losing her mind. She was dying. "No, I'm not." She whispered the words aloud at first, then shouted them. "I'm not! I'm not! I'm not!" She made a fist and pushed it into her mouth to stifle the screams, the hysteria she knew was coming. After a few seconds she ran to the door and pulled it open and dashed into the street calling his name. "Andy! Andy, where are you?"

The road mocked her with its emptiness and innocence, its peaceful ordinariness in the darkening gold dusk. Lili ran to the corner, looking for him. Nothing. No one. She kept running, some fifty yards to London Bridge, halfway across it. There was no sign of the tall, slim figure with the sandy hair and the horn-rims; there was no one at all. She was entirely alone in a universe tortured out of recognition, distorted by her grief.

Below the bridge the waters of the Thames were flat and opaque. Lili stared down at them. Then, crying openly now, tears running down her cheeks and falling from her chin and soaking the front of her blue cotton blouse, she walked back home.

For three days Lili was a wounded animal cowering in her lair, a shattered creature hiding from the world. She could not bear to leave her apartment. She phoned Ruth and their clients and pleaded illness. She really was ill—dizzy, and vomiting all the time. Andy leaving was like an amputation performed without anesthesia, a savage attack on the essence of herself.

Late Friday afternoon she dragged herself into the hall and opened the mailbox. Maybe Andy had written. He hadn't. There was only an advertising circular suggesting she take her winter holidays in the Greek Islands—and a letter from her mother.

Irene's letters were instantly identifiable. They were written on those pre-stamped foldup air sheets bought in the post office. Irene had a small, neat hand. She always managed to write quite a bit on the single sheet, but she seldom said much of anything. Usually her letters were brief reports of local doings, along with a line saying she was well and hoped Lili was enjoying herself.

This letter was different. In three sentences it said an enormous amount.

"I've decided to sell the house since you aren't returning. It's been on my mind to do so for some time and I've had a very attractive offer. Fielding is suddenly growing and lots of people from Boston want to live out here in the country."

Lili read the words twice. Then she screamed aloud and kept screaming. Andy's departure had all but paralyzed her; Irene's news destroyed the shattered hull that remained. Lili reacted with something more than hysteria or mere anger. What she felt was blazing, soul-destroying fury, a rage that demanded an outlet. Her screams went on for a long time, until she became aware that someone was pounding on her door.

"Miss Cramer! Miss Cramer, are you in there? Are you all right?"

Lili pressed her palms over her mouth and stopped screaming and stared at the door. The pounding and the questions continued. "Miss Cramer, please answer me. What's going on in there?"

Lili opened the door to find a neighbor, one of the architects who lived on the third floor. "I'm fine," she whispered hoarsely. "I'm really sorry. I had the television on and I didn't realize it was so loud." The lie came quickly, but she read disbelief in the man's face.

"You're sure everything's all right?" He was in his fifties, pleasant. She'd met him while she was moving in. Now he looked over her shoulder and his gaze swept the room as if he imagined someone was hiding with a gun, forcing her to deny some terror that would resume as soon as he left.

"Yes, really, everything's fine. Thank you, you're very kind. I—" His concern demanded more than lies. "I've had some bad news," she whispered.

"I'm sorry." He reached out a hand, then pulled back, too shy to make his sympathy physical, very British. "If you're sure—"

"Yes, positive."

He left and Lili closed the door and stared at Irene's letter. It was lying crumpled on the floor where she'd dropped it. She picked it up and put it in an ashtray and struck a match and watched it burn, as if she could make the whole thing not happen simply by destroying the thin sheet of blue paper with the terrible words.

There was a brass ship's clock on the wall; it tolled eight bells. It was four P.M. Greenwich Mean Time, so it must be eleven A.M. in Fielding. She went to the telephone; a few moments later she heard Irene's familiar voice.

"Mother, you can't!"

"Can't what? We have a poor connection, Lili. I can hardly hear you. Why are you calling? Are you all right?"

"No, I'm not all right. I'm terrible, furious! How can you sell our house?"

"Oh, that's it. My dear, you're being silly. Why should I keep it since . . ." A wave of static obscured her next words. . . . "the furnishings, then I can travel a bit."

"No!" She shouted the command across the wires. "No. Don't do it. I'll come back. I'll fly home tomorrow. Don't sell the house."

The line cleared. "Lili, don't be ridiculous. You're grown-up now. You're working in England. You have your own life. What would you do in Fielding? Whyever would you want to return? Anyway, I signed the purchase and sales agreement yesterday."

Lili couldn't give up. "You can have it annulled or something. Look, if it's a matter of money, sell the Constable. You can travel on the proceeds. You can lock the house up and never go back. Only don't sell it. Please, Mother, you mustn't."

Irene laughed softly. "My dear, you're being so foolish, I can't believe we're having this conversation. The Constable . . . No, I can't do that."

"For God's sake, why not? It's only a picture." There was a moment's silence. "Mother, are you there? Can you hear me?"

"Yes, I can hear you. But the Constable . . . isn't salable."

"What do you mean?"

"Lili, I can't explain on the phone. Believe me, I'm doing the only thing possible."

Lili didn't answer right away. When she did, she could merely repeat, "Don't sell my house."

"Look, this is a very expensive way to have a disagreement," Irene had adopted her firm, no-nonsense tone, "and there's really nothing more to discuss. I'll write again soon. Good-bye dear. Do take care of yourself, and be sensible."

For a long time Lili simply sat and trembled and stared at the phone. Once she even picked it up and started to call

again. But she didn't because she knew it was utterly futile.
As she'd known that calling Andy would be futile.

Don't leave me. Don't sell my house. Both were meaning-
less pleas that fell on deaf ears. Andy didn't want her and
her beloved house wasn't really hers, it was her mother's.
Irene had waited until she was convinced that Lili had, as
she put it, grown up, then extricated herself from what was
apparently a burden.

At last the shaking stopped. She could stand up and walk
to the little kitchenette in the corner and pour herself a glass
of water. She drank it quickly, gagging because her throat
was so sore from all the screaming and the weeping, and
leaned her head against the coolness of the refrigerator.

"Andy," she said aloud. "Andy." But he wasn't there. He
wasn't going to be there for a long time. Eventually, he'd
come back, she had to believe that. He cared more for her
than anyone he'd ever known, he'd said. And someday she
would marry Andy and take him to America to see her house
and they'd buy it back. She'd work hard and save every cent
she could and eventually she'd have enough to reclaim her
house.

Meanwhile, she could remember that it existed, that it was
waiting for her. Whoever bought it was bound to love it and
take care of it. The house had stood for a hundred years; it
would wait a few more for her. Irene had said something
about the furnishings. Lili hadn't gotten it all because of the
interference on the line, but she was pretty sure the house
was being sold furnished. Good, that was fine. When she
reclaimed it, the house would be exactly as it had been.

If the scenario was something less than realistic, that didn't
matter at the moment. It made it possible to bear the pain.

Andrew Mendoza never ceased to marvel at the family
home in Córdoba. It was set in a rectangle between four
narrow streets within the picturesque and ancient Barrio
de la Juderia, the neighborhood of the Jews. The Palacio
Mendoza turned to the world a façade of austere white
walls randomly pierced with old nail-studded wooden doors
and grille-covered windows. From the outside it did not

appear to live up to its grandiose name, but that was a deception.

Behind the walls, sunk deep in the ancient earth on which they stood, were the roots of a clan who had a past traceable through countless centuries. That was extraordinary in a world where most Jews had wandered so far and so often that their memories went back only a few generations. An incalculable price had been paid for such continuity, but one of the rewards was the palace itself.

Two huge doors seven feet tall and equally wide formed the main entrance on the Calle Averroes. They opened into a glorious square courtyard known as the Patio del Recibo. It was paved in cobblestones, had mosaic walls, and was over-hung by the spreading branches of a graceful chestnut tree.

From there one had a bewildering choice of arched doors and colonnaded passages. Andy still wasn't sure where each led, though he knew it was possible to walk along the arcades to each of the fourteen patios within the walls—and never once enter a room or retrace a path.

On Christmas day 1971 Andy wandered idly, glad to be alone. For the servants this was a day of fiesta, for the family a time to stay within the walls and be discreet about the beliefs that separated them from their Catholic neighbors.

He came to the southernmost corner of the grounds, to the Patio del Pozo, the patio of the well. Running water had long since come to Córdoba, but there was still a tiled and decorated well in the center of the small courtyard. Around it were plantings of bougainvillaea and jasmine and lantana. Only the bougainvillaea was in flower because the Andalusian sun was at its nadir. To Andy it still seemed hot. He was in his shirt-sleeves.

He made his way through three more patios, looking for his cousin Susan. Eventually, he found her in the Patio de los Naranjos, a precise square of orange trees dripping bright fruit above a smaller square reflecting pool.

Andy stood in the shadows and watched her a moment. Susan was English, but she had married a distant Spanish cousin and lived in Córdoba for thirteen years, the last four of them as a widow. She was a small woman, economically put together. She looked a bit prissy, a bit like an archetypal upper-class matron, but Andy knew that was a false impression. Susan was perceptive, bright, quick to laugh, lively—and sometimes very stubborn.

Her head was bent over some needlework and the sunlight picked out the strands of gray in her short dark hair. She hadn't turned and he didn't think she knew he was there until she said, "It's chilly today. Don't you want a jacket?"

"You must have eyes in back of your head." He went and sat beside her on the stone bench beside the reflecting pool. "I'm not cold."

Susan smiled. "You're good, hearty English stock. After all these years in Spain, my blood's thinned."

"Your brain too. Why the hell won't you tell me what you know?"

"You're becoming boring, Andy. I have told you what I know."

"No, you haven't."

"Boring and petulant," she said, and returned to the crewel work in her lap.

They were easy with each other because years before Susan had befriended the small boy cousin who was too skinny and wore glasses, and had that awful taint of workingclass Yorkshire in his blood. All during Andy's school years they had exchanged monthly letters, and after he was graduated from Cambridge, Andy had come to visit frequently.

"Look," he said now, "I can't do the damned book if you won't cooperate."

"Then do some other damned book. Do another novel."

Andy grimaced. "As well as getting thin-brained, you've forgotten how to read English. The critics aren't clamoring for another novel by Andrew Mendoza."

"Is that all you write for? To please the critics?"

He pulled an orange from a tree and began peeling it. "I've asked myself that a few times these past months. It is one reason, acclaim. Look at Andy Mendoza, never thought he had much purpose in life, but he can write. Only apparently I can't. Not novels anyway."

"Those are Seville oranges. Sour. Meant for marmalade." Susan broke off a strand of yellow yarn. "You can write."

"A moot point. If I can't have literary prizes and public homage, I'll settle for something else."

"What?"

"Money."

"Money! Andy, you don't *need* money. Nobody's disowned you while my back was turned, have they?"

"No." He took a bite of juicy flesh then spit it out. "Sour," he agreed. "I have my trust, if that's what you mean. Five thousand a year. Barely enough to survive."

"That's only the preliminary trust. In a couple of years you'll have more. When you're thirty, isn't it?"

"Yes. But I don't want to owe everything to them. Look, I have no intention of flinging my inheritance dramatically in their faces; that won't accomplish anything. But I want to earn money of my own. Achieve something in my own right."

Susan folded the crewel work away and stood and walked to the edge of the reflecting pool. "This conversation is going around in circles. All right, you want to earn money and garner fame. And you believe you can do it writing a certain type of book. Why does it have to be the Swanning murder?"

"Because my agent and my publisher think it will sell millions of copies. The Americans will gobble it up—seeing as Amanda Kent was one of theirs—and all our fortunes will be made, and nobody's better positioned to do it than I am."

She stooped and fished a dead leaf from the edge of the water. "Very well. But as I said, I don't know anything that will help you. I was eleven years old when Lady Swanning shot her husband. I'd never even been to Swanning Park."

"But you met her."

"Not exactly. Emery brought Amanda to Westlake for a hunt weekend soon after they were married. I was eight then, still relegated to the nursery. I spied from the top of the stairs. I do remember how young she looked, little more than a child. And that she was terribly pretty and gay. You can find out that much from any of a hundred people."

He went and stood beside her. "Susan, I've been digging around this thing for years. There's a thread that leads straight back here. To Córdoba and the family."

"You're mad." She didn't look at him.

"No, you know I'm not. And there's something I haven't told you about. Someone actually. A friend in London." He hesitated. "A close friend."

"The girl you mentioned, Lili?"

"Yes, how did you guess?"

"I don't know." She shrugged. "Your tone of voice perhaps." Then, apparently apropos of nothing, she asked, "Have you seen Cousin Charlotte lately?"

"No. They keep her locked in her room these days."

Susan was shocked. "I don't believe it!"

Andy chuckled. "I don't mean she's a prisoner in the tower. But her dottiness has gone the limit. She needs nurses round the clock and can't be allowed out in public, not even downstairs anymore. It's not surprising, she's ancient."

"No, she's not. What ever gave you that idea? I think she's sixty. That's not old. Poor Charlotte."

"Okay, then it's the price of a wayward youth," Andy said. "Imagine announcing to your Edwardian elders that you're a proud and active lesbian. Only she'd have said sapphist, I suppose."

"Yes, I suppose she would."

He cocked his head and eyed her speculatively. "Why are we talking about Charlotte?"

"I simply thought of her." Susan turned her face away from his scrutiny. "I remember her so well. She was . . . I think *splendid* is the word. She strode about the place in men's breeches and boots and silk blouses, with dangling earrings and ropes of antique beads. She collected the beads, whole drawers full of them. In winter she wore a great velvet cape."

"Funny I don't remember her," Andy said. "You're not that much older than me."

"I remember her best from when I was about fifteen. So it was probably 'forty-three, the year you were born. After the war she moved to Paris and didn't come back for ages."

"By the time I knew her she already seemed old," Andy said. "And she was definitely losing her marbles. I remember the Christmas of 'fifty-nine or 'sixty, coming home from school and seeing her with a faint mustache and stringy white hair.

Mostly she was vague, but she seemed to know a lot about the family history."

"Yes, that was one of her passions. She was our unofficial archivist."

"Then it's too bad she's prematurely senile," he said. "She might be able to help me. Though she'd probably simply clam up, like the rest of you."

Susan looked away. He was again staring at the back of her dark, well-groomed head when he asked, "Do the words *forget thee* mean anything to you? Connected somehow to the family?"

She turned to face him, smiling. "Of course they do. The words of the psalm."

"What psalm?"

" 'If I forget thee, O Jerusalem, let my right hand forget her cunning,' " she quoted. "The hundred and thirty-seventh, I believe."

"Sorry, I don't know what you're talking about."

"Andy, all your hostility has kept you from absorbing some of the most elementary things about us. Things every Mendoza is supposed to take in with mother's milk."

"I took in some good old-fashioned Yorkshire skepticism. Please stop talking in riddles and explain."

"The legend is that some of our clan fled to Africa in the sixth century because the Christians were persecuting them here in Córdoba. The Mendoza patriarch had those words inscribed over the gates of his house in Tangiers to remind the family of their religion, and of Córdoba and what they'd left behind. In the next century, when they came back here and lived under the caliphs, a brass plaque was made and inscribed with the same words. The plaque seems to have disappeared around the time of Moses the Apostate."

"Moses who?"

"The Apostate. He lived in the twelfth century. He was the first Mendoza to adjust his religious beliefs to suit the times."

Andy sat down on one of the stone benches, cocked his head, and looked at her. "Bloody fascinating. The twelfth century, you said. Why?"

"Because that's when the persecutions began again in Andalusia. Until then the Jews and the Arabs had lived

together peacefully for four hundred years. The Jewish
community was extremely wealthy, and well established in
government and the arts and professions. Supposedly, there
were more than three hundred synagogues in Córdoba alone.
Then the caliphate became Shi'a."

"Muslim fundamentalists," Andy murmured in astonishment. "My God, I thought they were a new invention."

Susan shook her head. "The Shi'a date back to the origins
of Islam. Anyway, to get back to the twelfth century, it was
suddenly very unhealthy to be a Jew in Córdoba. The old
choice yet again, convert or be exiled or killed. Good-bye
great houses and synagogues, and for the Mendozas, hello
Moses the Apostate. He chose to convert."

"He became a Muslim?"

"Exactly. And he had the plaque removed."

"Where is it now?"

"Nobody knows. I've been poring over the old records in
the library here. That's how I found out about Moses and the
Shi'a, but there's no mention of the plaque after 1150. Of
course, later the family turned Christian, when that was the
fashion, and the plaque would have been equally incriminating
to them. Because of the Inquisition and the constant hunt for
converts who still secretly practiced Judaism."

He nodded and she went on. "Tío Manuel says the plaque
must have been destroyed."

Something in her tone alerted him. "You don't think
so?"

"I suppose it has to have been. But there are hints in the old
stories. Half clues when you try to put the pieces together."

"Clues to what?"

"A hiding place. A cache of some sort. Not very likely, is it?"

"Why not?" he said, looking around. "This ancient rabbit
warren could have a hundred hiding places."

"It's been torn down and rebuilt and added to God knows
how often since the plaque disappeared. You'd think somebody would have found it if it was here."

"Maybe it was broken up," Andy said thoughtfully.

"What are you talking about?"

"Maybe it's scattered around in pieces," he said.

"I suppose it could be, but what made you think of that?"

"Because I've seen a little triangular piece of gold, about one inch by two, with the Hebrew words *forget thee* engraved on it. It's obviously part of something larger."

She furrowed her brow and thought for a moment. "Doesn't sound like a piece of our plaque," she said finally. "It would be much larger than that. There's a room here in the oldest part of the palace that still has a mark on the wall where the plaque is supposed to have hung. I'll show it to you, but for the moment take my word for it, your bit of gold must be something else. Probably nothing to do with the Mendozas. We're not the only people familiar with the psalm."

"We're the only ones known as the House of Mendoza in Córdoba, aren't we?"

She was startled. "Is that written on your piece of gold?"

"Not exactly." He didn't explain about the envelope Lili had found and shown him. Dear as Susan was to him, in this business she had become one of the enemy. He'd save some of his ammunition for later.

She realized he was going to say no more and didn't insist. "You'd better go put on a coat and tie. It's almost time for lunch. Cooked by Tía Rosa today. It's a family tradition you may not know. On Christmas and Easter the servants have the day off and the lady of the house cooks. Tía Rosa is very good at it."

Rosa wasn't his aunt or Susan's. She was the wife of Manuel, head of the house. All the family called her *tía* as they called him *tío*. "All right," Andy said. "I'm starving, I'll never get used to lunch at three." He started to leave, then turned back. "Susan, tell me one thing. Has anybody ever talked to you about Lady Swanning's secretary?"

"Oh, for heaven's sake! Andy, I keep telling you, nobody has talked to me about any of it in years. Why should they? When it happened, we discussed nothing else for a few weeks, then it was obvious that Amanda must have killed herself or had an accident. It was all forgotten. Why can't you forget it? There must be something else to write about."

He persisted. "The secretary was American, but after the first police interview she drops from all the records. I can't even discover her name."

"No doubt because she had nothing to do with the whole affair. She was only an unfortunate bystander."

"At least tell me if you remember her name."

"The secretary?" Susan busied herself picking a piece of yarn from her skirt. "I don't think so."

He took a step toward her. "Couldn't have been Irene, could it?"

There was one sharp, indrawn breath. He was too close to miss it, though she covered very well. "Maybe. I simply don't remember." No faltering and her gaze was level.

"And somebody named Harry Cramer?"

"Never heard of him," Susan said firmly. A bell tinkled. "That's lunch. Do hurry. The one thing our Spanish relatives are prompt about is meals."

As promised, the food was good; the setting was better. Lunch was served in the small dining room adjacent to the kitchen. There was a larger room for greater occasions, but Andy didn't like it half so well as this square space with colonnaded openings to a cypress-filled courtyard, and exquisite mosaic panels set into walls covered in dark blue velvet.

At the head of the long table was Tío Manuel, the patriarch, a man in his early seventies. He was extremely tall and despite his age his hair was still flaming red, a legacy of his Irish grandmother. Andy tried to remember her name. Lila Curran, yes, that was it. There might be a book in Lila's story too. He'd heard that she'd been kept a prisoner in this house for years, chained to her bed and made to eat like an animal from a dish on the floor. And there was yet another story about Tío Manuel, that he'd been a hero in the Second World War. Andy found that tale hard to believe. Spain hadn't been in the war. One more Mendoza mystery. He looked at the others.

Fourteen people were lunching today, a variety of cousins and in-laws ranging in age from seventeen to over seventy. The table was covered with a floor-length embroidered cloth, and the custom was to lift the cloth and drape it over one's lap. Underneath, on a slightly raised platform, were braziers of lit charcoal that warmed feet and legs in these few chilly months of winter. Thus comforted, the diners could gaze into the patio at a tinkling fountain and the slim evergreens clipped to look like ascending spirals of ruched green velvet. Today they ate arroz con pollo and garlic-scented green olives and avocados dressed with lemon juice and sea salt and bread fragrant with anise, and drank the clean, flinty Montilla wine that was made from grapes grown in the family's vineyards and aged in their own bodega.

Tía Rosa had insisted that Andy sit beside her. She kept heaping his plate and filling his glass, and nodding and smiling because she spoke no English. His Spanish was barely passable, and Susan kept correcting him and the others laughed at his mistakes, but not unkindly. They were always kind and warm and welcoming; and he knew in his gut that they were hard as nails, all of them, including the women—and that some of them had information he wanted and were united in seeing he didn't get it. Even Susan. Especially Susan.

After the meal the others disappeared for their sacrosanct siesta, but Andy didn't feel like sleeping. He roamed through the patios until he was at the easternmost corner of the property, in the Patio de la Reja. Wrought iron *rejas,* grilles, were ubiquitous in this part of Spain; they covered nearly every window, but this one was different. Immense and ancient, it guarded the entrance to a shallow declivity in an outcropping of rock. Centuries-old, the family claimed, used originally as a strong room for the Mendoza gold.

So it may have been, but now it was merely an empty, dusty space. In a kind of reverse alchemy the gold had become far-flung lands and countless great houses containing priceless collections of art and artifacts. It was mortgages and stocks and bonds and cash in dozens of currencies, controlled and ever regenerated by that multinational steel web known as the Mendoza Group. And all the deceptively gossamer threads led back here, to be knotted firmly behind the austere marble façade of the Banco Mendoza on Córdoba's Avenida del Gran Capitán.

That was the heart of it, the damned Mendozas had more money than God. Money didn't buy only this world's goods, it also bought power and the ability to circumvent laws that were inconvenient. But for an American girl who'd murdered a Mendoza relative? How? More important, why? The questions were without answers and they brought Andy back to thoughts of Lili.

He'd sent her a Christmas card the day before. In a short while he'd return to London and he was fairly certain she'd be waiting. It was time to fish or cut bait, as Lili might say. The low-slung sun westered behind the hills, and Andy stood watching it for a long time.

ও 9 ৯৹

New York, Madrid, Caracas: 1980, 1981

In November, soon after Loy returned from Florida, Peter managed to see her alone. He went to her house, ostensibly to ask about a Spanish magazine he'd discovered that might fit into his list. Would Loy translate some of the articles so he could be sure?

The phone rang while they were discussing the magazine. It was Lili. "I'm depressed," she told Loy. "After diddling around for two months, NBC said no to the pilot of the new show. CBS and ABC have already turned it down, so I'm stuck with cable and the lunatic fringe."

Loy made sympathetic noises. "Listen, darling, Peter's here. I'm translating some Spanish for him, but we'll be through in no time. Jump in a cab and come down. Peter and I will cheer you up."

Peter scowled, but if Loy saw, she didn't comment. By the time Lili arrived, he was resigned and cheerful, and he dutifully worked at raising her spirits. That wasn't easy. She really was depressed.

"I'm sorry, I'm being a bore," Lili said. "But I feel so down. And—" She hesitated. "So damned rootless."

"The national disease," Peter said. "All Americans are rootless."

"I wasn't." Lili's tone was bitter.

"You mean that little jerkwater town you're from?" He ruffled her hair even though he knew she hated it.

Lili shook off his hand. "Not exactly." She took a long sip of the glass of sherry at her elbow. Like Spanish brandy, it was a taste acquired under Loy's tutelage.

"What can we say to cheer you up?" Peter asked.

"Nothing. I think I'd better go. I'm obviously rotten company." Lili rose, but Loy's voice held her back.

"Sit down, please. Pay attention, both of you. I think this is the time to let you in on an idea I have." Loy paused for effect. "I want you two to go into business together."

"Crazy," Lili said.

"Doing what," Peter asked, "a song and dance act?"

They'd spoken at the same time. Loy held up her hand. "Stop being so negative and hear me out."

Essentially, Loy based her case on three simple assertions. Lili was overworked and underpaid, and her talents were largely unexploited. "This man Kerry, what does he really do for you? You're always mentioning possible deals he's working on, but as far as I can see, very few of them come to fruition. You've had a television show for four years and thousands of people know your name and your face, but what use is being made of that?"

Peter, Loy said, was stuck in a small pond that by definition could never get any larger. He worked hard and long, but there was such a limited market for what he did that no matter how skilled he was at it, growth was impossible.

"And third," she said, "you two have known each other a long time. You're good friends and care about each other. You'd make an excellent team, but you don't seem to recognize it. Moreover, you ignore the obvious similarity in your fields of expertise."

"Which is what?" Peter asked, apparently still unconvinced.

"The good life," Loy said. She was animated, enthusiastic, willing them to believe. "The *expensive* good life . . . as expressed in people's homes, what they eat, what they read."

It was that last point which set Peter thinking. Lili listened to Loy's arguments and nodded, and went home as depressed as she'd arrived. In a matter of days she'd forgotten the conversation. Peter remembered.

•   •   •

A couple of weeks before Christmas Peter rang Loy's bell a little after eight. "Sorry to arrive out of the blue," he said. "Is it all right? Am I bothering you?"

"Of course you're not bothering me. Come upstairs, it's cozier."

She paused long enough to instruct the butler to bring coffee and brandy, then led the way to the little sitting room off her bedroom. It was small and charming. There was a love seat and one chair and a desk. The walls and the furniture were covered in matching chintz printed with pale-blue birds and stylized lime-green trees. The fabric gave the room both character and warmth.

Peter had been up there once before, but Lili had been with them. This time the visit was disturbingly intimate. Loy was in the same green hostess gown she'd worn the first time he'd come to her house, seven months before. It seemed longer. He felt as if he'd known her all his life. No, amend that, he thought. He felt as if he'd been searching for her all his life. "You look beautiful," he said.

Loy busied herself putting away the writing things that covered the desk. "Thank you. Did you come only to pay me compliments?"

"No. But suddenly that seems much more important than what I did come to talk about." His voice was husky with feeling.

Loy stood quite still and didn't turn to face him. "Peter, very dear Peter, please let's talk about whatever you first had in mind."

"Why?" He took a step nearer. Loy stiffened. He could actually see her body tense.

"Because it's best if we do," she said. "Please, I'm enormously fond of you, I value your friendship, don't spoil things."

He was on the brink of forcing the issue, but he pulled back. "Okay. Relax. I came to talk about your nutty idea that Lili and I should go into business together."

"It's not a nutty idea."

He sat on the abbreviated sofa and pulled his tie loose. "Yeah, that's what I've been thinking. Maybe it's not. A couple of days ago I ran across something that made me think it through again."

"Good." She sat opposite him, in the chair. "What was it?"

Before he could answer, there was a tap on the door. The butler came in with a tray. Loy sent him away and tended to the pouring. She didn't have to ask, she knew Peter took black coffee with a scant teaspoon of sugar. Their lives were full of such superficial intimacies. She handed him the cup and a snifter of brandy and repeated her question. "What did you find?"

Peter had learned to respect Loy's quick intelligence. He didn't bother with any long preamble. "A small magazine publisher called Bass and Demmer. They own eight magazines. No Bass anymore, he's long dead, apparently. A guy named Randolph Demmer is publisher and chief executive officer. He's pushing seventy and there's no obvious heir apparent."

Peter took a folded sheet of paper from his inside pocket and handed it to her. "Here's what they've got."

Loy wore reading glasses, little half lenses in thin gold frames, suspended on a chain around her neck. She pushed them on to the edge of her nose and studied the paper. There were eight names. *Coin Collecting, The Rare Book Journal, Doll Houses, Your Vintage Car, Archaeology Today, The World of Food, Professional Chef,* and *House Remodeling Quarterly.*

While she read, Peter spoke. "The only monthlies are the two food magazines. The archaeology number's a quarterly, like the house one. The rest are bimonthly. It's a sluggish operation, low circulation in every case but one. Mostly aimed at loyal diehards with bees in their bonnets. Extremely high renewal rate, which keeps them ticking over and attracts enough advertising to let them survive."

Loy was still looking at the paper. "Which one isn't low circulation?"

"Guess."

She didn't hesitate. *"The World of Food."*

"Got it in one. A hundred thousand according to published figures. How did you know?"

"Why else would you be interested?"

He chuckled. "Right. That's the link. What interests me are the final three on the list. *The World of Food, Professional Chef,* and *House Remodeling.* I've taken a close look at them. They all have enormous scope for improvement. At the same time, they've got a base of advertisers and subscribers. I'm wondering if they could be bought. If so, Lili and I would have something to work on together. I'd publish, with Lili as special editorial consultant. Meanwhile the books would provide a platform from which we could spin off into other related things that she'd manage."

"What kind of things?" Loy asked.

"I'm not sure yet. But I feel in my gut the potential's there. Manufacturing probably. A line of cookware. Kitchen accessories. Something like that."

She slipped off the glasses and they fell to her breast, glinting softly against the deep green bodice of her gown. "Have you talked to Lili?"

"No. I came to you first. I haven't a hope of putting together enough capital to buy those magazines. Not by myself. And I don't think Lili's got much."

"Are you sure they're for sale?"

"Haven't a clue," he admitted. "But I think they could be. Everything points to a company that's run out of steam, that's barely keeping its nose above water."

"And this . . . what's his name?" She put the glasses back on and looked at the paper she still held.

"Randolph Demmer," Peter supplied.

"Yes. This Mr. Demmer owns the firm?"

"Not exactly. It's publicly held, traded over the counter. Do you know what that means?"

She smiled. "Of course."

"Okay. Apparently Demmer's got the single largest block of stock. And he's chairman of the board as well as CEO."

Loy settled back and thought for a moment. "I'm intrigued," she said. "I'd like to talk to Lili and think about it a little more."

• • •

Lili, too, was intrigued by Peter's idea. Loy told her about it over a Sunday brunch. Peter wasn't there. He'd had to go to Chicago for a business meeting. "It's a fascinating idea," Lili said. "But I don't have a lot of capital either. Probably less than Peter. How could I buy in?"

"Let's leave the finances to be settled later," Loy said with a wave of her hand.

"That's the worst business advice I ever heard."

Loy laughed. "Yes, I suppose it is. But it's not merely business, is it? We're friends. That must count for something."

"A lot," Lili admitted. "Only . . . Listen, why did you bring this up in the first place? Why should you become involved in Peter's business life or mine?"

"Do you think I'm interfering?" Loy asked quietly. "Butting in where I don't belong?"

"No, that's not what I meant. I'm not sure I can explain. I guess what I'm trying to say is that it seems out of character."

"You mean out of character for me."

"Yes," Lili said. "I think it is."

Loy toyed with her food and didn't answer right away. "You once accused me of being decorative," she said finally, "and I told you I'd never had a chance to be anything else."

"I remember."

"I can't go into the background, Lili, but at the moment I'm freer than I've been for many years. I would like to use my resources to do something that interests me. If at the same time I can make you happier—and Peter, of course," she added hastily, "what's wrong with that?"

"Nothing."

Loy leaned toward her. "Lili, is there something else you want, something I could help you get?"

The question could hardly be more pointed. Lili looked at her friend, opened her mouth to say something, then held back. She never talked about this to anyone, but lately the dream seemed to be receding beyond her reach. Lili needed to talk to keep it alive.

"My mother sold the house I grew up in. I want to buy it back."

"I see," Loy said softly. "It's in New England, isn't it?"

"Yes, in Fielding, Massachusetts, where I was raised."

"But you don't intend to go back there, do you?" Loy's eyes were dark with concern. "Your life is here in New York, Lili."

"I know. But I could use the house on weekends. If I could afford to buy it, that is. I tried last year, but the owners didn't want to sell. The real estate agent suggested they might if I offered an astronomical price. I can't do that. Not unless I get a network show."

"I could lend you the money for the down payment."

Lili shook her head. "That wouldn't work. I'd have asked you before now if it would. The problem is that I don't earn enough to support a second home, let alone pay you back."

"I thought you'd say something like that. So my way makes more sense, doesn't it?" Loy leaned forward and lay her hand over Lili's. "I care about you. I want you to be happy. I want to be part of making something exciting happen for you and for Peter. Is there any reason not to try?"

Lili looked at her and smiled. "None at all," she said.

"Good. That's settled. As for Peter's idea, I'm not sure what's involved or how to go about it. Peter's doing more checking, and I want some legal and financial advice. Perhaps the three of us can get together and talk again in a few days."

At the end of the week they met at a new Chinese place Lili was considering for the possibility of a show. After dinner Peter pulled a sheaf of papers and a stack of magazines from his briefcase.

"Copies for both of you," he said, distributing the materials. "I've also been asking around, very discreetly. There's no hint that old man Demmer wants to sell any bits of his decrepit little kingdom. And apparently he's hale and hearty." He made a despairing gesture. "It doesn't look good. Maybe I'm wasting our time."

"I've been asking too," Loy said. "I have a financial advisor, a man who deals in this kind of thing all the time. He also reports that Mr. Demmer has never shown any signs of wanting to sell."

"But that doesn't close out the possibility," Lili said. "We could make an offer. You never know until you try." She made a face. "Listen to me talking about an offer. If I liquidate everything I have I could maybe come up with forty thousand."

Loy held up her hand. "We're not dealing with that yet, remember? Right now we're only trying to figure out if the idea is . . . what's that word businessmen always use?"

"Viable," Peter said.

"Yes, that's it. That's what Mr. Crandall said."

"Who's Mr. Crandall?" Lili poured more Chinese tea into each little handleless cup.

"My financial advisor. I talked with him last Monday, and again this morning."

"And?" Peter leaned forward. The idea of being publisher of three magazines had begun to take root in his gut as well as in his imagination. He told himself to be cautious, but it wasn't easy. "What does he think?"

"Well, he's put a whole new slant on things." Loy took a small leatherbound notebook from her purse. "I made some notes so I'd be accurate. He points out that one possibility is a raid."

There was silence at the table. Lili and Peter stared at her.

"You know," Loy said. "A takeover. Peter, you're the one who first mentioned that Bass and Demmer's shares are publicly traded."

Peter began making notes on a paper napkin. "Currently selling at $6.25 a share. Declared profit of thirteen dollars a share as of last December. Which is a price-to-earnings ratio of something under five." He looked up at the two women. "I'm no expert on the stock market, but that sounds to me as if the company is undervalued."

Loy nodded. "Yes. That's what Mr. Crandall pointed out. He says they could be vulnerable. We could buy enough of the stock to control the company."

"We don't want the whole company," Lili said. "Look at this garbage." She thumbed through the magazines. "Coins and dollhouses and potshards from Nepal. More lunatic fringe. I've had a bellyful of that."

"That's not it." Peter spoke softly. He was looking at Loy and his eyes were shining. "If I'm not mistaken, that's not what this guy Crandall is suggesting."

Loy shook her head. "No, not at all. He says that once we control the company, we sell off all but the three magazines we want."

"Exactly," Peter said. "And use the capital the sales generate to finance an upgrade of the magazines we keep, plus seed money for our spinoff enterprises. Beautiful. It's simple and beautiful." He leaned over and put his hand beneath Loy's chin. "Sweetheart, you are the most amazing woman I've ever met."

Lili watched the two of them. Loy looked happy, but it was a general, unfocused happiness. Peter's pleasure in the moment was something different, more than the excitement of a possible business coup. His high, the adrenaline obviously pumping through his system, was partly the smell of a deal, but equally it was his feelings for Loy. Poor Peter.

Lying in bed that night, unable to sleep, Lili analyzed further her reactions to Peter and Loy. This time she didn't feel proprietary about Peter or jealous of the other woman because this time, Lili realized he cared desperately. And she was prepared to admit that she had no romantic feelings about Peter Fowler. But he'd been part of her life for a long time, a constant in the background.

Peter was her fail-safe date, her reliable shoulder to cry on. If he made a permanent alliance with somebody else, things would change. So be it. What bothered her now was that Peter was hungering after something she was sure he couldn't have. And probably shouldn't have. Peter refused to see it, but Loy gave no sign of being in love with him.

Convinced she wouldn't sleep, Lili got out of bed and made a cup of Constant Command tea. It was delicious, and comforting. She sipped the tea and gazed into the middle distance. In her mind's eye there was a far horizon and a shingled house with a roofed porch leading to a double dutch door.

No one could know the depth of her commitment, the savagery of her longing. Lili understood. It was a truth she'd come to accept.

Two things she had loved beyond price, beyond measure: A man and the house she'd grown up in. The man had left her. Once a year she saw a new book Andy had written and she always bought it and read it—and cried herself to sleep for a few nights. But she'd accepted the fact that he probably no longer remembered her name, and certainly didn't love her. She'd been force-fed that truth. It stuck in her throat and made her physically sick if she thought about it, but most of the time she didn't. The house was different. It still could be hers someday. It would be. Clinging to that thought, Lili returned to bed and eventually slept.

Two days before Christmas, Peter, Lili, and Loy had an appointment with the man Loy described as her financial advisor. Peter was on a tight schedule and would be a few minutes late, the two women were to go ahead. Lili and Loy met in midtown and took a cab to Wall Street. "I've never actually been inside anyplace on Wall Street," Lili said.

"You won't like this one much," Loy warned. "Lots of marble and hushed voices. Designed to be intimidating. But I do trust Jeremy Crandall."

"I'm still not exactly clear. Is he a lawyer or an accountant?"

"Neither," Loy said. "He's an officer in a financial company. Rather like a bank, but for businesses and governments, not individuals."

"You're not a business or a government."

"No, but they've looked after my affairs for years."

There wasn't time to ask more. The cab dropped them in front of a granite building with a severely classical façade relieved only by a pair of modern glass doors. Beside the doors was a brass plaque containing three words: The Mendoza Group.

Lili stopped walking. She stared at the plaque and grew very pale.

"What's the matter? Lili, are you ill?"

She shook her head. "No," she managed to murmur. "No, I'm all right." She wasn't. Her stomach was knotted and she felt dizzy.

Loy watched her for a moment. "Are you sure? We can postpone the appointment."

"God no," Lili said between clenched teeth. "Let's get it over with." It was a coincidence, a trick of fate. It was life giving her the finger.

A uniformed attendant opened the door before Lili or Loy could. "Good afternoon, Señora Perez." He led them to the elevators. "Mr. Crandall?" he asked.

Loy smiled and nodded. The attendant reached inside and pushed buttons.

"He doesn't want you to strain yourself," Lili murmured as the doors whooshed shut. Loy giggled.

The elevator was lined with mahogany and brass. It carried them soundlessly to the seventh floor, and its doors opened not to a corridor but a small reception room. Once more Loy was greeted by name. "Mr. Crandall's waiting for you, Señora Perez. I'll take you straight in."

Lili had expected an elderly man. Jeremy Crandall was around thirty-five. A Young Turk, she guessed, a whiz-kid graduate of Harvard Business School. With a slightly facile air of bonhomie.

"You look as wonderful as ever, Loy. And this must be the famous Lili Cramer." He turned a practiced smile in Lili's direction. She decided she didn't like him, then reminded herself she was predisposed not to like anyone she met in a place owned by the Mendozas.

"Peter will be here any minute," Loy said. "He had a scheduling problem he couldn't avoid. It has been absolute hell getting you three busy people in the same room at the same time."

"Busy people get things done," Crandall said. Lili wondered if he spoke only in clichés, but before her dislike could harden, his attitude became more natural and relaxed. "I've got some numbers for you to look at." He passed them each a sheet of figures. It was the last published financial report of Bass & Demmer.

Lili studied the paper. In the few weeks since she'd realized that it all might really happen, she'd embarked on a crash course, cramming on things like *Forbes* magazine and *The Wall Street Journal*. It was absurdly broad-spectrum, too little too late—but it was better than nothing. And she'd made up her mind not to be afraid to ask questions, no matter how dumb they might sound. "How does a company get to be this undervalued, Mr. Crandall? If we can see it, how come every sharp trader in the market doesn't see it too?"

"Because," Crandall said, "thousands of companies are traded daily. Nobody can watch them all. Thirteen years ago, shortly before Leo Bass died, his company entered the market with a limited public offer. Very small potatoes. Probably Bass had plans, but he died before he could realize them. Since then the company has sat still. Wall Street isn't interested in companies with their feet in lead. Besides, over-the-counter stocks aren't everybody's cup of tea. Most of the big funds avoid them. But finding something like this, the way you three have, that's what makes the stock market the world's greatest indoor sport."

Lili figured he probably slept cuddled up to Dow Jones reports.

A buzzer sounded on the desk. A disembodied voice announced that Mr. Fowler had arrived. Peter was shown in and the two men were introduced. They shook hands. Lili could see them sizing each other up. In seconds Peter was at a subtle disadvantage. Jeremy Crandall sat behind a huge desk of brass and plate glass, Peter was in a chair on his left. Lili was on the other side, Loy in the middle.

Crandall cleared his throat, Lili had the distinct impression that he was calling a meeting to order. This wasn't friendly conversation. This was business with a capital B. Crandall confirmed the impression with his next words. "First, let me say that I'm here solely in my capacity as advisor to Señora Perez. The Mendoza Group is not interested in any participatory role in your venture."

"Why not?" Peter asked immediately. "Does it look that bad to you?"

"No, at this point it's value-neutral as far as we're concerned. Any venture is until we decide to study it. But as a matter of policy, we don't get involved unless substantial sums are required."

"What do you call substantial?" Lili asked. She was always trying to get the bottom line spelled out, probably because her resources were the most limited.

Crandall shrugged. "Let's say we don't look hard at anything under twenty-five million."

The numbers dropped into a void of disbelief, but he didn't seem to notice. He went on speaking. "With that out of the way, we can talk. I've put out a few more feelers and learned that Demmer has no interest in selling the three magazines you want. Nor any of them, for that matter. The board is composed mainly of relatives, either his or the defunct Mr. Bass's. They do whatever he says."

"The shareholders may not be so tame," Peter said.

"I'm sure they won't be. But you're premature. It's not yet time to figure the shareholders into the equation."

Loy leaned forward. "Please tell Peter and Lili what you told me on the phone, Jeremy."

"Yes, I think I should. I have mixed feelings about this enterprise. On the face of it it's a profit opportunity, but by definition that implies risk. It's my understanding that Señora Perez will be the source of all the seed money, and her affairs normally aren't managed that aggressively. We have no need to seek a killing on her behalf, not when that means exposure."

Peter started to say something, but Crandall cut him off. "Let me finish, please. I said all this to Señora Perez because that's my responsibility. She insisted she wants to go ahead. On that basis we're having this meeting."

Loy sighed. "I didn't mean the lecture part, Jeremy. And you neglected to mention that I told you I hadn't had this much fun in years. I can afford to have a little fun once in a while."

This time Peter wouldn't be silenced. "I want something clear up front. If we go ahead with this, there's no way I'm going to agree to Loy taking the entire risk. I can raise a couple of hundred thousand, and that goes into the pot from the start."

"I agree," Lili said. "Only crooks gamble with everybody's money but their own. I probably can't come up with more than forty thousand dollars, and in this instance that's so little it's a joke. But if I'm not willing to risk it, I have no business being here."

Loy was agitated. "I talked you two into this. It was never my intention that you—"

"We're both set in our positions, Loy," Peter interrupted. "Let's accept them as a given and go on, okay?"

She sat back, but with the air of one who has conceded the battle, not the war.

Peter turned to Crandall. "On the working presumption that we're going ahead, what's the first step?"

"A game plan." Crandall took three more sheets of paper from his desk and handed one to each of them.

"Here's a memo outlining my suggestions. I'd like to go through it with you. First we set up a corporation naming the three of you as officers. Next that entity creates some others; eventually, there's a wholly owned company run by Mr. Fowler here. I'm suggesting him because it's still a fact of life that a man in charge attracts less attention than a woman. And in the early stage the last thing we want is attention."

"Why?" Lili asked. "I keep reading every day about people buying up other people's stock."

"By the time you read about it, those people are in a very strong position. It's getting there that requires discretion. Can I go on?" He looked at Lili and she nodded. "Okay, the entity headed by Mr. Fowler begins buying Bass and Demmer shares. When you own in the neighborhood of twelve percent, you'll start making waves."

"What happens on the beach?" It was again Lili who asked the question. Loy was silent and Peter was punching numbers into a hand-held calculator.

"More than likely the word will get out. A lot of small investors will figure that something's happening, that somebody knows something, and they'll buy on the strength of that alone. When a lot of people want to buy a stock, the price goes up. That rule at least is inviolable. One good thing: If it's invoked, you'll have cover of a sort. At that point you can elect to get out. And if you're very smart and your timing is perfect, you might not lose your shirts."

Peter looked up. "If my figures are even close to being right, your scenario means we'll be in to the tune of over a million bucks before we have that dubious cover."

Crandall grinned. "Yup. That's what's so delightful about this venture. It's business in miniature, a little dollhouse of a deal."

"A million dollars doesn't sound like a kid's toy to me," Lili said.

"It's all relative, isn't it?" Crandall shuffled some papers on his desk. "Getting back to our game plan, when you've made some noise, the risk really starts. If you don't sell, and you can't if you're still pursuing your original goal, you'll have to find ways to keep acquiring what will now be more expensive stock. Preferably in large blocks. And Randolph Demmer isn't likely to roll over and play dead. He'll fight back."

"Then what?" Lili's voice was subdued. Suddenly this business was for real. The stakes seemed staggeringly high considering that she had nothing but a glamorous job, a fox fur coat, a few valuable books, a small IRA, and thirty-some thousand in a mutual fund.

"Then we have a textbook situation," Jeremy Crandall said. "You're well into a raid. A hostile takeover."

Before they left, Crandall retrieved all three copies of his memo. "Safer," he murmured. "An accidental leak now would be fatal."

They were at war. Lili wondered if the Geneva conventions applied. No, she decided. Judging from her experience, the only rule the Mendozas followed was take no prisoners.

On the tenth of February 1981 Diego Parilles Mendoza arrived at his seventieth birthday. Later the family would have a large party in his honor, but for the moment he was alone in his Madrid office. He much preferred that.

Diego was still a handsome man. Thin and sere, he was not skeletal—rather, he was honed, sharpened, rubbed to a hard, high gloss. It was the kind of hardness many women found irresistible, the kind spoken of as masterful. Men immediately recognized him as one of those who make the rules but seldom follow them. There were some who said Diego was little different from a gangster, but they never said it very loud. He certainly didn't look like a thug. The head he bent over a report displayed a patrician profile, evidence of the generations of breeding which had produced him.

The report excited Diego. This business with the young woman who had an old-fashioned name intrigued him. He said it aloud. "Lili." In a long life he'd learned that nothing is predictable, but also to trust his instincts. An upheaval in a situation he'd thought stable could mean many different things. Whatever it turned out to be, it must be dealt with.

He glanced at a clock standing under a glass bell on a table the other side of the room. The clock had a rotating set of three brass balls at its base. They were perpetually turning, spinning away seconds and minutes that stretched into days and years. Time was a cheat, an instrument of confusion. Now it was three P.M. in Madrid, so it must be nine in the morning in Caracas. Leaning forward, he pressed a button on his desk. A secretary appeared in the doorway.

"*Sí, Don Diego?*"

"*Quisiera llamar a Caracas. El Señor Cortez.*"

The secretary nodded and disappeared. Two minutes later the phone on Diego's desk tinkled softly, the connection had been made. When he lifted the receiver he seemed transformed, suddenly full of energy. "*Soy Diego, amigo, cómo estás?*"

"*Don Diego, qué sorpresa. Estoy bien, y usted?*"

"*Más mayor, pero bien.*" The formalities were over, it was time to say why he'd called. "*Acabo de recibir información lo cual es raro. Tienes que ir a Nueva York.*"

"It is impossible," the poet protested. He didn't give a damn what information the other man had received or how strange it was. "I can't go to New York, I'm working on something new, a long epic poem about a horse. It's marvelous, Don Diego, after years of silence my muse sings again. I'm inspired. This will be my masterwork, I'm sure of it."

"Santiago, if you write the greatest poem in the history of man or horses, it will still earn less than you require to live on for six months."

"There is more to life than money, my friend."

"Is there? I hadn't noticed. You will go to New York, Santiago. Within the next few days. I'll arrange for a ticket to be waiting at my Caracas office. And you will be very diligent on my behalf, because otherwise your monthly check will stop."

"I am tired of this. Year after year I run your errands, do small, unpleasant tasks." Santiago's voice rose. "You think I am a puppet on a string, but I will cut the strings, Diego, and you—"

"New York," the man in Madrid repeated calmly, interrupting the futile outburst. He owned Santiago, had for years. No particular reason, except that men such as this sold themselves into bondage cheaply. "I'm sure the gracious Señora Perez will be delighted to receive you once more."

Later that same day the poet lunched in the restaurant of one of the better hotels in Caracas. He could not usually afford to frequent such places. Don Diego's check was small. Its great virtue was that it was regular, the only income he could absolutely rely on. And for his art, his poetry, he must sacrifice. So he would remain the Mendoza errand boy. But he would get back at his patron, prod him a little.

The poet was the guest of the man he'd telephoned after the call came from Madrid. "This is Santiago Cortez," he'd said. "We met the other night, do you remember?"

Andrew Mendoza had remembered; now they were having lunch.

Santiago's heart beat so fast he could almost hear it. Betrayal was ugly, yes, but revenge was sweet. And this young man was full of questions. He had been from the moment they met, when Santiago admitted that he knew the Mendoza family in Spain.

"I'm touched by your concern for your family," Santiago said now.

"I'm a loving relative," Andy said dryly. "Always interested in the doings of the aunts and uncles and cousins. You did say you were with them in the late thirties, in Córdoba?"

"Yes, I did."

"The period interests me," Andy said.

"Of course. It was an interesting time in Spain."

It amused Santiago to toy with the young Englishman. Mendoza was trying to maneuver the conversation back to what had happened in Córdoba in '39. Santiago knew a lot about that, but he would tell only a little. The arms of the family Mendoza were all-embracing. His publishers here in Caracas were a wholly owned subsidiary of a Mendoza company. He would say enough to put the young man on the scent, to cause Diego a bit of trouble, make the bastard squirm a bit—but not enough to allow Diego to know he'd talked.

The waiter arrived with their lunch. "I told you our food is marvelous," Santiago said enthusiastically. "This proves it, no?"

On the poet's advice Andy had ordered asado Venezolano, braised beef larded with capers and bacon in a rich sweet and sour sauce. It was served with a remarkable cake made of bananas and cheese. He sampled the beef. "Yes, sure, excellent."

Andy knew the other man was stalling. He understood why. A small man was somehow going to tweak the tail of the mighty Mendozas. Cortez wanted to enjoy his moment. Okay, he didn't mind. Going along with such charades had become a commonplace in Andy's life. Disgruntled underlings were often the source of startling information for an exposé.

He took a sip of his beer. The book that had brought him there dealt with the six richest families in South America. It was nearly finished and he was sick to death of marimbas and gauchos and haciendas. He longed for Europe. So why was he wheedling information out of an antique third-rate poet? Because another story still gestated in his gut, waiting to be born. He drank some more beer.

Santiago signaled the waiter and ordered another round. Andy's bill was mounting. Enough, he'd call time. "What do you have for me, Señor Cortez?"

The poet laughed softly. "You are like an American, impatient. They say the English are subtle."

"Proves you can't believe everything they say, doesn't it?"

"Perhaps. But sometimes yes, you can believe." The old man leaned forward and began speaking in a low, urgent murmur.

The following day Loy was awakened by the telephone. *"Querida, soy Santiago."*

Loy sighed, but she greeted him cordially. They exchanged pleasantries. Eventually, he got to the point. He had to be in New York for a while, there was a chance of a new translation of his collected works, and hotels were so expensive . . .

She knew what response was required. *"Pero, por qué un hotel, Santiago? Mi casa es tu casa."* The ancient Spanish politeness, my house is your house; she spoke the words easily but without conviction. Santiago didn't seem to notice. He gushed thanks and said he'd arrive by the end of the week. It was clear that the visit would be open-ended. When she hung up, Loy was seething.

Almost instantly the telephone rang again. This time it was Jeremy Crandall. "Look, Loy, I've been doing the numbers. If you're going ahead with your venture, you'll have to invade the corpus of the trust. You can do that only once in any given year, and only up to a limit."

"I know all that, Jeremy." She was crisper than she might have been. Blame it on the call from Caracas. "Do whatever's necessary."

"I'll have to inform the trustees."

"So you will." Her voice was flat. The only trustee who mattered already knew. Why else Santiago? "Do it," she repeated.

He said a few things more and broke the connection. Loy didn't put the receiver down immediately. She held it and stared into space. Finally the instrument began making protesting noises. She replaced it and pressed her fingertips to her temples. She had a raging headache.

Loy's bedroom was large, done in shades of red with ornately carved Spanish furniture. It was the only Spanish-inspired room in the West Tenth Street house, and at this moment she hated it.

She fled to the bathroom. It was pure American, full of gadgets that worked and white tile and mirrors. Loy studied her reflection. She was getting older, and more tired, and full of regrets. So she was prepared to take risks. How great they were only she, and perhaps Irene, realized. Shuddering slightly, Loy reached for the aspirin bottle, though she suspected it would require more than aspirin to soothe a pain so intense.

❧ 10 ❧

New York, Caracas, and Madrid: 1981

"You're sure you want to liquidate all the shares in your mutual fund, Miss Cramer?"

"Yes, quite sure." Lili held the telephone casually, looking out the window at the softly falling February snow. She was past being nervous about her commitment to the scheme Loy had initiated. After two months of talk, she was utterly convinced. "When can I have the check?" she asked.

"Five business days."

"Okay, I'll pick it up."

She did, on Friday afternoon at five to five. After the broker's commission, it came to thirty-seven thousand two hundred dollars and sixty-seven cents. Not bad, she'd almost doubled her investment in four years, lousy economic years at that. Moreover, she had two other checks in her bag. An antique dealer had paid her sixteen hundred dollars for fifteen old books, and one of the secretaries at the station had bought her fox coat for twelve hundred.

Lili deposited the total of forty thousand dollars and sixty-seven cents in her account. She didn't think of it as money. To her the cash represented thousands of shares of Bass & Demmer stock. It was also her ante, the stake she threw in the kitty in return for the right to play.

The entity they had created was named LPL Corporation. It produced nothing, but at the moment of its birth LPL had liquid assets of slightly under a million dollars. Most of the money came from Loy; between them Peter and Lili had supplied little more than a quarter of the total. But because Loy would have it no other way, they each owned an equal third of the company.

In a short time the cash would be used to purchase stock. It was only enough for the opening salvo, a million wouldn't buy victory. But they were still in the preliminary stages, the dream time when everything seemed possible. At the point where they needed more money they'd have a toehold; hopefully, they'd be strong enough to generate the additional capital. "At that juncture we should be able to negotiate a leveraged buyout," Crandall said. On paper it all looked simple, even straightforward.

The acquisitions would be made in the name of Fowler Distribution, Inc. Part of Peter's ante was his company. For the time being he would continue to run it and he was still titular head of the corporation, but the company was now a wholly owned subsidiary of LPL. He'd also insisted on turning over his apartment; he would live in it and pay LPL a rent equivalent to the mortgage payments and the maintenance. Jeremy Crandall was surprised at Peter's insistence on denuding himself so entirely. "You don't have to," he'd said. "Señora Perez doesn't think—"

"Prepare the papers," Peter had interrupted. "I go for broke or not at all."

Lili didn't think he was being very wise, but she understood. Precisely because he was in love with Loy, he had to do it. Peter believed he had a future with Loyola Perez, and he wouldn't be seen as using her. He wanted no one to think he was a fortune hunter after a wealthy older woman. Lili thought his hopes forlorn, but in a few months the money part wouldn't matter. She was positive they'd succeed—all three of them were.

The raid began on the second of March, a day of bitter cold and gray, threatening skies. At nine A.M. Peter bought the first block of five hundred shares of Bass & Demmer stock in the name of Fowler Distribution, Inc. Within a few days he and Lili had developed a system. Different brokers were approached, sometimes as many as a dozen in one week, and the biggest and busiest were used two or three times. By the fifteenth the raiders owned nine percent of outstanding Bass & Demmer stock, and they were still buying. The simple act of acquiring the shares had become a full-time job.

Peter didn't want to do it from his office. He trusted his secretary, but Crandall's paranoia about leaks had rubbed off. He left the secretary to run the distribution company— she could do it very well in the short term—and spent most of the day at what had become the base of operations, Lili's apartment. He'd suggested Loy's house, but surprisingly she demurred. "My friend Santiago Cortez is staying with me."

"Does that matter? We can closet ourselves away in one of the extra bedrooms," Peter said.

"No," Loy insisted. "I'm not comfortable with the idea, Peter. You have to work someplace else."

He was disappointed, but she was adamant, so they used Lili's tiny apartment. She installed a second telephone and allowed most of her own work to slide. The only thing she couldn't get out of was her show. For one thing, she was under contract, for another, Peter thought the fact that thousands of people saw her weekly on television was vital.

"Your celebrity is going to be very important to us. We're going to splash your name and your face all over. You can put the remodeling on hold and tell Kerry you're not available for any of his other schemes, but keep shooting off your mouth on the tube."

Lili did, but that left her plenty of time to sit in the Eighty-first Street living room with Peter and drink endless cups of coffee and talk on the telephone. Because of the tension, he was practically eating cigarettes. The air was blue with smoke and they were both hoarse by five P.M., but they quivered with excitement.

On the nineteenth Lili found a large block of shares that would bring their holdings to fifteen percent of the company. They had been worried that the easily available stock was drying up. Now this.

At noon Lili gave the buy order; at one twenty-five the broker called to say it was theirs. She hung up the phone and looked at Peter and they both began to laugh hysterically. Lili sobered first. "Come on! The market's got a little over an hour before closing. Let's get back and work the phones."

They didn't find anything more that day. The next morning there was a call at five past nine. Peter was already talking on one phone, Lili answered the second. "This is Crandall, I thought I'd better tell you right away. Bass & Demmer is up eighty-five cents. It opened this morning at seven ten."

"We're making waves," Lili said.

"Yup. Right on schedule. Buy anything you can find immediately. The rise will probably loosen a few blocks, but I suspect there's not going to be anything for sale within a couple of hours."

He was right. They bought a few thousand more shares, first at seven ten and then at seven twenty-five, but by noon no broker could find anything for them. "How much have we got?" Lili demanded.

Peter was already punching numbers into the calculator. He used one with a tape now. Before he spoke he ripped it off and compared it with a column of figures. "Unless I've made a mistake, and I don't think I have, nineteen percent."

"At seven twenty-five, what are they worth?"

More activity with the calculator. "Exactly $742,500. Subtract what we paid and we've made a profit of $112,000."

"On paper," Lili said.

"Yes, on paper."

She stretched. "Academic, since we're not selling. Anyway it's chicken feed. Especially cut three ways. What do we do now?"

Peter picked up the phone again. "Let's talk with Loy. Then I think the three of us should meet with Crandall."

That meeting took place after six. Crandall came to Lili's after he left his office. Loy was there too. They'd offered to go to her, but she put them off. "You're forgetting my house guest. It's awkward. I'll come uptown."

Lili poured drinks while the air crackled with tension. They were all equally affected, even Jeremy Crandall. "Time to look at the major shareholders list again," he said.

They did. The numbers hadn't changed. Randolph Demmer had the largest single chunk, he owned twenty-eight percent of the company. The seven members of the board of directors, all

Bass or Demmer relations, held between them another twenty-three percent. That left forty-nine percent spread among the buying public; that's what LPL had been raiding. The clearest way to think about it was simply to say that they'd bought up nineteen percent of what wasn't held by various members of the family.

Crandall kept examining the paper, sucking in his cheeks and blowing air out of pursed lips. Lili found the mannerism revolting; she looked away. Peter puffed hard on a cigarette; a few minutes ago he'd opened his third pack of the day. He was watching Loy, not Jeremy Crandall. Lili caught Loy's eye, smiled, and raised her glass in a small, intimate gesture of salute and affection. The silence lengthened.

"Willa Grayson," Crandall said finally. "She's Bass's daughter. Been on the board since her father died. I have a vague memory of reading something in the old clippings in our morgue. Nothing spelled out, only a hint that maybe she and old man Demmer aren't the best of friends. She's got ten percent."

"Ten percent added to our nineteen makes twenty-nine," Peter said softly. "That's more than Demmer has. That would make us the majority holders."

Crandall nodded. "I think you should go see her, Peter."

"My God," Lili half whispered. "We already own more than the daughter of one of the founders."

"So you do," Crandall agreed.

Lili wasn't sure if it was for Crandall's benefit, or for Loy's, but Peter was suddenly very cool. "Even if she hands them to us on a silver platter," he said, "Demmer can outvote us if the rest of the board hangs tough."

"Premature," Crandall said. "At this stage it's impossible to know who'll hang tough and who'll want a quick killing. Next step is for you to talk to Mrs. Grayson."

Loy had become a silent partner in recent weeks. Having set all this in motion, she'd removed herself from the day-to-day battle, but she spoke now. "What if we can't get Mrs. Grayson's shares? What if she won't sell?"

Crandall closed his briefcase and stood up. "I don't for a moment think you'll get them. Not right away. Whatever you offer her today, she'll be sure you'll offer more tomorrow. But now's the time to declare your hand. She lives in Morristown. The address is on the list. You'd better get over there right away. While they're all still reeling. My guess is today's the first day they've realized something was happening. Good luck, Peter."

Lili thought it sounded like the tag line from the old *Mission: Impossible* show. All it needed was a warning that the list would self-destruct in thirty seconds. "I want to go too," she announced.

Crandall was already at the door, but he turned back. "I wouldn't advise it. I think Peter will do better one-on-one. And she may particularly resent another, younger woman."

The door closed behind him. Lili turned to Peter. "Does he think you're going to get the shares by taking Mrs. Grayson to bed?"

"I don't think so. But I swear I'll do my duty. I won't fail the cause no matter what she looks like."

They held their breath as he phoned New Jersey. He cradled the receiver between chin and shoulder, lit another cigarette, and looked at Lili and Loy. "Ringing," he said quietly. Then he nodded and they knew the phone had been answered. In a few seconds they realized Willa Grayson was on the line.

"Mrs. Grayson, this is Peter Fowler of Fowler Distribution. Am I correct in assuming you know who I am?" There was a pause, and he grinned. "Yes, that's right. I'd like to speak with you. This evening. May I come over?"

Ten minutes later he left the house.

The two woman waited. Lili made some scrambled eggs and toast, but neither of them could eat. Neither did they talk much. Once Loy called her house and spoke to Santiago Cortez. She told him she was tied up for the evening and hung up quickly. Before he could ask any questions, Lili guessed.

Peter came back after midnight. Empty-handed. They'd authorized an outright buy at anything up to eleven fifty. "No go," Peter said. "She said she might consider fifteen, and she wasn't even sure about that. My guess is she was playing with me. At this point she hasn't made up her mind which way to flop."

"Fifteen is robbery," Lili exclaimed.

It was Loy who observed that they were not in any position to shout thief.

On March twenty-third Andy Mendoza typed "The End" on the last of six hundred and seventy-five manuscript pages. He spent two hours collating originals and carbons, then carefully packaged the original and addressed it to Barry Clark, his agent in London.

The Caracas *Correos* was a twenty-minute walk from his hotel. Andy stood in a long line, made out forms in triplicate, and got a little green card that had to be affixed to the package if it was to pass customs and travel halfway around the world. Finally he could drop it in the mail bin marked *extranjero*. He did so with a sigh of relief and moved to another desk in the post office. "HIDALGO FINISHED AND MAILED TO YOU THIS DATE," he cabled Barry. "ON MY WAY TO SPAIN TO FOLLOW NEW LEAD IN SWANNING AFFAIR. KEEP YOUR TOES CROSSED."

Twenty-four hours later he landed in Madrid.

The meaningful part of Andy's conversation in Caracas with Santiago Cortez had been brief. First the poet had spoken in riddles; finally he'd come to the point. "I had been to the university in Madrid with one of the Mendoza sons. We became good friends. In 'thirty-nine I was a guest of the family in Córdoba. They were also entertaining two young women. Americans, I think. Anyway, they were not staying at the palace in Córdoba but at the country place, the *cortijo*. Do you know that the Christian King Fernando III of Spain is supposed to have given that enormous tract of land to the family in the thirteenth century because they helped him overthrow the Muslims?"

"Yes, and it may be true," Andy had said. "The Mendozas have always been good at trimming their sails to suit the wind. What were the names of the girls?"

The poet sighed and made a great show of searching his memory. "Their names . . . Luisa, I think, and maybe Lotte. Something like that."

"Surnames?" Andy asked, pencil poised over his notebook.

"I don't remember. Don't forget it was 1939, a great deal was happening. Franco had just become el Caudillo, chief of the military and head of state. From exile in the Canary Islands to dictator of Spain in three years. But what a terrible war it had been. I recall—"

"Civil wars are always the worst," Andy interrupted. "I know the history. What did any of this have to do with the American women? Your Luisa and Lotte."

"I was never quite sure. There was some talk, only a hint . . . Look, you know the Germans had supplied Franco with arms? Well, some said the Mendozas were helping the Nazis."

"Jesus Christ." Andy took a long pull at his beer. "I thought that was one time they hadn't acted like complete bastards."

The Venezuelan leaned forward. "Later they weren't. They paid millions to ransom German Jews. And even in 1939 they were anti-Nazi. Pro Franco, so maybe Fascists, but there was opposition to Germany. That was a source of friction. I think one of the family had made a deal with Alfred Krupp, Hitler's munitions man. But the rest were opposed. They squashed it. Like that." He twisted his thumb on the white tablecloth.

"Luisa and Lotte," Andy said again. "They weren't Nazis surely?"

"No, of course not. Merely two pretty but rather silly girls. I was simply explaining why I don't remember more about them. The times were so difficult."

"Yes, I understand. But is that all you remember, their names?"

"Not quite all." Santiago sat back and gripped his wineglass but didn't drink. "Do you know Diego Parilles Mendoza? He's your cousin, isn't he?"

"Lives in Madrid? Yes, I've met him. And yes, we're cousins. God knows how many times removed. What about him?"

"He must be seventy now, and still women find him charming. In those days he was young and like a Greek God. I think he was in love with one of the Americans. Luisa. He was married, you understand, so it could never be anything but an affair. And I don't really know if it was that. But when he was in Córdoba rather than Madrid he spent a lot of time with the two girls."

Santiago still held the wineglass. He turned it by the stem and watched the dark red fluid move. "Once they went off alone and were gone for a couple of days. It was August; I remember that. The heat was stupefying. Anyway, the girls disappeared and there was a terrible fuss. They turned up again, perfectly fine. Seems they'd wanted only an adventure. But a few days later there was a picture in some gossip magazine. The two of them sipping sangria at a table in front of a bar in Málaga. Imagine, the world was about to blow up, Spain already had, and there were gossip magazines and sangria."

"Do you remember the name of the magazine?" Andy leaned forward urgently.

"No. But the family was very upset by the picture. The Mendozas keep themselves quiet. A . . . what do you call it in English?"

"A low profile. Did the magazine print their names?"

"A low profile, yes. There were no names, but the Mendozas thought the picture scandalous. I guess it reflected on them because the Americans were their guests. Anyway, Diego was sent to threaten the editor. I don't know why, the photograph had already been published."

Andy reached into his pocket and withdrew the old newspaper pictures of Amanda Kent, the ones he'd shown Lili years before in London. "Is this by any chance a picture of either of the Americans?"

The poet stared at them. His face was impassive. "They are all of the same woman, no?"

"They are."

"Such poor quality. It's hard to tell, but I don't think so."

Andy gave him a few seconds more to look at the pictures, then gathered them from the table, restored them to the plastic wrapper, and put them away. "Okay, if you're sure. What happened next?"

"I don't know. I returned to Venezuela and didn't see any of the Mendozas again until after the war."

"And Luisa and Lotte?"

Santiago at last sipped his wine. "I know nothing more about them."

With that Andy had to be satisfied. It wasn't much, but it was a lead.

On March twenty-fourth he flew to Madrid. It was a better choice than Córdoba because the research facilities were good, and because eventually he'd have to tackle Diego Parilles, who still lived in the capital.

Andy made the Melia Hotel his base. It wasn't far from the excellent public library. Fortunately his Spanish had improved enormously in the last couple of years. He'd worked hard on it in order to do the South American book. His accent wasn't perfect, but he had a sufficient grasp of the language to ask for the records he needed and to read them.

His first job was to determine the magazines most likely to have carried the picture Santiago Cortez had mentioned. That wasn't as difficult as it might have been because in the summer of 1939, while the rest of the world trembled on the brink of war, Spain was at the beginning of an impoverished peace. With the bloodiest of bloody civil wars recently ended, the country had few publications of the sort the Venezuelan had described. In two days Andy narrowed the field to four possible titles.

He'd found a sympathetic and patient librarian, a young woman with a warm smile and intelligent eyes. Her name was Marisol Ramirez and she told him that there were indeed back copies of periodicals, mostly on microfilm. "But 1939 was not a good year for us, Señor."

"I know. Still, if you wouldn't mind checking, it's terribly important to me."

She nodded and handed him a library form. Andy filled in the details of his request, then signed his name. When the girl saw it she smiled at him. "Mendoza is a Spanish name, Señor, but I don't think you are Spanish."

"English," he explained. "My ancestors were Spanish." There seemed no need to mention the particular Mendoza family to which he belonged.

He hung around the library for two days waiting for the rolls of film to appear. Modern Spain was still the land of mañana. When they finally arrived from wherever they'd been entombed, Marisol brought him to a reading machine, and after showing him how it worked, left him to it.

Four hours later he'd been through half the stack of films. Santiago Cortez had been sure the incident had happened in August, but Andy was checking every month of the year. He'd not come this far only to make a mistake because he wasn't thorough. His careful examination of the data was narrowing the field still further. Two of the four magazines he'd selected proved to have few pictures. Printing was entirely letterpress in '39. Reproducing photographs was expensive. They weren't scattered all over as they would be today. Nonetheless, Andy examined each issue before putting it to one side.

The third magazine he tackled was called *Los Dias*. In format and layout it was more like a tabloid newspaper than a magazine. It was a weekly, he discovered as he began scanning the pages and reading the captions under the pictures. At first there was nothing, but when he came to August, his gut tightened.

Los Dias seemed like exactly the right sort of publication. Maybe they hadn't run the picture Santiago had mentioned, but they easily could have. Based on what he'd read so far, it was exactly their kind of story.

The magazine came out on Tuesdays. As it happened, August 1, 1939, was a Tuesday. He checked that issue with infinite care, moved on to the eighth and the fifteenth being equally as painstaking, and found nothing. He wasn't discouraged. All Andy's instincts told him he was closing on his quarry.

He'd come to the end of a roll of film. He threaded the next one into the machine while trying to suppress a buzz of premature excitement. He turned the knob that brought the picture into focus, looked at the date, then looked again. What he had was the issue of the twenty-ninth. The twenty-second was missing. He checked again to make sure the material hadn't somehow gotten out of date order, then summoned Marisol. "There's an issue that isn't here."

"But that is impossible, Señor Mendoza."

"That's what I thought, only it isn't. You can look for yourself."

She examined the film he had in the machine, running it through with practiced expertise, then checked all the labels. "It seems that you are correct, it isn't here."

"Damn! Sorry, it's not your fault. But I think what I'm looking for is in precisely that missing issue."

"What bad luck, Señor."

"It's not luck," Andy muttered. "It's the damned hand of the Mendozas reaching out from Córdoba."

The girl's dark eyes opened wide. "You mean the Mendozas who are the bankers?"

"None other."

"And you are one of them?" It was an exceptionally direct question for a Spaniard, but it had been startled out of her.

"Yes, God help me," Andy admitted. "That's the bad luck, to be one of them. They have too much power for anyone's good."

Marisol shrugged. "I think all that is changing these days. Now we have *democracia* in Spain."

"Yeah, sure," Andy said grimly.

"It is true," Marisol insisted. She thought for a moment. "Señor, there is an archive of original documents from which these films are made. Perhaps what you are looking for is in that archive."

Andy's face lit up. "Marisol, you're terrific, *estupenda*. Where is it and how do I get there?"

"That is a problem, Señor. It is a few kilometers out of the city, and the public isn't allowed in the archives."

Andy spoke with some hesitation, unsure how she would react. "What about you, are you permitted entry?"

"Of course, I have my official identification and—" She broke off, glanced at the clock on the far wall. "It is three o'clock, Señor. My lunchtime." She walked away without saying any more.

As depressed and discouraged as he was, Andy went through all the rolls of film he'd not yet examined. There was nothing in them, as he'd known there wouldn't be. He thought about quitting, then decided to wait until Marisol returned from her two-hour lunch. He'd press her a little harder about the location of the archives and how he might get in.

By five-thirty she still wasn't back and he was half convinced he was wasting his time. Then, as he gathered his things together preparatory to leaving, he saw her in the corridor outside the reading room where he'd been working, motioning to him to join her.

Andy got up from the table and went outside. Marisol pressed a finger to her lips and indicated he should follow her. The way she led him ended on the landing of the fire stairs; a cold, deserted venue where a weak yellow bulb made the only light. Marisol smiled at him, then opened her leather jacket. Beneath it was a folded tabloid. "I am sorry it took me so long. There were many forms to fill out, and I couldn't take this until I was sure no one was looking."

"Holy shit!.." He didn't bother to translate that when he switched back to Spanish. "Marisol, you are fantastic. But how come—"

"I told you we have *democracia,* Señor, but I don't think you believed me. These days it is not so important that the bureaucrats have everything their own way. And we are not afraid of powerful bankers. Here." She held out the magazine, and when Andy had taken it she turned around and stared at the wall.

"See if what you want is there," she said. "Do whatever you wish to do, but do it quickly. I must get back to work, and tomorrow I must go again to the archives and return this thing."

Within seconds Andy realized that what he was holding wasn't a regular copy of *Los Dias.* It was the makeup dummy for the twenty-second of August, 1939, the sample that had gone to the printer to be set in type and to have the blocks cut for the pictures they planned to run. He searched his memory for the name of those blocks as he thumbed through the pages. They were called half-tones.

What he was looking for was on the fourth of six pages. The picture itself was glued to the paper, yellow and faded but still recognizable. The background had been cropped to show a small section of beach and two tables on a scruffy boardwalk. At one of the tables two young women sat smiling at each other. The photographer seemed to have caught them unawares. The caption read "Two elegant foreigners enjoy themselves in sunny Málaga."

Andy detached the picture carefully and slipped it into his pocket. *"Bueno,"* he said, folding the tabloid back into shape. *"Está."*

Marisol turned around and smiled at him. "You found what you wanted?"

"Exactly what I wanted." It wasn't perfect, in the best-case scenario the women's names would have been printed below the photograph, but he was satisfied. This picture wasn't worth merely a thousand words, it was worth a hundred speculations. "Thank you," he added. "More than I can say."

That night he sat for hours in his hotel room, staring at the black and white snapshot.

The two girls wore the dresses of the time, square necks and short puffed sleeves and exaggerated shoulders. The table obscured the length of the skirts. One of them had on a long rope of beads and a close-fitting hat with a shallow brim that partially shaded her face. The other girl's hat was small and round and had a feather and a wisp of a veil that obscured nothing. Each had a glass in her hand and there was a pitcher on the table. Santiago's sangria, wine laced with brandy and poured over fresh fruit.

Andy took his newspaper clippings and lay them next to the photograph, then found a magnifying glass in his briefcase. He looked. Back and forth, one to the other, over and over again. The minutes passed. Finally he sighed. It was inconclusive. There was a possibility that the woman in the feathered hat was Amanda Kent, but only if he worked hard at believing it. The resemblance didn't jump up and hit him. It didn't prove anything. He put down the magnifying glass and rubbed his eyes.

There was something in the magazine picture that tugged at his memory, something he was sure was familiar, but not in the face of the girl he thought might be Amanda. In the other one. It stayed in the back of his mind and teased him. Finally he decided he'd looked too long, that he was imagining things.

He applied himself to the other mystery—how this print had survived. Santiago Cortez had told him that Diego had been sent to threaten the editor of the magazine. Apparently the threats had worked. They had withdrawn every copy of the issue. That's why there had been the gap in the records on microfilm. Andy was prepared to bet a year's earnings that Diego had gotten hold of the negative and the print as well. What he'd missed, because he knew nothing of publishing and wouldn't have suspected its existence, was the dummy.

God, he'd love to rub the old man's nose in that. You screwed up, Diego. I've got you by the balls. But he didn't. The picture, as he'd admitted to himself, proved nothing. Moreover, he could not now confront Diego Parilles with its existence. Marisol Ramirez had signed her name to the forms in the archives. It would be all too easy for Diego to find her if he went looking for a leak. To expose the girl to Mendoza vengeance was unthinkable.

Andy had only one place to go, one direction to take—the one he'd been avoiding for ten years. The jigsaw was falling into place, but if he was going to put all the pieces together, he'd have to be man enough to look into his own pain and confront his own past as well as his family's.

❧ 11 ❧

New York: 1981

The short piece in *The Wall Street Journal* ran on the twenty-eighth of March. It was a single paragraph under the heading *"Street Signs."* "Why would a tiny, privately held magazine distributing company wholly in European imports enter the over-the-counter market to raid a sleepy fleet of U.S. mags with only one moderately successful flagship? Has greenmail fever infected the lumpenproletariat?"

"What's greenmail?" Loy asked.

She and Lili were lunching in the Russian Tea Room. It had been Loy's idea, because Lili's thirty-first birthday had come and gone unnoticed in the last week. Besides, they needed something to lift their spirits. At the moment they could only sit and wait—nobody approached them privately, no new stock came on the market, and the price was holding at seven twenty-five. It was driving them all mad.

Loy decreed a festive lunch to celebrate Lili's birthday and what they'd thus far accomplished. At the last minute Peter had to cancel, he was trying to catch up on Fowler Distribution business, so the two women were alone. It was Lili who had spotted the item in the *Journal* and brought it for Loy to see.

Lili cut a small bite of blini and pushed some of the glorious caviar onto her fork. "Greenmail is like blackmail," she said. "Only it's legal."

"That still doesn't tell me what it is."

"Say what we wanted was to make Randolph Demmer buy back our shares at well over the market price. He'd have to do it to avoid a battle and a possible takeover and we'd make a killing. That's greenmail."

Loy frowned. Her gray eyes were darker than usual. "That isn't very nice."

"No, but we're not doing it." Lili took another bite of caviar. "I wonder who first figured out that plain old fish eggs could be ambrosial if the fish was a sturgeon? Some Russian, do you think?"

"No, probably a Persian. The best caviar comes from Iran, doesn't it?"

"A minority opinion," Lili said. She stopped eating. "It's true we're not working the greenmail ploy, but sometimes I think what we are doing isn't so wonderful either."

Loy looked surprised. "Why not? Randolph Demmer has sat on his hands. The magazines could be much better and more profitable. He hasn't been fair to the shareholders."

"Okay, but what about the books we want to sell?" Suddenly it dawned on Lili that they were speaking openly in a public place. She looked around nervously.

"What's the matter?" Loy demanded.

"Nothing, I guess. It occurred to me that we were being indiscreet, but there's no one sitting near enough to hear."

"I would have stopped you if there had been," Loy said. "I'm expert at being discreet."

"I suppose that comes with being filthy rich."

Loy shrugged. "Something like that. What you were saying about the holdings we don't choose to keep, there's no reason we can't dispose of them responsibly. We don't have to be ruthless and simply look for the greatest profit. We can find buyers who want to continue publishing, assure the jobs of the present staff."

"Maybe then we'll be the ones who aren't being fair to the shareholders," Lili said.

They stared at each other in perplexity for a moment, then Loy signaled the waiter and ordered another bottle of champagne.

•   •   •

Two days later Peter took a call at his office. "Fowler, this is Randolph Demmer. What the fuck are you playing at?"

Peter had seen a picture of Demmer. He was a small, fragile-looking man with a thatch of white hair and delicate features. He hadn't appeared the type to be either so direct or so profane.

"I'm not playing, Mr. Demmer," Peter said.

"And you're not alone. Saying *I* doesn't mean you're in this by yourself. Somebody's in with you. I'm checking, I'll find out."

"We seem to be at an impasse. Have you some suggestion to make?" Peter's voice was absolutely neutral. He might be ordering a pizza to go.

"Yeah. Go fuck yourself."

"That's not very helpful, Mr. Demmer. Look, there's no mystery about this. I want control of your company. Perhaps you should think of that in a positive way. A lot of men your age would be glad to retire."

"Not me. And you don't want my company. You want a lot of money. Greenmail. Like it said in the paper."

"No, that doesn't happen to be true."

"You say," Demmer growled.

"I'm the one who should know." Peter was still mild. "I'm a busy man, Mr. Demmer. Do we have something to discuss?"

"Listen, you prick, I remember those inquiries about six months ago. The ones about selling off my two food books and *House*. You say you don't want to make a killing. Okay, maybe you don't, but I know you don't want the company either. You want three books and you'll dump the other five. That's right, isn't it?"

"I'll do what's best for Bass and Demmer's share-holders."

"Bullshit. You'd savage us, tear us apart. It's not going to happen. When the rest of the board know what you have in mind, they won't budge. You haven't a prayer, Fowler. And I'm going to love watching you take a bath for all those hundreds of thousands of dollars."

Peter was sweating when Demmer hung up.

"He sounds tough as nails," he told Lili later.

"Good," she said. "That makes it a fair fight."

Peter hugged her and after that he started calling her Amazon.

On April first there was another call. This one was from a young man named Harvey Michael Demmer. He was the old man's grandson, and he wanted a meeting with Peter. It took place two hours later in the place Harvey picked, St. Patrick's Cathedral.

"You come here a lot?" Peter asked.

They were behind the high altar in what was called the Lady Chapel. There were tourists, but not so many as in the main body of the church. A woman knelt at the communion railing and looked lovingly at the statue of the Virgin. Peter and Harvey were seated in the right rear pew. Harvey carried an umbrella and a raincoat and had a red handkerchief in his breast pocket. He'd arranged all that. So Peter would recognize him, he'd said.

"Not too often," the boy said in response to the question. "I'm not a Catholic."

"I see," Peter said. "Neither am I, as it happens. Mind telling me why we're here?"

"You know why."

"The subject of the meeting, sure. But in a church?"

"I have to be certain nobody sees us," Harvey said in a sibilant whisper. "I want to sell you my stock, Mr. Fowler. I have six percent of the company." It was a mark of the young man's inexperience that he didn't realize Peter already knew that. "I got it last year for my twenty-fifth birthday. My father left it to me in his will. He's dead."

"Most people are before their wills take effect."

"Don't make fun of me, Mr. Fowler. My grandfather does it all the time. That's why—"

A uniformed guard approached from the rear and lay a hand on Peter's shoulder. "Would you gentlemen mind saving the talk for later? We ask that visitors respect the silence here."

"Sorry," Peter whispered. He turned to Harvey. "Let's go. I know a little bar on First where it's so dark your mother wouldn't recognize you."

Over a couple of glasses of beer Harvey loosened up a little, seemed less frightened. "I want to go to Europe, I'm sick of this country. It's so plastic."

"Ever been to Europe?" Peter asked.

"No, but I'm sure it's better than here."

"Maybe. Depends what you're looking for. I take it, selling your share of Bass and Demmer is necessary to finance the trip."

"That's right."

"You could sell on the open market," Peter said.

"No, my grandfather would find out. He'd manage to stop me some way." Harvey took a long swallow of beer. "Besides, the stock's worth seven twenty-five on the open market. I think you'll pay more than that."

"I see. Not so innocent as you seem, are you, Harvey?"

"That's what I keep telling my mother and my grandfather."

"Okay, how much?"

"Make me an offer," Harvey said.

"No way."

"Then no deal."

Peter chuckled. "Stalemate. Let me think a minute. What about your mother? She has six percent too. Think she might like to throw her shares in with yours?"

Harvey shook his head morosely. "I already tried to talk her into that. She hates the old man. He never wanted Dad to marry her. Never got over it. Made their lives miserable. But she won't sell, she's afraid of him. She'd have hysterics if she knew I was talking to you."

"Your grandfather is beginning to sound like a real tough character," Peter said quietly. "Harvey, for the sake of discussion, say we make a deal. Are you going to get cold feet and welsh on me?"

"Not a chance. I went to the bank yesterday. I got the certificates out of the vault."

The palms of Peter's hands started to prickle, as if he could feel the precious pieces of paper. "You have them with you?"

"I'm not that stupid. They're in a safe place. You can have them whenever you want. In return for a certified check."

"What numbers have to be on the check, Harvey?"

"I told you before, make me an offer."

Peter sat back and studied the kid. After a few moments, he spoke. "Harvey, it's against all the best negotiating rules, but I'm going to do exactly that. Only there's one thing you have to understand. I'm not going to bargain. I'm going to make you a firm, legitimate offer, and you're either going to take it or leave it. I want the stock, but I don't have to have it. There are other possibilities."

Harvey was startled. "Somebody else is going to sell to you?"

"I didn't say that. I said possibilities. Now, let's score or go home, okay? One offer and you say yes or no and that's it. Understood?"

He nodded. Peter knew he had him. There was no way this boy was going to leave without accomplishing what he'd come for, getting his drop-dead money. Given his age and the obvious situation, it wouldn't take much to make him feel he had it. "Eight fifty," Peter said. "A buck and a quarter over the going rate."

For a moment neither of them moved. Then Harvey nodded again. They shook hands.

Twenty-four hours later LPL had twenty-five percent of the Bass & Demmer stock—three percent short of matching Randolph Demmer's majority holding. They were also out of ready money.

"It's time to look for allies rather than sellers," Jeremy Crandall advised when they met in his office. "You've got enough to carry the day if you can get one or two of the board members to vote with you and against the old man."

They had spent many hours analyzing the makeup of the board. Not counting Demmer himself, or Harvey, who was now out of the picture, there were six of them. Two seemed more likely to respond to Lili than to Peter. One was a man, a distant cousin of Demmer's. He owned a string of fast-food restaurants; maybe Lili could offer to put them on television. The second prospect was Harvey's mother, Randolph Demmer's daughter-in-law.

"The cousin lives in Cincinnati," Crandall said. "Let's opt for the bird in the hand. I think you should talk to Mrs. Demmer, Lili. Depending on what the response is, Peter can talk to the others."

"What response do we want?" Lili asked. "How much do I tell her?"

"It seems to me—" Crandall had no opportunity to finish. The phone on his desk rang and he excused himself and picked it up. He'd told his secretary to hold all calls except any that were urgent or related to Bass & Demmer. This one met both requirements.

Crandall didn't say anything his listeners could interpret, only "yes" and "no" and "I see." Then he hung up, looked at them a moment, and reported. "Randolph Demmer has found a white knight."

"Shit," Peter said.

Lili buried her head in her hands.

"Will someone tell me what's going on?" Loy demanded.

"A white knight," Crandall repeated. "Demmer's found someone to buy the company. Someone he considers friendly. He does not consider you folks friendly."

"Do we know who it is?" Peter asked.

"Yes. An oddball multimillionaire from New Mexico who happens to be an avid coin collector and a long-time subscriber. You can bet he won't make them sell off a damn thing."

"Isn't there anything we can do?" Loy demanded.

"Only offer the shareholders a better deal than the knight's proposing," Crandall said. "The problem is, that would take more cash than you can come up with."

"We have to go to the board anyway," Lili insisted at their next meeting. "We have to convince them that we're their best hope for future profit. All Demmer's white knight will do is hold the status quo."

"Quite right," Crandall agreed. He seemed different, less enthusiastic, maybe even a little bored. "But you'd have to sweeten the pot. The board would want to see cash money. You don't have any. Without it you're dead in the water."

Neither Peter nor Lili could control their reaction; instinctively, they looked at Loy. "I'm quite willing to put up more money," she said. "I'll have to sell a few things, perhaps some paintings. Jeremy can arrange it."

"I'm sorry," he said. "I can't authorize it. The trustees have made that clear."

"That's ridiculous," Loy said. "My agreement with them has always been—"

Crandall interrupted. "I had a telex from Madrid this morning, Loy. It was quite explicit."

Loy turned very white, and for a moment she looked old. What occurred to Lili was that a mask was crumpling. Then she thought she'd imagined it. In seconds Loy was subdued, but in control. "This has to be a misunderstanding," she said. "I'm sure I can straighten it out, but I need a little time."

Loy rose and left the office. Neither Lili nor Peter followed her. They both had the clear impression that Loy wanted to be alone.

It took Loy an hour to get through to Spain. Then there was no answer at the office. She had to call a private home. Finally she got an answer. "What is going on?" Loy demanded. "He's never done anything like this. Never. We had an agreement. It's worked for ten years. Why is he breaking it now?"

"It's difficult to explain on the telephone. These days his positions are . . . extreme. He feels strongly and he's become more single-minded than ever. I think there is reason for concern, *mi niña*. I might even say, *La Gitanita*." After that there was only the static of a broken connection.

Slowly Loy replaced the receiver. *La Gitanita*. A code devised years before, when everything was different. It meant "danger, exercise extreme caution."

Ten minutes later Loy phoned Lili. "I'm sorry I walked out with so little explanation today. Are you terribly upset?"

"Mostly numb," Lili said. "And puzzled. Loy, can you tell me what's going on?"

"No, I can't. But I promise you I'm going to make it all right. I'm flying to Spain tomorrow morning. I'll phone you from there as soon as I can. Probably within a couple of days. Hang on and don't worry. Will you tell Peter?"

"I think it would be better if you told him yourself. Look, this is none of my business, but you know how Peter feels about you, don't you?"

"Yes, I know. I'll call him."

Peter wouldn't accept a quick explanation on the phone, he insisted on coming to the house.

"I don't give a damn what happens to Bass and Demmer," he told Loy. "Not if it upsets you this much. You look terrible."

"I'm tired. And I have to be up early in the morning. Can we make this brief, Peter?"

He sipped the drink she'd given him and looked around. "Where's your tame Venezuelan?"

"Gone home, thank God. A couple of days ago. Look, it's going to be all right. My assets are tied up in a Spanish-based trust. The trustees are old and unduly cautious. I'll see them and explain and it will be all fine."

He had to be satisfied with that. And that she allowed him to kiss her when he left. Rather a brother's kiss than a lover's, but Peter was accustomed to accepting crumbs from Loy.

The next morning was damp and cold, more like December than April. Peter had insisted on taking Loy to the airport, and when they couldn't find a skycap, he carried her luggage himself. He was surprised that Loy had only three bags. It wasn't exactly on a par with a backpack, but it was traveling light for a woman like her. "I thought you'd have piles of suitcases," he admitted.

"I learned better in a wandering youth," she said, laughing. She was cheerful this morning, more like herself.

"I wish I knew more about what you call your youth. I want to know everything that happened during every minute before I met you."

Loy smiled and touched his cheek. "Dear heart, I don't think I can possibly live long enough to tell you all that."

He waited until they called the flight, then walked with her as far as he could. "At least you should get some sun in Spain. It will really be spring there, won't it?"

"Oh, yes. Sunny and warm, I imagine. It is for most of the year."

"Enjoy it," he murmured, and kissed her lightly before she disappeared through security control.

Loy's gaiety evaporated as soon as she was in the area reserved for passengers. The mood had been dragged from her reserves by Peter's concern. Once alone she could be herself: depressed and nervous and quite certain she wouldn't enjoy this trip.

La Gitanita. It harked back to events she'd almost forgotten, to at least one danger she'd thought long past.

"I think Crandall's screwing us." Peter spoke the words without apparent feeling, staring into the glass of bourbon he held. It was April 5, six P.M. on Sunday, the armpit of the week. He was with Lili in a bar called Southern Comfort on First and Seventy-second. They were drinking lethal mint juleps in frosted glasses.

"I should say, you're crazy." Lili stirred her drink with two short straws, waiting for the ice to melt and dilute the straight bourbon. "I'm not saying it."

"You think so too?"

"It has occurred to me."

"How come you didn't say anything?"

"Loy left thirty-six hours ago. The shit hit the fan the day before that. I'm still in the process of figuring things out."

"Me too, let's figure together." Peter downed the last of his whiskey and signaled the waitress to bring another. "It goes back to what Crandall said in the very beginning, doesn't it?"

"Yes, exactly. We knew from the start we didn't have enough loose change to do it all with cash out of pocket."

"Out of Loy's pocket," Peter amended.

"Largely, yes. But that's not relevant. Back then sweet little Jeremy said when we came down to the wire we'd be in a position to negotiate. Try and put a deal together. Probably a leveraged buyout."

"That's my memory too." The waitress arrived and set down two more drinks. Lili still hadn't finished her first and she started to protest. "No hassle," Peter said. "I'll drink it if you don't."

"Since when are you a candidate for A.A.? Don't get boozy on me, Peter. That won't help."

"You're right." He pushed the fresh drinks to the side of the table. "Taking the coward's way out. Because we've been had, sweetheart. That outfit calling itself the Mendoza Group should be world-class at doing deals like ours."

"Like the deal we're trying to do," Lili corrected him.

"Yes. And Crandall should have a dozen suggestions for how we proceed. Instead, he says, 'Sorry, no more money, Loy,' and pulls the plug. It doesn't add up. We never planned to get more cash from Loy."

"No, we didn't."

Lili sat silent, Peter lit a cigarette and puffed at it and thought. Finally Lili spoke. "Say we're right—"

"We're right," Peter interrupted.

"Okay, what can we do about it?"

"That's what I don't know. What the hell can Crandall's motives be?"

"Maybe the Mendoza Group is behind the white knight," she said. "Maybe they decided to buy the company themselves."

"Nuts. What would they want with a pissy-assed outfit like Bass and Demmer? Remember those numbers that were thrown around the first day? Twenty-five million or it's too small for them to look at."

"Yes. Well, what about Jeremy? Maybe he's playing a private gig."

"Could be," Peter agreed. But it doesn't feel right. Whatever you can say about Crandall, stupid he's not. I don't think he's suddenly got a yen to publish magazines. If it's merely an investment, bigger and better options must cross his desk every day."

"And all he had to do to make a few bucks was start buying

when we did or before. He had classic insider information. He could have made a killing. Maybe he did."

"The S.E.C. frowns on that kind of thing," Peter said.

"Doesn't stop it happening every day. But even if it were true, he'd probably have sold by now. And that wouldn't require his trashing our plan."

"Game plan. You're forgetting his business-school lingo." He picked up one of the untouched mint juleps and took a long swallow. "It comes down to one unpleasant possibility. He's deliberately trying to dump us in the shit. And since neither you nor I laid eyes on Jeremy Crandall until a few months ago, his target must be Loy. We simply got in the way."

"Oh, Jesus." Lili put her head in her hands. "Do you think that's it?"

"My gut tells me it's likely."

"She knows a lot more than she's telling," Lili said. "That's certain."

Peter was instantly protective. "I don't think Loy is anything but a victim in this."

"I'm not accusing her of anything, Peter. I love Loy too. And I'm feeling sick that she's gone to Spain by herself to do God knows what. Meanwhile we're sitting here about to lose everything we have and a lot that she has, and if you're right, somebody's got a hidden agenda we don't know a damn thing about."

"Crandall knows about it." Peter stood up and fished some money from his wallet. "C'mon, let's get out of here before we become candidates for skid row. We need some food."

When they were on the street Lili said she didn't want to eat. "I don't think I can tolerate anything but a bath and some sleep. Do you mind?"

"No, of course not."

It had turned surprisingly mild for April. They walked the ten blocks to Lili's building and said good night by the door. "We can't sit around," Peter said. "I think I should go see Crandall in the morning."

"I guess it's a good idea, I can't think of anything else.

If it's tomorrow morning, though, I can't come. I've got a taping session at the studio."

"That's okay. I think it's better if I tackle him alone. Don't hit me if I say man to man."

You mean so I won't be shocked when you tell him to go fuck himself."

He grinned. "Yeah, that's what I mean. You know, that's what old man Demmer told me to do a week ago. But we're being adequately fucked by everybody else, aren't we?"

"I always want to be kissed first," Lili said.

"We were. That was the high we had when we were buying."

"I'd laugh," she said, "but it hurts too much."

"Yeah, doesn't it just. Good night, sweetheart. I'll call you when the confrontation's over."

"Not until noon," she said. "I won't be back much before then. And Peter," she added, "be careful." She was suddenly filled with foreboding. "Be very careful. Crandall is smart, and I suspect if he feels the least bit threatened, he'll be ruthless."

Peter mocked a punch to her chin. "I'll outtough him. Don't worry. Take it easy, get some sleep."

Once upstairs, Lili decided against the bath, she was too keyed up to enjoy a leisurely soak. She showered quickly instead, then made herself some tea and toast. Her mind was racing in three directions at once. What could be done to salvage the takeover? Who wished Loy ill and why? What did Jeremy Crandall, who was really nothing but a well-educated lackey, have to do with it?

By ten-thirty she realized she wouldn't come up with any answers, and she had to be at the studio at the crack of dawn, so she might as well try and get some sleep. Before she did she remembered that she hadn't yet checked her answering machine.

She pressed the button. The first message had come in at six-fifteen, shortly after she left the house to meet Peter. It destroyed her ability to listen to any others there might be, and certainly it banished any thought of sleep.

"Lili, this is Andy Mendoza. I know you hate the sight of me, but I must speak with you. Please, it really is vital." He added the telephone number of the New York Hilton on Sixth Avenue and said he'd wait all night for her to return the call.

PART TWO

Lili and Irene

∿ 12 ∿

London and Paris: 1972–74

In March of '72 Lili still had the Christmas card Andy had
sent from Spain the previous December. She looked at it
every day. The card was signed "love." True, there had been
no other communication, but he'd said he needed time. Lili
was determined to be patient.

Irene, meanwhile, was on a trip around the world. She
sent postcards from places like Hong Kong and Kashmir.
Lili couldn't bear to think about the source of Irene's funds,
but she reminded herself that the present state of affairs was
temporary. She was working hard, saving every penny she
could get her hands on, moving closer to her goals. She
certainly wasn't sitting at home and brooding.

Her circle of friends and acquaintances was widening. Most
weeks Lili went out two or three evenings with friends who
gathered in places such as the hottest restaurant of the moment
or an after-hours discothèque—spots the smart set favored.
Lili wasn't yet easy with such people, but she was learning,
beginning to truly believe that she was seen as clever and
talented, someone worth knowing.

When she was invited to an April Fool's party at the home
of a woman she hardly knew, it was natural for her to accept.
When she arrived, Lili didn't see a familiar face. She began
moving casually around the margins of the room, looking for
a congenial group, when she heard someone say, "Have you
heard the latest about Andy Mendoza?"

Lili made her way to the man who had spoken. He was standing with a few other people, none of whom she recognized. "Did I hear you mention Andy Mendoza?" Lili asked.

"Yes. Do you know him? I'm told he's doing a new series for one of the papers. Tells all about the idiotic doings of some fool with a title. There's bound to be weeping and wailing and gnashing of teeth."

"Well, if there is, Andy won't be here to hear it," Lili said confidently. "He's in Spain."

"Was," someone corrected her. "He's been back since New Year's. I've seen him around a few times."

She kept a smile glued to her face. The others were so busy talking, she didn't have to say anything. After a few seconds she moved away and managed to get to the table with the drinks.

She stilled her trembling fingers long enough to pour a large brandy, gulped it, and poured another. Then a third. Lili stopped counting after that.

Andy had been back in London since New Year's and she hadn't heard a word from him. April Fool.

The next morning Lili woke fully clothed in her own bed. She had no memory of getting home, and she felt worse than she'd ever felt in her life. In seconds she remembered. Andy was in London. He'd been home since the new year, somebody at the party said so. And he hadn't come near her.

Waves of nausea engulfed her and she stumbled into the bathroom and hung her head over the toilet and vomited for what seemed like forever. Finally she was retching nothing and she could crawl back to the bed.

She wanted to get out of her clothes. She fumbled with the buttons of her silk blouse, but she couldn't manage to undo them. The combination of hangover and grief paralyzed her. She could only sob and shove her fist in her mouth to keep from screaming.

She lay for many hours staring at the ceiling, ignoring the ringing telephone. Toward evening she was able to get up and strip and stand under a scalding shower for twenty minutes. Then, with a zombielike calm, Lili carried the heap of clothes she'd worn the night before to the fireplace, cut them into tiny pieces with scissors, and lay them on top of the coals and set the whole thing alight.

She watched the flames for a long time, until it was dark outside; by then she'd made up her mind that she was not going to do anything crazy.

At nine she made a cup of tea with lots of sugar and drank it even though it made her gag, because somewhere she'd read that was a good treatment for shock. She was not going to be destroyed, she told herself. She was going on with her life. She'd dust off the dreams of her childhood, the ones she'd replaced with Andy Mendoza. She'd become rich and famous. She'd buy back her house and spend holidays there and invite her English friends and give wonderful parties.

Shortly before ten Lili dialed Ruth's number. For a moment she had an insane, almost irresistible urge to pour out the whole terrible story, to cry and shout and demand sympathy. She took a deep breath and overcame the impulse. "Hi," she said brightly, forcing her voice to sound normal, even cheerful. "I imagine you were trying to get me earlier. Sorry, I was out late last night and had a bit too much to drink. Yes, I'll be on the job tomorrow."

Lili worked like a demon, burying her anguish in as much hard labor as she could cram into her painful days and nights. As well as jobs for clients, she had another project. When the owner of her apartment on Bankside returned, Lili decided not to look for another rental. She used every penny of her savings to buy a tiny four-room house on Masbro Road in a section called Brook Green. It was a slum when Lili moved in, but the area was due to be gentrified and she was sure it would be an excellent investment.

A few months later she was terrified that she'd made a big mistake. Early in 1973 OPEC turned off the West's oil and recession set in. It was Ruth who saw to it that Owens and Cramer survived while swinging London became penny-pinching London.

Lili had long since stopped going out; she couldn't bear the thought of running into Andy accidentally, of perhaps seeing him with someone else. Ruth, on the other hand, intensified her already frantic social life. She partied and cajoled and schemed, did anything to get them work. There was even an episode with a sixty-year-old Lord-somebody who needed to be spanked before he could fornicate.

"All for the cause," Ruth told Lili when she described the encounter. "His lordship wants his drawing and dining rooms put back the way they were before his last wife knocked down the walls."

"Put back?" Lili was incredulous.

"Yes. 'Make 'em look old-fashioned again,' he says. You can do it, Lili."

Lili could and did—and the job was large enough to keep them alive during that cold and rainy autumn.

As the difficult year drew to a close with Owens and Cramer remaining a going concern, both women let up a little, convinced their business would survive. So when Irene wrote in early December suggesting Lili join her in Paris for Christmas, Lili felt she could go.

Irene had arrived in France a few days ahead of her daughter. When she met Lili at Orly Airport she announced that she'd found them lodgings in the palace of some impoverished duke who now discreetly housed a few tourists.

"Isn't it charming?" Irene asked when she ushered Lili into the high-ceilinged bedchamber with its faded damask and faintly lingering smell of damp. "I knew you'd love it. Breakfast and dinner are included in the price of the room. The food's quite nice." She eyed her daughter. "You're very thin, Lili. Have you given up eating in England?"

"No. I wasn't well last year. I lost a lot of weight and haven't gained it back."

Not well was a euphemism for destroyed, betrayed, in mourning—but she had no intention of telling Irene about her broken heart. She would not report that Andy Mendoza remained present on the fringes of her universe, keeping alive the dull ache that was the residue of agony. Lili did not say that she frequently saw his by-line on magazine and newspaper articles, that there had been a picture of him with some gorgeous creature in a fabulous hat at Ascot, that he was often on television sounding off on the meaning of class differences in England.

Irene seemed unaware of any undertones in her daughter's explanation. "Being thin becomes you, but I hope you're well now."

"Oh, yes," Lili said. "I'm fine."

Irene turned and peered into one of the impoverished duke's ancient mirrors. She was fifty-seven, but her hair showed no gray. She still kept it ash blond, still wore it upswept. Irene tested the pins that kept the hairdo rigidly in place and sought her daughter's eyes in the shadowy glass. "Lili, are you happy? Is everything going well?"

"Everything's great," Lili said firmly. "I love my work and I'm very good at it. All my clients adore me."

"Life isn't simply work," Irene said softly. "Are you planning to live permanently in England?"

"I don't know." Lili preferred to ignore the statement that preceded the question. "Maybe, but I never make any plans beyond a few months."

Irene smiled. "You're young so you can do that. And these days I can too."

That was the other topic Lili had promised herself would not be discussed. Irene must have gotten a fortune for the house. She'd been traveling for over a year. Apparently, she did it frugally—guest houses and cheap tours—nonetheless, she couldn't have afforded even that before the sale. Lili allowed herself one question. "Mother, did you sell the Constable?"

Irene didn't look at her. "No, it isn't salable. I told you that."

The same crazy statement she'd made before. Only one explanation made sense, maybe somehow the Constable belonged to someone else. But it had hung in the house on Woods Road since the days of Amanda and Sam, so how could that be? Lili bit back the question. The whole subject was an emotional booby trap. She had vowed she wouldn't let this visit turn into a battle. "What are we going to see in Paris?" she asked instead.

In minutes they were involved with studying brochures and scheduling trips to the Louvre and Versailles.

Three days went by before Irene again questioned Lili about the shape of her life in London. "Darling, I don't mean to pry, but you're almost twenty-three. Do you have a boyfriend?"

"Not really." Lili kept her eyes on the omelette on her plate. "I have plenty of friends, but no one special."

"Is that natural? There was someone, wasn't there? When you first went to England? You only wrote a little about him, but I sort of read between the lines. Andy, wasn't that his name? Short for Andrew, I imagine."

"The Honorable Andrew Mendoza." Lili saw Irene flinch, her mouth tighten. Irene was sensing the emotional swamp behind Lili's words. Lili didn't want that to happen. She had to put the subject aside. "Can we please not talk about Andy?"

Irene regained her composure so quickly Lili thought she'd imagined the reaction. "As you wish," Irene said. "Do finish your lunch, Lili. It's good for you."

And later, when they were drinking coffee and getting ready to leave the café and look for a small furniture museum Lili wanted to see, "One more question, dear, then I won't mention it again. Am I correct in thinking you don't still keep company with this Andy Mendoza?"

"You couldn't be more correct. Put more accurately, and using your quaint term, he stopped keeping company with me. Nearly two years ago."

Irene wiped her lips delicately with a paper napkin. "I don't mean to intrude on your privacy, Lili. It's only that I want you to be happy."

"Yes, Mother, I understand. Shall we go? It's getting late."

In some ways Irene seemed more relaxed during their time together in Paris, as if now that Lili was grown she needn't feel so responsible, be so constantly alert to any flaws that needed correcting. Except for one that didn't escape her.

"Lili, your hair is as lovely as ever, but shouldn't you do something with it?"

Echoes of the old refrain, *You're not pretty, Lili, but your hair is very nice* . . .

"It's okay as it is," Lili said. Today the heavy dark mane was tied at the nape of her neck; sometimes she let it hang loose in a burnished curtain that framed her face. "I wash it at least three times a week," she added. "Like Mother always told me."

"I didn't say it wasn't clean." Irene betrayed a hint of exasperation. "But you aren't a child anymore. It should have some style."

"It's too straight to have a style. And I can't be bothered with sets or permanents."

"No, it shouldn't be curly." Irene thought for a moment. "Do you remember that picture we saw in the gallery on the Left Bank?"

They'd looked in dozens of galleries at hundreds of pictures. "No. Which picture? What does that have to do with my hair?"

"The Egyptian scene. The enormous one that filled the whole wall. I'm thinking of the hairstyles. You had bangs for a while when you were little. I think they might look nice on you now."

Lili scoffed at first, but the idea took root. The day before they were to leave Paris she happened to go out alone to buy some last-minute gifts and spotted a likely looking beauty salon.

Lili walked in and communicated what she wanted with sign language.

The hairdresser, a quite beautiful boy, smiled and nodded.

In forty minutes Lili's lovely hair was shorter, blunt cut, with longish, straight-across bangs, a shining cap of vitality that moved when she did and fell into perfect repose when she was still.

Irene was delighted. "It looks very nice, dear, shows off your cheekbones," she said when the newly shorn Lili returned to their room. "We could shop for a few new clothes before you go back to London. A couple of skirts perhaps?"

"Look, I've had a new haircut on your suggestion. I don't want some women's magazine makeover."

"Suit yourself, dear." Irene turned away from the jeans and peasant blouses and bright colored shawls which were her daughter's signature outfits and adjusted the folds of her own neat wool dress.

Something about the gesture set Lili's teeth on edge. She perched on the bed and began sorting the presents she'd bought. She didn't look at Irene when she said, "You have quite a bit extra to spend on things like clothes these days, don't you, Mother?"

She knew it was a bitchy remark, the kind of thing she'd promised herself she wouldn't say, but somehow she couldn't keep her mouth shut.

"Not exactly," Irene said quietly. "In fact, I have to start watching my pennies. I've been meaning to tell you, I bought a house."

Lili stiffened, stopped in the middle of folding a purple silk scarf intended for Ruth. "What house? Where?"

"Well, not a house exactly. A condominium apartment. In Stuart, Florida."

"Florida. Good God, why?"

"It's warm and pleasant." Irene dismissed the subject with a wave of her hand.

All the pain of losing her beloved home in Fielding welled up in Lili. It had never gone away, only been buried. The scarf dropped unheeded to the floor as she stared at her mother. "You got a fortune for our old house, didn't you?"

"No, not a fortune," Irene said. She seemed unaware of the raw wounds into which she was pouring salt. "Fifty-two thousand dollars. But the furnishings brought a great deal. I was amazed, I never thought they'd—"

Some maddened animal sank its teeth into Lili's belly. It clawed at her intestines, it was tearing apart her guts. She gasped aloud and hugged herself, almost doubling over in agony.

Irene took a step forward. "Lili! What is it? What's the matter?"

Lili lifted her head and stared at Irene, her eyes smoldering with something close to hatred. "You sold the furnishings separately?" she asked in a hoarse whisper.

"Of course. At auction. I told you that. I'm sure I did. The auction house sent a truck and they cleared away everything, even all the old linens and things. It was wonderful, so convenient. I had nothing but my clothes to pack afterward. And the auction earned over fifty thousand, almost as much as the house. Why, the flow-blue china and the cranberry glass alone made— Lili, are you listening to me?"

Lili had gotten up while her mother spoke, moved as far from her as she could. Now she stood with her back pressed to the door of the room. "I'm listening, but I can't believe what I'm hearing. Jesus God almighty! I can't believe it!"

Her voice spiraled upward; it beat against the paneled walls and the rococo ceiling. "You bitch!" Lili screamed, her throat thick with tears. "You rotten, greedy, selfish bitch!"

The words rushed out of the past; they were torn from her. For a moment Lili was both child and woman, and her grievances had become a monster that must be attacked. "You knew how I loved that house, every stick of furniture, the china, the old Kent linens, everything. You knew! And you did it anyway. You never even thought about what it would do to me. When I called and begged you not to sell, you said I was being silly. I thought at least you'd sold it intact, you never admitted you scattered everything to the winds, that you—"

Irene pressed her hands over her ears as if that would shut out all the hurtful words, the terrible catalog of crimes. "Lili, stop it! Stop shouting. I'm sure you can be heard by everyone."

"I don't care! I don't care who hears me. I don't care who knows what you've done. I want—"

"Shut up!" It was those two ordinary words, so out of character for Irene Petworth Cramer, that finally stemmed the flow of Lili's accusations.

Like her daughter, Irene was white and trembling. Like Lili, she too had ancient grievances to air. "All your life I did everything I knew how to do for you. Nothing mattered except that you should be cared for, grow up safe and secure. Nothing. I made all that happen for you. By myself. From the moment you were born until you left for London, you came first. Only when I knew you were settled and happy did I think of myself. That house and its contents were my only asset. Don't you understand how—" Irene broke off. "No, of course you don't. Why am I bothering to explain? You were born totally egocentric. That's your legacy," she added bitterly.

Then there was silence.

Lili had her hands over her face, her fingers pressed against her forehead as if they could dig the pain out of her brain. Slowly she dropped her arms to her sides, looked at her mother. Irene's face had crumpled. She looked like an old woman, but there was no remorse in Lili. Remorse required emotion, and she had none left.

"I'd rather not speak to you again until you're prepared to apologize," Irene whispered.

"I'll never apologize," Lili whispered. "Never."

"Never say never," Irene had told Lili repeatedly when she was a little girl. It wasn't bad advice. Lili walked for hours after the terrible argument, roaming the streets of Paris but seeing nothing. She didn't bother to eat because she wasn't hungry, but shortly before eleven she realized she was cold. And that she felt terrible. And that a large part of the source of that feeling was guilt.

She returned to the room she and Irene shared.

Her mother was sitting up in bed, wearing a pink knitted bedjacket and holding a magazine to the dim glow of the low-wattage bulb in the reading light. "Hi," Lili said, closing the door behind her and slipping the bolt into place.

"Hello. Did you have supper?"

"No, I wasn't hungry." Lili went to the closet and hung up her jacket.

"They had chicken in some sort of sauce here. It was very nice, but I wasn't hungry either."

"No, I don't imagine you were. Mother, I'm sorry I exploded."

Never had lasted about six hours.

"Yes, dear. I'm sure you are. We'll simply forget about it, shall we?"

• • •

Less than twenty-four hours remained of Lili and Irene's time together in Paris, and they survived it. By mutual consent and long habit they allowed the quarrel to bury itself in that limbo of unknowing which had existed between them always, descend into the sinkhole of things they did not mention. When they parted, it was with chaste kisses and admonitions to take care and promises to write.

Lili, of course, had forgotten nothing. She couldn't stop thinking of the furnishings of her beloved house, of the fact that as she'd shouted at Irene, everything she had so loved was now scattered to the four winds.

She struggled with her grieving all during the short flight to London. She was being stupid, ridiculous. Things were not the most important elements of life. She was alive and well and . . . And she ached so inside. Oh, God, it was all gone, all destroyed, her beautiful house had been raped, violated, it no longer existed. Yes, it did. It could have been worse. There could have been a fire, everything could be truly gone. But it was so unnecessary. Irene could simply have sold the Constable.

The plane landed uneventfully. Lili went home but could find no comfort in her familiar surroundings. She stayed only long enough to leave her single suitcase, then she went out again and took a bus to the National Gallery in Trafalgar Square.

Why had she never done this before? Lili recognized that her reasons were complex, but that essentially she was afraid. She knew there was something strange about the painting Amanda Manning had brought as part of her dowry when she married Sam Kent, something strange about the house on Woods Road, something strange about her own childhood. She had not wanted to probe those anomalies and inconsistencies. Now she felt she must. She had a compelling need to see again something of what she'd lost, to possess for a few moments what had once been hers. And to try to understand.

She had picked a terrible day. The schools were still closed for the Christmas holidays and the National Gallery was full of children being dragged around by parents attempting to force-feed culture. Lili struggled past the family groups and located a guard. He told her the Constables were on the floor above, in Room 7A.

She climbed the stairs, made her way down a long corridor, and found the right room. Miraculously, it was empty. Nothing and no one obstructed her vision of the four paintings on the wall immediately in front of her. She paused and stared and held her breath.

These pictures were like nothing she had imagined, certainly not like the dark two-dimensional scene that had hung over the fireplace in Fielding.

One in particular was a revelation. It was called "The Hay Wain" and depicted lush farmland bisected by a shallow stream. Two men sat talking in an empty oxcart, perhaps they'd left their grain at the nearby mill. A dog stood on the bank watching. The colors sang, the depth was incredible. You could hear the men's rural twang, smell the summer countryside, feel the warmth of the sun setting on the red brick of the mill, almost see the dog's tail wag. "My God," Lili murmured.

She stood there for fifteen minutes, drinking in the beauty, the vitality, the love that had obviously moved the artist. Then a group of the ubiquitous children came in and shattered her peace, but it didn't matter. She knew now. Irene had not sold the painting because, as she'd long ago said, it wasn't salable. The Fielding Constable didn't look anything like these because it was a crude fake. It had to be. And her mother, knowing Lili's passion for everything under the roof of Sam Kent's house, hadn't wanted to tell her.

Lili could not forgive—the hurt was too deep—but one small part of the mystery she could understand.

Because it was January, Irene could descend the Spanish Steps without tripping over tourists and hucksters, and the Via Veneto was almost deserted. She walked quickly, it was too cold to enjoy the sights. Her coat was dark tweed wool, a classic cut and warm. She pulled it closer to her body and defied the facing wind and made her way to the lobby of the

Excelsior Hotel. Loy was waiting. She was swathed in furs, haloed with the faint scent of expensive perfume.

They pressed cheeks, then found a secluded corner of the lobby and ordered coffee and little glasses of crystal-clear licorice-scented Strega. "How was Lili?" Loy asked, shrugging out of her sable. "Did you enjoy Paris?"

Irene stood up to take off her coat, folding it neatly over the back of a nearby chair. "Lili's fine, amazingly thin. And Paris was charming. But . . ."

"What?" Loy demanded. "You look disturbed. What happened?"

"We had a terrible quarrel. Lili said dreadful things, accused me— No, that's not fair. She was upset, that's all. We made it up."

"Mothers and daughters often have disagreements," Loy said gently. "It's to be expected."

"Yes," Irene agreed. "I'm sure you're right. And under the circumstances—"

She stopped speaking, the two women looking at each other before nodding knowingly. There was no need to put their shared memories into words. Then Loy broke the spell. "Tell me more about Lili, did she seem happy?"

"Sort of, there are gaps though," Irene said pensively. "I did manage to ask about Andrew Mendoza."

"And?"

"And it really is over, for two years now."

"Thank God. What about Harry Cramer?"

"She didn't mention his name. I decided I'd best let sleeping dogs lie."

"Yes, very wise." The Strega was sipped with grace, more coffee requested by a raised eyebrow and quickly brought by an attentive waiter.

"That's enough about Lili," Irene said firmly. "Tell me what we're going to do. Why did you pick Rome now? It's cold and damp."

"I know. It seemed like a good idea until I got here. I've been thinking of Sicily. A cottage in the country somewhere. We can wait for spring. It comes early in Sicily."

"That sounds wonderful," Irene said with genuine happiness.

• • •

Two months after Lili returned from Paris, in February of 1974, Ruth announced they had been offered a job adding a conservatory to a house in a village on the south coast called Lymington. It was two hours away by train and they didn't usually accept jobs so far from London, but since work was so hard to come by, they decided to go there and check out the possibilities.

Lymington turned out to have lots of winding lanes snaking up from that strip of the Atlantic known as the Solent, views of the Isle of Wight, and a shopping street that still boasted an outdoor market. The little town oozed charm. "In some ways it reminds me of Fielding," Lili told Ruth when they'd finished with the client and were in a café next to the train station.

Ruth wrinkled her nose. "I hate everything rural. Which makes me some kind of a freak. English people are supposed to be born with a love for the country in every cell and pore."

"Maybe that's why I have it," Lili admitted. "I mean because I'm half English."

Ruth had recently given up her diet of all natural food. She swallowed a mouthful of toasted teacake before she asked, "How old were you when your father died? You've never said."

"I wasn't born. He was killed in an automobile accident while my mother was pregnant."

Ruth's eyes narrowed. "Lili, how come you've never mentioned your father's family? Have you met them?"

"No. I have sort of looked for them, but I never had any luck. And I don't think it was a happy marriage, because my mother won't tell me anything about Harry Cramer."

"It's a fairly ordinary name, but not like Smith or Jones. It shouldn't be impossible to check."

"No, it shouldn't. But I've come up empty trying to trace him. Andy was helping me look, then—" Lili broke off.

"To hell with Andy," Ruth said firmly. "There must be Cramers everywhere. Even right here in Lymington. I'll prove it." She disappeared for a moment and came back carrying a telephone directory. "Now," she said as she opened it, "I'll bet—" Ruth stopped speaking.

"What is it?"

"There's only one Cramer."

"And?" Lili demanded.

"And his first name is Harry."

Ruth had suggested that Lili immediately call the number in the Lymington directory. Lili had copied it down, but she pointed out that the London train was due to leave in less than fifteen minutes. She would call from home. Nothing more was said. In a few days Ruth had apparently forgotten the incident. Lili, of course, had not.

"Maybe he's alive," Andy had said years earlier. Perhaps that idea wasn't as ridiculous as Lili had always believed it to be.

A dozen times she picked up the telephone in her living room, but she never actually dialed. There seemed something magical about the casual conversation with Ruth that had produced such startling results. Lili wanted to return to Lymington and see if she could rekindle the sense of excitement she'd felt when she saw the name Harry Cramer in print. She could do it by herself. She didn't need Ruth Owens, and she certainly didn't need Andy Mendoza.

She made the trip on a Sunday. The connections weren't as good as they had been during the week, and it took hours. She didn't reach Lymington until well past two. The station was deserted, the streets empty. Lili stood for a moment in the chill afternoon air. It felt like snow. Maybe she'd be stranded. She ought to turn around and go straight back. No, she'd come this far. Silly to give up now.

The café where she and Ruth had waited for the train was shut tight. And if there was a hotel with a comfortable lobby, she couldn't see it. It was too cold to wander around looking for someplace warm with a telephone. Her only choice was a public booth on the corner.

The door to the booth didn't close properly. The wind was cutting and made Lili's eyes tear and her nose run. She picked up the receiver.

What in God's name was she going to say? Hi, I think I may be your daughter? No, of course not. Only that she thought perhaps they were related. And if he said no, that it was impossible, she'd hang up. What was the harm? She had nothing to lose. She got her change ready and dialed with cold stiff fingers.

A man answered on the third ring. Lili pushed her coin through the slot, waited for it to drop and for the surcease of peeping sounds that announced a call made from a pay telephone. "May I speak with Mr. Harry Cramer?"

"This is Harry Cramer speaking." He had a nice voice, pleasant and firm.

"Mr. Cramer, we haven't met, but my name's Cramer too. Lili Cramer. And I'm trying to find some relatives."

"I see. You're American, aren't you?"

As usual, her accent, little affected by nearly four years in London, had given her away. "Yes, I am," Lili admitted. "But my father was English."

"How interesting. Don't think I've any American relations, but you never know, do you? Small world we live in today. Look, I realize you're calling from a public phone—"

"Yes. As it happens, I'm in Lymington for only a short while."

"Come along and see me, why don't you? Delighted to give you tea. Can you come now?"

Fifteen minutes later Lili was seated in a small cottage overlooking Lymington Harbor, sipping hot delicious tea and eating freshly made scones topped with Devonshire cream. The sitting room was filled with faded chintz and comfortable cushions and a log fire scented the afternoon. Across from Lili was a short, frail man with a fringe of white hair. He had a large cane with a heavy gold top that he kept fondling and he wore dark glasses. Harry Cramer was blind.

"Glaucoma," he explained. "Lost my sight ten years ago. Don't know what I'd do without my Claudette." The hand that didn't hold the cane patted the knee of the woman sitting beside him. He was able to locate her without hesitation, as if between them there was a secret means of communication that didn't require ordinary senses.

"I must explain about my wife," he said. "Claudette's French. She doesn't speak English. She's one of those people who finds it impossible to learn any language but her own. We met in Paris in 'forty-six and never left until a few years ago. Pity to bring her back here. Had to because of my health. Difficult to uproot a couple of old fogies like us after so many years. But I'm chattering, and you came for a purpose. Now, Miss Cramer, tell me about your family and I'll see if I know of a connection. All we Cramers have excellent memories."

Lili looked at Harry Cramer, and at his wife. Claudette was a large, motherly looking sort of woman, big bosomed, wearing a blue sweater and a gray skirt. Her hair was twisted into a bun and her lap was full of knitting. And while it might be true that she didn't understand a word of the conversation, she was looking at Lili with knowing eyes. She murmured a few words in French.

"Claudette says I seem to have disturbed you," he said. "Sorry my lack of sight makes me such a blundering old fool. Would you care to tell me what's troubling you, my dear?"

"Nothing. Really." Lili couldn't very well say that he wasn't supposed to have a wife or to have been in Paris in 1950.

"Very well. Now, what can you tell me about your father's people?"

He was kindness itself, they both were. Which made it all the more difficult. "Not a thing," Lili stammered. "That's why I'm here. As I said, he was English. My mother was Irene Petworth before she married. From Fielding, Massachusetts. She told me my father died in an automobile accident before I was born and that his name was Harry Cramer. She's never liked to talk about it, so when I heard that was your name I thought perhaps she hadn't told me the exact story and—"

"You thought I was worth a try," the old man said gently. "I understand. And I really am sorry. I've never been married to anyone but *ma chère* Claudette. For almost thirty years. And we have no children."

Cross off one very outlandish possibility. Lili apologized for bothering them and left soon afterward.

Claudette Cramer returned from seeing her out and picked up her knitting. For a few moments the couple sat in silence. Harry Cramer spoke first. "I probably should have put her off when she phoned, but it seemed such a heartless thing to do. Still, I gave my word. I couldn't tell her anything, could I? Pity. She seemed a nice young woman. Is she pretty?"

"Very pretty," his wife said. "And yes, it is a pity. But you had no choice."

"No," Harry murmured. "I don't think I did."

Claudette leaned over and kissed his cheek. The room was cooling, so she put another log on the fire and thought of how comfortable they were here, of the peace of their lives. Thank God Harry hadn't taken it into his head to rattle skeletons long buried.

❧ 13 ❧

London, New York, Fielding: 1975–76

"Look this way please, Miss Cramer. Thank you, that will do nicely."

The man with the light meter made mysterious motions and moved away. Lili shot a desperate glance at Peter Fowler, the only familiar face in the room. Peter was absorbed in conversation with a middle-aged man wearing makeup—which added to Lili's sense of the surreal.

A woman approached the blue-carpeted dais on which Lili sat. It was supposed to look like a living room, but it was a set in a television studio. Lili was surrounded by lights and cables and wires, and people who scurried around looking as if they knew what they were doing. Only Lili had no idea what she was doing.

"You can relax, Miss Cramer," the woman said smiling. "I'm Sharon Wright, the producer, and I promise you, this is a very informal show. You'll do fine." She raised her voice. "Places everyone, please. We're on the air in three minutes."

My God! What was she doing here? How had Peter talked her into this? Lili's mouth was dry, her palms were sweaty. Peter and the other man, Ian Chambers, the show's host, came and sat beside her. A red light flashed somewhere in the darkness beyond the island of glare. There was zingy music. A man holding a camera moved in and pushed it in Ian Chambers's face.

"Good afternoon," Chambers said. "Today my guests are Peter Fowler, British editor of one of America's most up-market art of living magazines, *Lifestyle,* and Lili Cramer, a kitchen designer. So you won't be surprised to hear that we're going to talk about the new kitchen consciousness. When did we all become foodies?" His delivery was relaxed and low-key, a neighbor who'd dropped in for a chat. Lili was so tense her nails were making grooves in her palms.

"It was supposed to be a chef," Peter had explained when he called her at six-thirty that morning. "I should say a chefesse, some English dame with a regular TV program of her own, but she chose last night to have a burst appendix. Chambers just telephoned to ask if I minded doing the show alone with him. I suggested adding you instead."

Which was how Lili came to be sitting here under the fierce heat of the lights, listening to Peter and Ian Chambers talk about the kitchen as status symbol, barometer of affluence.

"No more coziness," Chambers said. "That's what I miss. My wife did ours over recently. Now it's like a laboratory, all steel and black glass."

"High-tech," Peter agreed. "Every gadget and gizmo that's been dreamed up. But I think the only thing modern ladies use a kitchen for is to heat up precooked or frozen dinners."

For a moment Lili forgot where she was. She leaned forward. "Listen, you're both talking rot." The men turned and looked at her. "A great kitchen is one that makes your heart sing. It's the nerve center of the house now that almost nobody has servants. It has to be beautiful as well as convenient and serviceable. And all that frozen-fish-fingers nonsense went out with the miniskirt. Women are busier than ever, but when we have time we really cook, with love and attention and skill. That's honest."

"Honest about what?" Chambers asked. "I thought simple food lovingly prepared was honest."

Peter made a noise of agreement, and Lili bridled again. "You guys are fantasizing about some woman who stays home and bakes bread. A woman today is likely to be a doctor or a lawyer or a stockbroker. Maybe she still bakes bread, but when she does it's for her own satisfaction, not simply to cater to your whims."

It was the lens of the camera zooming in almost to her chin that made Lili conscious of the fact that she'd spouted off to thousands of people. She clamped her mouth shut. Her knees began shaking and she thanked God that she was sitting down. Peter grinned at her.

"A statement for women's lib," Ian Chambers said. "Are all your clients women, Lili?"

"No, and what you're calling 'women's lib' has nothing to do with what we're discussing." The rhythm of the discussion was taking her over again, supplanting her nerves with conviction. "It's a simple matter of fairness," Lili continued. "Everybody eats, men as well as women, so why shouldn't everybody know how to cook? And want a beautiful, convenient kitchen in which to do it?"

Peter shook his head and leaned across the talk show host to confront Lili. "But at *Lifestyle* we've found that the most glorious kitchens are in the houses of people who wouldn't dream of cooking for themselves, the jet set, the super rich. In the end, isn't it simply a matter of money, getting it and flaunting it?"

"No. You think that only because your magazine draws its stories from a preselected pool," Lili countered. "Usually it's interior decorators who suggest the houses you photograph. Most of them won't accept a client who only wants advice and supervision for a smallish job on a budget. They'll do the whole house in imported silks and antique furniture, or nothing."

She'd completely forgotten the cameras now. Lili was engaged in the argument, sparring with Peter and Ian Chambers, tossing her bouncy dark hair, waving her hands when she wanted to make a point, being eloquent about a subject she knew and about which she cared deeply. Until she was cut off in midsentence.

"Thank you, Lili Cramer, kitchen designer, and you, Peter Fowler, British editor of *Lifestyle*. I'm afraid that's all we have time for today. Next week my guests will be . . ."

Chambers spoke to the red eye of the camera a few

moments more. Then the hot lights went out and Sharon Wright emerged from a booth in the rear. "Terrific, Ian. It's in the can. Thanks, both of you." She turned to Lili. "Especially thanks to you for coming at such short notice. You were great. Don't forget to watch the show. Tomorrow afternoon at five."

"Tomorrow afternoon?" Lili's eyes opened wide in surprise. "But before we began you said we were on the air."

The others chuckled. "A hangover from the days when we did everything live," Sharon Wright said. "We tape now. It's a lot less risky."

"So if I'd been terrible or said awful things, nobody would have known except you?"

"Not another soul," Ian Chambers agreed. "Sorry, I should have explained. But you weren't terrible. I only wish my wife had talked to you before she spent a fortune on that damned new kitchen."

In the taxi Peter and Lili shared after they left the studio, she found herself thinking not of her debut on television but of the kindness of the man sitting beside her. Peter Fowler was a very special kind of guy.

Their friendship had begun eight months earlier, when Peter called to say that *Lifestyle* was thinking of running a feature piece on Lili's work, because she'd carved a unique niche—"Something between an architect and a decorator," was the way Peter had put it. While he was doing the story, Lili and Peter and a photographer had lived in each other's pockets. When it was done, Lili had discovered two truths about herself.

The first was relatively simple. Her best and most exciting work was connected to cooking and eating. Peter's text had summed it up. "All Lili's designs are imaginative and witty, but her kitchens and dining rooms are a revelation, a synthesis of New England kitsch and Old England pomposity that somehow works . . ."

The second truth was more complex.

Lili and Peter went on seeing each other after the article was finished. Lili wasn't sure exactly how she felt about that. Peter was fun, easy to be with, she cared for him, but not, apparently, the way he cared for her.

Things came to a head one night when they were having dinner in her little house, in the combination living and dining room she'd made into something close to perfect, at least for its miniature size. "Lili, am I muscling in on somebody's territory?" Peter had suddenly asked.

Lili looked up from the seafood-stuffed crepes she was serving. "I don't think I understand."

"Are you involved with somebody else?"

"Another man you mean?"

He grinned. "I suppose it could be another woman these days. Doesn't alter the question."

She passed him a plate. "Neither. Not in any special way. What made you think that?"

"You. It's May. I've known you since January, but now that the article is finished, you make it very clear that my time is rationed. I see you once a week, maybe twice if I'm very insistent. So I'd like you to set me straight on how things are. Or are not."

"Is all this because of last Thursday?" she'd asked softly.

Peter frowned and nodded. "I guess so."

Last Thursday. A long walk on a warm and sunny afternoon, Peter's gorgeous Mayfair flat, a bottle of wine—the result was inevitable unless she stopped it. Lili had not stopped it. And she had learned something about herself. She wasn't cut out for sex as sport. Peter might be a world-class player, but she saw only Andy's face, heard only his voice, felt only his once-beloved hands.

Peter Fowler had made gentle, caring love to her on the Oriental rug in front of his fireplace, and below the level of purely physical response, Lili had felt nothing. The frost was too deep to melt, and he had known it.

Later, in the house on Masbro Road, when Peter asked for an explanation, she had toyed with the crepes on her plate. "I'm sorry. It wasn't your fault. I was tense."

He had reached over and taken her hand. "Hey, you don't have to explain anything. It's not a test; we don't have to give each other marks. Good sex needs time to ripen. Only I thought we'd passed to the next stage of what I have to call our relationship, though I loathe the word. Afterward you were as cool as ever. 'Give me a ring next week, Peter . . .' What gives, Lili?"

She had thought for a few moments. "I guess I don't want anyone in too close, not even you. I'm not very trusting. I'd like to be, but I can't manage it."

He got up and began searching through the bottles in one of her cupboards. "Do you have some scotch in here? Wine doesn't seem tough enough at the moment. Right, here it is." He poured a stiff drink and moved back to the table.

"Listen, I've heard all about you and Andy Mendoza. There were plenty of gossips simply dying to tell me about it."

Lili started to say something but Peter held up his hand. "No, let me finish. If we follow the classic scenario, this is where I ask what happened and you tell me about your terrible experience. As they say here, it's not on, Lili. We've all got scars and bruises that still ache. Life's like that. Grown-ups pick up the pieces and keep on going."

"Okay," she said after a while.

"Okay? What does that mean?"

"It means I see what you're saying."

"But nothing's going to change. You still only want someone to share a few laughs with once in a while." He finished his scotch and stood up again. "Sorry, Lili, I'm too old for this. I've reached the point in my life where I only have time for quality. Cheap imitations of the real thing bore me."

And from that moment in May until he'd called at the crack of dawn this August morning, she hadn't heard from him. Now Lili chose her words carefully. "Peter, getting me on that show was very generous. Thank you."

He chuckled without much humor. "That's me, ole generous Petey." He took her hand. "Let's be friends, Lili. I'm not a sore loser."

She squeezed his fingers. "Friends," she said.

The next day Lili switched on the television at five, expectant and nervous. In a few seconds she heard the distinctive zingy theme music; this time she identified it as unaccompanied voices singing in parts an old English madrigal. There was a clever display of graphics representing talking heads, then Ian Chambers appeared, and a few seconds later herself and Peter. Lili watched in amazement. It was as if she were looking at a stranger, a view from a distant place of a woman she didn't know. The television Lili was so animated, so full of gestures and opinions, even of wit.

Forty minutes after Chambers bid his viewers good-bye, her phone rang. "Miss Cramer, this is Sharon Wright of *Talking with Chambers*. Since we went off the air people have been calling to ask where they can reach you to discuss redoing their kitchens."

Lili grinned. That was exactly what Peter had promised would happen; it was how he'd induced her to do the show despite her terror of being on television. Moreover, it was exactly what she needed at this point in her life, because a few months previously Ruth had announced that she was marrying an interior decorator and wanted to work with him. Maybe it was best if Owens and Cramer was dissolved.

Lili had been devastated, but there seemed little she could do. She'd signed the dissolution agreement Ruth waved under her nose without legal advice, though she'd later realized she should have insisted on being paid something for the goodwill the business had built, and began looking for clients on her own. That had proved a very difficult undertaking.

Ruth had always been the up-front member of their team. Lili had labored in relative obscurity until Peter's article, and even that was seen by a small number of people compared to the audience who watched *Talking with Chambers*. After the television show, everything changed. Suddenly Lili was on her way to being remarkably successful, maybe even a little bit famous. It wasn't merely potential clients who clamored for her services, Lili was invited to fill guest slots on two more TV shows and half a dozen on radio. Lili sometimes looked in the mirror and grinned. She was becoming a celebrity.

As if to confirm that judgment, in August she got a call from an American named Dan Kerry, an agent, who urged her to sign up with him. He was high on something new in television, cable, and wanted her to consider moving to New York to start a talk show. Lili found the idea preposterous— but she kept his card.

Shortly before Christmas, Peter telephoned to tell her that *Lifestyle* had been sold. "Some hotshot young team of accountants are running things now. They're going to change the thrust, whatever that means. Lots of shake-up at the top. Half a dozen editors are out, including me."

Lili grieved for him, and felt vaguely guilty because the Ian Chambers show that had turned out such a marvelous break for her had been a kind of swan song for Peter, but there didn't seem a lot she could do.

In late February 1976, less than a year since her debut appearance on *Talking with Chambers,* Lili was so busy, she decided to hire a secretary and a bookkeeper. But if she was to have a staff she couldn't continue to operate out of her tiny living room. She began to look for office space. The quest took her on a rainy March afternoon to a London suburb known as Maida Vale, where quite by chance she was seduced by the display of cookbooks in one window of a corner bookstore.

Lili glanced at her watch, decided she could spare fifteen minutes, and stepped inside. She paid no attention to the crowd at the far end of the selling floor. What caught her eye was a huge stack of identical books. The jackets were blue and white, the artwork a Star of David surrounded by barbed wire, and the title, *Agony, A Study of Israel's West Bank Policy.* The book's author was Andrew Mendoza.

She picked up a copy. Andy peered at her from the back cover. The angular face, the knowing eyes gazing at the world with slight disdain from behind the horn-rimmed glasses, the half grin—he was unchanged, achingly familiar. Lili studied the photograph for a moment, felt tears prickle behind her eyes, and put the book down.

She looked up to meet his real-life gaze.

Andy was autographing books at a table a few feet to her left. The crowd that had hidden him when she came in had dispersed. Now he was alone, watching her. They stared at each other a moment. He half rose.

What did she want to do, turn and run or stand her ground? Spit at him? Weep? Be casual and sophisticated? The choice was an illusion. Seeing him without warning and with no time to array her defenses, Lili was immobilized by sudden melting joy and bottomless despair.

The electrified instant of potential seemed to last forever, but it was only seconds.

A woman approached and walked along the ionized path made by their two pairs of eyes and broke the spell. "Mr. Mendoza, I've wanted to meet you because—"

Andy turned to the woman and smiled, took the book she held out, said something. Lili dropped the copy of *Agony* she'd been holding and fled.

For two days she was nauseated, fevered, cold no matter how high she pushed the thermostat. Ridiculous, Lili told herself. It was over. It had been over for four years. She had the flu; it wasn't seeing Andy Mendoza that had made her sick. But she knew it was—and that she could never predict when it would happen again. London was an enormous city, but she and Andy had both become celebrities of sorts. In that rarified world their paths were bound to cross.

On Sunday she dragged herself out to get the papers in hopes that they'd take her mind off him. *Agony* was on all the bestseller lists. There was a feature in the *Observer,* a transcript of a meeting between Andy and the Israeli ambassador. "Since when are you an expert on foreign affairs, Mr. Mendoza? It seems to me you've made your reputation in other fields."

"I'm an expert on how the privileged misuse power, Mr. Ambassador. That's what's happening on the West Bank. And as someone whose ancient roots are the same as your own . . ."

Lili crumpled up the paper and shoved it in the garbage with the old tea leaves.

Later that day she flicked the dial on the radio—and heard Andy being interviewed in tandem with the Foreign Secretary. There was no escape. Andy Mendoza was suddenly larger than life, seeming to fill the horizon, to float above the Thames, to walk the streets and avenues and parks. He ravished Lili's beloved London.

But was that bad? There had been a moment in the book-store when he'd been on his way to speak to her. Maybe now that he'd come out of wherever he'd been hibernating, they would meet, talk. Maybe they could begin again.

That was one truth she admitted to herself in those two horrible days. She'd give her soul if it could begin again. Another was that Andy didn't share her feelings. If he did, he'd have telephoned long before. Even if he hadn't had the nerve to do that because of the way he'd ended their affair, he wouldn't have let her leave the bookstore. "Lili," he could have called. "Wait a moment, please." Then he'd have whisked her off to a café or a pub and they'd have talked and . . .

And it was all fantasy. Andy Mendoza was clearly no longer interested in Lili Cramer.

Suddenly England was stifling. It wasn't really her turf, it was Andy's. Here she would always be prey to his power to make her feel mortal pain. She needed to get away.

She called Peter Fowler. "Peter, what's New York like?"

"New York? Everything you've heard and read and seen in the movies. The Big Apple. Drop-dead city. Home of the biggest and the brightest and the meanest. Where the stakes are sky-high, and no guts no glory. Shall I drag out a few more clichés?"

"No more," Lili said. "Those will do for the moment."

"Yeah, I guess so. Lili, are you thinking of going to New York?"

"Maybe." That was all she would say, but it wasn't the truth. There was no maybe about it; she'd made up her mind. She found Dan Kerry's card in her desk and on Monday she telephoned him.

Throughout the long hours of Lili's flight to New York she kept her fingers wrapped around a triangular piece of gold. It was her good luck charm, the token she'd found so long ago in Fielding. She'd had a loop attached and now she wore it on a chain around her neck. She thought of the enigmatic Hebrew words with which it was engraved, *forget thee.* . . . She was going home to forget, but also to remember.

Lili's first few months in America were a blur of frantic work. The show Dan Kerry dreamed up for her and sold to a small cable station was her first priority. Lili's original idea was to call the program *A Moveable Feast,* but the creative types at the station nixed that and came up with the more pedestrian *Dining Out, Eating In,* which they said was more accessible. Lili was quickly learning the rules of play in her new world. She shrugged and agreed to the title change, though she thought it was terrible.

Once her career was back on track, she had to find a place to live. Lili had brought home a nest egg of twenty-two thousand dollars, mostly profit on the sale of her London house, but she decided not to try to buy a place to live in Manhattan, where real estate prices seemed to her astronomical. Dan helped her find a rental in a new building on East Eighty-first Street, the last one in the city he told her, and Lili signed a long lease, quelled her nerves by remembering that it had a sublet clause, and furnished it and moved in. The eighteen thousand left of her capital she put in a mutual fund that promised a high rate of growth.

All this took an enormous amount of time and energy. Labor Day weekend of '76 was Lili's first chunk of leisure time since she'd arrived in New York. The holiday began with an incredibly hot Friday evening. Her apartment was air-conditioned, but the streets of New York were unbearable. She regretted that she'd made no plans to escape the city for her three free days.

The next morning at six, when dawn was a pink glow in the sky, Lili came suddenly awake and realized she'd made a decision while she slept. She dressed in jeans and a T-shirt and threw some clothes in an overnight bag.

By seven-thirty she was at LaGuardia Airport. At nine she

was in Boston. Forty minutes later she was in a cab approaching Fielding. Lili hung out of the window—watching, waiting for a sense of coming home.

There was a new gas station with serve-yourself pumps on the outskirts of town and a new shopping mall. The parking lot was jammed with cars. "This is Fielding, Miss," the cabbie said.

"Yes, I know."

"Okay, so where you wanna go?"

"Turn down that road over there on your right. I'll tell you when to stop."

Lili had the taxi drop her at the far end of Haven Avenue, by the public library. It was closed for the holiday. The street was absolutely silent. Lili walked south toward the stores, wondering if she'd see anyone she knew. If she did, would they recognize her? A moot point. There was no one to see. Haven was all but deserted. A few places were open, Petworth's Department Store among them, but only a handful of shoppers browsed in the aisles. Doubtless the effect of the new mall.

She walked slowly, regretting the change but telling herself it was inevitable. The sun climbed higher and she was uncomfortably hot. She'd be turning on to Woods Road in a minute, and it would be cooler.

When she rounded the familiar corner, Lili felt a stab of true delight. The old trees still marched along the roadside. They seemed to welcome her.

She slowed her pace even more, a lover suddenly grown shy, then sat down under a pine, savoring the moment, delaying its fulfillment. A boy came along carrying a fishing rod. He might have stepped from a Norman Rockwell painting; a child of about ten, with tousled brown hair and a few freckles. He eyed Lili curiously. "You okay, Miss?" he asked after a few seconds.

"I'm fine," Lili said. "Thanks for asking. You going to fish down at Willock's Stream?"

"Yeah. The yellow bellies have been great lately."

"Good luck."

"Thanks." He still lingered, obviously wanting to know more. "You live around here?"

"No, I used to, but I don't anymore."

"Oh, come back for a visit, huh?"

"That's right." Lili couldn't resist. "You know the old Kent place?" she asked.

"The big house down the road? Sure. That where you're going?"

"Not really. I remembered it was here and I wanted to see it again."

"Driveway's a little beyond that bend. But yesterday the gate was closed, people who own it aren't here much."

A gate was a new addition. There'd never been one before. Lili got up and dusted pine needles and grass from her jeans. "Do you know them?"

"Nah, not really. No kids. My dad says it's crazy for people without kids to buy a big house like that. 'Specially since they're not here most of the time."

Lili murmured an assent and they walked together in companionable silence for about ten minutes, then came to the beginning of the driveway. Lili paused. Two tall, spiked iron gates set into stone posts were secured with a chain and a padlock. The exuberant summer growth made it impossible to see the house.

"See, I told you it was shut up," the boy said.

"Yes, so you did. I guess I'll go back to town. Good luck with your fishing."

He waved good-bye and moved on. Lili took a few steps in the opposite direction, waited a few seconds, then turned to check. The boy was gone, the road empty.

She ducked into the woods. There seemed to be more underbrush than she remembered, and she was glad she'd worn sneakers. Just in time she remembered a virulent patch of poison ivy. It was still there, and she'd almost walked straight into it. She veered off on a westerly angle and finally came to the path that led past an achingly familiar stand of shadblow. In June the trees were white with blossom, now their leaves were the first to be speckled with autumn red. She expected to see the chicken coop after a few paces. Instead, Lili suddenly found herself on a closely mown green lawn.

Her heart began beating a tattoo. The ruined chicken coop was gone and in its place was a large rectangular swimming pool with a tiled surround. The pool had a fiberglass cover stretched across its top. To one side was a small building, obviously a pool house. All its windows were shuttered. She stood still for a few moments, trying to assimilate the implications.

People without kids who didn't use the house much and put up gates and built a pool and a pool house must be wealthy. What, then, would they have done to the house itself? She squeezed her eyes shut, trying to force back tears. It was crazy to cry when she didn't know if there was anything to cry about. The loss of the chicken coop didn't mean much. Hell, the pool was a great addition. And the pool house was clad in brown shingle and trimmed in blue. Why build a pool house to match if you'd changed the main house?

The only way to know for certain was to go on. She did, walking easily along a path that had been widened and edged with angled bricks. That was okay too. The paths in the old formal garden were edged the same way. In former days this one had led to the door to the back hall and the kitchen. It still did.

Lili came upon her house from the side, and she knew instantly that everything was fine. Nothing was changed, only better cared for than she remembered.

She stood for a long time looking at the windows, seeing each room in her imagination. Eventually, she made her way to the rear. The screened porch was still hung with wisteria, entirely green now because its flowering season was past, and the bow-fronted window of the dining room was intact. "Thank God," she whispered in a genuine prayer of thanksgiving.

Because all the curtains were drawn, Lili never saw the inside of her house denuded of the furnishings she knew and loved. Better that way, she decided when she was back in New York. It was better not to have any mental picture of what had been put in place of what she knew belonged. Someday when the house was hers she'd begin a search of every antique shop in New England. She'd attend every auction. However long it took, she'd duplicate everything. Someday.

❧ 14 ❧

New York: 1981

Lili listened a second time to the message on her answering machine. ". . . this is Andy Mendoza. I know you hate the sight of me, but I must speak with you. Please, it really is vital . . ."

She pushed the button that silenced the familiar voice, and stood where she was, paralyzed by emotions to which she could put no name. How many times had she imagined this exact scene? A million? But that was years earlier, and now she'd stopped dreaming about Andy. Consciously perhaps. But it was filling her again, rushing through her blood—a flood of longing, of despair, of hope.

Jesus! Lili pressed her fingers to suddenly throbbing temples. He wasn't going to do this to her again. She was not going to suffer through another dose of the kind of misery Andy Mendoza dealt out. Even as she thought the words she glanced at her watch. It was eleven-ten. He had left the number of the Hilton and said he'd wait all night for her to return his call. Lili picked up the telephone.

"You're not chubby anymore," Andy said.

"And you're not so skinny. Sit down."

He dropped into one of the floral-strewn chairs in Lili's living room. It was almost midnight, but still balmy. She'd opened a window, and outside the street was quiet. They might have been alone in the universe.

"How did you find me?" Lili asked. She wanted also to ask why, but she wouldn't, not yet.

"Easy. I had heard you were in New York. When I got here, I looked in the phone book."

"Yes, of course, easy. And this is the first time you've come, right? And you didn't return to London from Spain for years and years. Is that it?"

"No," he said quietly. "That's not it."

"No, it isn't." Lili forced the words from between clenched teeth.

She'd told herself she'd be cool, reserved, maybe convince him she had all but forgotten the whole thing. But the accusations surged up and wouldn't be choked off. "It was such a rotten thing to do," she whispered. "Why? That's what I've always wanted to know. Why did you have to be so cruel?"

He slumped in the chair, long legs sprawled out before him, and stared at the tips of his shoes. "I told myself it was kinder. Why gnaw at the wound? I didn't see any future for us. I thought if I dropped out of your world you'd forget about me."

Lili stared at him. The same sandy-blond hair, the same sharp-planed face, the ubiquitous horn-rims—all so familiar, once so beloved. Half of her was melting, wanting to fling herself on top of him, wrap her arms around his neck, feel the solid reality; Andy was actually here with her, breathing the same air, occupying the same space. The other half was rigid with fury; she'd waited for so long and imagined so many answers. Now she had an opportunity to ask the questions. "Really? You honestly thought it was kinder to leave me hanging, never knowing what had happened? I don't believe it. And you're a worse bastard to lie about it after all this time."

"Lili, don't. I can't bear it, love."

She shuddered and had to turn away to swallow tears. She wouldn't let him see her cry, not at this late date. But a thousand times she'd heard his voice in her mind, heard him call her "love" in that way that meant so little to him and had meant so much to her. "You can't bear it," she said bitterly. "My heart bleeds for you."

She clenched her fists to keep from lunging at him in a mixture of longing and rage, and shoved them in the pockets of the white terry jump suit she wore. She'd pulled it on after they spoke on the phone. It was an instinctive, self-protective choice; nothing sexy or self-consciously pretty, just the zip-front one-piece she wore to do her shopping on Saturday mornings.

"I like your hair like that," he said. "Sort of Cleopatra. Suits you."

"Don't charm me," she spat out through clenched teeth. "For God's sake, Andy, don't try and charm me."

"Nothing I say is going to be right, is it?"

"I guess not."

"I'd better go."

She didn't want that either. "No. What about your vital need to see me?"

"It's still there, still vital."

"Okay, then stay. Do you want something to drink?"

"I'd love a cup of real tea. Do you have any?"

"Sure. All those years in London tamed the savage colonial. Wait a minute."

She went to the kitchen and boiled water and put three spoons of Assam tea in a warmed teapot, and fixed a tray with mugs and a small pitcher of milk. He didn't take sugar, she remembered because she remembered everything. In the living room he was still sitting as he had been, staring at his shoes. Lili poured the tea and handed it to him. "Here, it beats lukewarm water with a paper-wrapped tea bag on the side."

"It does indeed. Are you going to jump down my throat again if I ask how you've been?"

She shrugged. "Okay. Good, in fact. I have a television show now, restaurant reviews and chat about kitchens."

"I know."

That surprised her. "You do? Have you been in New York a long time?"

"No. I come maybe once a year to see my U.S. publishers. But I've always kept up with what you were doing."

"How thoughtful. And you've become quite a success. I see your books everywhere."

"I've been lucky with topics. They seem to catch the notoriously fickle mood of the public. Sometimes I even do book signings in shops."

"Oh, yes, that," Lili said with a grimace. "Another of your wonderful exhibits of concern for my feelings."

"Wait a minute, that wasn't my fault, it was yours. You turned your back and walked out. It was painfully clear you hated the sight of me."

"Is that what you thought?"

"Yes." Defiantly. He was tired of being whipped.

"It wasn't true. I waited for you to give some sign, you didn't."

"It was a short wait, all of about twenty seconds as I recall. There wasn't time to give any kind of sign."

"You're a liar."

He sighed. "Lili, I admit I acted very badly. But my motives were not what you think they were. I honestly thought I was doing the right thing. I hurt you and I'm sorry. I was pretty hurt myself. I loved you, you know."

It was the first time he'd ever said it. She clutched the mug of tea but she didn't drink. The words were rushing up into her throat, I loved you too, I still do. . . . She wouldn't say them. Nothing would make her expose herself like that. Not again, not after peace had been so dearly won. But she still couldn't leave it alone; she couldn't dismiss the past. "And you still can't tell me why?"

He was thoughtful for some moments. "I suppose I can try. I'll have to if you're going to understand what I'm doing here in the middle of the night ten years after the event. Lili, do you remember the Swanning story?"

"The murder of your distant cousin by Amanda Kent, the stately home in Sussex? Yes, I remember. Are you still working on that?"

"I've never stopped working on it. I can't help it. It's what is called an idée fixe. I've suspected for years that the Mendozas were up to their eyeballs in the murder and Lady Swanning's disappearance."

"Okay. You should know, I suppose. But you were going to explain why you walked out without a word. I keep listening, but I don't hear anything that relates to that."

"I'm getting there. How's your mother?"

"My mother? Ah, I see. The connection you always believed in. Irene's fine. She lives in Florida. I don't see a lot of her."

"Listen, I still think she's deeply involved in the whole thing. I think she was Amanda Kent's secretary and helped her escape after Swanning was shot. I've suspected it ever since you told me that she had grown up in Fielding with Amanda and come to England soon after Amanda did. And there was that business with your father, my family warning us off when we were looking for Harry Cramer. He'd be important to them only because of your mother, because Irene was involved in the Swanning affair."

Lili was staring at him. She put down her mug and pushed her hair back from her face, as if seeing him more clearly might clarify all else. "And because that was a far-out possibility, a shot in a million, you—"

"Walked out," he finished for her. "But when I did, it wasn't a shot in a million anymore. It's not important how, and it would take too long to explain, but while I was in Spain over that Christmas of 'seventy-one I had confirmation that the secretary's name was Irene. At least, what I took as confirmation. How the hell could I go on with you when I knew that?"

She shook her head. "You're going too fast for me. I'm not following. Say you were right, say Irene was part of it, you didn't have to tell me. Apparently nobody but you is interested anymore. All you had to do was drop the whole thing."

"I couldn't," he whispered. "I can't."

"Why not?" She was almost shouting. "For Christ's sake, why not?"

"Because all my life I've wanted to disassociate myself from them. The Mendozas are a plague on the universe, Lili. They're vultures. They feed on anybody that's weaker than they are. And most people are. I think I can prove they covered up a cold-blooded murder. If I can and I don't, then I'm no better than they are."

He'd never put it into words before, not so explicitly, not even to himself. After he said it, Andy realized he'd spoken more truth than he meant to reveal. She'd twisted it out of him with her demands and the calling in of a debt he'd owed for so long. "I'm sorry," he whispered. "You were well shot of me. I never should have come here and picked at the remains."

He started to rise and she motioned him to stay. "Don't, you can't undo it now. You're here, we're talking. If we don't get to the bottom of it, I'll never have any peace."

"Neither will I," he admitted.

"You still haven't told me everything, have you? Something new has come up, otherwise why this visit?"

"Yes, something new to me, though it's quite old."

He reached into his breast pocket, withdrew an envelope, and from that the photograph that had been stolen for him in Madrid. "This picture was taken in 1939. I believe it's the only copy in existence. Apparently a great effort was made to destroy the prints and the negatives, but this one slipped through. I got it in Madrid a few days ago. It was taken in Málaga in the south of Spain. Will you have a look?"

Lili held out her hand. Andy passed her the picture and she looked at it for some moments, fascinated by the dresses, the long rope of beads around the neck of one smiling girl, the silly little hat on the other. "Am I supposed to recognize either of these women?" she asked at last.

"I thought you might."

She shook her head. "No, I don't. You think one of them is Irene?"

"Yes. With Amanda Kent, Lady Swanning."

"Do you still have the newspaper clippings from right after the murder? The ones with the pictures of Amanda."

He nodded and she held out her hand again, knowing he'd have them with him. Lili looked, moving her head from one side to the other like a spectator at a tennis match. "I'm not sure. Maybe the one on the left with the little hat and the feather could be the same woman. As for my mother, I suppose the one on the right could be her. But that's only a vague feeling. Irene was thirty-three when I was born, she's sixty-six now. In 1939 she'd have been—" Lili paused and did the math. "Twenty-two. I don't know what she looked like at twenty-two."

Andy took the picture and glanced from it to Lili. "You don't look anything like your mother, do you?"

"No. I never have."

"I thought maybe I saw something familiar. If you looked like Irene at the same age, that might have explained it." He put the photo in its envelope and the pieces of newspaper in theirs and returned everything to his pocket.

"I don't look like Irene. The Cramers, I suppose, except not him."

"Not who?"

"The Harry Cramer I talked to."

"What? When?" He leaned forward. "You found Harry Cramer. He's alive?"

"Was. He may well be dead by now. In '74 I found an old gentleman in Lymington named Harry Cramer. I went to see him. He was blind, and well into his seventies. And he had a French wife and they'd been married for forty years and never had any children. So no hits, no runs, no errors. I never even got to bat."

Andy took off his glasses and twirled them by the frame. "Maybe he had an affair with your mother. Maybe all her secrecy was related to the fact that you're illegitimate."

Lili shook her head. "No. I don't think so. It's not like Irene, for one thing. For another, all my instincts said the old man was telling the truth. He'd never heard of me. He was simply the wrong Harry Cramer."

"Okay, if you say so." He looked at the photograph again. "There must be something we can compare with this, pictures of your mother as a young girl, a young woman."

Lili got up and stacked the tea things on the tray. "I've never seen any. I always told you Irene was reserved. She's not the type to show me old snapshots and gush stories of her youth."

"You implied more. We talked about it a few times and you made it seem that she'd always treated the past as taboo. Something not to be discussed. And for her generation, that would tie right in to my illegitimacy theory."

Lili went to the kitchen and he followed her. "That's true," she admitted. She didn't say anything more immediately. Being with Andy seemed to have thrown her into a time warp. Lili ignored the dishwasher and washed the mugs and Andy automatically reached for a towel and dried them. "Listen," she said finally, "my mother's a tough customer. We had a terrible fight several years ago because she had sold the Fielding house."

He put down the towel and lay his hand on her arm. It was the first time he'd touched her since he walked in. "The house you loved so much?"

"The very same. I heard about it right after you left. I never got over it. I still haven't. Mother and I are barely on speaking terms these days. All the same, I don't believe she could be an accessory to murder. She's basically naive, and . . . gentle. There's no violence in her."

He hadn't really listened to the last bit. "Your house," he said softly. "Poor love. What a rotten thing. Any chance of getting it back?"

Andy understood. In all these years, not another soul ever had. When she'd dared to hint that she dreamed of regaining an old house in Massachusetts, Peter or Loy, or Irene, for that matter, acted as if she were insane. But Andy didn't. This time the tears wouldn't be stopped. She was crying and there was no way to hide it.

Andy pulled her close and Lili sobbed against his chest. She was crying for the whole thing now; for the young lovers they'd been, for his obsession with an ugly piece of history and all it had driven him to, for the anguish of losing him, for the pain of losing the house. "Nobody but you has ever understood how I felt about it," she gasped between sobs. "Nobody."

"A lot of people don't have a sense of place," he said. "These days we all move around and it doesn't seem to matter. But there is such a thing, and if you feel it, then it's overwhelming."

A sense of place. Yes, that was it. But a phrase, no matter the insight it held, wouldn't stop her crying. Andy picked her up and carried her back to the living room and sat down with her on his lap and let her cry and rocked her as if she were a child. She wasn't, of course; she was a mature woman. And if she let this continue, it would lead to only one thing, and she didn't want that to happen. Not by default, as it were, not by accident, not without thinking out the implications and having the ground rules clear. With an enormous effort of will, Lili pulled free of his arms.

"Not like this," she said.

"No," he agreed. "Not like this and not now. I'm going to go, love. Can I ring you tomorrow?"

She nodded because she couldn't trust herself to speak.

Lili had a six-thirty call at the studio the next morning. They were taping sections of the next three shows, segments that involved only her and some diagrams. It was a special little series within the series, Lili showing layouts of typical kitchens, the sort of thing developers had spread all over America, and discussing how they could be changed to something more exciting.

"Been out on the town, Lili?" the makeup man asked. "Your eyes are all red."

"Yes," she lied. "Big party last night. Can you repair the damage?"

He stepped back and studied her. "Yes, but I'm going to put in for a raise for all this extra work."

"I'll buy you a drink," Lili promised.

It was banter, not serious complaining. The makeup man wielded his long-handled brushes and kept stepping back and biting his lip. After ten minutes he turned on a powerful spotlight and studied her in the glare. "Okay, your public will never know you've been a naughty girl."

"Thanks, I owe you one. I won't forget."

She went down the hall to the room where her set was permanently in place. They used it for other shows as well, but after six years she thought of it as hers. Joanie Fine, her producer, was waiting. "Good morning. You look as tired as I feel."

"Oh, terrific. That sets me up. I thought the makeup covered all."

"Probably will on camera. You ready?"

"Yes."

But she wasn't. The diagrams were on a standing easel, and periodically she had to flip them back and expose the next one. The sheets of paper kept slipping out of Lili's fingers. Once she fumbled and moved two at a time and didn't realize it until she was halfway into her spiel. "Sorry," she murmured. They began again. This time she forgot her lines.

"Lili, is something wrong? Are you ill?"

"No. I'm sorry, Joanie. Give me five minutes, then we'll take it one more time from the top and I'll get it right."

She spent the short break down the hall at the coffee machine, sipping hot brown water masquerading as the real thing and trying to sort out her seething thoughts. What was wrong with her was Andy Mendoza. No, not only him. Peter and Jeremy Crandall as well. The three men and their various roles in her life were chasing each other through her brain. It had to stop, at least for a couple of hours. Right now she faced a task that had nothing to do with any of them, and everything to do with herself. She was supposed to be a pro. Lili squared her shoulders and walked back to the studio. This time she was word-perfect.

It was noon before she got back to the apartment. She heard the phone ringing as she unlocked the door and dashed to answer it, noting as well that the red message light on her answering machine was flashing.

"It's me, sweetheart."

"Peter, hi. Did you see Crandall? How did it go?"

"I saw him. I'm not quite sure how it went. No fisticuffs, not even any shouting. We were both laid back, very cool. In the end I don't think anything important was said. He certainly didn't crack. I don't think I did."

"Does he suspect we think he's lying through his teeth?"

"Yeah, I think he does. But it's all underground; at this point nobody's giving anything away. Any word from Loy?"

"I just this minute walked through the door. Hold on and I'll check my machine."

She put down the receiver and played through her messages. Andy had called twice. Hearing his voice startled her almost as much as it had last night. "Nothing from Loy," she reported to Peter.

"Shit. Lili, what the hell do we do next?"

"Look, there's been a kind of crazy coincidence." She hesitated, choosing her words. "You may not believe this, but Andy Mendoza turned up last night."

"You're right, I don't believe it."

"It's true. And remember, Andy has never had anything to do with his family. He's no part of the Mendoza Group we know and love, so it's only a chance in a million that he'll know anything, but it can't hurt for me to ask."

"Lili, are you sure you can trust this guy? I don't mean personally, that's your business. But the Mendozas are real powers. Major league. Like the Morgans or the Rothschilds, only more so."

"I know that. And it's okay. I can trust Andy."

"How can you say that after—"

"Don't ask a lot of questions, please, Peter," she interrupted.

He took a long breath. "Okay, sweetheart, the ball's in your court. Don't fumble."

"I won't. Call you as soon as I've anything to report."

"Or if you hear from Loy. Ditto this end."

The messages from Andy both asked that she call him back right away. She did. He must have been waiting by the phone in his room; he answered on the first ring. "Where have you been? I was worried."

As if it were the old days. As if they always knew each other's schedules. "I'm a working woman, Andy. I had an early call at the studio."

"Yes, of course. Silly of me." He sounded chagrined. "Look, I don't think I explained very well last night. It's been bugging me for hours." He'd been storing it up, now it all spilled out over the impersonal wires. "I didn't get in touch only because I thought you might identify Irene. I hoped so, of course, but I also couldn't go ahead without telling you first. Do you understand?"

"Yes. Andy, it's all right, about that part I do understand. Anyway, I told you before, there's no way I'm going to worry about my mother being mixed up in something like that. It's simply not her style."

He didn't respond to that. "Have you had lunch? Can we have it together?"

"Okay. Why not?" She almost told him to come over, she had salad makings in the refrigerator. But she didn't, she wasn't ready to go into the kitchen and fix a meal for him, to slide so easily back into the pattern that had once given her such joy. It would hurt too much when it ended. "There's a good place near you. Blue Billy's, Fifty-sixth between Broadway and Seventh Avenue. On the downtown side. It's a short block, you won't miss it. Meet you there in forty minutes."

The restaurant was crowded. He was waiting for her at the bar up front, but he'd requested a table. "Ten minutes, they said. Will you have a drink?"

"Perrier with lime."

"Still dieting?"

He smiled, and it was the same old smile, and she was sitting with him in a bakery in Brighton eating cream cakes and moaning about being too fat and trying to figure out why this wonderful man was paying her so much attention.

"Still doing a lot of things," Lili said.

"The same but different," Andy said softly. He touched her cheek with one finger. "I'd forgotten how your eyes change color when you wear blue."

She had on a deep-blue crepe blouse and Calvin Klein trousers in a pale blue-and-gray plaid with a matching jacket. Blue was Andy's favorite color. Had it been deliberate? She didn't know, subconscious anyway. His finger burned against her skin and she moved away. He stared at her for a long moment, the tiger eyes intense behind the horn-rims, then he looked down at his drink.

A few seconds later the maître d' tapped Andy's shoulder, picked up their drinks and led them to their table. A waiter appeared, very young and fresh-faced and aggressively extrovert. "Hi, folks, I'm Bobby, your waiter this afternoon. Today our specials are . . ." He recited a long list of dishes; it was impossible to register what they were—and, of course, there was no way to know what any of them cost.

"Did you get any of that?" Andy asked when the boy left.

"Not a lot. It's a deplorable habit and it's spreading. I'm always slamming it on television. Shows you how much influence I have. This place does a great pasta salad though."

"I don't like cold spaghetti."

"Stop being so horribly English. They're fresh out of roast beef and Yorkshire pud."

In the end he was convinced and they both ordered the day's pasta salad. It was delicious. "I guess I like cold spaghetti after all," Andy said.

"It's nothing to do with spaghetti, these are fusilli." Lili waved a forkful of twisted corkscrew pasta. "Different pastas have special tastes and each has an affinity for particular sauces and treatments."

"If you say so."

She stopped. "I'm nattering on, as you'd say, aren't I?"

"Maybe a bit. To avoid less pleasant topics. Have you thought any more about what I said?"

"Of course I have. But I want to change the subject for a while. It's waited since 1939, Andy, can it wait a little longer?"

"Sure."

He'd always had the knack of giving her his complete attention and making her know it. He still could do it. And not only with her, she thought. It was one of his talents, probably what made him able to get the people he wrote about to bare the intimate details of their lives. In a way that's what she was about to do. "Do you remember a conversation we had years ago? About coincidences."

"I remember. More like a fight, is my memory."

"Parts of it. Anyway, I've got a beauty for you."

"Coincidence seems to plague us. Okay, carry on, I'm listening."

"I'm up to my eyeballs with the Mendoza Group. And I think they're trying to shaft me. Or somebody who works for them is."

"No surprise, they shaft everybody. How in hell did you get involved with them?"

"It's not only me. I'm part of a takeover bid for a company. I have two partners. One of them has a long-term relationship with your high-powered family, and we naturally went to them for advice. What we're trying to do is their specialty."

"Taking things over, yes, they're good at that. Are you the only one who thinks they're doing the dirty, or do your partners agree?"

"One of them does, the other one can't be reached at the moment." It was on the tip of her tongue to explain about Loy, but she didn't. It was too complicated and there were already too many things to explain. "The guy we're supposed to be working with is named—" Lili stopped and looked around. "Maybe I'd better not say."

Andy shook his head. "I'm beginning to feel like a character in a Robert Ludlum novel."

Lili ignored that and fished a piece of paper out of her bag and scribbled Jeremy Crandall's name on it. She pushed the message over to Andy's side of the table. "Does this name mean anything to you?"

He looked at it and shook his head again. "Not a thing. Sorry. But I have nothing to do with the business, you know that."

"Yes, I only hoped. Andy, could you find out anything? Very, very discreetly."

He pursed his lips and thought for a moment. "Asking's easy. It's the discreet part that's tough. When it comes to closing ranks and enforcing discipline, my relations make the Mafia look like amateurs."

She was crestfallen. "That's what I was afraid of."

"Don't give up so easy, love. Where there's a will, etcetera. Let me think about it for a couple of hours."

He wanted to stay with her after lunch. "A walk in Central Park," he suggested. "Or a film, if you'd rather."

"I can't, I'm sorry. I have a lot of business to take care of." She really had nothing pressing for the afternoon, but she was terrified of what was happening, what she was feeling. Andy and Lili together again, as if the past ten years hadn't happened. But they had and she still had the scars, and she wasn't going to walk into the quagmire so easily a second time. They parted and she promised to call him the next day.

As it turned out, she phoned him that evening after a conversation with Peter, who was touching base as arranged, but had nothing to report. "What about your tame Mendoza?" Peter asked.

"Tame he's not. And he couldn't come up with anything off the top of his head. He promised to think about it. Listen, Peter, I'd like you to meet him. It can't hurt, and if he does get anything, it's better if you've sized him up before evaluating it."

"Fine. Anyway, I'd like to meet Wellington."

"Wellington?" She questioned.

Peter chuckled. "I was thinking of Waterloo."

"Oh. And I'm Napoleon. Is that it?"

"That's it."

"Screw you. I'll see if I can set something up and get back to you. What's your schedule like for the next twenty-four hours?"

"Busy, but this takes precedence. Only give me as much notice as you can. By the way, did you see the closing market quotes?"

"No. Tell me."

"Bass and Demmer's slipped half a point."

"Terrific. Exactly what I needed to hear."

When the three met for breakfast the following morning, Andy put a different slant on it. "If the stock's sliding, it means things are cooling off. That could be good for you, I'd think."

Peter nodded. He'd come to this meeting with prejudice. Years ago, when he was a little in love with Lili, and ready and willing to be a lot in love, it was the ghost of this man that had wrecked everything. Besides, he wasn't prepared to like anybody named Mendoza. But Andy impressed him in spite of that. Friendly, very frank, no false modesty when Peter mentioned having read and enjoyed most of his books. He had everything Peter had warmed to in the English writ large— politeness and charm and a dry sense of humor. Brains as well. Andy seemed to have sized up the situation very accurately.

"I've got something for you," he said. "Not much. I wish I could say I'll get more, but I don't think I can."

"Fast work in any case," Peter said. "Shoot."

They were in Lili's apartment, there was no need to speak in code. Andy flipped open a small notepad. "Jeremy Crandall went to work for the Mendoza Group seven years ago. Fresh out of the Wharton School of Business."

"I always thought it was Harvard Business School," Lili said.

"Same thing," Peter interjected. "They clone them. Go on, Andy."

"He's always been in the New York office and that would seem to make him less than favored. Their pattern is to ship the best and the brightest to Europe, usually Spain, to be indoctrinated."

"So he could be acting privately," Lili said. "Throwing us to the wolves for reasons of his own, nothing to do with his bosses."

"I said *seems* to make him less favored," Andy reiterated. "It also turns out that he speaks fluent Spanish and spent two of his undergraduate years at the University of Salamanca."

Peter whistled through his teeth. "He could have been co-opted, then, is that it?"

"Yup." Andy closed his notebook with a snap. "That's a very wild supposition. It could also be that the facts of Salamanca and fluent Spanish made him apply for a job with the company, and made the Mendoza Group hire him. There's nothing sinister in that."

Lili rested her head on her hand and pushed croissant crumbs around the table with one finger. "No, there isn't. We're really grasping at straws. Anyway, what good is it going to do us to know what Crandall's up to? Unless we can find a way to beat him, it's irrelevant."

Peter had another concern. "Mind telling us where you got the information? If somebody's been alerted to our suspicions, it's better if we know about it."

"Not to worry," Andy said. "I decided the best disguise was no disguise at all. I got it from a secretary in the London office. I told her a paper here had asked me to do a piece on the family firm in New York. My relatives never much like what I write, but they know I'm going to write it anyway and the standing orders are for me to be given any information I require. My illustrious half brother figures that's better than what I might imagine. Only that's why it's so pedestrian. I'm not in sufficient good graces to get you the secrets out of the office safes."

"Not safes these days," Lili said. "Data bases in whirring computers." She rose and started to clear the table. Both men helped. When it was done, they returned to the living room. "Okay, guys," she said. "Any ideas about how we proceed?"

Peter glanced quickly at Andy. He didn't like him that much.

"I'd better go and let you two lay your plans," Andy said instantly. "May I call you later, Lili?"

"Yes, do." And when she came back from seeing him out, "Well, did you like him?"

"Very much. I can understand the attraction." Peter's voice gentled. "You're still in love with him, aren't you, sweetheart?"

She sank heavily into a chair. "I guess I am. I've never been out of love with him. But I'm scared to death he'll be around for a while, then up and leave me again. I don't think I can go through that a second time, Peter."

"Don't," Peter said softly. "Look after yourself for once, your own best interests. Unrequited love's a bore. Ask the man who should know."

"Yes." She smiled at him. "I wish I'd fallen in love with you instead."

"Once upon a time I wished that too." He got up and kissed her on the forehead. "Advice to the lovelorn's closed for the day. Lili, we've got to do something. I'm sick that we haven't heard from Loy, but we can't wait any longer."

"I know. Only what do we do?"

"Look, the operative commands up to now have all come from Jeremy Crandall. He's been acting as chief honcho, right?"

"Right."

"Well, you and I know he's double-dealing, or acting for someone else, or whatever. Not to be trusted. So we should follow our own instincts. What are yours?"

"Talk to some of the board members," she said immediately. "That's what I said as soon as we heard about the white knight. Why should they take Randolph Demmer's advice and sell to the guy from New Mexico, if they can be convinced they'll make more money with us?"

"My thought exactly," Peter agreed. "And we have two options, though we won't necessarily mention them up front. Either we get assurances that some of them will vote with us and we force a stockholders meeting, or we go back to the original scenario and try and buy one or two of them out and have the controling interest ourselves." He lit a cigarette. "That brings us back to money."

"No," Lili said. "Not the way you mean. I don't think money's a problem, Peter. I think that was a smoke screen Crandall put up. With what we've got and our plans, I don't see why a bank wouldn't back us. If we can get a commitment to sell to *us* and not the nutcase millionaire, I think we can put a deal together."

"Okay, it makes sense. So buying is what we really want. That's our opening negotiating posture."

"Yes, that's it." She crossed to her desk and pulled the list of board members from the drawer. "Whom do we start with?"

"I don't have to look again," Peter said. "I know them all by heart. And I know who I think is likely."

"Willa Grayson? The disgruntled daughter of the dead Mr. Bass?"

"Nope. Bass has been dead for twelve years. I didn't get the feeling that Mrs. Grayson was still mourning him. Somebody with a fresher grudge. Harvey Michael Demmer's mommy."

The next day was Thursday. Lili had to tape a restaurant appearance in the afternoon, but she was free until three P.M. They'd decided that she should be the one to call on Mrs. Demmer. "According to Harvey Michael," Peter had said, "Mommy's not only afraid of the old man, she hates him. So maybe she hates men in general. It's only a hunch, Lili, but I think you've got a better chance than I have."

And she agreed. Which was why she was standing in the lobby of a building on East Sixty-fifth Street at eleven A.M. Thursday morning, being ogled by a lascivious doorman. She'd called the woman the night before. In theory an unannounced visit would be better, but in practice it was impossible. These days you couldn't get to the upper floors of any decent Manhattan building without being vetted and announced. She had to telephone and imply that she wanted to discuss something related to her show.

"Lili Cramer," the woman had said. "Hey, what do you know? But my kitchen isn't anything fancy. When my husband was alive we ate out a lot. And now I don't—"

"It's a series on Manhattan apartments. I'd simply like to talk to you," Lili had interrupted smoothly.

"Well, there's no harm in talking. Come over, then."

So now the doorman was studying her and talking into the house phone. "Yeah, that's right. The lady what talks about restaurants on TV. I seen her plenty of times. She's Lili Cramer, I'm sure of it."

Lili was grateful for human nature. She could walk down any street, eat in any restaurant, shop in any store and be unrecognized. But if she jogged people's memories, said who she was, put on her television smile and asked if they recognized her, they almost always did. Maybe they didn't, but they said they did. Nobody wants to admit to ignorance of popular culture, not in New York. She thanked the doorman and headed for the elevator.

Louise Demmer was a brassy bottle-blond. In her mid-fifties, Lili guessed. Not a pretty woman, she had a long, narrow face and no chin, but she was tall and what had obviously once been a fabulous figure was still very good. She was wearing one of the old Diane Von Furstenberg wraparound dresses. It wasn't the height of fashion anymore, but it showed off her shape.

She shook Lili's hand with a mixture of wariness and avidity and drew her into a living room that was a jumble of periods and styles, crowded with furniture and knickknacks, every inch of wall space hung with something. "Sit down. Over here, the light's better." Mrs. Demmer perched on the edge of a brocaded slipper chair and indicated the embrace of a plushy sofa.

"It's very kind of you to see me," Lili said, "But I have to tell you up front, it has nothing to do with my show."

The other woman's mouth fell open, then she jumped up. "Look, lady, I don't know who you are or what this is about, but—"

"Mrs. Demmer, I *am* Lili Cramer. I'm not here with any criminal intent. But I had to see you, and I was afraid you wouldn't agree if I told you the real reason."

Louise's eyes were close-set and pale. They narrowed as she studied her caller. "Maybe you better tell me quick, then get out of here."

"Okay, if that's what you want me to do when I've said my piece, I'll do it. But hear me out, will you do that?"

"It's not going to cost me anything? You're not selling something?"

Robbers, rapists, murderers, and salespeople, New Yorkers considered them equally dangerous. "Definitely not," Lili said. "The other way round. I want to buy something."

"What?"

"Your shares in Bass and Demmer Publications."

"Jesus," Mrs. Demmer said. She repeated it. "Jesus. Is that what this is all about? What's it got to do with you? Besides, my father-in-law is selling the company to some coin collector–type from New Mexico."

"He can't do that without the consent of the board. And nobody can make you sell your shares to anyone unless you want to."

"You don't know my shithead father-in-law." The woman had sat down after her first outburst, now she got up again. "Jesus." It seemed to be her favorite word. "I need a drink. You want something?"

It was quarter past eleven in the morning. But this was in the line of duty. "I'd love a little sherry if you have it."

"Maybe, let me see." She pawed around in the liquor cupboard in the corner. "My son, Harvey, he sometimes buys stuff like that. Yeah, Tío Pepe, that's sherry, isn't it?"

"Yes, it is," Lili said. And when a large wineglass full of it was handed to her, "Thank you." The other woman had a water glass half full of scotch. With one ice cube.

"Me, if I want a drink, it has to be a belt," she said. "Is the sherry okay? It's not turned to vinegar, has it? God knows how long it's been in there. Harvey must have bought it, like I said. He's been gone a couple of weeks. Went to Europe. Too bad you didn't come sooner. Harvey sold his shares. I thought the old bastard would shit a brick when he found out." She chuckled.

"I already own Harvey's shares, Mrs. Demmer." Lili made the announcement and waited.

The thin-lipped mouth fell open once more. "How can you? He sold them to that smartass who tried to take us over on the quiet. Peter somebody."

"Peter Fowler of Fowler Distribution. He's my partner."

Mrs. Demmer sat back and sipped her scotch. "I think I'm beginning to see what you're doing here."

"I hope so. Look, I'm prepared to pay you a substantial sum over the going price. In the past two days the stock has slipped to six ninety from seven fifty. Give it a few days and it will be back at six twenty-five or lower. Because Wall Street knows this coin collector isn't going to do a thing but sit on the magazines the way your father-in-law's been doing for years. There's no percentage in that for you. Not unless you have a sentimental attachment to the status quo."

The blond laughed. "Sentimental, that's a good one. No, I've got no sentiment where those goddamn magazines are concerned. When my husband and I got married we were a couple of kids crazy in love. I was a showgirl and the old man didn't approve of me. Jealous, that's why. I always swore he had the hots for me." She stretched out one leg. It was sheathed in the sheerest nylon and shod with the highest possible heel. "Still pretty good, huh?"

"Great," Lili said. It wasn't flattery, it was true. "You make me green with envy." That was true too. But it wasn't the other woman's legs she envied.

"For my gams or my stock?" the blond demanded, laughing again. So she wasn't stupid.

"Both," Lili admitted.

"Yeah, I bet. Anyway, the old man put my Harvey through the ringer. I mean my husband, my son's Harvey Michael Junior. Not that randy Randolph didn't lean on him too. He did. And my life's been hell because of him."

"Then why—"

"Why don't I jump at the chance to do something that'll make him squirm, huh? It's not that simple. See this apartment? I don't own it outright. It's in a trust and Randolph Demmer's the trustee. Same goes for my income. Comes from the trust too. I don't think he could get everything away from me in the end. My lawyer says he couldn't. But he sure could make life rough on me while we battled it out."

Lili sipped the sherry. Her brain was racing. She had a few extra seconds because Louise Demmer had finished her drink and gotten up to pour another. "You want some more of that stuff?"

"No thanks. Look, I'm trying to put something together off the top of my head. You've got six percent of the stock."

"Yup."

"And we have twenty-five percent. So if you sell us yours, we have thirty-one percent, and we outvote your father-in-law."

"The rest of the board will go with him, and all together they've got . . ." Louise stopped to calculate.

"Minus your shares and your son's, they have eleven percent," Lili said. She'd long since worked all this out. "Twenty-eight and eleven makes a possible thirty-nine percent that Randolph Demmer can control. But I think we can get one or two members of the board to come with us. Why shouldn't they? We represent a genuine profit opportunity. Your father-in-law and his tame buyer do not."

"You mean you can get Willa, right? She's the only other one with a big chunk. The rest are distant cousins and things like that. One or two percent each."

Lili didn't answer; she didn't have to, the numbers were obvious.

"But, like I said," Louise continued, "I can't sell to you. The old man can make it too tough for me."

"What if we don't merely pay an attractive price? What if we give you preferred stock in the holding company? You'll share in the future profits and get a lump sum now. The best of both worlds."

"You really want it, don't you, sweetie pie?"

Lili stood up and she didn't smile. "Yes, we really want it. I'm not trying to kid you about that, Mrs. Demmer. And you're not kidding me either. You really want to sell. You'd absolutely love dumping that old man in it up to his ears."

The other woman shrugged. "There's no secret about that. Yeah, I would."

"Okay, I'm showing you how to do it with practically no risk. Are you going to play?"

"Practically no isn't the same as none," the other woman said.

"No, it's not. Life doesn't work that way. As I'm sure you've noticed."

"Yeah."

They faced each other for a few moments. Lili was determined not to speak first, and she didn't have to.

"I'm tempted." The blond took a gulp of her scotch. "I'm very tempted. But I gotta think about it and talk to my lawyer. I'll let you know."

"Fine. But I can't give you more than twenty-four hours. I'll call you tommorow morning at eleven."

"If you had to bet your life," Peter asked later, "how would you bet? Which way will she go?"

Lili thought for a moment. "She'll sell to us," she said at last.

And that was how it turned out. There was a condition however. "I have to hear it from Willa Grayson that she's going to vote with you and squeeze the old man out. Until I do, we haven't got a deal."

That was Peter's task. Lili had been to Louise Demmer's on Thursday, her answer was received on Friday morning. Peter phoned Willa Grayson immediately but was told she was tied up for most of the weekend. She didn't refuse to see him, just said she couldn't manage to do so before Sunday night.

"Maybe by then we'll have heard from Loy," Peter said hopefully. "I hate doing all this without telling her about it. It's probably not even legal."

They were at the counter of a midtown coffee shop, eating soggy tuna sandwiches. "We can't wait," Lili said. "It's all talk and promises at this stage anyway. Probably not legally binding."

"But in something like half an hour we're going to be committed," Peter said. In thirty minutes they had an appointment at the bank across the street.

It was the bank where Peter had done business for years. Both his personal and business accounts were there. It was a logical place to begin looking for financing. "I wish to hell we'd come here first and never got tied up with the Mendoza Group," he said to Lili as they waited in the busy lobby for the man they were to see.

"Me too, but it was Loy's money that started everything, and she had a right to pick the team."

"Yes, don't remind me." He was really worried about Loy. Lili understood. But while she agreed that it was odd that they hadn't heard anything for almost a week, and even odder that Loy had left no word of how to reach her, she didn't share Peter's concern.

"Loy's not fragile," she said. "I think she can take care of herself very well. It's stupid to be upset unless and until there's something definite to be upset about."

They were ushered into a private office in the rear. The banker shook their hands and settled back and indicated he was willing to listen. He sat patiently while Peter made the presentation, with occasional additions from Lili.

They laid it all out. The nature of Bass & Demmer, the history and content of the magazines, the makeup of the board, and LPL's future plans. It took over half an hour and the man behind the desk never rushed them or made them feel they were wasting his time. Finally they had said everything they could say and used every argument they knew.

"So we're going to need something under a million to take control and start operating," Peter finished up. "Will you guys play?"

It was the banker's turn. He didn't rush to bat. He tamped tobacco into a pipe after asking Lili if she minded, and fussed with getting it lit. Finally, "By today's standards, it's a very small deal, Peter. Normally small deals aren't worth the paperwork."

"Okay, are there exceptions to 'normally'?"

"Sometimes, sure. But one thing still puzzles me. You say your advisor was a man with the Mendoza Group. They're masters at this sort of thing. Why are you coming to us now?"

They'd anticipated this question and planned for it. Lili took over. "As Peter explained, they were acting only by virtue of their relationship to the third partner, Señora Loyola Perez. The Mendoza Group has already told us that anything under twenty-five million is too small to interest them."

The banker sucked on his pipe and nodded. "I'm sorry this Mrs. Perez isn't with you today. I'd like to meet her."

"We're sorry too," Lili said. "But she's in Spain. That's where most of her assets are. A second line of economic defense. Loy's trying to see if she can free up some capital, in case we can't float a leveraged buy."

The banker nodded again. "I see. That's part of the problem, however. It's not a straight leveraged buy. If it were, it would be much simpler. For one thing, the five magazines you want to sell are unlikely to bring enough to recoup the cost of acquisition of the whole package. For another, you have a hostile corporation on your hands. That can lead to a lot of trouble."

"Not once we control it," Peter said. "It's only Randolph Demmer who's hostile. The rest just want peace and profits. Once we've squeezed him out, they'll play ball."

"Maybe." The pipe was creating a haze of blue smoke. "I need to speak to my loan committee, of course, and I will. I think I know what they'll say, and at this point that's my answer too. Maybe. I'm impressed with your plans and the initiative you've shown. Not to mention the degree of your personal financial commitment. I know you're a first-class manager, Peter, and I think Miss Cramer here is a remarkable asset. Her reputation is going to mean a lot to the future of those magazines you elect to keep and publish. But I still have to say maybe. It depends first on how my committee sees it. Second on whether you can actually bring these two stockholders to heel." He looked through the papers Peter had given him, "Mrs. Demmer and Mrs. Grayson, right? You've got to get them to cooperate or I'm afraid we definitely won't be interested."

And that's how they had to leave it. "What about tomorrow?" Peter asked as he and Lili went through a post mortem over coffee at the lunch counter of the small restaurant across the street. "You working?"

Lili shook her head. "No, I'm going out of town. Only for twenty-four hours. I'll be back by late Sunday afternoon, before you tackle Willa Grayson."

Peter stirred half a spoonful of sugar into his cup. "Tell me to mind my business if you want, but are you going out of town alone?"

"No, not alone."

"I see." He turned and covered her hand with his. "Be careful, sweetheart. Don't lead with that pretty little chin."

She shook her head again. "It's not like that, not the way you think. I'm not running off for a romantic interlude. It's business of a sort."

"I'd have thought you had enough business on your plate at the moment."

"Not my business, Andy's. I'm only going along to help."

Which was what he'd asked. "Lili, I can't put it off any longer, I have to go to Fielding. Will you come with me and help?"

❧ 15 ❧

New York, Massachusetts, Spain: 1981

They'd decided to drive to Boston, and to leave very early. Andy picked her up before dawn on Saturday. He'd rented a Porsche. The powerful car swallowed the empty Manhattan streets. "We'll go by the George Washington Bridge, won't we?" Andy asked.

Lili was navigator. She glanced at the map on her lap. "We can, sure."

"Please, let's do that. When I was a kid I had a book, *Cities of the World*. It had a picture of the George Washington Bridge. It looked to me like the most fantastic thing in the universe."

They rolled up the Henry Hudson Parkway, watching the darkness fade and the Jersey Palisades on the other side of the river emerge from the night. When they reached the bridge, the sun still wasn't up and festooned lights hung like jeweled necklaces in the sky. "Whoopee!" he shouted. "There it is. Hello, bridge. I told you I'd see you someday."

"Did it seem an impossible dream?" Lili asked. "Why, when you were so rich?"

"Being rich in that way doesn't feel like it, not to a child. It felt like being confined instead. Big house, lots of servants, everything always having to be done according to some preordained ritual."

"But not anymore," Lili said.

"No, not anymore. Definitely not today." He leaned back, stretching his arms full-length, leather-gloved hands gripping the steering wheel. "Free at last!" he sang out. "Good God almighty, we's free at last!"

His enthusiasm was contagious, and Lili laughed with delight.

In a pink dawn they turned east onto the Cross River Parkway, still innocent of traffic, and headed for the Merritt. "More scenic than the New England Thruway," Lili said. Andy's mood definitely called for the scenic route. It also dictated a breakfast stop at a McDonald's.

"There are McDonald's in London," he said. "But it's not the same."

"Next you'll be telling me you want to see Disney World."

"Absolutely. And Hollywood so I can take a coach tour of the homes of the stars."

"Bus tour," Lili corrected him. "This side of the water, coaches are only trains and horse-drawn carriages."

"What about cheap flights in the back of an airplane?"

"Yes, you're right. Only now we say economy."

"Fair enough," Andy said. "But last night I was invited to dinner at my editor's and she gave me scones and called them biscuits. With the main course, would you believe?"

"Yes, because biscuits are bread. What you're thinking of is a cookie."

"Yes, and braces are suspenders and suspenders are garters."

Lili leaned back, more relaxed than she'd been in weeks. "And kirby grips are bobby pins, and a solicitor is a lawyer, and the dole is unemployment, and sweets are candy, and a pavement is a sidewalk, and a hundred others I've forgotten."

"Forgetting the Queen's English must be high treason. Your lot have been traitors for years." He turned and grinned at her. "But I like you. I like you very much indeed." His look made the pronoun singular and personal and the miles dropped behind them and the Porsche rushed forward and the time passed in gaiety and banter.

By nine they were on the Massachusetts Turnpike and by

ten-fifteen at the Framingham exit. "It's better if we get off here," Lili said, looking at the map. "We don't need to go into Boston itself. Not if you want to go directly to Fielding."

"Yes," he said. "I do." Then, "Lili, you're wonderful to do this with me. Considering."

"Considering nothing. I've told you and told you, your suspicions are insane, at least as far as my mother is concerned. Besides, I love Fielding."

And years ago, when she was young and believed all things could be wonderful she had dreamed of taking him there and showing him her house. It was to be their honeymoon and Andy was going to love the house as much as she did and they would buy it. And he'd also love her and they would live happily ever after. Years ago in her dreams.

Lili braced herself for the shopping center at the edge of town, glad she'd seen it before and the shock was past. It was bigger and busier than she remembered, but that was to be expected. "This is all new since my day."

"The ubiquitous American 'mall.' Not exactly the original, is it?"

He referred to the historic tree-lined mall leading from Buckingham Palace to Admiralty Arch. Kings and queens rode along it in sumptuous royal carriages, and if they had the permission of the Lord Mayor, they might proceed and enter the City of London. "Not exactly," Lili agreed. "But Fielding has history too. It's one of the oldest towns in New England."

She directed him to Haven Avenue. "The library's on the next corner. I suppose we should start there."

He glanced at the clock on the Porsche's elaborate dashboard. "We've made excellent time. Want to show me a bit first?"

"I'd like that, but it's up to you."

"We tour first," Andy decided. "I'm not indulging you, I need to get a feeling for the background."

"Okay, head straight to the next set of lights. That's Kent's Pharmacy coming up on your left." But when she turned her head, it wasn't there.

Where the drugstore had always stood there was a restaurant. It had gingham tie-back curtains and window boxes.

"That *was* Kent's Pharmacy," Andy said. "Or did you mistake the corner?"

"No mistake," Lili said. She was staring at the stores on either side of the road. Not one was as she remembered. These were boutiques and gift shops; there was even an art gallery. "I was here when I first returned to the States in 'seventy-six," Lili said. "It's all been done over since then."

"Competition from that juggernaut on the outskirts," Andy said. "Happens all the time. Change or die, it's been a rule on every High Street in the western world."

"Main Street," Lili corrected him automatically. "What's High Street in England is Main Street here—my God!"

"What?"

"That's Petworth's Department Store."

Andy glanced quickly in the direction she pointed. He saw a red brick structure with large globe lights punctuating its exterior and wide steps leading to an angled entrance marked by tubbed trees. A sign said FIELDING ARCADE. He'd come to the light and it was red. Lili rolled down the car window and stared.

"Looks like the town's been tarted up," Andy said. "Somebody's idea of eighties chic."

"Petworth's has stood there for over a hundred years. They've all gone crazy."

"Boom on economy. Once more unto the bank . . . Which way from here?"

The light had changed. "Left on to Woods Road," Lili said. The Porsche took the turn smoothly. She started to speak again, then covered her mouth with her hand. "Stop," she whispered through her fingers.

He sidled to the edge of the road and braked. Beside him Lili was breathing hard and her face was white. "What's the matter, love?"

"Look. Just look."

He didn't know what to expect, and what he saw wasn't to his eyes particularly surprising. It was another standard American vista. A wide verge of grass fronted a complex of one- and two-story buildings with decks and sliding glass doors. There were cement paths lined with sapling trees. The construction was all wood, natural gray cedar shingling, and there was a large wooden sign a few feet ahead of them on the opposite side. WOODS HAVEN FARM ESTATES. Next to it was another, more temporary-seeming sign that advertised MODERN LIVING WITH TRADITIONAL CHARM—ONE- AND TWO-BEDROOM CONDOMINIUMS. SHOW HOUSE AND OFFICE STRAIGHT AHEAD.

"I take it this is all new too?" He reached over and lay his hand on her knee. Lili wore jeans and he could feel her trembling beneath the heavy cotton fabric.

"Yes," she said. She was still whispering. "Oh, my God, they cut down all the trees."

He waited a few seconds, knowing her pain, not knowing what to say to ease it. "Shall we go back, love, or go on?"

"Go on," she said.

He moved the car forward slowly, fearing what she would find, hoping that he was wrong.

"There's a gate about a mile down on the left." Her voice was low, slightly tremulous. "It's an addition since my day, but I saw it in 'seventy-six."

The gray-shingled buildings were behind them now. They seemed to have passed the development and Andy breathed a little easier. Two huge maples and a stand of pines came into view. "Those are your old trees, aren't they?"

Lili nodded, her tension quivering, setting up an almost audible hum. "There it is!"

The iron gates stood open, nearly obscured by heavy underbrush. Andy would have missed the spot if he were alone. "Do I turn up?"

"Yes," she murmured. The Porsche entered the long driveway. It was still lined with trees. "You can't see the house from here," Lili said. "Not until you go around that bend." She was leaning forward, reassured, almost unbearably excited.

"Any idea what we're going to say to whoever lives here now?" Andy asked. "I think—"

He never said what he thought. When they rounded the bend they were facing a construction site.

It was raw and new, but there'd been time for the house to be totally demolished. A huge hole in the ground had been prepared for foundations, but none were yet laid. There was a wide dirt road gashed through the land behind the hole. It came from the direction of Woods Haven Estates and two tractors and a bulldozer were parked on it. Because it was Saturday, the site was deserted.

He stopped and turned to pull her into his arms, but she'd already yanked open the door of the car and was running across the scarred ground. He followed her. "Lili! Please, love, let's go. You won't do yourself any good here."

She ignored him. She was at the very edge of the hole, staring into it. Andy joined her and tried to take her arm, but she pulled free. "Lili," he said again. She shook her head fiercely and he was silent.

A few yards away was another temporary sign. After some minutes she turned from the gaping wound in the earth and crossed to it. Andy followed and read over her shoulder. THIS SITE WILL BE THE WOODS HAVEN FARM ESTATES CLUBHOUSE. At his feet was some sort of booklet that had been dropped and forgotten. It was mudstained and damp. He picked it up.

A four-color job. Expensive, definitely up-market. The cover showed the complex they'd driven past. The first page was a brief history. "The town of Fielding was founded in 1649 and incorporated in 1690. By that time two families were already an integral part of Fielding's past and future, the Kents and the Petworths. Josiah Kent had built a mill near Willock's Stream and established himself at Haven Farm. In 1682 he bought the stand of woods between his farm and the mill from Adam Petworth for twenty-six wooden shillings . . ."

Beside him Lili still hadn't moved or spoken. Andy folded the brochure and shoved it into the pocket of the leather battle jacket he was wearing and turned to her and put both his hands on her arms. "Come away, love." He spoke softly, respectful of her grief. "Staying and looking will only make it worse."

She raised her face and he saw that tears were streaming down her cheeks, though she hadn't made a sound. "Come away," he said again.

Gently, he started to lead her back to the car, but they'd gone only a few steps when Lili broke from him and ran down the drive. Andy stood uncertainly for a moment, then decided not to follow. He watched her go. When she was out of sight he got back in the car and drove to the foot of the drive and parked and waited.

Lili didn't know where she was running, or why. To what? From where? From nothing. Where her house had been there was nothing. Inside her there was nothing. She felt empty, removed from space and time and feeling. Her feet didn't seem to be touching solid ground, it was as if she moved suspended in a fog.

She rounded the bend in the drive and went on past the trees to the road. Left. She must turn left because the condominiums were on the right. Straight on along the black asphalt surface, unaware of either passing cars or people. Fast. Faster than she'd ever run in her life. Because she was not bound by gravity, not on the earth, the fog enclosed her.

Finally she became aware of her pounding heart, of racking pain in her chest when she tried to draw breath, of a thudding in her head. And she could go no farther. Where she was she dropped. On her knees, palms pressed to the ground, hunched over, head hanging, sucking in air because the organism demanded survival.

Time passed, how long she could not say. The fog began to thin, her eyes to focus. She was on the bank of Willock's Stream. The grass was brown beneath her, but a patch of seedling nettles had started into growth a few inches from her left hand. She studied them; the leaves were miniature at this stage, but the veins showed. She counted the veins in the leaves. Six. She raised her gaze. The bank was deserted except for one man some ways downstream. He was standing in the water in hip boots, holding a fishing rod. He didn't seem to have noticed her.

Lili got to her feet, still not truly present to reality. She could absorb only small things, tiny inconsequential details such as the fact that seedling nettles had leaves with six veins. Nothing more. When she stood she staggered slightly. Suddenly there was nausea, great waves of it rising from her stomach to her gorge. She was going to be sick. A primal shame forced her to seek cover among the trees a few yards back.

She dashed for them. There was a struggling sapling growing between an old pine and a clutter of fallen, rotted logs.

Lili clung to the wiry trunk of the infant tree and vomited repeatedly over the logs.

At last she was heaving only yellow bile that burned her throat and she straightened and took a deep breath, then another. The nausea passed. She was weak and sweating, but she was no longer sick. She broke some branches from the pine and lay them over the mess she'd made. Then returned to the stream.

She knew it so well, knew so thoroughly every inch of this ground that she didn't have to investigate. She longed to drink and to bathe her face, but the water was inaccessible here. The bank was high and steep and the streambed six feet below. She'd have to go downstream some fifty yards before the bank sloped off and the stream rose and she could touch the water without diving in. The fisherman was still where he'd been. Lili turned away and headed back up the road.

Andy was sitting in the car waiting. When he saw her approach he got out. He didn't say anything and he didn't come to meet her, but when she was at his side he put his arms around her and held her close. "I decided you'd rather be alone for a while," he said.

She nodded because she still didn't trust herself to speak and he led her around the car and opened the door and helped her in, then got behind the wheel and turned the key. "Can we get out of here if I go straight ahead?"

"No." They'd be cut off by the stream.

"Too bad," he said, but he backed up into the drive and changed direction and drove out the way they'd come. When they passed the condominiums Lili looked neither right nor left, only stared straight ahead. He didn't speak nor did she, not until they'd passed the shopping center and were headed back to the turnpike.

"Where are you going?" Her voice was dull and lifeless. "You want to go to the library. It's all right, I'm okay."

"I'm not going to put you through that," he said. "Not today."

"It's all right," she said again. "Really. Nothing's going to undo it. You might as well get what you came for."

He slowed. "You're sure."

She nodded again.

"No," he muttered. "I don't have to be that much of a selfish bastard."

"Andy, go back. Let's go to the library. I want to. When we drove past, it looked exactly the same."

So they did. It was twelve-thirty when they walked up the broad granite steps and into the big room that was still full of golden oak chairs and tables and shelves, and still smelled of books and furniture polish. There was a water cooler by the entrance and Lili stopped and drank and noticed that something had been added. There was a sign saying NEW WING AND PUBLIC LAVATORIES. An arrow directed her down a short hall she didn't remember.

She murmured something to Andy, then went in the direction the arrow pointed and came to a door marked WOMEN. Her canvas shoulder bag had been in the car through the whole ugly time, and she had it now. She washed her hands and splashed water on her face and touched up her eyeliner and her lipstick and brushed her hair. Ordinary, automatically done things happening on the surface while the pain seethed somewhere below. Fortunately, she hadn't soiled her clothes. She was wearing jeans and a wool plaid lumberjack's shirt on top of a black turtleneck sweater. Except that she was pale, she looked fine, as if nothing had happened.

When she returned to the main library Andy was seated at a table staring into the raised eyeframe of a machine for viewing microfilm. That was new since her day too. She sat beside him and he looked up. "Okay?"

"Okay."

He returned to his task and she glanced around. Whatever the new wing might house, in here nothing much had changed. She was so grateful for that she almost wept again. She noticed that the librarian kept looking at her. Lili wondered if she should know her. They were about the same age. She remembered Miss Demel and she smiled. The librarian thought Lili was smiling at her, and she grinned back. Lili got up and approached the desk.

The librarian spoke first. "You're Lili Cramer, aren't you?"

"Yes. I'm sorry, I think I should know you, but I can't remember." Her throat was still raw and sore and she was surprised the words came out so normal and ordinary sounding.

"Oh, no, I don't think so. I'm from Kansas City. My husband and I moved here last year. I know you because of your television show. And because everybody in Fielding always talks about how you grew up here."

It was as if she were being reminded of another life in another time. Television and New York and everything that had been important until that morning seemed a distant, not quite real world. "Oh," she said. "I see. Did you say you've been here a year?"

"Yes, my husband's a computer programmer. He works in Boston, but we wanted to live in the country. Fielding is perfect; it's near enough, but it's still kind of rural."

"Not as much as it used to be."

They spoke in hushed tones. Miss Demel had always said that you had to be quiet in a library, but you didn't have to act as if your tongue had been cut out. Apparently, younger librarians felt the same. "Was the new development on Woods Road built when you came?" Lili asked. She needed to know, needed to keep probing the wound.

"Oh, sure, it's been up a few years, I think. The apartments are real nice, we looked at them. Didn't buy one though. Too expensive. We wanted at least two bedrooms and those are over a hundred thousand."

Lili nodded. The lump in her throat was swelling again. She didn't think she could speak without the tears starting. "We bought a house on Mill Street," the librarian volunteered. "It's real old and we're doing it over ourselves. I sure wish I could have a kitchen like the ones on your show."

Lili dragged a smile out of her quivering insides. "You will. Do things slowly, one room at a time. A great kitchen takes more careful planning and imagination than money. You'll see."

A woman came in and approached the desk and the librarian turned to her and Lili wandered away and rejoined Andy. His head was still bent over the microfilm machine. The old clippings and the photograph of the two women in Málaga lay on the table beside it. When she sat down he lifted his head and smiled at her and lay his hand next to her cheek. "You're a strong woman," he said.

"Tough Lili, that's me." There wasn't much humor in her voice, but she was trying. "What have you found?"

He frowned. "A lot, but I don't think it's much help. Have a look."

He wound back the film and showed her how to move it forward and she took his place and peered into the viewer. She was looking at the front page of the *Fielding Post Times* for April 25, 1939. The headline was big and black. "Amanda Kent Wanted for Murder."

The story ran five columns and had pushed everything else off the front page. "Police in England are seeking the former Amanda Kent, daughter of the late Thomas Kent and his wife, Jane, of Woods Road, for the murder of her husband, Emery Preston-Wilde, the Viscount Swanning . . ." It went on to describe the killing and Amanda's disappearance.

Halfway down the page was a picture of Amanda that had been taken five years before, when she was nineteen. It was a formal portrait that showed her in an off-the-shoulder gown wearing a double string of pearls. Her hair was shoulder-length and waved. She was very pretty, but in a rather boring and pedestrian way. Maybe that was only because of the photographer and the conventions of the time. Lili moved the microfilm forward. The *Post Times* had been a weekly, as far as she knew it still was, and for two months every issue featured a major story on the murder and Amanda's disappearance. She scanned them all, but there was no mention of Irene.

Lili looked up. Andy was staring at the newsprint pictures of Lady Swanning. Lili peered over his shoulder, then back at the microfilm. "You can see that they're the same girl," she said.

"Yes, but in this one it's still not clear, is it?"

She looked at the Málaga snapshot. "No, it's not clear. Maybe, but that's all."

He said something under his breath. She thought it was a curse and didn't ask him to repeat it. He turned back to the machine. "Have a look at something else." He changed the film and threaded it forward until he found what he was seeking. "Here, see what you think of this."

This time the date at the top of the newspaper was March 17, 1935. The headline read, "Petworth's Department Store Sold." Underneath was a picture of Irene shaking hands with a baldheaded man. Irene wore a dress with long sleeves and a peplum, the man had on a dark double-breasted suit. They were both smiling self-consciously for the camera.

Lili read the story. "Miss Irene Petworth announced today that her fourth cousin, Henry Davis Petworth of Newton, has bought Petworth's Department Store on Haven Avenue. The store has been a landmark in Fielding for more than a century. It was the Fielding General Store until Miss Petworth's late father enlarged it and gave it its new name . . ."

The article went on to say that Irene had inherited the business after the tragic death of her parents a few months earlier and ended by quoting her as saying that she was, " . . . very gratified because Petworth's is remaining in the family."

That sounded exactly like Irene. And the picture looked exactly like her. Lili studied it for a long time. She'd have known her mother in that photograph even if it was shown her with no explanation or caption. It wasn't so much her features as an attitude. The tilt of the head, the way she was standing. It was Irene beyond any question or shadow of a doubt. She turned her attention to the Málaga snapshot. Wordlessly, Andy handed her a small magnifying glass.

Despite its size, it was very powerful, the sort of thing used by photo editors. She adjusted the distance between the lens and the picture until she could see it clearly. The grain of the paper was now very pronounced, but so were the dresses, the hats, the beads, the sunlit faces of the two young women. Lili looked at them for a long minute, then she looked back into the microfilm machine. Finally she pointed to the photograph on the table. "Neither of those women is Irene."

"That's what I think too," Andy said. His tone was neutral. If he was disappointed, it didn't show. "That's presuming the one in the paper looks like your mother."

"It does. I'd recognize her anywhere at any time." She pointed to his snapshot again. "The other night I thought one of these two might have been her. It's the period and their ages, I guess. But when I compare that shot with Irene as she was four years before it was taken, I'm sure. She wasn't in Málaga that day."

"Looks like she wasn't," Andy said. "And even with the glass you can't be sure about the other one. That it's Amanda Kent, I mean."

Lili pursed her lips. "Let me look at the one in the *Post Times* again."

He'd started to change the microfilm once more, when the librarian approached. "I just remembered this." She put a stack of leather-bound books on the table between them. "Same period as the papers you asked for."

The books were about twelve by fifteen inches, bound in dark red leather. The word *Memories* was embossed in gold on the top and *Fielding High School* below. Andy looked puzzled.

"Yearbooks," Lili explained. "It's a standard American practice. A memento of their high school years for the graduating class." She flipped through them. "Here's 1934, that's the year my mother was graduated."

They paged through the book together, and were able to identify three candid shots of Irene involved in various school activities. The new information simply confirmed their earlier conclusion. Neither woman in the Málaga photo was Lili's mother.

"Amanda Kent was born in 1919," Andy said. "What year would she have been graduated?"

"Let's try 1937." Lili found the appropriate volume, but Amanda wasn't in it. A little more looking and they discovered that she'd been a member of the class of '36. "Graduating at seventeen's not unusual," Lili explained. "It depends on when your birthday comes."

Andy wasn't listening. He was turning the pages of *Memories* for 1936. "She's on almost every page," he said. "A popular kid. Pretty too."

"The Kents were a power here in those days." Lili moved closer to look over his shoulder. Amanda Kent smiled up at her in a dozen different poses. She was sitting on a sled and waving during the class's winter carnival. She was a member of the cast of the senior play. She was Prom Queen. All the pictures were black and white, of course, so there were only gray hints at her coloring. Her hair and her eyes were medium. And her nose was turned up and she was always smiling. She was adorable.

"She doesn't look like she could murder anybody," Lili murmured.

"In cold blood at that," Andy said. "But murderers seldom look the part."

A man had come in during the past ten minutes and sat at a table near theirs. Now he turned and shushed them loudly. He looked to be in his seventies. Lili thought she half recognized him. "Shh," he said again. "This is a library, not a dance hall."

Andy grimaced and went back to the yearbook. He used his magnifying glass to study it further, then lay the Málaga snapshot next to one of the clearest of the high school pictures of Amanda. He compared the two for a moment more, then motioned Lili to look.

She did, very carefully. Then she turned her glance to him and shook her head.

"Shit," Andy whispered, ignoring the withering glance of the old man. "That's what I think too."

He'd been in Boston once before, on a promotional tour for a book, and he'd liked it. They'd talked of going there after Fielding. Instead, they headed west toward the Berkshires. "Someplace quiet and peaceful," Andy decreed. He'd studied a map and some tourist guides and when they left the library, and he'd made a telephone call and a reservation.

Great Barrington was another quintessential New England town. Nearby was Tanglewood, famed summer venue of the Boston Symphony Orchestra, and two miles from the center of the city was the Garson House Hotel. It had been the estate of a man who made a fortune in the nineteenth-century cotton mills that once studded the area. Now it was a luxury hotel where the Victorian character had been preserved and the gardens promised to be lovely when spring really arrived.

"You asked for two rooms, Mr. Mendoza," the woman behind the reception desk said. "I can do that, but I wondered if you might prefer a two-bedroom suite?"

"If it's the very nicest you have," Andy said.

She smiled at him. "Yes, it is. It's booked way ahead for the Tanglewood season. But at this time of year we're not busy."

That had to be an understatement. It seemed as if Andy and Lili were the only guests in the place. "We serve only breakfast at the moment," the receptionist said. "The full dining room doesn't open until June. There are two or three very nice restaurants nearby where you can have dinner. Will that be all right?"

"Fine," Andy assured her.

The suite was fine too. A large sitting room looked over the garden and a distant pond, two bedrooms opened off it. One was done in soft green carpeting and chintz printed with overblown roses, the other in blue-and-white plaid set off by a darker blue rug. "Flowers for the lady?" the man carrying their two small suitcases asked.

"Definitely," Andy said.

Lili took no part in the decision. As soon as they were shown to the suite she went to the window and stood staring out at the garden and left the two men to settle everything. She was still standing there when Andy tipped the bellman and closed the door behind him.

He went to where she was, started to reach for her—and pulled back. Thus far all the touching had been precipitated by crisis. In the normal way of things he had no right. So instead he sat in one of the comfortable armchairs and began fiddling with his pipe. She still didn't speak. After five minutes he said, "Lili, can I tell you a story?"

"As long as it doesn't end. '. . . and they lived happily ever after.' I'm not up to that." She didn't turn around.

"No, it doesn't exactly. But it begins once upon a time. A long time. It's about the Mendozas. I know we're not high on your list, but I think this applies anyway." He tamped more tobacco into the bowl of the pipe and lit it.

"In Córdoba they say that the family was founded before

the Romans came to Spain, before the birth of Christ. No one can prove that, of course, but that's what they say. And sometime in the fifth or sixth century A.D. the Mendozas were supposed to have fled to Africa because Jews were being persecuted."

"Nothing new in that, is there?" It was the first sign she'd given that she was listening to him.

"No, nothing. Anyway, so the legend goes, they prospered in Africa. But they were never happy, never considered themselves at home." He thought about telling her about the motto they had supposedly adopted, *If I forget thee, O Jerusalem, let my right hand forget her cunning. . . .* He could ask if she still had her bit of gold. But it didn't seem like the right time. He skipped that part.

"They're supposed to have been moneylenders and financiers even back then. And very rich. Because they wanted only to return to Córdoba, they colluded with the Moors and backed the invasion of Spain. When the conquering hordes overran the country in seven hundred and something the Mendozas were right behind them. And they got back their land in Córdoba and built their house. I don't know whether any of that is true, but one thing is. There have been Mendozas in that house in Córdoba from that day to this."

"Good for them," Lili said. "I don't know anybody who wants to invade Fielding. And my house isn't there anymore."

"No, that's the point." The pipe went out and he lay it in the ashtray and ignored it. He leaned forward, hunched over his knees, willing her to look at him. "Two points really. First, what they've done to stay there for twelve hundred years is beyond belief. Murder, rape, thievery, the stories would curl your hair. Nothing was ever too much, no price too high. They've changed their religion for whatever happened to be in fashion, helped to topple governments. Parents have murdered children and vice versa. You name it, the Mendozas have done it."

"All for a house?"

"I don't think so. That's what I'm getting at. The house, and it's not the same house naturally, it's burned down and been rebuilt and God knows what, but it's in the same place. Anyway, the house is a symbol, staying in Córdoba is a symbol. It's who they are. Rich, powerful and *Cordobéses*. That seems to be all they are. You're not like them, Lili. You're something more than a house and a piece of land."

She left the spot by the window finally and wandered around the room, picking things up and putting them down, eventually slumping in a chair across from his. "I know that. I'm not going to die, I'm not even going to go crazy and run screaming down the street, although I might have been slightly psychotic when I saw the house was gone. No matter, the pain isn't any less. I loved it so," she added, putting her hands over her face as if to shut out the world.

"Why, Lili?" He got up and went and knelt beside her. "Why did you love it so much? I know it was a beautiful house, you've told me. I remember the snapshot you had. But making beautiful houses is what you do best in the whole world. You can have another one. For that matter, if you really want to, you can build a duplicate. All it will take is money. But that's not the same, is it?"

"No, definitely not." Spoken from between her fingers. Her hands still covered her face.

"Look, I know this is twopence worth of psychiatry, forgive me. But I think it's accurate. In your head you've mixed up being Lili with having a particular house in a particular place. Maybe because of the way your mother was, maybe because you never knew your father. Whatever the reason, in your mind that bloody house was a symbol of something fundamental. But you're wrong. It's a loss and of course you've every right to mourn. But it's only the house that's been knocked down. Not Lili. What you are doesn't depend on any configuration of bricks and mortar."

"Not bricks and mortar," she said dully. "Wood and stone."

"The same thing."

"Yes, it is." Lili finally looked at him. He was still kneeling beside her chair and she leaned forward and put her palms on either side of his face. "You know, now that you've grown up, you're kind of a nice guy. Thanks."

He took her hands in his. "Doctor Andy's instant cure. Sometimes it takes a while to work."

For a few moments they stayed like that, then she pulled free and stood up again. "It's getting late. If you want your dinner, we'd better see about finding a restaurant."

They went to a place the hotel recommended, Pritchett's Forge. The remains of an old blacksmith shop had been turned into the kind of eating place that attracted travelers from Boston and New York. It dripped with atmosphere and served traditional New England fare. "Lobster or clams or scrod," Lili said. "All famous Massachusetts foods, but I think we're too far inland for them to be at their best."

She was really trying and so was he. They studied the menu and discussed every offering. "What about the duck?" he asked.

"Not a local specialty, so probably not the kitchen's star attraction."

"Roast beef, then," he said. "I am addicted to thick cut, rare American roast beef. I may get thrown in the Tower if anybody at home finds out."

They both ordered the prime rib, and clam chowder to start. Lili did little more than play with the food. "Sorry, I'm not very hungry."

"Eat a few bites at least," Andy insisted. "So I know you're not going to drop dead before I get you back to New York."

Lili tried to oblige, but she stopped with her fork halfway to her mouth. "Andy, that story you told me, about your family. It was all about Spain. How did the Mendozas get to England?"

"Also a long tale. It had to do with the sherry trade. I'll save it for another day. The moral's different, and I may need it sometime."

Years ago he used to talk as if they would part any moment and that had filled her with anguish. Now he sounded as if he were going to be around forever, and that raised emotions of a different sort. She preferred not to deal with them. "We've been concentrating on me," she said. "You've had a disappointment today too."

He smiled. "Not in the same class. And I'm not crushed, it simply means I have to try harder."

"Try what? If that picture isn't of Irene or Amanda Kent, what do you have?"

"My instinct," he said slowly. "What I do is largely based on instinct. When I have a story, I know it. I know it's there. I keep digging and eventually it falls into place."

"So that's what you're going to do, keep digging?"

"Yes. I'm going all the way with the Swanning thing this time. I've been brooding on it far too long." He poured some more of the burgundy they were drinking. "Are you very angry with me?"

"Angry? No, why should I be?"

"Your mother—"

"Is not in your picture and isn't going to wind up in your story. I'll say it again for the last time. Nothing will make me believe that Irene Petworth Cramer is mixed up in anybody's murder." The waiter appeared and cleared their plates. Lili waited until he was gone. "Funny thing is that I'm in such a rage about her at the moment, I almost wish she were."

"You mean if she hadn't sold the house in the first place, the developers wouldn't have got close."

"Yes." She felt herself starting to choke again. "Let's change the subject. Tell me more about what you've been doing these last years. Where do you live, for one thing? Not that grubby bed-sit in Hackney, I presume."

He chuckled. "Not quite. I bought a house in Kensington, off the bottom end of the Brompton Road."

Lili raised her eyebrows. "Very nice."

"It is rather. Listen, I'd better tell you something else. I got married a few years ago."

She'd been sipping wine and she set down her glass with slow, deliberate motions. "I see. Well, yes, I think it's a good thing you told me."

"Don't look at me like that, I may shrivel up. It's not what you think. It was a disaster. Wed in 'seventy-eight, divorced in 'seventy-nine. She wanted a cash settlement, so I got to keep the house."

Her stomach settled back into place. It had been climbing up so, she thought it would collide with her pounding heart.

Damn him! Why could he still do this to her? "What was her name?" She didn't care, but it was something to say to cover her reactions.

"Don't laugh. Fiona. Fiona Farraday."

Lili giggled. "I'm not going to apologize, you deserve it. Good evening, Nigel. I bet you made an adorable couple."

"Oh, yes, didn't we just. She married a French count the minute the divorce was final. Why are we talking about this?"

"It started because you were telling me about your house. Is it beautiful? Do you love it?"

He picked up something in her voice, a return of the despair of earlier. "I don't want to talk about houses either. We've had enough of that today."

Lili had changed for dinner. She was wearing a dress made of a soft, clinging fabric. It was dark but vibrant, something between blue and purple. "You look lovely," Andy said. "What's that material called?"

"Silk jersey. Thank you. You don't look so bad yourself. This is how I've always thought of you, in a three-piece suit straight from Savile Row."

"I thought we'd be in Boston this evening; it seemed in order." He reached across the table and touched the pendant she wore, then realized his earlier unspoken question had been answered. She still had the fragment of gold. "That's the thing with the Hebrew writing, isn't it?"

"Yes, I had the chain put on a few years ago. I wear it a lot."

"It's definitely connected to the Mendozas. That was one of the things I found out that Christmas of 'seventy-one."

"One of the things that made you decide to—"

"Yes," he interrupted quickly, not wanting her to dwell on his betrayal yet again. To divert her, he told the story Susan had told him about the motto adopted in Africa and the plaque made in Córdoba.

"She's sure the plaque was bigger than this?" Lili asked.

"Yes. And she's probably right. Susan's very clever about things like that. Good at solving puzzles and putting pieces together. But your bit is related to my family too. I'm dead certain."

"Perhaps," Lili said. She didn't want to go on talking about old mysteries. The waiter appeared and Andy ordered coffee and brandies.

"Do you like Spanish brandy?" Lili asked.

"Sometimes. In Spain it seems right. A bit rough everywhere else. I don't know why."

"I don't agree. A friend introduced me to it a while ago. She lived in Spain for years and developed the taste. I like it a lot."

"Shall we see if they have some?" Andy raised his arm to signal the waiter.

"Don't bother. They probably don't. Anyway, I like cognac too."

"Where in Spain did your friend live?" It was merely idle chatter as an antidote to all the emotions of the day.

"Madrid, I think. She doesn't talk about it too much. But she still uses her Spanish name. Everyone calls her Señora Perez."

Andy made a face. "Sounds affected."

"No, it isn't. It suits Loy. She's a wonderful person. You'd like her."

"Introduce us, then."

"Maybe. If you're still in New York when she gets back. She's in Spain at the moment."

He cocked his head. "I'm beginning to put two and two together. Is this Señora Perez the third partner, the one Fowler mentioned the other morning when he was giving me a bit of background relative to checking out Jeremy whatshisname?"

"Yes."

"I see. She must be something special. I noticed the light in Fowler's eye when he talked about her."

"Is it that obvious? Peter's in love with her, you're right. Not reciprocated, I'm afraid, at least not in the same way."

"Bad luck for him." The cognacs came. Andy swirled his round in the snifter. "Listen, I'm planning to be in New York quite a while. If it's all right with you."

His words should have made her feel happy . . . not afraid. She clasped her hands around the coffee cup, looking for warmth, but like her flesh, the coffee had developed a chill. "It's not up to me what you do, Andy."

"Yes. In this instance it is."

It was after eleven when they got back to the Garson House. There was a first-class stereo in the living room of the suite. Hotel management apparently took seriously the musical bent of its guests—but expected them to bring their own records, for there were none in the room. Andy fiddled with the radio and found some Mozart. It lasted two minutes and was over. A man began talking about bee keeping and honey production in Nigeria. He twisted the dial again. Dance music. The old-fashioned big-band style. He held out his arms.

Lili fitted into them with ease. "We must be getting old," she said. "We didn't used to dance like this."

"I had to learn how, though," he said. "When I was a kid. Dancing classes were de rigueur for the little sons of the privileged."

She lay her head on his shoulder and they moved slowly to the beat of a mellow saxophone and lots of strings. She could feel what was happening, so could he. "No more," she said when the music faded.

"Okay." He released her without protest. "Not until you say so."

Lili didn't think she'd sleep, but she dozed off almost instantly. She was awake again, though, in a few hours. It was still night. She found her watch on the bedside table. Four A.M. She lay still and listened. There was no sound from the next room. But then, he never had snored.

Each bedroom had a private bath. Lili went into hers and looked at her face in the mirror over the sink. Nothing of what had happened that day showed. She looked fine. Not twenty-one any longer, but that shouldn't be a surprise. Time passed and things changed and you kept on keeping on. Who was it who said he was prepared to live out his life in quiet desperation? She couldn't remember. But she wasn't. And she wasn't prepared, either, to live on promises for the future. She'd seen today where such dreams led. To a big hole in the ground.

His door was ajar. There was no sound from the bed. "Are you sleeping?" she whispered.

"No. Lying here thinking."

"I'm not sleeping either."

"I rather assumed that. Are you coming to join me, or am I living on false hope?"

"That's what I've been thinking about. It depends. For tonight, no, not false hope. Afterward, I don't know."

"Fair enough."

He held up the covers and she got under them and he tucked them around her. "Warm enough? I can close the window."

"No, leave it. Andy, kiss me please."

"I will, in a moment. I want to say something first."

"Yes?"

"I love you, Lili. I've loved you a long time. That used to scare me; it doesn't anymore."

She didn't reply. She could say that she loved him too—it was the truth—but she had to hold something back. There was too much pain and the memory of pain inside her. She pressed herself against him instead. It felt absolutely familiar and natural. And wonderful.

He found her mouth with his, and they held the kiss a long time. She was wearing a small silk nightshirt that reached only to the middle of her thighs. He put his hand beneath it and stroked her skin. His hardness pressed against her leg. Lili fumbled with the tie of the pajama bottoms which were all he had on. "Now," she whispered urgently. "Don't wait. Now."

Andy pulled up in front of Lili's building at five-thirty Sunday afternoon. "Can I leave the car here?" he asked.

"No, it's illegal, you'll get a ticket. Besides . . ."

"Yes?"

"Andy, please don't be hurt. I'd rather be alone this evening. It's all too . . ." She shook her head, and the dark hair moved around her pale face. "I don't know."

"I do. It's okay, love. I'll turn this thing in and go back to the hotel. Can I ring you later to say good night?"

"Yes, I'd like that." The familiar street and the sounds and smells of the city were working on her, returning her to the world she inhabited now. "But if the phone's busy, don't be surprised. Peter has a critical business meeting this evening. He'll be calling me right after it. It may involve a lot of telephoning."

"Go-go America. Nothing's sacred, not even Sunday night. Okay, but I'll keep trying until I get through."

Peter's call came at nine-fifteen. "Hi, how was your weekend?"

"Very nice in parts, terrible in others. I'll tell you about it sometime. Not now. Peter, don't keep me in suspense. Did you see her?"

"See who?" he asked innocently.

Excitement began in Lili's toes and crept upward; he wouldn't be fooling around if the news was bad. "You damn well know who. And I have a strong suspicion Willa Grayson was a pussycat who rolled over and waited for you to scratch her tummy."

He laughed. "Not exactly. She's not quite the type. But Lili, do you know what?"

"No, what?"

"Well, it just so happens we've got a deal."

"Fantastic! Peter, is she likely to back out? Are you sure of her?"

"Positive. She's a 'do it now' lady. She phoned Louise Demmer before I left. I was on the extension. The two of them were cooing with pleasure while they sharpened their claws. They're going to love sticking it to the old bastard."

Lili sighed. "I'm going to love it too. And I never thought I was a bitch."

"The nicest kind of bitch. Slight change of subject. You haven't by any chance heard from Loy yet?"

"No, I checked my machine as soon as I got in. Not a thing."

He was silent for some seconds. Then, "If there's nothing by tomorrow night, I'm going to do something."

"What can you do?"

"I don't know. Call the American embassy maybe, get them to do some checking. I can't simply let her fall into a black hole over there."

Lili remained convinced that when Loy wanted to be in touch with them she would be, but there wasn't any point in saying that to Peter. "Okay. But give it another twenty-four hours."

"Yes, agreed. Can you phone the bank in the morning? I'm supposed to see some distributors. I keep reminding myself that it's in LPL's best interest to keep my company chugging along."

"Yes, of course. Our friendly banker's going to want more than our word though. How do we convince him Grayson and Demmer are going to play?"

"A letter of intent's being prepared. We're all going to sign it. Probably late tomorrow afternoon. So hold that open."

Lili said she would and they hung up. Quid pro quo, she thought. You win some and you lose some. Her loss had been terrible, but her gains of the last twenty-four hours were rather remarkable too. She'd started to tally them, when the phone rang again. She put her hand on the receiver and waited for a moment. It would be Andy. The sheer pleasure of knowing that was a sensation to savor.

In Madrid it was very early Monday morning. Loy woke in a white and gold and pink and gray bedroom that was the epitome of fin de siècle taste. More French than Spanish, but then, the Ritz in Madrid had always been like that. White-gloved footmen in pale blue livery, crystal chandeliers, gold damask walls, patterned carpets in delicate pastels—the hotel had not changed in the forty years she'd known it.

Loy pressed a button beside her bed. In less than three minutes there was a discreet tap and the door opened. "*Su desayuno, Señora.*" A white-coated waiter set a tray beside her and disappeared as quickly as he'd come. Ignoring the basket of warm rolls and the little silver dishes of butter and preserves, she poured streams of hot milk and thick black coffee into a porcelain cup and sipped it while she dialed the legendary *conserje* of the Ritz and asked him to have her car ready in half an hour.

The coffee was cold. Loy put it down. Her stomach was

tied in knots. In twenty-five minutes she'd showered, dressed in a skirt, sweater, jacket, and boots, and gone downstairs. In ten more she was heading out of Madrid in the rented car the *concierge* had arranged, and toward the little village of San Domingo de la Cruz. It was a long name for a hamlet deep in the mountain forest, consisting of a dozen or so houses, a single all-purpose store, and at its far edge the shooting lodge of a wealthy Madrileño.

If she didn't know it so well, she'd have missed the cutoff to the dirt track that rose at an alarming angle and narrowly skirted deep gorges and dry rocky *barrancas*. In season they would rush with water tumbling toward the plain and sweeping away everything in its path.

Now the winter rains were over and the late spring had arrived, almonds and peaches beginning to open pink flowers in the April sun. She'd never been quite sure which season was the most beautiful in these high hills, though once she'd known them intimately in every month of the year. It all seemed a long time ago, another life. Loy shook her head as if to brush away the cobwebs of memory, and lessened the pressure of her foot on the accelerator as she took yet another hairpin curve.

San Domingo de la Cruz appeared without warning on both sides of the narrow road. There were two gas pumps in front of the *tienda*. She remembered when the store-keeper poured fuel into your tank from a rusty watering can he'd filled from a barrel behind his house. The houses themselves hadn't changed. They were low white structures with red-tiled roofs and green-shuttered windows. She drove swiftly through the village; any local with a long enough memory would have no time to recognize her. The farmers had been up for hours. Now it was after ten and, their housework done, the women were shopping for the makings of lunch.

A dozen pairs of eyes watched the low-slung Ferrari speed through San Domingo. They saw it turn right at a track that climbed yet higher into the hills and thought, yes, of course, someone going to the lodge. El Madrileño often entertained strangers.

The caretaker was an ancient woman. Doubtless she had

a name, but no one remembered it. She was called only Mamacita, little mother. She'd stood less than five feet when she was young; now she was even shorter, stooped and wizened, and she looked like an evil gnome. It seemed impossible she would remember anything. But she smiled when Loy parked and got out of the car. *"Hola, mi niña. Estoy contenta al ver tu cara una vez más antes de ir a mi lecho de muerte."*

Loy kissed the old woman on both cheeks. "You will never die, Mamacita. Don Diego won't permit it."

The woman shrugged and laughed. "Sometimes he cannot have everything his own way, not even Don Diego. You and I, we know that, no?" She smiled and winked.

"Yes, we do. Is he here?"

"Not yet. He told me to expect you. Last night after midnight the telephone rang." She said it with pride, not annoyance. The phone had been installed less than a decade earlier. Mamacita remained amazed that it worked after everyone had gone to bed as well as during the day. "I have coffee. And *churros*. Come inside, it's cold."

The old woman had made a log fire in the big stone sitting room and drawn a table and two comfortable chairs to the hearth. Loy sat down, stretched her boot-clad feet toward the blaze, and warmed her hands. Mamacita brought a tray with the promised food. The coffee was the strongest in the world, the *churros,* long, twisted crullers made of fried yeast dough, crisp and hot.

Despite her nerves, the drive had made Loy hungry. She ate. Somewhere a clock chimed eleven times. "Did Don Diego say when he'd get here?" she asked.

Mamacita had the outrageous familiarity of the very old servant who has been in the same job so long she considers her employers her children. She smiled wickedly. "No, he wants to make you wait. He wants to pretend it is the old days and when he arrives you will—"

"Yes, I know." Loy cut her off with a wave of her hand.

The old woman settled in to chat. She said Loy's clothes were nice and she was glad to see that her tits hadn't sagged. "Mine hang like a cow's udders. *Mira*." She opened the front of her black cotton dress. "Because I have had seven children and you none. Is it true that in America the young women don't want any babies until they're over thirty?"

"Sometimes. More and more these days," Loy admitted. "They're busy with careers."

She didn't listen to the stream of comment this produced. She wanted Mamacita to go away and leave her alone. It had taken a week of probing and questioning and thinking to bring her to this meeting. A week of fierce interior struggle while she tried to find a way to get what she wanted and protect what she loved. Now she'd made up her mind. She would have liked to be alone for a few minutes and think it through again, but Mamacita stayed with her by the fire until nearly noon. Then they heard another car approach.

"That will be him. I'll go see," the old woman said.

She left. Loy remained where she was. A minute later two pairs of feet walked up the path to the front door. Mamacita opened it and stood aside to allow Diego to enter.

He did not greet Loy immediately, just looked at her. *"Sal,"* he told the old woman. Get out. The command used to a dog. She went, but she didn't slink away. She left in a wave of cackling laughter and comments about her employer maybe being too old to get a hard prick anymore.

"She needs horsewhipping," he said to Loy. "Hello," he added finally.

"Hello, Diego. You look well."

"And you. You are as young and beautiful as ever."

"Thanks to you," she said softly.

"Yes. So you remember that? Lately I'd thought you'd forgotten."

"No. Why did you think that?"

"Because of what you are doing in New York. Because you've been in Spain a week and you did not call me until yesterday."

She wasn't surprised. She'd assumed he'd know. So had the others with whom she'd spoken. That's why they were so cautious. "You have everyone cowed, Diego. I found no allies. Not even Manuel. He hasn't the courage of the old days."

He shrugged and walked to the table and poured himself a large brandy from the bottle Mamacita had left for him.

"In the old days you and Manuel were mad with courage. He used up all his. But not you, eh?"

"Yes, I think perhaps I did. I'm not feeling very brave. Diego. Only . . ."

"Desperate?" He supplied the word with some pleasure.

She shook her head. "No. Not desperate because I believe that once you understand, everything will be all right."

"What you are doing in New York will not be all right."

"Why not, for God's sake? Diego, I have a very small project involving myself and two friends. How can that possibly bother you?"

"It bothers me."

Loy took a sip of her brandy before she asked, "Why?"

He smiled. "It isn't necessary for me to answer questions, *querida*. This meeting is at your request. And I seem to recall your saying some time ago that you needed nothing more from me."

"It was over, Diego. We both knew it."

He shook his head. "That was your feeling, not mine."

"But we agreed to part friends. You provided for me very generously. Why have you suddenly interfered in my life?"

"I am not a man to forgive easily, you know that."

"I did nothing you need to forgive."

He shrugged. "Perhaps. But the corpus of the trust reverts to the family after your death. Why should I allow you to squander it on this magazine business?"

She countered with another question. "Diego, why haven't you retired? You and Manuel should have turned everything over to your sons by now."

He was normally a fastidious man; now he spat into the fire. The flames protested with a moment's sizzle, then continued burning steadily. "Our sons are corrupted."

"How? By what?"

"By *democracia*. By the music they listen to, the filth they read and watch on television. All Spain is corrupted. Juan, my oldest, will be fifty in a few months. And do you know how he spends his time? Whoring in Monte Carlo. And playing tennis. Already he has had two wives. To such a man I should give the keys to the Mendoza kingdom?"

She understood. Partly this was what had driven her away,

the increasing right-wing fanaticism, the rigid inability to recognize any truth but his own. She would say no more of Juan, who suffered the fate of being the son of a remarkable father. "What of Manuel's son Roberto?"

"Worse, he's stupid."

There was silence between them for some moments. Finally Loy spoke again. "I know a young woman who is not corrupted, who deserves your help. And I know that by blocking me you are acting against your own best interests. That is not the Mendoza way."

His eyes were hazel. They narrowed and he studied her. "*Querida*, you know a great deal about the Mendoza way. You had to learn. So what are you talking about?"

"Sit down," she said. "Sit down and pour another drink for yourself and one for me and I will tell you."

By six Loy was back in Madrid. She left the car with the doorman of the Ritz and asked the concierge to book her a flight to New York the next day. "In the late afternoon," she said. "So I can do a bit of shopping first."

"There's a TWA flight at five. It arrives at seven-thirty New York time."

"That will be perfect."

In her room she rang for a maid, ordered tea and a bath to be drawn, then sat staring at the ivory and gold telephone. She had to call Lili . . . Peter. . . . And she had to call Irene. Tomorrow.

She gave in to the bruising emotions of the day and wept for a long time.

❧ 16 ❧

New York and London: 1982

"You look so tired, was it a terrible flight?" Lili added Loy's carry-on case to the two in the foyer and followed Loy and Peter into the living room of the Tenth Street house.

"Not the flight, the time in Spain was difficult."

"And all for nothing," Peter said bitterly. "All because that schmuck Crandall had some kind of private deal going."

Loy shook her head. "No. Jeremy was following orders." She sank onto a sofa and slipped her shoes off and put her legs up. "Get us drinks please, Peter. Lili, sit over there, where I can see you. Now, tell me again what's happened. I don't think I got it all in the cab."

Peter was busy with bottles and glasses, so Lili explained. "It's beautifully straightforward. We've done it." She glanced at her watch, it was eight P.M. "To be precise, for the past four hours we have owned thirty-one percent of Bass and Demmer's stock. We outvote Randolph Demmer."

"But how? Who sold you the shares? Where did the money come from?"

Loy sounded particularly agitated, and Lili decided she must be even more exhausted than she looked. "We bought them from Louise Demmer, Harvey Michael's mommy."

Peter handed drinks around. "Remember what the kid told me? That his mother hated old man Demmer? We figured that made her a likely target, so Lili went to see her. Turned out we were right."

"But what about the money?" Loy asked again. "Jeremy said there was no point in talking to any more board members until we had replenished LPL's liquid assets. That's why—"

"Jeremy lied through his pearly white teeth," Lili interrupted. "He took advantage of our innocence."

Peter had given Lili a sherry, which she clutched but didn't drink. "You have to understand that first of all. We don't know why, but halfway through what he liked to call our game plan, Crandall began giving us bad advice. The worst was the smoke screen about needing more money to complete the takeover. Peter and I saw that soon after you left, so we marched into Peter's friendly neighborhood bank and got the cash."

"Not so simple and not so friendly," Peter added. "But simple enough. We're committed to selling the five magazines we don't want. Which is okay since we don't want them. And . . ." He looked at Loy. "Lili's right, you seem much too tired for any of this. I'll save the details of the bank deal for another time. For the moment, trust me, we can live with them."

"There's only one other thing you have to know right away," Lili said. "We have Willa Grayson's signed assurance that she'll vote with us. In return for some preferred shares in LPL. So we not only outvote Demmer, we have control of the board. Demmer's lost and we've won."

Loy wasn't looking at either of them; she was staring into space.

Peter was on the couch next to her. He got up and went behind it and began massaging her neck and shoulders. "If you're thinking we had a hell of a nerve to do all this without consulting you, can I say we had to act quickly and you weren't here and we didn't know how to reach you?"

"No, it's not that." Loy put her hand over his and smiled up at him. It was rather a weak smile, but she was trying. "You did exactly the right thing. Winning always means you've done the right thing."

Which, she realized, was what Diego had done. He'd squeezed her until she was wrung dry, turned her inside out and examined all the parts. After all these years, he had beaten her. Diego had won. Loy looked quickly at Lili and felt tears sting behind her eyelids.

Lili didn't notice. She was still thinking of the triumph of the afternoon. "Loy, one question. Have you any idea what Jeremy Crandall's motives were?"

"He had no motives of his own. He was following instructions." She wanted to leave it there, but Lili was studying her so intently she didn't feel she could. "Look, I can't explain the whole thing. It has to do with me and . . . someone in Spain."

Lili almost asked if that someone was one of the Mendozas, if Loy's involvement with the Mendoza Group had personal origins. She decided against it. Not here and not now. "Okay, that will do." Lili finished the sherry and stood up. "What you're saying is that it had nothing to do with LPL or me or Peter. And that makes it your business. Which is fine, since it's come out all right. Now I think we should get out of here and let you get some sleep."

"Don't go," Loy said. "I won't sleep anyway. I'm too keyed up. Stay. If you haven't eaten, I'm sure some kind of supper can be produced."

Lili shook her head. "I can't, pet, maybe Peter can."

"You're sure?" Loy asked. It was obvious she didn't want Lili to go.

"She's sure," Peter said. "Something else has happened while you were away. An old boyfriend's returned. Lili's in love." He spoke lightly, teasing, sure she'd not mind Loy knowing.

"Not yet," Lili said quickly. "I'll tell Loy about it later." Her tone was brusque and sharp. Peter shrugged. "Whatever you want."

Loy glanced from one to the other, then started to rise, but Peter put a restraining hand on her shoulder. "Stay where you are, I'll see Lili out."

He followed Lili into the foyer and she rounded on him with a harsh whisper. "For God's sake, Peter, she may be involved with the Mendozas in some way we don't know a thing about. I need time to explain about Andy."

He smacked his forehead with the palm of his hand. "Right. Sorry to be such an ass."

"It's okay. But don't say any more. And don't stay too late, she looks terrible."

"I like to think of my presence as soothing and welcome," he whispered back. "What's known as tender loving care."

Which for once seemed to be how Loy saw it. It was long past midnight when he left.

Lili had promised to meet Andy at the Hilton for a nightcap. It was quarter past ten when she arrived. He was waiting in the bar, staring into his glass, shoulders hunched over. She slipped onto the stool beside him. "Hi. Why the hangdog look?"

He leaned over and kissed her cheek. "You."

"Me? Why?"

"Because you're late. I was convinced you weren't coming."

Lili didn't reply. The bartender came and she said she'd have Perrier and lime. They waited for it, then moved to a small table in a quiet corner.

"Were you undecided about coming?" Andy asked.

"Not at all. I got held up. My friend was a little late getting in and we had to go back to her place and talk. It all took a while."

"I'm paying for my sins, aren't I?" he said softly. "Expecting you to disappear without a word because I did."

She toyed with the short straw in the glass of mineral water. "That's not exactly how it happened, but it's interesting that you perceive it that way. It's not a very good basis for going on, is it?"

"Not very."

"So what do we do?" She leaned forward. "What do we do, Andy?"

"That rather depends. I know what I want to do."

"Maybe you'd better tell me," she said. "This time I'd like to know exactly what you want."

Very deliberately, he loosened her fingers from around the glass and twined them with his own. "I want us to spend the rest of our lives together. I want to get married."

Lili waited a moment, gripping his hand, dealing with a storm of emotions she couldn't sort out. It was too much too fast, it had come at a time when her life was too much in flux. She was still frightened of how vulnerable she was to him. "Not yet," she said finally. "It's my turn to say I need time."

"Okay. But does that mean you don't want me to go away?"

"Yes, it definitely means that." Her voice was a whisper. "Please don't go away."

"I won't," he promised.

Two days later, telling Loy about Andy, Lili was better able to put it all in words. "I loved him so much once upon a time. I hurt so much when he dropped me. I still love him, but I can't unlock the defenses all at once. Does that make sense?"

"Yes." Loy stirred her coffee in a repeated spiral because she needed something to do with her hands. "It makes sense to me. Maybe if he weren't a Mendoza, I wouldn't understand so well."

"Your friend in Spain, the one who tried to stop us getting the magazines, he's a Mendoza too, isn't he?"

Loy nodded. "I expected you to guess that. Yes. They're an extraordinary family. Not always easy to like, but remarkable." She lay her hand over Lili's. "And they can be very dangerous, darling."

Exactly what Andy had told her years before, and undoubtedly true, but with an exception. "Andy's not dangerous," Lili insisted. "He's nothing like his family. I told you, he can't stand them. Please, don't judge him by his relations. I want you to like Andy."

"I want to like this unusual Mendoza," she added smiling. "I will, I'm sure of it. When do we meet?"

"Soon," Lili promised. "We'll make it a foursome. You and Peter and Andy and me."

"A double date at my age," Loy said wryly.

"You're ageless." Lili insisted. Today Loy was rested, not tired and drawn as she'd been the other night.

"Nobody is ageless. I keep telling Peter that. He's being very foolish. He deserves someone closer to his own age." She held up her hand to forestall Lili's comment. "All right, maybe not you. But someone like you."

"People don't usually care much about what they should have or what they deserve," Lili said. "Most of us want what we want."

"Yes. Whether or not it's good for us."

Lili's loyalty to Peter demanded a protest. "I think Peter would be good for anyone. He's such a darling, and he loves you, you know."

"I do know. What I meant was that I'm not good for him. But Peter's addictive. I find it hard to keep saying no, though at my age I should have learned."

Lili couldn't resist. "How old is that?"

"No you don't." Loy laughed. "Not even you. Some secrets I shall take to my grave."

She made it sound frivolous and silly, and Lili didn't mind indulging her. "Okay, I won't even speculate." She glanced at her watch. "I have to be at the studio in an hour. We'd better get out of here."

It was almost three. The restaurant was practically empty. The waiter saw Lili's signal and quickly produced the check. Loy insisted on paying. They gathered their things and went out onto First Avenue. "I'll drop you," Loy said. "I'm headed back downtown, it's on my way."

They crossed the street to a better spot for flagging a taxi. They were standing in front of an elegant antique shop. A little card in the window said, TO THE TRADE ONLY. It was forbidden to cross the threshold without a decorator in tow. Lili glanced at it, then looked again.

Loy lifted her arm to signal a cab. One pulled up. "I have a taxi—"

"You go ahead," Lili said in a choked voice, still staring into the window of the antique shop.

Loy murmured an apology to the driver and let the cab go. "What is it? What's wrong?"

She moved closer so she could look at the display that had apparently mesmerized Lili. It was six mahogany Queen Anne dining chairs with beautiful needlepoint upholstery. She caught her breath, hesitated only a brief second, then said casually, "Lovely, aren't they?"

"They're from my house," Lili said. She had told Loy about the hole in the ground that was all that was left of her house in Fielding. Loy hadn't been particularly sympathetic. Neither was she impressed now.

"Maybe not," she said. "You can't be sure, can you?"

"I'm sure. My mother made the seat covers. They're a replacement of the originals. It took her years. I never knew she'd finished." The last was spoken over her shoulder as she moved to the door. It was locked, but that didn't mean the shop was closed. Lili pressed the buzzer.

The man who admitted them was beefy and sharp-eyed. He looked as if he might have a gun under the counter, as if he could deal with anything the New York streets could produce. "What can I do for you?"

"Those six chairs in the window, there should be eight of them," Lili said. "Do you have the other two?"

"Yes, as a matter of fact I do. But they don't have the needlepoint cushions."

"They're covered in brown velvet, aren't they?"

"That's right." He cocked his head and studied her. "How did you know?"

"They came out of my old house. Years ago." The window display was on a raised platform not separated from the interior of the shop. Lili stroked the red-brown wood of one gracefully bowed leg, ran her finger over the slightly raised petal of the rose on the seat.

"Where was your house?" the man asked.

"In Fielding, outside Boston."

"Could be," he said. "I got them in Boston. I believe the couple who sold them to me bought them at auction some years back."

"In 1972," Lili said. "How much do you want for all eight."

"Darling, where are you going to put eight dining room chairs?" Loy protested, uttering her first words since they'd come inside.

"I don't know. In storage. It doesn't matter. How much?" Lili asked again, taking her checkbook from her bag.

"Two thousand two hundred," the man said. "They're classics, and quite old. That's with the trade discount, of course. I presume one of you is a decorator."

"No, neither of us," Lili said dismissively. She turned to Loy. "Look, I can't cover twenty-two hundred. Will you lend me the money?"

"Of course, but I don't think—"

"We don't sell to the general public," the man said, cutting off her words.

Lili ignored Loy's objection and looked at the dealer. "I'm not the general public. Do you watch television?"

He cocked his head again and studied her some more. "Wait a minute, I thought you looked familiar." He snapped his fingers. "Got it. *Dining Out, Eating In*. Lili Cramer."

"That's right. So you're going to sell me the chairs without making me go through the hassle of finding a decorator to do it, aren't you?"

He chuckled. "Sure, why not? Maybe you'll put some of my stuff on your show. I've got a great dining room table coming in."

"That was my next question," Lili said. "Do you have the table that goes with these chairs?"

"No, sorry, I don't. As far as I know, it wasn't for sale."

She had to content herself with that, and a promise that he'd look up the name of the Boston people he'd bought from, and get in touch with them and see if maybe they'd acquired other things at the same auction and might want to sell them now.

Lili wrote a check for the dealer, Loy wrote one for her. "I'll give you an IOU later," Lili promised. "I'm already late for work."

Loy waved the comment away. "That doesn't matter. But I still don't know what you're going to do with these chairs."

Lili didn't answer. It was something that was either understood or not. You couldn't explain it. She turned to the man. "Hold the chairs for me for a few days. I'll find someplace to store them and let you know where to send them by the end of the week."

She thought Loy might offer to keep them for her, but she didn't and Lili didn't ask.

• • •

Finding and buying the chairs should have thrilled Lili; instead, it made her loss more poignant.

"It keeps tearing me up," she admitted to Andy later in her bed in the middle of the night. "Every time I think about it I get the same sick pain in my stomach."

He didn't try to argue her out of it. He stroked her hair and kissed her and drew her closer. "Think about the practical problem instead," he said. "What do you want to do with the chairs?"

"I don't know. They sure as hell won't fit in this place."

"How about a nice big house in the country somewhere? Commuting distance to Manhattan, but out of the proverbial rat race."

"How about heaven? But it's a little beyond my reach at the moment. I had to borrow the money for the chairs from Loyola Perez."

"You should have called me. Listen, love, maybe I haven't made it altogether clear. Things really have changed since Hackney. I'm . . . stinking rich is, I believe, the phrase."

"Lucky you. But it's okay, Loy is too."

"About that house," he said. "What would you really think of a place like that?"

She drew back and tried to make out his face in the moonglow coming through the windows. "Are you serious?"

"Why not? I want to tell you a couple of things. First, I've made a big decision. I'm dropping the Swanning book."

"Andy, you don't have to do that. If it's my mother you're worried about, I've told you—"

"I know what you've told me. It's not Irene, only that the damned thing has already made so much trouble for us. And a bloody sight more for a lot of other people. Lord Swanning for starters. I'm sick of it. Besides, I want to try another novel. I recently finished a nonfiction book about South America. My publishers are happy with it and I can take a breather. So if I'm going to take a second stab at fiction, this is as good a time as I'm likely to get."

She remembered what he'd said so long ago, that reporting wasn't really writing. "Good, I think that's a great idea. You said you had a couple of things to tell me. What else?"

"That I can write a novel here as well as in England, so I'll be staying for a while. That's okay, isn't it? Even though you're not ready to say you want me around for always."

She hugged him. "It's very okay. Where are you going to live?" She didn't say anything about his moving in. He didn't seem to expect it, perhaps because her apartment was too small, perhaps because he truly understood her feelings.

"That's what I meant when I mentioned a house in the country. It's what I'd really like. I'm going to look around. Meanwhile I may as well stay at the Hilton. I'll talk to them tomorrow about a monthly rate."

On Tenth Street Loy didn't sleep at all. It was a long night, one spent largely in worry. At dawn she gave in to an impulse and called Florida. "I shouldn't be bothering you with this," she told Irene. "But coming on top of everything else, it makes me uncomfortable. She really loves this man."

"Andy Mendoza," Irene repeated. "You're sure that's who she said it was?"

"Of course I'm sure. How could I make a mistake about a thing like that?"

"You couldn't, I guess. But he jilted her. I didn't think Lili would ever forgive a thing like that."

"Well, he's unjilted her. And she's forgiven him because, as I said, she really loves him."

Irene sighed. "What a shame. Lili deserves better than one of them."

"Irene, I'm worried about Lili. She's living in the past. Yesterday she did something insane." She explained about the chairs.

"Imagine her finding them after all these years," Irene said. "How extraordinary."

"Buying them was extraordinary. She has a two-and-a-half-room apartment. Irene, I'm out of my depth. You're the only one who probably knows her well enough to help. I think you should come to New York, talk to her again about why you sold the house. I think it's time you reached a real reconciliation with Lili."

"Maybe," Irene said. "I'll think about it."

Two days later she telephoned Loy and said she'd decided against it. "As you pointed out, I know Lili. Forcing the issue isn't wise. We have to trust her enough to let her work things out for herself. I'm sure she will."

A few days after that conversation Lili called her mother. They exchanged the usual pleasantries, then Lili said, "Remember the magazine deal I wrote you about? We've succeeded in getting control of the company."

"Did you, dear? I suppose that's very exciting."

Irene didn't sound excited. Lili didn't care, she hadn't called to talk about Bass & Demmer. "I went to Fielding a couple of weeks ago. Do you know what's happened there?"

"A lot of changes, I imagine."

"Yes. A lot." Lili took a deep breath. She'd promised herself there wouldn't be another scene. What was the point? Everything she'd had to say she'd said long ago. She wasn't calling to reproach Irene with the terrible results of her folly. Still. "There's a condominium development on Woods Road."

"Oh."

That was all, oh. It was like beating your head against a stone wall. If she told Irene about the hole in the ground where their house had been, the result would be the same. Lili thought she might go mad if that happened. "Listen," she said, "did you ever finish making the covers for the dining room chairs?"

"The ones from the house?"

"Of course. What other chairs would I be asking about?" No, that wasn't the way. "I mean the covers you worked on for such a long time, the ones you said were a replacement of the originals."

"Needlepoint roses. Yes, I remember. No, I'd finished only six when the set was sold."

"You won't believe this, but I saw the chairs in an antique shop here and I've bought them. All eight. But as you said, only six have covers. I thought maybe you had the other two."

"No, I sold everything."

Lili gritted her teeth. "Mother, is there any chance you could make me two more? So the set would be complete?"

"I suppose I could. It will take a bit of time though. It's slow work, and my eyes aren't as good as they were."

"That's okay. I've put the chairs in storage. I don't have any place for them."

"Then why did you buy them?"

Lili had to grip the receiver to keep from screaming. How could her mother ask such a question? Why did she buy them? Why had she been brought up in a home so beautiful, nothing would ever be the same again? Why had she been allowed to love it so passionately?

"I bought them because they used to belong to us," she said slowly, desperately trying to be patient. "Someday I won't live in a dinky apartment and I'll have a place for them. Meantime, I'd be enormously grateful if you would finish the covers. It's beyond me. I don't do needlepoint."

"No, I know that. All right, fine. I'll get the thread and start tomorrow. Luckily, I still have the pattern and the measurements. Somewhere."

Another deeply satisfying conversation with her mother.

A week later, the first Friday in May, Lili and Andy and Loy and Peter went to Le Perigord for dinner. It was a classic French restaurant, one of Lili's favorites. The ambience was delightful and the food excellent. Everybody tried to make the evening work. All the same, Lili decided that it hadn't.

"You didn't like Loy, did you?" she asked Andy later.

"Hard not to," he said. "She beautiful, she's charming, she's intelligent, she's rich. What's not to like?"

Lili giggled. "Do you realize you're picking up New York syntax? But you didn't answer my question."

"Actually, I did like her. Only I have the distinct impression she didn't like me."

Which, when she came to think about it, seemed accurate. Lili had waited to tell him about Loy's connections to his family. Now she decided not to mention it. And maybe it would be as well if they avoided what Loy had called double dating.

๛ 17 ๛

New York, London,
and Lymington: 1981

Lili had long ago decided that New Yorkers were a little crazy. Ecstatic when spring came and for a brief time the sun was pleasantly warm and the breezes soft, they forgot how soon the baking heat and tremendous humidity would descend. Short memory was a New York disease.

"What a gorgeous day," Loy said on a glorious June Monday.

"For the moment it's perfect," Lili agreed as she squeezed lemon into her paper cup of iced tea.

It was nearly two months since they'd gained control of the company and they were in a shabby office on the fourth floor of an old building on West Twenty-ninth Street. The office was naked of beauty or creature comforts. It had belonged to Randolph Demmer; now it was Peter's. He was away from his desk for the moment and the two women were alone.

"What's going to happen if they don't get the air-conditioning installed before the party?" Lili asked.

"We and our guests will probably fry," Loy said.

"Answer this question too: How are we going to make this place look like something in time for Thursday?"

Loy laughed. "You're supposed to be the expert on that."

Lili shook her head. "My specialty is raze the whole thing and build it back up. I don't think I can manage that in three days."

"Not on our budget." Peter had returned in time to hear Lili's comment. "Air-conditioning yes, so people can work. But decorating the offices can wait."

"I know," she said. "But we were talking about sprucing up the place before the party."

"I thought we deliberately decided to have it here rather than a restaurant." He repeated the arguments he'd used earlier. "We agreed we'd be completely honest about where we are. This party's about our new direction, the new look of our magazines. We're telling the movers and shakers, okay, this is a shitty office, but listen to our plans."

"I know," Lili agreed. "But is grubby the same as nobly impoverished?"

Peter looked around. "It is pretty ratty, isn't it?"

"An understatement. And we definitely don't want a ratty party. We need a little *ambiente,* as the Italians would say."

"Why don't you leave that to me?" Loy said. "You've both got so much to do and I'm so useless. I can at least take on the party decorations."

"You're already handling the catering," Peter said. He persisted in thinking of Loy as fragile, despite all the evidence to the contrary. "It's not too much, is it?"

"Of course not. Consider that settled." She turned to Lili. "What are you going to wear?"

Lili grinned. "What do you suggest? You're my favorite fashion consultant."

Loy cupped her palm beneath Lili's chin. "You're looking so gorgeous these days, it almost doesn't matter. Isn't she, Peter?"

"Gorgeous," he agreed. "Ah, what love can do."

"Cut it out, you two. I'm going to look tough and businesslike. Maybe I'll dress for success in a pinstripe suit and running shoes."

On Thursday, when Lili arrived to greet the food critics, the publishing competition, the TV types, and the big-name chefs and restaurateurs, she wore amber-colored linen, a small, closely fitted dress with cap sleeves and a drawstring waist. It was utter simplicity sustained by perfect cut.

Loy approved. "Very nice. Bill Blass, isn't it?"

Lili's eyes widened. "How did you know? Is the label showing?"

"No, I saw it in Bergdorf's a while ago. It has a matching sweater, doesn't it?" Lili nodded. "I should say I thought of you at the time," Loy added. "But I didn't. Suits you though."

"I didn't pay Bergdorf's price. Got it over on Broadway at a discount house. Paid for it with plastic. All the same, it didn't suit my finances," Lili looked sheepish. "Pretty soon I'll be wondering if I can pay my Visa with my MasterCard. I seem to be a little crazy these days."

"Crazy nice." Loy smoothed the seam of one shoulder. "Love becomes you, darling. Enjoy it."

Lili frowned. "While it lasts, you mean."

Loy didn't reply to that. "How does the place look?"

The launch party was being held in the outer office because it was the largest space they had. Loy had pushed all the desks against the walls and covered them with yards of cheap but pretty printed cloth. And she'd filled the room with flowers, large-scale bouquets of massed purple lilacs and white baby's breath.

The caterers were somebody new Loy had found, a Spanish couple just starting up. They weren't as expensive as the famous names that usually did parties such as this. They were also more pliable. They'd brought their own tables for the bar and the buffet, but they didn't object when Loy put skirts of the printed fabric beneath their white linen coverings.

"It looks fabulous," Lili said.

"I wouldn't go that far, but it will do." Loy smiled at her. "Is Andy coming?"

"Later probably, toward the end. In time to take me to the airport."

Lili was going to London for six days because of a commitment made by Dan Kerry months before. He'd sold a dozen of her shows to Britain's independent television channel, ITV. The whole nation was addicted to *Dallas* and *Dynasty,* so why shouldn't they love seeing glitzy New York restaurants? Lili had promised to go over and hype the series as soon as they started showing them, and the time had come.

"How's Andy going to survive with you away?" Loy asked.

"For a week? Fine, I'm sure." Then, impulsively, "Loy, do you like him? At first I thought you didn't."

"Let's say at first I wasn't sure." She made a dismissive gesture and the loose, floating sleeves of her dress moved in a graceful arc.

Loy wore black chiffon printed with scarlet tulips. The dress had an uneven hem that drifted when she moved and she'd added a long rope of many-faceted jet beads to the simple round neck. She removed the necklace and dropped it over Lili's head. "Here, when I put these on I decided to give them to you. Have them now instead of later; they look nice with the Bill Blass."

Lili ran a few of the beads through her fingers. Each was intricately and differently carved. "How lovely. I've never seen anything quite like them."

"They're Victorian," Loy explained. "Mourning jewelry from the time when ladies were concerned with such things. Not really valuable, but a collector's item. Enjoy them. I've had them a long time, now it's your turn."

"Not to mourn, I hope."

Loy started to protest, but there wasn't time. The glitterati were arriving and Lili was center stage.

"Lili, how marvelous you look . . ."

"Congratulations, Peter darling. I keep hearing wonderful things about what you're doing . . ."

"That's Loyola Perez, isn't it? I heard she had a piece of the holding company. Must be true . . ."

"Look, I know Lili Cramer can talk, and I know she can design, but can she write? What good is she going to be to Fowler in this venture?"

The hum of voices became a buzz and soon a roar. That pleased Lili. Once the decibel level was deafening, she was sure the party was a success.

"Great food, Lili." Pepe, the restaurateur from Greenwich Village, took a delicate bite of a ringlet of fried squid. "Maybe tapas will be the next Manhattan rage."

"You can bet on it, Pepe." Lili's face was beginning to ache from smiling. "And don't forget you had them here first. That's what our new magazines are going to be like, all the best new ideas first."

"No." He shook his head. "First I had them in Spain. You didn't invent them, darling. Not even you."

The scent of the lilacs began to mingle with that of the pungent food on the buffet table. The room was very hot. The air conditioners were in, the installers had worked frantically to be finished in time for the party, but something must be wrong. They weren't doing a thing. Lili caught a glimpse of Loy deep in consultation with the head bartender. They must be getting worried about the ice. She listened to Pepe with half her attention while she searched over the heads of the crowd for Peter.

At first she couldn't find him, then she saw him coming from the direction of the elevator. She knew instantly that he wouldn't want to be distracted by a discussion about the temperature. He was carrying a stack of magazines.

"Listen, everybody!" Peter shouted. "Hot off the presses, as they used to say. The first issues of the new *World of Food* and *House Remodeling*."

That was a triumph; as late as this morning the printer had said he couldn't have them ready in time. Lili managed to catch Peter's eye. She raised both hands clasped in a champion's salute. He grinned at her, then he was surrounded. The magazines were passed among the eager guests.

They weren't yet entirely updated, not as they would be within six months. Magazines took time to change. But they'd managed to get new covers printed and with judicious cutting and pasting a few new features had been added, including Lili's column, which ran simultaneously in both books.

"Why not?" Peter had asked. "Two separate markets, practically no overlap. And *Remodeling*'s a quarterly while *World* is monthly. Let's try it, at least this first time."

So they had. Lili was nervous about the column. "I've never done this before," she'd wailed when the time came to write the first one.

"Don't chicken out on me at this late date," Peter admonished her. "I'll assign you a tame editor of your own. Get the ideas down and we'll write them up in house."

In the end it didn't work that way. It was Andy who took Lili's virgin efforts and put them in publishable form.

"I see your boyfriend's fine hand," Peter said when Lili gave him the typescript.

"A little polishing," she admitted. "But not the title, that's strictly my idea. What do you think?"

"I think you're a bona fide genius. It's terrific."

Lili's page in both magazines was called *"The Home Front."* She would write about the things that made a house a home, concentrating on the kitchen and the dining room, since that was what the public associated with her name. Her first article was about the placement of dining room furniture—how you could be creative and do different things for different occasions, as long as your background was carefully planned.

She was talking about the piece with the wine expert from the *Times* when Andy arrived. "Judging by the sound of things, you're a success," he shouted in her ear.

"Yes. I think so. Andy, this is—" She turned to perform the introductions, but the *Times* man had disappeared. "A story breaking in Napa Valley, no doubt," Lili muttered. "The noble rot, or something."

Andy looked puzzled. "Mind telling me what you're talking about?"

"It's not worth it. Have a drink and something to eat."

He made a face. "Not here, too much like feeding time at the zoo."

She grinned and then Peter was calling her and she had to leave Andy to fend for himself.

He was waiting by the door forty minutes later when the crowd had thinned and there remained only a few old friends chatting with Peter and Loy. Lili thought Loy looked like she wanted to get away, but Peter had a firm grip on her hand.

"We'd better get out of here or you're going to miss your plane," Andy said.

She reclaimed the sweater that went with her dress, and a raincoat and her two suitcases. Andy eyed her speculatively. "Two suitcases for a week doesn't seem like the old Lili. She would have traveled with a backpack."

"The new Lili is doing a dozen television appearances and will have to change three times a day."

The elevator was ancient and slow. Andy kept studying her as it inched downward. "I'm probably crazy letting you go to London alone when you look so spectacular."

"Not to worry, Mr. Mendoza. I'm a one-man woman." She reached up and kissed him and they held it until the door creaked opened on the lobby.

Her flight didn't go until eleven, and they were at Kennedy a little before ten. There was time for a drink in the lounge. Andy was still looking at her as if he needed to store up a vision that would last a week. "I really like that dress. New?"

"Yes." The sweater was tiger-striped in black and the same tawny amber as the dress. It had frankly fake topaz buttons. She undid them and shrugged it off.

"Those beads are new too, aren't they?" He fingered the length of black jet round her neck.

"New to me. A present from Loy. She says they're Victorian. What ladies wore when they were in mourning. Why are you looking like that? I'm not really anticipating your funeral."

He frowned. "I just thought of something. These reminded me." He started to say more, but her flight was called. "Tell you about it when you get back," he murmured.

He still looked preoccupied when Lili grabbed her carry-on case and the sweater and raincoat and they headed for the gate.

ITV did very well by her. They put her up at the Connaught on Carlos Place, near the American embassy in Grosvenor Square. The Connaught was all mahogany and brass and marble and soft subtle velvet—perhaps London's most elegant small hotel, a last bastion of the idealized England of Edwardian fiction. Lili loved it, and she loved being back. The only sad thing was that she simply couldn't make time to see old friends.

There was a publicist, a woman named Shelley Cooper, in charge of all the arrangements. She had Lili on a schedule that barely allowed time to sleep.

Breakfast-time television was new since Lili's day. Now there were two programs, one on ITV and one on BBC, and Lili was to be on both. "How did you get BBC to let me show my face when the series is running with the competition?"

Shelley Cooper grinned. "Piece of cake, love. Because it's you, the famous fabulous Lili Cramer. Come back to where it all began. You're doing two other BBC slots as well. The Terry Wogan show, that's early evening, and *Pebble Mill at One,* so we cover the afternoon audience. There are five ITV shows. Including *Talking with Chambers,* of course."

Lili grinned. "That's really returning to the scene of the crime. It's all great, but it's a good thing I'm staying only a week. By the end of it everyone in the country's going to be sick of my face."

Monday she did one of the breakfast shows live, then taped the Terry Wogan show for the following evening. After a hurried lunch she did a radio call-in program. It too was live and lasted an hour. At the end of it she was exhausted and counting on a short rest at the hotel to recoup her strength before dinner with some people the Cooper woman said were important.

The Wogan show aired at six. Lili watched it from her glorious room at the Connaught while she was dressing for a dinner with the trade association of makers of kitchen equipment. She was putting the second pearl stud in her ears when the telephone rang. "Miss Cramer, I'm with the Terry Wogan show. We just aired your segment and—"

"I know," Lili interrupted. "I watched it. Terrific, you all did a great job."

"Thank you. I'm calling about a man who rang to say he saw you on the show. He claims he has to get in touch. He insists it's urgent."

"It probably has something to do with a kitchen he wants done over," Lili said, still fumbling with her earring. "I no longer take private commissions."

"That's what I said," the young woman agreed. "But he was really insistent that it was personal and important. Naturally, I wouldn't tell him where you were staying, but I did agree to give you his name and number."

"Fine," Lili said. She reached for a pencil and paper. "Okay, go ahead."

"He gave his name as Harry Cramer, and a telephone number in Lymington."

"Hello, my dear. It's been some time, and now you're famous."

The little cottage in Lymington looked shabbier than Lili remembered, but the blind man still moved through it with surprising ease. She followed him into the sitting room and looked for his wife.

As if he could see her, Cramer said, "Of course you were expecting to find Claudette. Sadly, my wife died a year ago."

"I'm sorry." It was an automatic response, but she meant it. She remembered how close they'd seemed.

"So am I," Cramer agreed.

It was midmorning on Wednesday, she'd managed to make the time free only by disappointing a breakfast meeting of restaurateurs and infuriating Shelley Cooper. Harry Cramer had fixed a tray with coffee and little cookies. He fumbled for the edge of it on the table. Then, assured it was there, he said, "Will you pour, my dear?"

Lili studied him while she filled the cups. He hadn't changed much. Harry Cramer had the same white hair, the same air of being extremely fragile, held together by paper clips. Yet he was alive while the placid, healthy-seeming Claudette was dead. Lili put the coffee in his hand, noticing while she did so that the cottage was indeed run-down. The upholstery and the curtains were threadbare, the tables looked as if they hadn't been polished in months.

Once more he showed that uncanny facility of the blind to read minds because they couldn't read faces. "I'm afraid the house has gone downhill since I lost Claudette. I do try, but—"

"Do you live alone now?"

"Oh, yes, I quite prefer it. The social-worker types wanted to put me in a home, but I resisted. They send someone to check on me once or twice a week and the neighbors pop in regularly. I manage."

"Mr. Cramer, I don't want to sound rude, but I have very little time. It was extremely difficult to get here. I'm in England for only a few days."

"I know." He held up a forestalling hand. "I heard you say so on television. Quite a lucky stroke that. I'd been thinking of getting in touch, but I wasn't quite sure how, since you'd gone back to America."

"Did you know I'd gone home?"

"Oh, yes. For years one of the neighbors has come in to read me the newspapers and magazines. Terribly kind, and it means I've kept up with you."

"Please, why did you say it was urgent that we meet? The last time you insisted you knew nothing about me, that we weren't related."

He sighed. "I've been troubled by that ever since. I never was quite sure I'd done the right thing. But by the time I'd made up my mind, you had left the country and Claudette had died. There seemed nothing I could do to change a decision I'd made and regretted. Until last night, when you were on the Terry Wogan show and said you were in London for a week."

She was longing for him to get to the point, but there seemed little chance of hurrying him. He was still speaking. "Now's my chance, I said to myself. If you're going to undo that old wrong, Harry Cramer, this is the time to do it. So I telephoned the station and they agreed to give you a message."

He kept nervously fingering the heavy cane that he didn't

use in the house, but which was propped beside the chair. Once he dropped it and Lili reached down and picked it up and placed it back in his hand. "Thank you. You're a nice girl. Claudette and I thought so from the first, that's why—" He broke off, hesitated, then started again. "You see, my dear," he said softly, "when we met in 1974, I lied."

Lili drew a sharp breath. It really wasn't a surprise. His long, rambling approach made it obvious that he had more to say than he'd said before. But she couldn't be patient any longer. She wanted to know immediately the only thing that mattered. "Are you saying you really are my father?"

He smiled. "No. I am not."

Oddly, she was relieved. She hadn't admitted to herself that she wanted it to be so, but she did. Lili felt no kinship with Harry Cramer, no electric spark of discovery. She didn't want him to turn out to be the man she'd dreamed about and fictionalized and searched for. "Then, who are you?" she asked.

"I'm not your father," Cramer repeated. "But I was there when you were born. I lent you my name." He hesitated.

Lili could only wait.

"Loyalty is fine," Harry Cramer continued, "but after all these years it seems less important than other things. To live your whole life not knowing the truth about something so basic, it simply does not seem right."

She'd started shivering and couldn't stop. Lili sat trembling for the entire hour he took to tell his story.

Somehow she got through the next day and a half, and no one guessed that her world had turned upside down. Except for Andy. He telephoned her Thursday evening at midnight, while she was lying in the big hotel bed staring into the dark. Hearing his voice almost destroyed the rigid self-control she had maintained since her meeting with Harry Cramer.

"What's wrong, Lili?" Andy asked within the first ten seconds. "You sound awful."

"Something's happened, but I can't explain on the phone.

I'll be home late tomorrow afternoon. Will you meet the plane?"

"That's what I was calling about, love. I'm not in New York."

"Where are you?"

"At Westlake. My family's place in Grasmere."

"You're here in England?"

"Yes. I can't explain on the telephone either. I'll be staying a day or two more I think. I should be back in New York by Sunday." His voice softened, "Unless your crisis can't wait. Darling, do you need me? I'll come down to London tonight if you want."

Of course she needed him. But maybe not yet, maybe a couple of days on her own in New York would be a good thing. "I always need you," she said softly, "but I can wait until Sunday. I'll go home as scheduled. Only, Andy, come as soon as you can."

Because of the time difference, she was at Kennedy Airport Friday at five and in her apartment by six-thirty. She sat staring into space for a few moments, then got a piece of paper and a pen and began making notes. She'd tried to do this on the plane but she had been too exhausted. Now she had a kind of adrenaline-inspired resurgence and her head was clearer. She wanted to have it all down in black and white— the answers Harry Cramer had provided and the questions he'd unknowingly raised.

It was after ten when she put down her pen. Lili stared into space for a while, then made up her mind. She would not live with this secret, pretend an innocence she no longer had. Whatever the consequences for any of them, she was going to bring things into the open. They owed her explanations and she would have them.

She reached for the telephone, took a deep breath, and lifted the receiver. She'd call Irene first, then Loy.

On Sunday Andy went to Lili's directly from the airport. She was there waiting for him. They held each other a long time;

finally she pulled back and looked into his face. "You're tired."

"I am a bit. And . . ."

"And what?"

"Come and sit down." He led her to one of the oversize chairs, made her sit, and perched on the arm. "I've got a lot to tell you. Some of it is going to make you unhappy, but I've decided I can't keep it from you for that reason."

Lili didn't appear to react. "Okay, I'm listening."

Andy took the Málaga photograph from his pocket. He pointed to the woman in the brimmed hat, the one wearing the beads. "This is my cousin Charlotte. She was famous for her beads. That's what finally jogged my memory. The night of the party, when you wore the jet necklace, I realized that the familiarity I'd always thought I saw was because my subconscious had recognized Charlotte. Even though she was only thirty in this picture and it was taken before I was born."

"I see," Lili said. "And the other one? Do you know who she is too?"

"Amanda Kent Preston-Wilde. Lady Swanning, as we first suspected. By the time this photo was taken she'd had plastic surgery. That's why it didn't look like the pictures of Amanda we compared it to."

Lili got up without saying a word. He followed her into the kitchen and watched her pour drinks, straight scotch without ice for both of them. He was unnerved by that; it was so out of character for Lili. So was her silence.

"Will you let me spit out the rest of the story while I still have the courage?" he asked. "I hate hurting you and I know I'm going to."

Lili turned her face to his. "Go ahead," she said.

He couldn't meet her eyes. "I'm sure Amanda had further plastic surgery." He took a deep breath. "I'm equally sure Loyola Perez is Amanda Kent."

Lili didn't say anything. His words echoed in the silence between them.

Andy cocked his head and studied her. "It seems insane, but I have the feeling this isn't news to you."

"No, not exactly. I had another meeting with Harry Cramer

while I was in England. Let's go back in the living room. It's my turn."

This time Lili insisted on sitting across from him so she could see him more clearly while she spoke.

"There's something very important that you don't know," she said quietly. "Amanda Kent is my mother."

PART THREE

Amanda and Irene

❧ 18 ❧

Fielding and London: 1935–36

It was Irene's father, Bill Petworth, who enlarged the Fielding general store and renamed it Petworth's Department Store. Bill was the same age as Sam and Amanda Kent's son Thomas, who was a graduate of Andover and Harvard, and a Boston businessman with substantial investments in stocks and bonds. In 1911 Bill married Mary Simms, a Fielding girl. Thomas had married two years previously, and brought his wife Jane to the big house on Woods Road.

Neither Thomas nor Bill became a father easily. Mary Petworth miscarried three times before she produced Irene in 1917. And in 1919, after ten barren years and after she had all but given up hope, Jane Kent gave birth to a baby girl. The child was called Amanda after her grandmother.

In the normal way of things the Petworths and the Kents did not socialize, but both little girls attended the Abraham Lincoln School. Amanda and Irene met on the playground swings when grades one and three had recess together, and some particular chemistry which knew nothing of social divisions made each recognize in the other a kindred spirit.

Later, the town and the families presumed, their ways would part. Amanda Kent would do whatever wealthy young women of her generation were doing, and eventually marry well and perhaps distantly. Irene Petworth would marry a local boy and likely he'd take over the store. She would remain in Fielding as countless Petworth women had before her.

Partly as a result of the new mores that swept America in the twenties, it did not work out that way. There were no flappers in Fielding, no marathon dancers or women who smoked in public—but change was in the air. There was a definite sense of the old order passing. Maybe that's why the two girls remained, against all tradition, inseparable friends.

The friendship was seen as peculiar, but while Irene and Amanda were young, the town reserved most of its disapproval for Irene. People in Fielding did not like the Petworth girl. Cold, they said, gives herself airs. Pretty enough in her blond way, but no warmth or naturalness in her. They felt more kindly toward Amanda, and not only because she was a Kent. Amanda was sweet and remarkably pretty, with a ready smile and an appealing natural gaiety.

The hard times of the thirties followed the craziness of the twenties. During the boom Thomas Kent had sold much of his land, all but the acreage surrounding the house itself, and put every last cent in the stock market. When the crash came in '29 he hung on by his fingernails. After that things got worse rather than better.

"There's nothing else to do," he told his wife in late 1935. "I have to raise some cash or we'll lose everything."

"Thomas," Jane said softly, "what about the Constable?"

"I've been thinking of it," he admitted.

A few days later an art expert from Boston came to tea at the Kents'. They received him in the parlor with its rosebud-strewn wallpaper, its red velvet furniture, and its marble-topped tables. Jane served little jam tarts and her best brew of Earl Grey.

"What do you think of my Constable?" Kent asked his visitor.

The Boston man studied the picture of the hayfield for some moments before he spoke. "Mind telling me where it came from?"

"My grandfather is supposed to have brought it from England sometime around 1835. He made it part of my mother's dowry when she married my father in 1870."

The art expert nodded. "A plausible story. Constable died in England in 1837. He was painting until the end of his life. But . . ."

Thomas and Jane leaned forward eagerly. "Yes?"

"Look," the man said with obvious discomfort. "I'm not the last word. You might want another opinion."

"I'm told that you're the most knowledgeable man in Boston as regards English landscape painting," Thomas said. "That's why you're here."

"I see. You're thinking of selling the painting?"

"Possibly," Thomas admitted.

The art expert sighed. "I'm sorry, really I am. In my opinion, it's a fake. You can go through a lot of testing and investigation, but there's absolutely no doubt in my mind. Walk into any museum and look at real Constables, even the very early work. You won't have any doubts either."

"That bad, eh?" Thomas asked quietly. As if the other man had not pronounced his doom.

"That bad."

"Wouldn't you like to take it down and have a look in better light?" Jane asked. "It is rather dull in here this afternoon."

"Mrs. Kent, forgive me, but there's really no need for a closer examination."

So the financial crisis could not be salvaged by the Constable, and the situation worsened. Five months later Thomas Kent went one morning to his Boston office and hung himself.

He was buried on the first Monday in May, in the Kent family plot in the graveyard beside the Congregational Church. It was a bright and sunny day with high puffy clouds scudding across a cerulean sky. Seventeen-year-old Amanda wished it were raining. If it were, perhaps no one would notice that she could summon no tears for her father.

"I can't help it," she told her mother later, when finally they were alone in the house. "I can't feel anything but fury that he'd do this to us."

Jane was more tolerant than her daughter. "Everybody has a breaking point," she said. "A place where they come to the end, where they can't hold on anymore. Daddy reached his breaking point."

Amanda had chestnut-colored hair with blond highlights, worn long in a soft pageboy. She pushed it back from her temples with nervous fingers. "Well, he's brought me to mine. I can't face it, Mama. What must people be saying? What are we going to do?"

"People are saying what they always say, a tiny bit of the truth fancied up with a lot of imagination. As for what we're going to do, we'll simply have to pull in our belts and make some hard choices. The ones Daddy couldn't make."

Four days later Jane had spoken to her lawyer about selling off part of the land around the house to raise money to pay the most pressing debts. Fortunately there was a buyer who had long been interested and whom the Depression had not totally impoverished. Jane agreed to take a price that she knew represented half what the property would have been worth in good times.

"Beggars can't be choosers," she told her daughter.

"I can't be a beggar, Mama," the girl whispered. "I can't face it." Amanda spoke with such utter desolation, her words demanded to be taken seriously.

"No," Jane murmured. "Perhaps you can't. Daddy couldn't either."

For a time Jane said no more, but she was thinking. Her husband's weakness had come as no surprise. Jane had realized early in their marriage that Thomas was a man sustained by his name and his wealth and his assured place in the scheme of things. Perhaps Amanda had inherited the same flaw.

Jane's way of coping was to maintain as much normalcy as she could manage. Sunday lunch was always served in the dining room at one; it was always formal. The Sunday after Thomas's burial was the same, though only Amanda and Jane sat at the mahogany table, and there was only one woman to both cook and serve the roast beef and the mashed potatoes, and the turnips and carrots and biscuits.

"Eat your dinner, Amanda," Jane said when the girl picked at her food. "Daddy wouldn't want you to starve because he's gone."

It wasn't grief for her father that had taken Amanda's appetite, her mother knew. The comment was merely a commonplace. Amanda didn't reply, and silence hung heavy in the dining room of the bay window and the cranberry glass and the flow-blue china.

"I think these seat covers have had their day," Jane remarked a few minutes later. "They're shabby to the point of being threadbare."

Amanda looked at the now-ragged pink roses on the needlepoint covering of the chair next to hers. "Yes," she said sadly, "they are." Amanda had always delighted in the fact that she lived in the nicest house in town. In the last few years, while the noose tightened around her father's neck, no money had been spent on keeping it up. Yet another charge to be laid against him. "Will you find someone to make new ones?"

Jane sighed. "Dear heart, I'll have to cover them myself with some old brown stuff I happen to have. There's no money to pay for fancy needlework. You simply don't understand, do you?"

"No." Amanda put down her fork. Were she a less well-bred girl, she'd have slammed it down. "I don't. I'll never understand. Look, I have an idea. Why don't we sell the Constable? It should be very valuable."

"The Constable is worthless," Jane said quietly. "Daddy had an expert look at it last December. It's a fake. If it were not, a great deal could have been salvaged." Her voice broke slightly. "Your father would be sitting here with us today."

Faced with such a contradiction of reality, Amanda was speechless.

Later, after Amanda and her mother had retired to the parlor, and the cook had brought a pot of coffee to complete the familiar ritual of Sunday lunch at the Kent place, Jane returned to the subject of her daughter's misery. "I have a plan, Amanda, but not much money to back it up. A lot will depend on you."

"Depend on me how? A plan about what?"

Jane plunged. "I think you have to leave Fielding. There's no way you're going to resign yourself to being less than you've always been. And if you stay here, you'll have to do exactly that."

Amanda's eyes were gray; they narrowed as she studied her mother. "Leave and go where? Boston?"

"No, that won't be far enough. In Boston everybody knows who you are and what has happened. I'm thinking of

Europe, England perhaps. Because of the language. Besides, our ancestors were English. It's fitting."

"What would I do there?" Amanda demanded.

"That's the part that's up to you. But it seems to me that for a girl raised as you've been, a pretty, intelligent girl, there may be opportunities. You'll be on your own, dear heart. All I can do is set you on your way. I have to stay here and see things through."

Amanda's mind was racing ahead. "If there's no money, how am I to go to England?"

Jane had worked out this part in advance, her cleverness inspired by urgency. If she was right and Amanda shared Thomas's flaw, his fatal weakness, then she did not have a lot of time. She was the widow of a suicide. She did not intend to sit back and wait to become the mother of something equally terrible. "I can whittle three hundred dollars from the down payment on the land," she explained. "I won't pay the Petworth's bill right away. It's three years overdue, but I expect Bill Petworth will wait a little longer."

"Surely three hundred dollars isn't enough," Amanda said.

"No, but I can give you something else. I still have my pearls. I've wanted to sell them a dozen times, but Daddy wouldn't permit it." Her voice softened and trembled slightly. "At first they were a symbol to him, a promise that our troubles were merely temporary. Later, well, they wouldn't have brought enough to change anything."

Jane took a handkerchief from her sleeve and dabbed at her eyes, and when she spoke again her voice was steady. "The pearls are appraised at a thousand dollars. So you should be able to sell them for at least half as much. And there's your grandmother's brooch. It has real diamonds around the edge and a sapphire in the middle."

"I bet I could do well if I sold them in England," Amanda said. Excitement was beginning to well in her, to raise again some of the spirited gaiety that had always been such a part of her personality.

"Yes, I think so," Jane agreed. "I'll begin checking on sailings, shall I?"

"Oh, yes!" Amanda crossed the room and knelt by her mother's chair. "Mama, thank you. You're an angel. I see some light at the end of the tunnel, and I was beginning to think I'd entirely lost my way."

Jane lay her hand gently on her daughter's hair. "Not you, dear heart. I will not permit you to lose your way. Now I suppose you'll run off and tell Irene, but be sure she understands it's a secret. We can't have any of this talked about before we're ready."

Amanda had discovered years before that her dearest friend was a good keeper of secrets. She and Irene spent countless hours together—by the edge of Willock's Stream, or in the ruin of the old Kent chicken house, or on the wisteria-covered screened porch at Amanda's, or the big double swing in the backyard at Irene's. They told each other everything and swore always to be the same best friends they were now.

On the Sunday when Jane made her proposal and changed the shape of Amanda's world, the girls had agreed to meet at three at the foot of the Kent driveway. Amanda grabbed a black wool jacket from the closet next to the butler's pantry and tossed it over her black silk dress—she had to at least pretend to be in mourning—and raced down the gravel path to where Irene was waiting.

The two girls hugged as they always did when they met or parted. It was a habit formed years before, like so many others. They were the same height. Amanda was thinner, Irene a bit more plump. Irene had lighter hair, a pale true blond, but she too had gray eyes.

Though Irene was two years older than Amanda, the younger girl was always the leader. It was almost as if Irene had willed her development to slow to keep pace with that of her friend.

Irene's first period didn't come until she was fourteen, three months after Amanda had her first at age twelve. It was about then that they began locking themselves in one or the other's bedroom and stripping off their clothes and examining each other's newly pubescent bodies with clinical attention. The episodes were entirely innocent, nothing else would have occurred to them, but as they got older they had pulled back from behavior they knew wasn't quite right. Now only the hugs remained.

"Bliss!" Amanda chortled as she pressed her cheek against her friend's. "Bliss! Bliss! Bliss!"

"What are you talking about? Amanda, what is it?"

Irene was always the more reserved of the pair, the more reticent and conventional. Perhaps that was why she so adored Amanda, whose enthusiasm and ready joy made up for all she sensed was lacking in herself. But sometimes, like today, it was overwhelming. Amanda's father wasn't even cold in his grave. "What can possibly be blissful when your poor father's hardly dead a week?"

"Don't mention him to me," Amanda said fiercely. "I don't want to hear his name. All this trouble is his fault. And it's only because Mama is so brave and so smart that everything's going to work out."

"What's going to work out? How? Amanda, sometimes you're so . . . imprecise. Calm down and tell me what's going on."

So they walked to the stream and sat on the high bank and Amanda Kent told Irene Petworth that she was going away.

"For how long?" Irene asked in a small voice.

"I don't know." The sun was warm. Amanda took off her jacket and rolled it up and made a pillow of it and lay back on the tender spring grass. "Years perhaps. Maybe forever. I have to find a wealthy Englishman to marry, Irene. Don't you see? That's the whole point of everything."

Irene didn't answer immediately. A robin circled them warily, then snatched a piece of reed it coveted and flew swiftly away. At last she said, "I'm going to miss you a lot."

Amanda turned and took her hand. "Not as much as I'll miss you. Irene, I have a brilliant idea. Why don't you come with me?"

Irene shook her head. "I can't do that. My mother's been feeling poorly for months. I couldn't leave her. Besides, things aren't especially good at the store now. My folks couldn't afford to send me to England."

"Speaking of the store reminds me. Can you get your father to wait a little longer for my mother to pay his bill? I'll send the money from England as soon as I can."

"I can't tell him that if you want me to keep your going a secret. But I'm sure he won't press your mother. I heard him say so a couple of nights back."

"Good. That's all right, then." Amanda stood up and dusted herself off and held out her hand. "Come along, pussycat. Let's go back to my house and you can help me decide what to pack for England."

In the whole world Amanda was the only person who called Irene by a pet name. She wondered how she was going to survive not hearing anyone address her as pussycat ever again.

On the first of June Amanda sailed for England. By the time the *Queen Mary* docked in Southampton eight days later, one of the gambles, taken on Jane's advice, had paid off.

A small first-class cabin aboard the floating palace cost a hundred and seventy-five dollars. That was a great part of what Amanda had, but she spent it. "It's an investment," Jane said. "You won't meet the right sort of people in anything but first class."

Amanda agreed, and so she traveled in style. And she made a friend of the tall, dark woman who always wore beads and breeches and smoked skinny black cigars and wasn't at all beautiful, but was remarkably attractive and enormous fun. It occurred to the American girl that she should be cultivating men, not women. But you couldn't choose your opportunities.

"I'm not very typical," Charlotte Switham said the night before they docked. "You mustn't expect everyone in England to be as mad as I."

"More's the pity," Amanda said gaily. "But then, the whole world is probably not big enough for two of you, so how could England be?"

And they laughed and Charlotte took Amanda's arm and pressed it close to her side in that way she had that always made Amanda feel a little peculiar, though she didn't yet know why.

At Southampton the sunlit, magic existence aboard the great liner was replaced by demanding reality. Suddenly the world was grimy docks and eagle-eyed customs men and shouting porters and sullen gray skies. Amanda knew her first moment of fear.

"Cheer up," Charlotte said, seeing her companion's expression. "Welcome to the Empire. And don't worry about anything. I'm being met. I'll give whoever it is instructions to look after your things as well as mine. We'll be out of this pretty quickly. Meanwhile, hang on to my cloak and do as you're told."

So Amanda literally clutched the folds of Charlotte's dashing red cape and followed instructions. And her miraculous luck held, because with very little fuss she soon found herself in a Rolls Royce limousine complete with a uniformed chauffeur and a bud vase holding a single rose and a decanter of sherry and tiny crystal glasses. The great black car carried them to London, to a wonderful late-Regency house in Gordon Square.

"Have you read any books by Virginia Woolf?" Charlotte asked. "Or Vita Sackville-West? Do you know what's meant by Bloomsbury?"

Amanda shook her head and Charlotte laughed with delight. "You innocent little foreign lamb! Bloomsbury's all around us. We're smack in the middle of it. The Woolfs actually live nearby in Tavistock Square. But don't worry, you'll learn. I'll teach you and you'll be a good girl and do exactly as I say."

Charlotte was twenty-five, seven years older than the American girl. This time Amanda was the follower, not the leader, as she'd always been with Irene. She didn't mind. She needed to snag a rich husband, and Gordon Square seemed the ideal place to start looking.

The invitation to stay with Charlotte had come soon after the pair met. Amanda had no hesitation in accepting. She'd already questioned her cabin steward and discovered that Miss Switham was related to somebody named Lord Westlake. In England, Amanda believed, titles usually accompanied wealth.

"I'm not in the mood for that great pile we live in up in the Lake District," Charlotte had said. "And you want to see

London, not the provinces. So we'll stay in town unless the family demands a command performance."

Thus Charlotte decreed and thus it was. Amanda couldn't have been better pleased.

Within a week of arriving in London, Amanda quietly sold her mother's pearls and her grandmother's brooch for two hundred pounds. As things turned out, she needed the cash only for pin money, whatever small luxury Charlotte might overlook, but there weren't many of those. The English woman assumed all expenses and paid all the bills.

Amanda not only had found free food and lodging, but also was plunged into fashionable society. Often they were guests at dinner parties attended by elegant men and women who regarded remarkable Charlotte and her pretty little American friend as a bit of color to liven up the proceedings. The social grouping known as Bloomsbury determined what was done and not done among a certain segment of the elite. Their tastes were "modern." In such circles Charlotte's eccentricities were seen as amusing. Besides, Charlotte had an interesting, supple mind. And she was supremely well connected.

"My mother was the youngest daughter of James Mendoza, the second Lord Westlake," Charlotte explained one lazy June afternoon when the two women sat in the conservatory of the Gordon Square house sipping after-lunch coffee amid the ferns and potted orange trees. "The Mendozas were originally a Spanish family."

The American girl wasn't particularly interested in the history of her benefactor, but she knew Charlotte was devoted to studying the murky past. She asked the appropriate question. "When did your ancestors come to England?"

"In the sixteenth century, because of the sherry trade. Sherry's made in Spain, but guzzled over here—and a thriving business. So naturally the Mendozas were involved." She paused and cast a sideways glance at Amanda, who was examining a selection of chocolates in an exquisite silver dish. "And something else," she added.

"What?"

"Before I tell you, will you swear to give an honest answer to a question?"

Amanda looked up, intrigued at last. "What question?"

"Swear first."

"Very well, I swear." The words were accompanied by a little giggle that contrasted with Charlotte's intent expression.

"How do you feel about Jews?"

"Jews! What an astonishing question." Amanda considered for a moment. "I really don't know," she said at last. "I've never met any. They're all foreign, aren't they? The men have beards and the women wear shawls and they speak with a funny accent."

Charlotte snorted. "See, you are prejudiced. What an absurd idea. They're not all like that. I'm not, for example."

"You! Charlotte, you're not a Jew. How can you be?"

"My ancestors were. That's what I was explaining. The Mendozas of Córdoba were originally Jews. When the Arabs ruled southern Spain they became Muslims. A few hundred years later the Christians defeated the Arabs and the family went back to being Jews for a while. In 1492 all the Jews in Spain were exiled, thrown out of the country. Rather than go, the Mendozas converted to Christianity. But a century later there was one named Ramón who wanted to be a Jew again. So the family sent him to London to organize this end of the sherry business."

"Here, to this house? How fascinating." Amanda really was interested now. She ignored the chocolates and fixed her attention on Charlotte.

"Not this house, you goose. It wasn't built until 1825. Ramón went to a place called Creechurch Lane in the East End. It's a slum now, but in those days there were lots of Spanish and Portuguese Jews living there. They were running away from the Inquisition. They pretended to be Protestants, but everyone knew they were Jews. The English had banished all their own Jews in the thirteenth century, but they let these few come in because they were good for trade."

Amanda cocked her head and stared at the other woman. "Then you really are a Jew?"

"Not the way you mean. My great-grandfather Joseph Mendoza bought Westlake, our estate in Grasmere, in 1825, the same year he bought this house. Then he started to worry. English law wasn't clear on the subject of Jews. Joseph couldn't be sure he could pass the property to his heirs."

Charlotte curled her long legs beneath her and lit another of her little cigars. In her breeches and her strings of beads she looked nothing if not foreign and exotic.

"It was one thing to have a little unobtrusive house in the East End," she went on, "but another to own a splendid town house and a two-hundred-and-forty-room Tudor mansion. Someone might become jealous and make difficulties. Joseph didn't plan to let everything he owned go to the Crown on some legal technicality. So when his father died in 1835, he became a Christian and joined the Church of England."

Charlotte sucked on her cigar and exhaled a stream of blue smoke into the warm sunlit air. "There were numerous Mendoza cousins who didn't follow Joseph's lead. Some of them are Jews to this day, but both branches of the family go into the family bank, at least the men do, and Westlake is rather the hub of the wheel, sort of a meeting place for all of them."

Amanda sensed something of importance to herself in this story and was now genuinely trying to understand. "How did your great-grandfather get a title? Did he buy it with the house?"

Charlotte chuckled. "You're learning how things are done, aren't you? It wasn't quite so blatant. Joseph donated a lot of money to defray the costs of Queen Victoria's coronation, and a short time later she created a territorial baronetcy for him." Charlotte snapped her fingers. "Presto-chango, from then on he was Lord Westlake and the Mendozas were hereditary peers of the realm."

"Just like that," Amanda said thoughtfully.

"Just like that," Charlotte agreed. Amanda looked pensive. She seemed moved by the story. "What are you thinking?" Charlotte asked.

Amanda waved a dismissive hand. "Oh, nothing much, just about history and about how life can be so . . . unpredictable."

Bliss was it in that dawn to be alive/ But to be young was very heaven!

Amanda closed the book in which she had read Wordsworth's lines about the French Revolution and savored a thrilling shiver of recognition. The poet had expressed exactly her sentiments about this very summer of 1936 in London. She looked at the matched sets of leather-bound books in the library of the house in Gordon Square, at the paintings of horses which Charlotte had told her were by somebody terribly famous named George Stubbs, at the antique mahogany and oak, and at the splendid carving of the plaster ceiling—and she purred with pleasure.

Thanks to her mother's inspiration and a stroke of luck, she had come to exactly the right place at precisely the right time. Here everything that had been jarred out of kilter in her life could be made whole again. No, it could be made better than she had dreamed.

Her smile of pleasure became a slight frown of determination. She would let nothing stand in the way of the golden possibilities unfolding, certainly not Charlotte's whims. As long as she was clever, everything would be perfect. It wouldn't matter that some of Charlotte's tastes were not merely eccentric, they were downright peculiar.

Charlotte accepted invitations for dinner nearly every night in the week, but she insisted that they have tea at home every day, and she wouldn't let Amanda wear ordinary clothes for the ritual. At five o'clock Amanda must exchange whatever she was wearing for the extravagant lingerie Charlotte had purchased for her at Harrods.

"I adore seeing you like some decadent *belle époque* courtesan, my sweet. Indulge me."

Amanda always did. Each day at a few minutes before five she went to her bedroom across the hall from Charlotte's own and removed her dress and her slip and her hose and her "all-in-one," and put on a pair of pink silk panties with loose legs and lace trim. Over it she wrapped a pastel satin kimono and tied it tight so it hugged her body. When the clock in the corridor outside the bedroom chimed five times, Amanda joined her hostess for tea.

It was served in the small sitting room adjoining Charlotte's bedroom, where the walls were hung with old tapestries and the furniture upholstered in dull gold damask. If it was chilly, there would be a fire in the grate, but so far that summer most days had been warm. When Amanda arrived, the tea tray was in place. No servants disturbed the perfect peace. They would not reappear until Charlotte rang.

Charlotte always poured. She did so on the afternoon of the July day when Amanda had discovered her soul's image in Wordsworth's lines. Amanda was thinking of the poem as she reclined on the damask sofa watching Charlotte.

The English woman added sugar and milk to Amanda's tea, but when her guest stretched out a languid hand, Charlotte did nothing. She seemed unaware that she still held the fragile porcelain cup and saucer. "I'm quite mad about you. You do realize that, don't you, Mandy?"

Charlotte was the first person who had ever called Amanda Mandy. She didn't like it, but she didn't protest. Charlotte called herself "she who must be obeyed" and it was not entirely a joke. "And I'm mad about you," Amanda replied as she gently pried the saucer from Charlotte's hand. "You've been so kind to me, how could I help but adore you?"

Charlotte didn't reply.

Amanda sipped her tea, then helped herself to a buttered muffin from the silver dish on the table between them. She'd not yet bitten into it when Charlotte flung herself forward and knelt beside the couch and knocked it from her hand.

"Stop it! Stop eating and acting as if I haven't said anything important. I know you're innocent, but surely not as innocent as that."

Amanda was alarmed. Charlotte sounded genuinely angry. "Darling, I don't understand what you mean." That was a habit she'd quickly acquired. Calling other women darling. It was terribly British and that was what she was trying to be. "Darling, if you'll only explain, I'm sure—"

"I shan't explain," Charlotte interrupted. "I'll show you."

A moment later her mouth was pressed to Amanda's, and she was fumbling with the tie of the satin kimono. It came apart easily and there was Amanda exactly as Charlotte had dreamed her to be, as she'd arranged—pale flesh naked except for the little pink knickers, soft breasts, soft belly, soft thighs emerging from a band of handworked lace. Charlotte broke the kiss and pulled back a bit, her dark eyes devouring the sight.

Amanda was frozen, not with revulsion but with surprise. Charlotte wore men's breeches and smoked cigars, but those were simply affectations. She was a woman. So why was Charlotte suddenly lowering her head and licking her breasts? Why was she tugging at the waist of the silk panties? Men did those things. That's what you had to be so careful of if you weren't married. Amanda knew all that, but what she knew did not fit the facts of this extraordinary circumstance.

"Charlotte, listen, darling, I don't think . . . ah . . . oh dear . . . you must stop, you're making me dizzy. Charlotte . . ."

"Shh," Charlotte whispered. "Don't say a word. Don't think, only feel. It's harmless. I love you, my adorable Mandy. I'm going to show you what love is."

What took place that golden afternoon on the couch in Gordon Square might have been termed a rape—except that after the first five minutes, during which Amanda was too conscious of her dependence on Charlotte to seriously protest—it became a mutual sortie into hitherto unknown delights. By the time they were dressing for dinner with friends in Belgravia, sharing Charlotte's dressing room so they could stop every few moments and kiss and fondle, the older woman could say with glee, "I knew you were a sapphist! I knew it the moment we met."

Perhaps.

Amanda quite soon realized that she adored the things she and Charlotte did together. She went weak at the thought of the other woman's mouth, her hands, her long, hard body and small, hard breasts. But when she analyzed everything she now understood about Charlotte Mendoza Switham and her family, Amanda recognized that she could make no long-term plans based upon this remarkable relationship. Charlotte was her entree into the world where true security was to be found. She was not, however, a source of such security.

So in September when Emery Preston-Wilde—whom she'd met at a dinner party and who was widowed, titled, rich, handsome, and apparently mad about her—proposed, Amanda accepted. A few days later she screwed up her courage and told Charlotte she was engaged to be married.

"You can't do it," Charlotte said, tight-lipped with anger, white with shock. "I won't let you do it. He was married to my cousin Phillipa until she died. He's twenty years older than you. And worst of all, he's a man. Don't you understand, Mandy!" She was shouting now. "A man!"

"I know."

"You can't. If you do, you can't understand what it really means. Or maybe you still don't realize what you are. Damn you! I'll show you."

And once more she threw herself on the younger woman and ravished her, and within minutes Amanda was reduced to a quivering heap of vibrating nerve ends. But when the passion was spent, nothing had changed except Amanda's understanding of how cautious she must be.

"Emery darling, would it be too awful if we eloped?"

Lord Swanning regarded his fiancée with mild surprise. "Awful? No, I suppose not. But why? I thought all girls wanted a fancy wedding. And isn't your mother coming over?"

"My mother isn't well enough to travel." Amanda had said nothing about Jane's impoverished circumstances. "Daddy's only dead five months. I don't think I can face the fuss of a big wedding without Mama."

"Of course, my dear." Emery was immediately solicitous and understanding. "Stupid of me not to have seen all that before. As long as I get you, precious, the wedding matters not a bit. Elope we shall."

❧ 19 ❧

Swanning Park and London: 1936–39

A week after the Preston-Wildes returned from their surprise elopement and honeymoon in Greece, Charlotte drove herself to Sussex to confront Amanda. "How was it?" she demanded of her unfaithful lover. "How was your wedding night with him? You slut! Did he make you feel what I can make you feel?"

In fact he hadn't, but Amanda had no intention of admitting that. "Charlotte, you and I had better come to an understanding." She was Lady Swanning now; she could speak her mind, dictate the terms of the relationship. "I'm married to Emery and I won't allow any scandal to touch me or my husband. If you try and make any, I'll heap it back on your own head so liberally that not even being one of the Mendozas will save you. Is that clear?"

Charlotte's dark eyes looked into Amanda's with a mixture of longing and pain and fury and supplication. She opened her mouth but no words came, and after some seconds she turned her face away. Her shoulders were quivering slightly, but if she were sobbing, it was without tears.

"Good," Amanda said softly. "I think you appreciate the realities, as Emery might say."

They were in one of the glass houses near the cottage of the head gardener, supposedly admiring the regal lilies. The flowers were not, Charlotte thought, half so regal as Amanda. In a mere thirty days she had changed completely. The naive little American had become Her Ladyship, and like a great actress she had assumed every nuance of the role.

Amanda lifted her wrist in an elegantly casual gesture and looked at her gold watch. With a stab of pain Charlotte saw it was the very watch she'd given Amanda to celebrate that first afternoon of love in Gordon Square.

"Forty minutes until luncheon," Amanda said, her voice now infinitely sweet and soft with promise. "We must go back to the house. And if you swear never ever to call me Mandy again, you can come up to my room." Amanda parted her lips, drew her tongue over them. "There's enough time to show you my wedding lace," she whispered.

Swanning Park made few demands on its new chatelaine. Nearly four hundred years the house had stood, its rituals were graven into the very stones, its manner of life ordained and sustained by a perfectly trained staff, most of whom had been born within its walls. Amanda had little to do.

This circumstance did not trouble Emery. He had married the young American because he found her charming and decorative, and he'd somewhere heard that Americans were particularly fertile.

He desperately hoped she would present him with a son. Lord Swanning was the last of his line. He'd been the only child of an only child. His first wife, Phillipa Mendoza, had developed a cancerous uterus which remained empty and eventually killed her. Within the terms of the grant made originally to his ancestor by Elizabeth Tudor, only males in the direct line of succession could inherit the title. So the need for a son was pressing. Apart from that, he expected little from Amanda.

Months went by and Lady Swanning did not conceive though her husband tried his best. Sometime during this period of fevered and regular thrusting and twisting beneath the silk quilts and linen sheets, Emery noticed that his new wife didn't enjoy his attentions. Maybe that was it. Maybe the fact that Amanda was apparently frigid affected the likelihood of her becoming pregnant. If she'd only move a bit beneath him, show a trifle more enthusiasm, perhaps moan once or twice. But she never did.

Emery came to resent this fact, and his resentment turned ugly. His lovemaking soon had nothing to do with love. It was a harsh assault made on a dry citadel. "You might try a bit, you know," he muttered often.

"I do try," Amanda whispered. "And I never refuse you."

Both statements were true, but they changed nothing of his style or her response. And she didn't become pregnant.

Emery never connected Amanda's behavior in the bedroom to her continuing friendship with the outrageous Charlotte Switham, or the slightly outré set Amanda had run with before he married her. He was not the kind of man to think of such a thing. He simply lived with the situation by day, and took his festering anger out on Amanda's docile body by night.

On the surface nothing changed between them. They appeared devoted and were seen in all the best places. The Preston-Wildes went to the appropriate venues at the appointed times, gave parties and attended them, traveled up and down the country to take part in weekends given over to hunting or fishing or croquet or, in the dead of winter, bridge. Amanda was always bright and gay and pretty, and Emery could not fault her behavior. It had to be enough.

As for Amanda, she very much enjoyed large segments of her life; the rest she gritted her teeth and bore. One annoying fact, however, did rankle, and for a long time she could find no way around it. She had no money.

As Lady Swanning, she never had to pay for anything. There was a housekeeper who managed all the household accounts and anything Amanda might see in a shop and want was automatically charged to her husband. Emery paid these bills without a murmur, so she had no reason to ask him for anything as vulgar as cash, but not having any meant she couldn't help Jane.

Amanda had not forgotten her mother's difficulties, but she couldn't figure out how to ease them. Explaining the situation to Emery was unthinkable, and while Charlotte would probably give her money, Amanda didn't dare grant Charlotte any additional hold over her.

For almost a year she was at an impasse. Until in 1937 she received a letter from home in which her mother enclosed a newspaper clipping from the March 17 edition of the *Fielding Post Times*.

There was Irene, whose parents had been killed in a train crash a few months before, turning over the store to her fourth cousin. At last Irene was free of her responsibilities, and she must have a bit of money in hand. Amanda decided at once to invite Irene to visit Swanning Park. Before she saw the picture in the newspaper she hadn't realized how much she missed her oldest and dearest friend. The letters they exchanged weren't the same as seeing each other.

Amanda wrote that same day and she felt happy simply having mailed the letter. Soon afterward she had a conversation which widened the possibilities.

She and Emery were entertaining guests for dinner. When Amanda led the ladies into the drawing room and left the gentlemen to their port and cigars, she heard one of the women say something about a secretary. "Do you have a secretary?" Amanda asked in surprise. "Whatever for?"

She was still young enough and American enough to be able to get away with such forthright questions. The lady with the secretary chuckled. "Don't look so shocked. It's certainly not business, my dear. A social secretary. So necessary to keep one's appointments sorted. Especially if one is active in charities and village things."

Before the month was over Amanda had involved herself in two church societies, an annual music fete, and a fund for the widows of seamen. Emery murmured approval of her assumption of the duties proper to a squires lady.

In November 1937 Irene Petworth arrived at Swanning Park. "Oh, pussycat, I can't believe you're really here!"

They hugged, they talked, they took long walks; Amanda showed Irene all the facets of her life as Lady Swanning. Well, almost all. She didn't discuss what happened when the door connecting her husband's bedroom and her own

was opened—and she certainly never admitted to what was
between herself and Charlotte.

"Your friend Charlotte terrifies me," Irene confided soon
after she met her.

"Terrifies you? How silly. Charlotte's eccentric, that's all.
It's an old English custom, being eccentric."

"Maybe. Is it an old English custom to look at someone
you've just met as if you wish they were dead?"

"Irene, that's absurd! Charlotte didn't."

"Yes, she did. It doesn't matter though. I didn't come to
see her, but you."

If Irene was willing to dismiss the animosity so easily,
Charlotte was not. Perhaps because she remained hopelessly
in love with Amanda, she recognized what Irene did not
suspect and what even Amanda had yet to admit to herself—
Amanda was in love with Irene. Internally, Charlotte hated
and raged, but she didn't see that there was much she could
do about it.

Emery, on the other hand, liked Irene immediately. Her
tranquillity appealed to him. Some people might see Irene as
placid, or even cool. Emery detected the deep streams that
ran in her. Besides, she was a relief after Amanda's brittle
chatter and the eternal gaiety that covered his wife's lack
of feeling. When Amanda suggested asking Irene to stay
on indefinitely, he was pleased. "But do you think she'll
want to?" he asked. "Hasn't she a life of her own back in
America?"

"No, not anymore. Her parents were killed a while back,
as I told you. But—" Amanda hesitated.

"But what?"

"Irene wasn't left very well off," she said. "I can't simply
ask her to stay. I have to provide some sort of an income.
Emery, I was wondering, could I hire her as my social
secretary?"

Emery was already thinking of something else. "Secretary,
yes, why not? Makes sense when you've all these charity
commitments."

"And can I say I'll pay her three pounds ten a week?"

He raised his eyebrows. "Seems a bit over the top, my
dear."

"I know. But Irene isn't a servant. She's a lady, accustomed to living as a lady should. I do so want to help her, Emery."

He shrugged. "Very well. Do as you like."

"Your secretary?" Irene said when she heard the proposal. "At three pounds ten shillings a week?" She did the necessary calculations on a scrap of paper, then looked up in astonishment. "Amanda, that's almost seventeen dollars. What duties am I to have?"

"Very few. And listen, pussycat, it *is* a lot more money than normal. I deliberately asked Emery to make it so much. For Mama." Amanda explained that what she wanted was to secretly send ten dollars a week of Irene's pay to Jane in Fielding. Irene, of course, understood and agreed.

For almost a year life was peaceful at Swanning Park, but the fiery potential of the relationships smoldered beneath the surface. Charlotte continued to visit, and she and Amanda continued to find stolen moments for their clandestine affair. Irene suspected nothing until an afternoon in the late summer of 1938 when she happened on the other two women in the boathouse near the pond.

They weren't exactly doing anything, but Amanda's blouse was unbuttoned. She was flushed and her hair was oddly tousled. Moreover, Irene could have sworn that in the instant before she arrived Charlotte had been kissing Amanda's breasts. She would have dismissed the idea as absurd, except that the look Charlotte turned on her was one of such venomous loathing.

For days Irene agonized about what to do or say. Amanda was a married woman, a titled woman. Surely what she did in that way was none of Irene's business? Besides, she, too, had grown up a great deal in the last few years. Irene was still a virgin, but she knew about life, even about lesbianism.

She'd sailed second class on a small, unglamorous ship and been bored by most of her fellow passengers, so she'd read a lot. Among the books she'd found in the ship's library was Radclyffe Hall's *The Well of Loneliness*. Irene had read it with great interest and sympathy. She'd even wondered for a while if she might be a lesbian and if that was the true nature of her love for Amanda. She'd decided it wasn't, and the last several months had convinced her she was right, but that didn't explain what might be between Amanda and Charlotte.

It would not have mattered so much if Irene had not also suspected Emery's feelings. She was more and more convinced that Lord Swanning was no longer in love with his wife, perhaps because she had not provided him with the heir he wanted so badly. If Amanda gave Emery cause, she might find herself banished, pensioned off. Irene was torn, unable to decide what she should do.

It was Amanda who created the situation that brought a temporary resolution of the dilemma.

The day Irene stumbled on Amanda and Charlotte making love in the boathouse, Charlotte became insanely furious. She managed to contain herself until Irene left, then she ranted and raved and hurled accusations. Among them was the one she'd promised herself never to make.

"You despicable little slut! You can't be true to anyone, man or woman. You're in love with prissy Irene and you haven't even the courage to do anything about it."

As soon as she said it Charlotte wanted to cut out her tongue. She knew Amanda very well, knew there was a kind of stupidity that accompanied her shrewdness. Amanda had probably never admitted to herself what she felt. Now that the idea had been put in her head, she would.

Two weeks later, on a stormy September night, when the wind howled about the countless chimneys of Swanning Park and the old fabric of the house creaked and groaned, Amanda crept into Irene's bed. "You're not sleeping, are you? I couldn't, not with this storm. I'm frightened." She cuddled up to her old friend. They had not been this physically close since they were children.

"You'd better go back to your own bed, Amanda. What will Emery say if he comes looking for you?"

Amanda giggled. "Don't worry, he won't. Emery sleeps like the dead. Especially after he's had as much wine as he had at dinner tonight."

Irene decided to chance it. "Since you've brought it up, don't you think Emery's drinking a bit much lately?"

"Maybe. I hadn't noticed."

"Amanda, you'd better notice. I think Emery's unhappy. I think you have to do something about it."

Amanda lay her hand lightly on Irene's thigh. "Pussycat, I don't want to talk about Emery. I want to talk about you and me."

Irene took a deep breath. "There's nothing to talk about."

"Yes, there is, even if you don't know yet."

Gently but firmly, Irene removed Amanda's hand from her leg. "I do know. I know what you mean, and I think I know about you and Charlotte."

"Charlotte is a whore. She's only a diversion. It's you I love, my darling pussycat. I've always loved you and you've always loved me."

"Yes, but not in the same way." Irene reached over and switched on the bedside lamp and sat up. "Amanda, I don't blame you, and I don't care what your . . . tastes are. But they're not mine, and if you can't accept that fact, I'll have to go."

Amanda was too clever to force the issue. She knew Irene well enough to understand she meant what she said. "Okay, if you're sure," she said easily. "Give me a cigarette and we'll chat."

They talked about life and love and men and women, the kind of intimate confidences that emerged from a lifetime of shared experiences. That was also what made it possible for Amanda to say finally, "Irene, do you realize that Emery's in love with you?"

"You're crazy!"

"No, I'm not. He's working up his courage to say so. If he hasn't declared himself yet, mark my words, he will."

"Oh, Amanda, that's awful." Irene was close to tears. "If that's true, then I really must go."

"Don't you dare! Haven't you been telling me to mind my p's and q's if I don't want to get tossed out of the manor on my fanny? Well, I don't. And I can't live without my kind of love. If you won't have me, I'll go on with Charlotte. So you'll have to stay around and take Emery's mind off me, won't you? Isn't that what a truly loyal friend would do?"

It was an absurd demand to make on any friendship, but theirs had always been special. Moreover, Irene didn't have anyplace to go, and if she was honest with herself, she had to admit she was flattered by the notion that Lord Swanning found her desirable.

Amanda proved a good judge of her husband. In early November he made his move. He and Irene were alone in the drawing room having coffee. Amanda had pleaded a headache and gone early to bed. Emery stood by the tray of liqueurs the butler had left. "A cordial, my dear? Something to warm you on such a chilly night?"

"Mmm, perhaps a tiny bit of apricot brandy."

Emery poured it and carried it to her. Their fingers touched. "Drink some," he whispered huskily. "Then let me drink from the same glass. It seems to be all I'm likely to have of you."

Irene stared at him for some moments, took a sip of the brandy, and passed him the tiny crystal glass. Emery downed the liqueur in one swallow, then leaned over and kissed her.

An hour later Irene Petworth was no longer a virgin.

Soon after Christmas she realized she was pregnant. Neither she nor Amanda had mentioned the affair with Emery, but Irene suspected Amanda knew. It seemed vital that Amanda not know about the child. That was a complication Irene simply couldn't deal with.

There was no question in Irene's mind of what Emery would do if she told him. He'd be delighted and he'd set her up in a household of her own, somewhere away from Swanning Park. If she had a son, he'd quietly admit parenthood and thus provide himself with what he desperately wanted, an heir for the title.

None of this suited Irene. She wasn't in love with Emery. She'd given in to him because his attentions were flattering, because she had a sense she was drifting, because she didn't know how to cope with the conflicting emotions in this ancient and imposing house. But if she admitted her pregnancy and had this child, she was tying herself to a lifetime as Emery Preston-Wilde's mistress. The thought appalled her.

She dithered for a week, then decided what she would do. There was only one person she knew who could help her do it.

On a bitter January day Irene took herself to London. Emery and Amanda were in Monte Carlo for a two-week holiday. Charlotte, Irene knew, was at Gordon Square.

The butler took her name and went away and returned a moment later and showed her to the drawing room. "Miss Switham will be with you shortly," he said as he bowed himself out.

Charlotte appeared after a few minutes. She didn't greet Irene until she'd lit one of her slim cigars and poured herself a drink, and pointedly not offered one to her caller. Then Charlotte leaned against a painted Venetian rococo console and examined Irene from head to toe. "Well, what have you come here for? To plead with me to leave Amanda alone?"

"No, nothing like that."

"I see. What then?"

"I need help. You're the only person I can think of who can give it to me."

"Why the bloody hell should I help you?"

"Because it will cost you nothing. Because I'm not your rival for Amanda's affection, and I think you know that now. Because my problem could rebound and cause Amanda problems, and I don't think you want that."

Charlotte narrowed her eyes and thought for a moment. "All good reasons," she said quietly. "What is it and what can I do?"

"I'm pregnant. I've decided to have an abortion but I don't know how to arrange it."

"Christ!" Charlotte lit another cigar from the stub of the first. "Am I permitted to ask who the father is?"

"Can't you guess?"

"Yes, I suppose I can. It's bloody Emery's bastard you're carrying, isn't it?"

Charlotte waited a moment. Irene said nothing and Charlotte knew that was confirmation of her statement. "Sit down," she said. "I'll ring for tea. After that I'll telephone a few people and make some inquiries. Don't worry, I'm sure it can be worked out."

• • •

By the time Amanda and Emery returned from Monaco, Irene had done what she'd set out to do and was back at Swanning Park. She looked as if nothing had happened, but that was not how she felt.

No one had warned Irene of any emotional repercussions. No ladies' magazines of the time admitted to the existence of abortion, no psychologists wrote articles about it in the popular press, women didn't send letters to the editor about how it had felt before, during, or after. Irene had nothing against which to measure her feelings.

Her experience had been better than many. Despite the fact that abortion was illegal in England, Charlotte had found her a competent man operating in a quite nice nursing home. She was properly anesthetized, cleanly aborted, and not exposed to anything sordid. But the aftermath was horrendous.

Irene walked through her days and endured her sleepless nights with the sense of a terrible void, a feeling of having both betrayed and been betrayed. What primitive instinct she had waked, what irrational taboo she'd broken—that she didn't know. But she wept all the time and she hated herself, and perversely she began to blame Emery, though he'd had no part in the decision and would have violently opposed it.

At the height of all this emotional chaos she was trying so hard to hide, Lord Swanning gave Irene a concrete reason to despise him. In February 1939 Emery joined Sir Oswald Mosley's British Union of Fascists, the Blackshirts.

Irene was not a political animal. She had not before now felt deeply about any social question and she had no particular sympathy for Jews. But the Blackshirts' ethos, their philosophy, and their vision of the future violated all her notions of the right ordering of things, that American sense of equality bred into her bones. Worse, Emery's fascism came as Adolf Hitler was making his presence felt internationally. All that Germany was becoming, all that it hoped to be, was what the Blackshirts seemed to desire for England. Irene was incensed. For entirely different reasons, so was Charlotte Mendoza.

"The bastards are all the same," she told Amanda. "Remember, I come from a long line of Jews, even if I've never been in a synagogue in my life. When you've read as much history as I have, you learn things. I *know* what Jew haters have done to us. Now Mosley and his lot mean for it to happen here. And Emery and the rest of the anti-Semites are falling in behind. Which is what they always do. Nothing changes very much."

Amanda listened to this diatribe, but she wasn't especially interested. "I don't think Emery's planning to run you out of the country, Charlotte darling. You mustn't make such a big thing of it."

Charlotte knew better. So did Irene. In their separate ways and in their separate provinces, the two of them worked on Amanda. The campaign wouldn't have succeeded except that while this secret undermining of anything she felt for Emery was going on, two other things happened.

First, Amanda learned that Emery had made some spectacularly bad investments and run up a huge overdraft at his bank. She found out when she accidentally opened a letter addressed to her husband. She immediately resealed it and said nothing, but she suspected that to pay his debts Emery would have to sell large parts of his holdings.

What would that mean to her? Were her jewels safe? Her furs? The house, the servants, the motor cars? She decided to do a little discreet probing, which was how she discovered the second devastating fact. Emery was attempting to make good his losses by becoming an agent for a German named Alfred Krupp von Bohlen und Halbach.

Herr Krupp was Hitler's munitions man and Emery had secretly met him while they were in Monaco, and apparently convinced the German that all England would soon be devotedly Fascist. It would be smart to locate a proper site for a weapons factory in Britain and get it ready. Emery was seeing to everything, so the moment His Majesty's government made an alliance with Herr Hitler, they could start production and give immediate aid to the Nazi cause, and incidentally make a fortune.

Amanda was no more politically minded than Irene, and she didn't have Irene's sense of moral rectitude. But her instincts about human nature were sound, and she was quite certain that the scenario Emery imagined would never come to pass.

The British public wasn't going to succumb to Mosley's hate-mongering on any large scale. More important, at least to her, was that if Emery's part in all this pro-Nazi business and his deal with Krupp were ever made public, he'd be a laughingstock, shunned by all the best people. Worse, if England actually went to war with Germany, he might be tried for treason. The prospect of being wife to a man in either situation was once more beyond Amanda's ability to bear.

So when Charlotte suggested that Amanda murder her husband, it did not seem too preposterous an idea.

The two women discussed the proposal in Amanda's bedroom on a wintry March afternoon. "The thing is," Amanda said matter-of-factly, "even if I did do it, how would it help me? Certainly it would remove Emery, and that would suit you. But what would I get out of it?"

"Freedom," Charlotte said.

"Freedom from what? To do what?"

Charlotte didn't answer directly. What she said was, "You could get away with it."

"How? You mean make it look like an accident? Then face down all the investigation and wait to inherit? Like an Agatha Christie book? I couldn't go through all that. Anyway, the only thing Emery has to leave me at the moment is this house, which is entailed and couldn't be sold, and a lot of debts."

Charlotte shook her head. "You've got it all wrong. I don't think you need any elaborate scheme. Simply get a gun from the gun room and shoot him. Pick a moment when there's no one around to hear and come running. Then you walk out and I meet you and whisk you out of the country."

Amanda giggled softly. So far the whole thing was only a silly charade, a verbal game she was playing to amuse herself. She didn't for a moment imagine she could really murder Emery and get away with it. "Whisk me away to where, Zanzibar? Or perhaps never-never land. Charlotte, you're living in a dream world."

"No, definitely not never-never land. Spain. Amanda, have you any idea who the Mendozas really are? Do you understand my family's wealth and power?"

"Perhaps not, but it's very un-British of you to point it out. Not the done thing, darling."

Amanda was applying a coat of polishing cream to her nails. Charlotte reached out and knocked the silver-handled buffer from Amanda's fingers as she'd knocked away the muffin long ago in Gordon Square. With the same earth-tilting results.

"I'm serious, Amanda. And you'd better be, or you're going to find yourself in a position you won't enjoy one little bit. Which will be a pity when you could have had the fabulously rich Mendozas in your debt."

Thus were Amanda and Irene and Charlotte brought to that momentous Good Friday in April 1939.

∾ 20 ∾

Madrid and Córdoba: 1939

Diego stared first at his English cousin, then at the American woman she'd brought with her on this surprise visit the day before Easter. "She did what?"

"Shot her husband. Twenty-four hours ago," Charlotte added. "The police will be looking everywhere for her by now."

"I see. So you brought her here. To my house, where my wife and my children live. Where the Mendoza connection can be immediately identified and pinpointed." Diego didn't raise his voice and his English was perfect, almost without accent. "Why is that, Charlotte?"

"Because she did it for us. Because you can make her disappear. Nobody else can do that half so well."

Charlotte had weighed her options carefully before deciding to come to Diego in Madrid. Manuel, the head of the house, lived in Córdoba. There were reasons why Manuel might have been more sympathetic, but Charlotte believed Diego more likely to envision the extraordinary. She watched him and held her breath, hoping she was right.

"I see. She murdered her husband for us." Diego repeated Charlotte's words as he poured three sherries.

He looked closely at Amanda when he handed her the crystal goblet filled with nut-brown oloroso. Very pretty now that she'd pulled off the absurd red wig she'd been wearing. Also very frightened. She was white with shock, trembling.

"So you want me to make her disappear?" Diego did not turn to face Charlotte, he kept staring at Amanda. "Do you mean I should kill her? Are we acting out some American gangster film?"

Amanda gasped and shrank back in her seat, terrified by Diego's lack of emotion, by the coldness of his hazel eyes.

"Stop it!" Charlotte commanded. "Stop scaring her and patronizing me. You know damn well what I mean."

Diego sat down and sipped his wine. "Yes, perhaps I do. But even if I could do what you ask, I don't see why I should."

"I told you why. She did it for us. Emery was a Fascist. He was making a deal with Krupp. He wanted to turn Britain over to Hitler. How do you think the Mendozas will fare under Hitler, Diego?"

"Not very well," he admitted. "We've pulled out of all our interests in Germany. But that's only Hitler's brand of fascism, my dear. Here in Spain we support Franco and the Falange. And here in Spain we have laws against murder, other laws governing the hiding of known criminals."

"Diego! Will you stop this nonsense? Amanda's here. So am I. You have to help and you can, easily. So bloody well do it, will you? And stop lecturing me."

He came within a millimeter of simply tossing them both into the street, or shipping them back to England and letting them take their chances. Then he looked again at the American woman.

"Please," Amanda whispered.

She really was very pretty. "All right," Diego said. "Tell me exactly what's happened. What you did. From the beginning. Then we'll see what's best to do."

Charlotte had not overestimated Diego's skills or his influence. He had begun accreting power in 1931, when he was twenty-five.

At that time the head of the house was Diego's half-Irish half-Spanish cousin, Michael Mendoza Curran. Michael was larger than life, a physical giant and a visionary. He'd had to plot and scheme to secure what was rightfully his, and the experience had made him far-seeing and willing to take risks. After the First World War Michael widened the family's nets. To the interests in Spain and Britain he added others in Europe and Latin America. The Mendoza Group was born.

Diego's mother had been a Mendoza. Like Michael, he was descended from Robert the Turncoat and his Gypsy wife, Sofía. As a boy he'd lived in the Córdoba palace and observed the increasingly international character of the family's affairs. When he was nineteen, Diego had seen his chance to ease the hard lump of ambition lodged permanently in his belly.

Michael's eldest son, Manuel, would inherit the patriarch's mantle, but Diego had a skill unique among the Mendozas of his generation. He was a linguistic sponge. He absorbed languages the way some people acquired a tan—naturally, with a minimum of effort. His fluent English and French and Italian and German proved invaluable, and by 1931 Michael had put him in charge of the Group's nonfiduciary foreign investments. Diego had a power base.

The year was momentous in other respects. The Spanish monarchy was overthrown and the country came under the rule of the Republicans. It was also the year that Michael died of pneumonia, so Manuel assumed the patriarchy at a time of intense political upheaval.

Spain endured a vicious civil war, and when the carnage ended Franco and the Falange had triumphed over the Republicans. It was Diego who had advised that Franco was sure to win because he had the backing of the Germans and the Italians. By the time of Charlotte and Amanda's arrival in 1939, Manuel had learned to rely on the younger cousin whose intelligence he respected, and who knew so much about their overseas operations. Nonetheless, Diego thought it prudent to tread carefully. On Easter Monday Diego drove himself to Andalusia.

The two men met at the *cortijo*. The Mendozas had been given their vast country estate in the thirteenth century by a Christian king grateful for their help in expelling the Moors. The house had been kept simple; it had none of the opulence of the palace in Córdoba. Diego and Manuel sat on leather-covered chairs in a room of bare whitewashed walls. A log fire blazed in the fieldstone fireplace, and above the mantle hung a portrait of Theodor Herzl, the founder of Zionism.

It was Michael's wife Beth who had returned the Spanish Mendozas to the practice of Judaism. According to rabbinic law, to *halakah,* Michael was a Jew because his mother had been. Lila Curran was born to Jewish immigrants in Dublin. Beth, on the other hand, was a convert. But it was Beth who instilled in her four children a deep love of the ancient faith. It was thanks to her that Manuel was a devout Jew and had recently become a fervent Zionist.

"So, Diego?" Manuel asked. "Why this sudden visit? What's happened? You said it was family, not business."

"In a manner of speaking." Diego glanced at Herzl's portrait. "Do you remember the Englishman Emery Preston-Wilde, Viscount Swanning?"

"I've never met him, but isn't he married to one of us?"

"He was. His first wife was Charles Mendoza's daughter Phillipa. She died five years ago when she was thirty."

Manuel nodded. "And?"

"Two years later Swanning married an American girl, Amanda Kent. A friend of Cousin Charlotte's as it happens."

"There is a point to all this romantic history, isn't there, Diego?"

"Yes. Recently the viscount became enamored of the glories of the Third Reich. He joined Mosley's Fascists. More important, he apparently had a number of clandestine meetings with Krupp. There seems to have been a plan for a secret munitions factory in Britain. To supply the Nazis, naturally."

"Bastard," Manuel muttered. "Can you squeeze him a little?"

"There's no need," Diego said quietly. "Two days ago little Amanda shot him."

"He's dead?"

"Very. Two bullets through the heart at close range."

"Excellent," Manuel said with satisfaction. "But I suspect you have something else to tell me. I'm listening, Diego."

"Charlotte brought her friend to me. She wants us to 'make Amanda disappear,' as she puts it. At the moment they're at my lodge in San Domingo de la Cruz. No one will find them there, but it's hardly a permanent solution."

Manuel lit a cigar and stared at the ceiling.

Diego watched him and waited. He did not doubt that Manuel was sympathetic. If Charlotte had wanted to enlist the family in her scheme for any reason other than to reward a heroine who had rid the world of one more Jew hater, one more prop in the growing power of Herr Hitler, it would be different. As it was, Diego expected Manuel to tell him to go ahead and do whatever he thought best.

He had underestimated his cousin's hatred of the Nazis.

"It should be easy," Manuel said finally, leaning forward to drop thick blue ash in a brass ashtray. "To make one young woman disappear and reappear as someone else shouldn't be that much of a challenge. She needs a new face. I know a man in Switzerland who is a miracle worker."

Diego was surprised. Manuel's Zionist connections had taken him to Switzerland a number of times in the past few years, but why had he had dealings with a plastic surgeon? "Your breadth of experience astounds me. Very well, can we bring this Swiss doctor here?"

Manuel shook his head. "No, I think we'd better take her to him. He'll need his own clinic, his regular assistants. It's best if she goes to Switzerland."

"That means a passport," Diego said, frowning. "Charlotte got her across the border while she could still use her own, but there's a worldwide search for her now."

"Not a problem," Manuel said with a wave of his hand.

Diego raised his eyebrows. "Are you sure?"

"I'm sure. Certain friends and I are smuggling people into Palestine every week. I can produce a passport. And she can travel to Switzerland with me, as my secretary. Since I go often, no one will think anything of it."

Diego nodded. He had reaped an unexpected benefit from this escapade. He'd discovered that Manuel was more deeply involved in the Zionist nonsense than he'd suspected. Knowledge was power and Diego banked it with far more satisfaction than mere money. He glanced at his watch and stood up. "I'll leave those arrangements to you."

Manuel walked with Diego to his car. "There is one thing," the younger man said as he left. "Tell your miracle-working Swiss to make sure Amanda is as pretty when he's through as she is now."

Within a week of their flight from Swanning Park, Amanda had gone to Switzerland and Charlotte home to England.

In June, Manuel brought Amanda back to Spain and Diego went to Córdoba to see her. He couldn't decide if his request had been honored. She was still pretty, but it was a strange, blank kind of prettiness. It was absolutely neutral. She didn't look like Amanda Kent Preston-Wilde, but she didn't look like anybody else either.

Meanwhile Manuel had grown quite fond of her. He had suggested Amanda stay at the *cortijo* to recuperate and he'd invited Charlotte to come and have a holiday with her there. Diego was quite annoyed by the last arrangement. Charlotte irritated him. And he had developed a real yen to bed the little American fugitive. That would be difficult with Charlotte around.

It was not, however, impossible. There was a young Venezuelan staying in Córdoba, an aspiring poet who was a friend of one of Manuel's boys. On a weekend when he'd come to Andalusia from Madrid, Diego used the Venezuelan in a ruse to separate Charlotte and the girl who now called herself Luisa, because that was the name on the passport Manuel had provided.

A group of the young people went on a picnic to the *cortijo* and Diego arranged that Santiago, the Venezuelan, would take everyone but Luisa for a ride in a donkey cart. Luisa was under strict medical instructions to avoid the sun.

Diego entered the house as soon as he saw the cart drive away. Luisa was surprised to see him, but she didn't seem displeased. He had to work quickly; Santiago had been told to keep the others away for about an hour, but the American girl made no difficulties. Diego had her on the floor in front

of the fireplace—with Theodor Herzl looking down. It was
not particularly satisfactory. She was entirely without enthusiasm. Still he thanked her warmly afterward, and kissed her
and petted her and promised her a present the next time he
came from Madrid.

"There's one thing I specially want, Diego darling."

"And what is that?"

"I should like Irene to come here. My secretary from
England."

"Irene?"

"You remember. She knows everything, she helped us.
Charlotte and I told you about her the first day."

"Ah, yes, so you did."

And he'd chosen to forget. Because the only danger in this
business was that too many people were involved: Amanda
who'd become Luisa, Charlotte, himself, Manuel, a Swiss
doctor. . . . Life could get dangerous when a secret was too
widely shared. "Irene," he repeated now. "Yes, perhaps that's
wise. I'll see if it can be arranged."

He needed to size up this unknown woman, to see if she
was a threat to them. Perhaps he'd have to do something dramatic, something out of an American film as he'd jokingly
said to Charlotte that first day.

So Irene came to Spain in late July. And that changed
everything.

Diego had Irene brought to him as soon as she arrived. He
interviewed her in his office in Madrid, questioning her
relentlessly, asking the same things over and over, subjecting
her to a ruthless interrogation that uncovered a number of
details Charlotte had deliberately kept from him.

Through Irene, Diego discovered that this wasn't simply
a slightly silly plot with too many players, it was a fully
fledged conspiracy. Charlotte had involved the head of the
English family, Ian Mendoza, the fourth Baron Westlake.
And Ian was so violently anti-Mosley that he'd gone along.
And God knows who else he'd involved. There had been a
great meddling in England. Nothing had been allowed simply
to run a normal course.

Irene's voice grew thin with exhaustion as she responded to the endless questioning, but somehow when this man looked at her she wanted—no, needed—to please him. Diego Parilles Mendoza had a kind of strength she had never before encountered, and it wakened in Irene a unique response. She dared not tell him everything, but she would tell him as much as she could.

"A few days before it happened, that is before it was scheduled to happen," Irene said, "Lord Westlake came to the house. He destroyed every picture of Amanda in Swanning Park."

"Didn't the servants notice?" Diego demanded.

"No one suspected anything. His Lordship was very clever. I helped him, of course. And later he got my name erased from the police reports and kept out of the papers."

"How? Why?"

"I don't know why. Lord Westlake thought it was best. As for how . . . When a newspaper or a county police force is told to do something by a peer of the realm, they're inclined to do it unless there's a pressing reason not to. In this case they saw no harm in complying."

"And was there?" Diego asked, studying her. She was a remarkable one, this Irene. Very cool. Very intelligent. Quite a different piece of work from Amanda or Charlotte.

She didn't meet his gaze. "I suppose not, no."

"And now? What are you going to do after your holiday in Spain?"

"I haven't decided."

"I see. Well, there's no reason for you to rush back, is there?"

"No, none."

They looked at each other a moment. Then both looked away.

Diego insisted that Irene mustn't go to Córdoba. "There are already too many people involved. Let's at least keep you from the mad scene in Andalusia. My family is notoriously hospitable. The place is crawling with guests. A

Venezuelan, our two fugitives, God knows who else. Charlotte and Amanda, I mean Luisa, can come here to see you."

They did and Diego put the three women in a conveniently empty flat belonging to a Mendoza company. It had three bedrooms, but as Irene expected, and as Diego probably never knew, she had one and Charlotte and Amanda shared another. In a few days Irene found this uncomfortable. Why, she couldn't say, but she did. Diego sensed her distress one afternoon when he called, ostensibly to see if they needed anything.

"You seem unhappy, Irene."

"No, not really. A little restless perhaps."

"I have a small place up in the mountains northwest of here. San Domingo de la Cruz, a marvelous old village. Very typical of a Spain that won't last forever. Would you care to see it?"

"How kind of you. I'd enjoy that very much, Diego."

What transpired is what they both expected, what each had been waiting for since that first meeting. There was a chemistry between them, an instant fateful attraction.

"I keep this place simple," Diego said as he ushered her into the lodge. "There's a woman to look after me when I'm here and keep things tidy when I'm not. She's not likely to disturb us."

Irene turned to him. She wore a pale pink linen skirt and a matching tunic. Her shoes and her gloves were white leather, and loosely over her shoulders floated the pale pink chiffon scarf that she'd tied around her hair during the drive. "I see," she said gravely. "Well, since we're alone, I would like you to make love to me, Diego."

"I, too, *querida*."

He took her hand and led her to the bedroom which looked out on the rear patio and which had an enormous high bed piled with feather mattresses. Irene was not in the least shy with him. She took off her clothes slowly and deliberately, glorying in the fact that he watched.

"I am not the first man you've been with, am I?"

"No."

"But you have never been married?"

"No, never married. Does that displease you, Diego? Do you think me a loose woman?"

"I think you are the most remarkable woman I have ever met. But I don't know exactly why I feel that way."

"Isn't that enough talk for now?"

He agreed that it was, and they lay together and made love for long hours. Swiftly at first, with an urgent need to have the initial time of not knowing over, then more slowly. Little animal cries of pleasure and delight were wrested from Irene. They were sounds that came from the deepest place inside her, and until this moment she had not realized that such a hidden well of feeling existed at the center of her being. In ways that he could not, would not ever understand, Diego freed her spirit.

It was well after dark when he drove her back to Madrid. Diego parked the car in front of the building where the three women were staying and turned to her. "I can't arrange to take you up there again until next week. I don't think I can wait that long. I'm besotted with you, Irene. That's the correct English word, isn't it?"

"It's a word." She didn't say anything more, only kissed him good-bye.

When she went upstairs she found the apartment empty. Neither Amanda nor Charlotte was there. Irene was glad. She needed time alone to examine the truths she had discovered about herself and her feelings for this Spaniard, who was, among other things, a married man.

It was after midnight when it occurred to her to start worrying about the whereabouts of Amanda and Charlotte. There was nothing she could do. It was unthinkable to telephone Diego at his home. Irene waited all night. The next morning she reached Diego at his office and told him the other two women were missing.

There was a great fuss, but Charlotte and Amanda turned up twenty-four hours later in Córdoba. They'd been bored, they said, wanted an adventure. So they'd taken a train all the way to the Andalusian coast and spent the day in the old port city of Málaga. And of course they'd been careful. Charlotte even took off her breeches and put on a hat and a dress so she wouldn't be recognized.

Diego was furious when he told Irene this story. "They have no idea of how much trouble they cause. Or that they're still playing a dangerous game. I've charged that young Venezuelan with never letting them out of his sight, but it's going to be some job."

"Well," she said quietly. "Whatever else, it does mean I'm alone in this flat."

Which was true, and they made the most of it.

It was a week later that the picture ran in *Los Dias*. The magazine was on the newsstands only a single day before Diego had every issue pulled, and obtained and destroyed the negative and all the photographs.

"Why are you so worried, since Amanda doesn't look like Amanda anymore?" Irene asked when he told her what he'd done.

"Because Charlotte still looks like Charlotte, of course. Even when she's wearing normal clothes. And because her friendship with Lady Swanning was well known."

"I see. Yes, very stupid of me. You're making me stupid, Diego. My head is so full of you, I don't seem to be able to think of anything else."

"Does that mean you love me, *querida*."

"I'm not sure," Irene said gravely. "Perhaps it does."

Irene couldn't answer Diego's question with more certainty because nothing in her controlled life had prepared her for what she felt, for the rapture she discovered in Diego's arms, or the sense of deprivation she suffered when he wasn't with her. But certainly what she felt for Diego was the reason Irene listened to Amanda's improbable scheme a short while later—and why ultimately she agreed to it.

The Swiss plastic surgeon was as marvelous as Amanda had promised, and the process wasn't unbearably painful. When it was over, Amanda, who had been the blank-faced Luisa, looked exactly like Irene Petworth.

"We've always been a bit alike. After all, there was probably some intermarrying in our families way back when,"

Amanda had said when she made her incredible proposal. "We're the same height and we both have gray eyes. Mine are a little lighter, but no one will notice that."

No one was likely to. Amanda now had Irene's nose, her chin, her hairline. All that was the doctor's doing, Amanda herself accomplished the rest. The gift for mimicry which had made her so able to assume the role first of a Bloomsbury ingenue and later of Lady Swanning, once more served her well. She knew every one of Irene's gestures, her mannerisms, her way of speaking and standing and walking. She ·copied them to perfection.

"Glory, glory!" she enthused on the day she stood before a full-length mirror wearing clothes that had belonged to Irene and holding Irene's passport. "Now I can go back to England!"

That had been the chief point of the exercise.

"There's going to be a war," Amanda had said. "England will be cut off. And Charlotte's been told by the family in Britain that she *must* come home for the duration or they'll stop her funds. I don't trust this phony passport I have. It says I'm Spanish, but I'm not. And maybe the British won't let a Spaniard come in and stay, the way they will an American. But I have to be able to stay in England. I can't bear being separated from Charlotte."

Irene would probably not have gone along with the scheme only because once more Amanda couldn't bear something, but she had reasons of her own for agreeing to it.

"You want to stay in Spain, don't you?" Charlotte had asked. Trust Charlotte to have figured out that there was something between Diego and Irene. "America says it will be neutral, so does Spain. But who knows what's going to happen in a war? You may be ordered to leave."

Irene had pondered this and discussed it with Diego. Amanda and Charlotte wanted to keep the whole thing secret, but Irene definitely would not agree to that. So she told her lover what Amanda proposed and at first he was violently opposed.

"Why should you give your identity to this little *arriviste*?" he demanded. "It's too much, she's mad. She thinks she can make us all jump through hoops because she did the world a

favor and got rid of one Nazi. There are plenty of them left
and she's not become the Virgin Mary to command and be
obeyed. Besides, I can get you a Spanish passport without
all this craziness. I've discovered that my cousin Manuel is
an expert at producing them."

Irene had shaken her head. "No, I don't want to do it only
because of Amanda. Listen . . ."

And she'd told him the thing she had not dared to tell him
that first day when he had questioned her so intently. Diego
listened to the remarkable story, and when it was over he
was silent for a long time. Then he agreed she should go
with Amanda to Switzerland.

"And who will you be?" Amanda had asked Irene on the
journey. "There can't be two of us, two of you, I mean."

"I'll leave that to the doctor," Irene had said. "As long as
he doesn't make me ugly."

Which he did not. Neither did he make her the sort of
neutral-faced nonentity Amanda had been after her first
operation. He made her exquisitely beautiful.

Geneva, Madrid, and Paris: 1939–50

"It was all there, Mademoiselle," the surgeon told Irene when he removed the bandages and she looked at herself in wonder. "You had remarkable bones, a face with structure. Nature herself came close to making you a beauty. I simply finished the work."

Irene added one further touch. She indulged a childhood fantasy, and when Amanda lightened her hair to Irene's original color, Irene herself became a brunette. The change was wonderful with her gun-metal gray eyes and pale skin.

The doctor would not allow either woman to leave his Geneva clinic immediately. They were still there on the first of September, when Hitler invaded Poland, and two days later when the voice of Prime Minister Neville Chamberlain addressing the British people came over the shortwave Empire Service. "This country is now at war with Germany."

Two days later the Amanda who was no more, who had become Irene Petworth, left for London, absorbed into waves of returning British citizens. A day after that Diego joined the real Irene in Geneva.

He looked at her and for a long moment he was speechless. "The thing that's so extraordinary," he said finally, "is that it's still you. Purified somehow. All the potential realized. You are exquisite, *querida*. And I've brought you something that's also wonderful. At least I hope you'll think so."

What he'd brought was an American passport. "Manuel outdid himself this time. It's not a forgery, it's real. Don't ask me how it all works, but as I told you, my cousin has become an expert in these matters. This is a genuine passport. All we have to do is have your picture taken and inserted. I have arranged for us to meet a man here who'll take care of that. But you haven't told me what you think of your new name. I chose it for you myself."

Irene looked carefully at the name typed on the inside cover of the passport. Loyola Perez.

"Only one surname," Diego explained. "We're saying you're an American of Spanish descent, not a Spaniard."

"It's a lovely name, Diego. I think I will enjoy it."

Odd that the thought of being Emery Preston-Wilde's mistress for a lifetime had been so distasteful, but that she never expected to tire of being Diego's. The woman who everyone now called Loy knew she could never be anything else. Diego was married and in Spain there was no divorce. Moreover, he was the father of four children and often spoken of as a possible candidate for government office. A good deal of discretion was required.

But her life was not without compensations. She had the man she now admitted she loved. Diego and his wife had made their peace years before—she, too, had lovers and a life of her own—and there was no trouble from that quarter. Diego gave Loy her own apartment in Madrid, as well as a maid, a car, and a generous allowance. And for the first few years she had the work she did with Manuel.

During the war they were active in rescuing from Hitler's "fortress Europe" first Jews, then resistance workers and downed airmen. It was during this period that Manuel gave Loy the code name La Gitanita. It had first been applied to Sofía Valon, the Gypsy who married Robert the Turncoat and who became a symbol of her country's resistance to the French in the Spanish War for Independence.

In this later war Loy and Manuel made common cause with the Basques in the Pyrenees close to the French border. The Basques were agitating for independence. It suited them to oppose the official Spanish government position of neutrality in favor of the Axis. They were hard mountain men, heroic themselves and capable of appreciating the heroism of a remarkable woman. The phrase La Gitanita came to be used to signify that there was great danger, that much courage was needed to overcome it.

After the war Loy's life in Spain retained a full measure both of being loved and needed—and of the independence she came to realize she prized. Which is why she was so shocked and frightened in late 1949 when she suspected she might be pregnant.

At first she didn't believe it. She'd been so careful always, because of what had happened with Emery. And she was thirty-two years old. It didn't seem possible she could be pregnant. But she was. She went to Barcelona, where no one knew her, and saw a doctor and he confirmed it. "Two months at least, Señora. Possibly three."

She was beside herself.

A dozen times in the next few weeks Loy came close to telling Diego, but she couldn't. He was an extremely pragmatic man. Much as he loved her, he would not be prepared to face such an upheaval in his life. Diego would insist on an abortion and make all the arrangements—which would no doubt be excellent. She'd had excellent arrangements the last time.

Loy couldn't go through it again. Some women could, but she could not. She decided to call in her debts.

"Diego, I'm going to Paris for a while. I need a change."

"Paris? Very well, but I hope you won't stay away too long. I'd go with you, only I can't take a holiday this year. There's too much work."

"I realize that. As to how long, I'm not sure. Six months perhaps."

He looked horrified. Loy stroked his forehead and gently kissed his cheek. "Try to understand," she whispered.

"I'm trying to. But you're not doing much explaining."

"I simply need a change for a while."

She loved him deeply, and Loy knew she was taking a risk. At forty, Diego was a man of such overwhelming strength and vigor that women melted when he merely looked at them. But she also knew he adored her, that he always would, that she was the love of his life. What was between them could sustain this strain. "Don't look so bereft," she added. "I'll be back, I promise, darling. Give me this little breathing time, please."

He always knew when to give in to her, when she really wanted something. He agreed.

Loy had chosen Paris because since the end of the war Amanda—she still thought of her by that name—and Charlotte had been living there. They would see her through this time and help her make plans about afterward.

"But what do you want to do with the child when it's born?" Amanda/Irene asked.

"I'm not sure. Right now I only know I have to have it. I had an abortion years ago. I can't have another."

Amanda/Irene looked at her with genuine sympathy, but Charlotte laughed.

"Don't pay any attention to her," Amanda/Irene said. "I swear she's losing her marbles."

Which was what the woman who had become Irene genuinely suspected, and she wasn't quite sure how she felt about it. In recent years many things had changed in her relationship with Charlotte. It had been love and passion and sex. Now it was passion, and sex of a sort, but certainly not love.

Charlotte had been different after Amanda returned to England as Irene. Perhaps because she knew that now she owned her utterly. She must do whatever Charlotte said, whenever she said it. No matter what. And this wasn't the playful, half-joking tyranny of their first months together. This was serious. Sometimes it was ugly and even painful. There were scenes with riding crops and once even with a lit cigarette, though she'd threatened to run away after that and Charlotte knew she meant it and didn't do it again.

After the war Charlotte decreed that they move to Paris, and since Irene had no money of her own and no life apart from Charlotte, she had no choice but to go. She'd hoped things might improve in France. Instead, they had grown worse.

Charlotte associated with the darkest elements of the lesbian sorority. She brought her new friends to the flat she and Irene shared on the Left Bank, and Irene had to take part in whatever entertainments they decided on. Sometimes she was herself the entertainment. She had grown to hate her life, but she didn't know how to change it.

The old friend whom Loy met in Paris was a frightened, timid woman whose degradation showed in her eyes. Loy's reaction to this might have been more acute if she were not so caught up in her own new experience.

Loy took a room in a small hotel in Montmartre and stayed there throughout her pregnancy. It was not as difficult a time as she might have expected. A very nice Englishman and his French wife came to stay in the same hotel, and they befriended Loy and helped her enormously.

The Englishman was named Harry Cramer and his wife was Claudette. It was she who made inquiries and found an excellent obstetrician for Loy. Careful to follow his advice exactly, Loy ate properly, often with the Cramers, took long walks, usually with Harry, and got plenty of rest. The presence of Irene and Charlotte and her friendship with the Cramers made Loy feel secure and protected. In a strange and perhaps irrational way, she was happy.

"But what about afterward?" Irene asked repeatedly. "What are you going to do about the baby?"

"I don't know. Give it up for adoption perhaps," Loy said softly. "There doesn't seem to be anything else I can do." That thought made her miserable, however, and she never dwelt on it or discussed it in detail.

On the twenty-second of March, 1950, the daughter of Loyola Perez and Diego Parilles Mendoza was born in a small private hospital in Paris. "I'm going to call her Lili," Loy said, pressing her cheek to the so-soft cheek of the infant.

"Lili's a nickname," Irene said, stroking the tiny fingers. "Why not Liliane? She can be Lili for short."

"Yes. I agree. Liliane, but she's to be called Lili."

Irene bit her lip and took a deep breath. "You know, if you give her to strangers for adoption, they'll probably change her name. I think they always do."

It seemed an unnecessarily cruel reminder, and Loy squeezed her eyes closed, as if darkness would make the terrible reality go away.

"No, don't shut me out," Irene whispered urgently. "Open your eyes and listen. I have an idea."

Loy looked at this woman whose ideas had so often changed her life.

"Give the baby to me," Irene said. "Let me raise her."

"You?"

"Yes. Don't look like that. I don't mean with Charlotte. I'm finished with Charlotte. At least, I want to be. But I have no one and nothing. That is, I won't, unless you let me have Lili. I could take her to America, to Fielding. My mother died a while ago; the house on Woods Road is for sale. Did you know that?"

"No. How could I? For that matter, how do you know it?"

Irene lowered her eyes. "Your friend Harry Cramer found out for me."

"Harry? How on earth did he think of such a thing?" Loy's voice dropped to a harsh whisper. "My God! You haven't told him you're Amanda Kent?"

"No, of course not." Irene said. "But one night a couple of months ago he asked me where I'd like to live if I could live anywhere in the world and we got to talking and I told him about Fielding. And a few days ago he told me he'd made inquiries and the old Kent house is for sale."

She leaned forward and gripped Loy's hand. "Don't you see? I could buy it if you got the money from Diego. I *am* Irene Petworth, you know. No one would ever question it. Certainly not after all these years. I'd go home and buy the house and raise Lili and she'd have a normal life. The kind you and I had before we left."

She made it sound like the saddest, most bitter leavetaking in the whole world. So it had become for this creature in front of her, Loy realized. That's why she wanted to wipe out the last fourteen years and start again. "Are you sure you really want to go back there?"

"Yes, oh yes, oh yes. It's the only thing I want."

Loy looked at the infant snuggled next to her breast and was overwhelmed by the notion. This precious child could be raised in Fielding, in the beautiful old Kent house. She would play by the banks of Willock's Stream, go to the Abraham Lincoln School, use the Fielding public library. . . . Not a foundling pushed into the arms of chance, a Petworth in the place where Petworths had always been. Her daughter, though she never really could be. But more hers than if she simply gave her away to she knew not who.

It took two days for Loy to decide to do it. Then they made their plans.

"I can't give you as much money as I'd like," Loy said. "Because I don't dare tell Diego about Lili. But I've saved quite a bit over the years and there are a few things I can sell that he'll never miss. And I can get some money from Manuel without having to say too much. I think I can raise two hundred thousand dollars. How much is the house selling for?"

"Thirty thousand."

"Okay, and we have to put ten thousand away for her future. Money for college if she wants to go. That will leave you a hundred and sixty thousand to invest. I don't know a great deal about these things, but I've heard Diego talk. I think with very safe investments you can count on a return of about five percent. That's eight thousand a year. You could live on that, couldn't you?"

"Of course I could. And give Lili a good life. I will, you know. I swear it. I'll raise her exactly as Irene Petworth would."

Loy smiled. "Fine, but you can't be Petworth when you go home. You have to be a widow with a married name."

"I know." Irene's hands were folded in her lap and she stared at them. "Harry made a suggestion."

"Harry? My dear, have you also discussed this idea with Harry Cramer?"

"Yes," Irene admitted. "I had to talk to someone." She would not tell Loy that in fact it was Harry Cramer who first suggested that Irene take on the raising of Lili. Loy might think she'd been talked into it. And she hadn't; she had nearly died with joy when the idea was first broached.

She looked up and met Loy's gaze. "Harry's on our side. He says I can use his name. He'll help me get all the right papers. So we can be the Widow Cramer and her daughter, Lili. Come home to Fielding."

The year 1951 was when the woman everyone believed was Irene Petworth went home—as a thirty-four-year-old widow named Irene Cramer who had a year-old baby girl called Lili, and apparently plenty of money. She bought the Kent house lock, stock, and barrel.

It was exactly as it had been, right down to the scarlet velvet furnishings and the Constable in the drawing room. Irene moved in with little Lili and hired Rose Carmichael to come three days a week to clean. And nobody dared mention that terrible business with her old friend Amanda, who was said to have murdered her titled husband in England, then disappeared.

In fact, nobody talked to Irene Petworth Cramer about much of anything. She was as aloof and icy as she'd always been, and folks didn't like her any better. But Petworths were part and parcel of the town. Fielding kept its collective mouth shut and tolerated the widow and her child.

For a time after she returned to Madrid, Loy thought Diego suspected that her sojourn in Paris had been more than an idle whim, more than the breathing space she'd told him she needed. He was slightly preoccupied, distant. Perhaps he was angry with her. Perhaps he loved her less after the separation.

"Diego, is something wrong?"

Loy dared the question on a hot July evening when they were on the balcony of her flat on the Calle Toledo in the heart of the old city. Diego had recently moved his wife and children to a newly built district west of the town, a quiet, clean, aggressively modern suburb populated by the professional class. By her own choice Loy remained between the eighteenth-century Royal Palace, from which the last king of Spain had fled twenty years earlier, and the Prado Museum,

where the art of Goya and Velasquez and El Greco bespoke
so eloquently the character of the people among whom she
chose to live.

The balcony was lit only by the moon, the street below them
was dark, but as usual the noise of the crowds in the nearby
Plaza Mayor provided a steady background cacophony. In
the closely packed dwellings surrounding them, hundreds of
suppers were being prepared. The smell of onions and garlic
frying in olive oil wafted through open windows and scented
the humid air.

"Nothing's wrong." Diego said in answer to Loy's question.
Then he added, "This is the real Madrid, you know. The real
Spain. Noisy and dirty and crammed with people."

"Yes. That's why I love it so." Loy refilled their glasses
with the heady red Rioja wine they were drinking. "Is
that what's troubling you? Do you think the old order is
passing?"

"I know it is. It must. That's the way the world works,
querida. It always has."

"Then why are you so disturbed? Lately, since I came back
from France, I've felt as if you were angry with me."

He looked at her, so exquisitely beautiful in the moonlight,
and his astonishment showed in his voice. "With you? What
an extraordinary idea." His eyes narrowed. "Should I be angry
with you, *mi amor*?"

Loy did not flinch. She knew she had ventured onto dangerous ground, but she was accustomed to confronting danger
and beating it. "No. I only thought perhaps you were."

The moment of doubt passed. Diego shook his head. "I'm
not. I'm sorry if I've seemed preoccupied, but I am."

"Very well, I won't say any more about it."

He shrugged. "There's no reason you shouldn't know
what's happening. You are my other self, *mi amor*. I trust
you completely, you know that." He drained his glass
and turned his face from her to the dark street below,
dropping his voice as if he feared spies and enemies
even here. "I have proposed a plan to the generalis-
simo. It's . . . unusual. I'm waiting to see if he's convinced."

"Franco usually listens to you."

"But not always. This time I think he must. No one lives forever. We must plan for what will happen after he's gone."

"But he's a young man! You're all young men."

"Not for ever," Diego insisted. "And if we don't begin now to build a future for Spain, the whole ugly drama will take place again. Listen to them down there." He jerked his head toward the plaza from which the noise was coming. "Songs and wine and pleasure. That's all the average Spaniard thinks about. Until someone suggests spilling blood, a man's or a bull's. They're always willing to think about that too."

"You believe there will be war after Franco is gone?" Loy asked.

"It's a possibility. Unless we give them something so dramatic to hang on to, so compelling a part of the Spanish folk memory, that they can focus all their passion on it rather than killing each other."

"What?"

"A king."

Loy stared at him. "There hasn't been a king since 1931. Do you imagine they'll take Don Juan back from exile? He has thousands of enemies."

"No, not Don Juan. His son, the grandson of the deposed Alfonso XIII. Prince Juan Carlos. He's only twelve years old, but I arranged a secret meeting with him in Greece. He has the makings of a ruler, that boy. If we begin now, if Franco makes the proper arrangements, Juan Carlos can be educated to take the throne when the time is right."

The maid came then to announce that their meal was ready and they went into the small dining room lit with candles in heavy wrought iron sconces. The flames danced and shadows played over the seventeenth-century white walls and oak beams. They drank more Rioja and ate tiny pigeons fried with onions and almonds and cinnamon. Loy thought of the Moors to whom such dishes owed their origin, and the warring Christian kings who had eventually defeated them, and all the long history of this, her adopted land.

Later, over coffee and brandy, she asked, "You really believe the people will accept a reinstatement of the monarchy?"

"I believe they must," Diego said quietly. "Other than Franco, it is the only thing that can hold this nation together. If we don't do it there will be fools screaming for *democracia*. But this isn't England or France, and democracy is totally foreign to us. It can never work here. Spain must be ruled by a strong hand, a dictatorship, if you will. Benevolent, but a dictatorship nonetheless."

That remained his position, and at least in the matter of the young prince, he prevailed. Quietly the forces that controlled Spain under Franco began grooming Juan Carlos to take over after Franco's death.

Loy met the prince a few times and found him as impressive as Diego had. It wasn't the idea of a king that disturbed her. It was the notion, Diego's idée fixe, that the Spanish people could not be trusted to elect genuine leaders rather than puppets. Sometimes she argued with Diego about it. It was fruitless; he could see no virtue in her position.

"Liberal idealism," he said repeatedly. "A sop for fools, *querida*. Stop worrying about such things. Only be my beautiful love and leave the politics to me."

Franco aged and grew ill and it became obvious that Prince Juan Carlos was being won over by those who supported an experiment in democracy for Spain. Diego was fighting a rear-guard action and he knew he might lose. His positions became more and more extreme.

Coupled with Loy's dismay over this was her agony over the lie in her past, the child she had given away and whose life was now so totally removed from hers. It was the only secret she'd ever kept from Diego, and she began to blame him for making it necessary. Paris and the irrevocable decisions made there had planted a poison seed in their love. Slowly it grew and eventually it blossomed.

In 1971 Loyola Perez was fifty-four years old. She looked like a woman many years younger, still as extraordinarily beautiful as she'd been after plastic surgery in 1939. She was, however, a woman with a heavy burden of sadness which seemed to her forever woven into her life in Spain, her life with Diego.

"I must leave," she announced on a golden afternoon at the lodge in San Domingo de la Cruz.

"Leave? I thought we were remaining here until Sunday?"

Loy shook her dark head. "That's not what I mean. I'm leaving Spain."

"I see." He turned away from her, his aquiline profile outlined against the mountains beyond the window. "You're leaving me, that's what you mean."

"Yes."

"You no longer love me? Thirty-one years mean nothing?"

"They mean a great deal. Everything. And I do still love you. Only I can't live with you anymore. You've become a fanatic, Diego. You're obsessed with the idea of making the world as you want it to be. And because of your gifts and the Mendoza power and wealth, you may succeed. But I don't want to stay and watch you do it."

"Politics have nothing to do with us. They never have."

She shook her head stubbornly. "Yes, they do. I've loved the whole man, Diego. Even though I've never been your wife, only your mistress, I felt that I had all of you."

"You had," he agreed. "You still do. I adore you, *querida*. That will never change."

She couldn't explain, she wouldn't try. She would only ask for her freedom in the terms he would understand. "If you love me, let me go. It's over, Diego. I want to leave before the dream dies."

"It will never die for me. Never," he repeated. But he released her.

PART FOUR

Lili, Loy, and Irene

✤ 22 ✤

New York: 1981

Lili stopped speaking.

In the thirty minutes it had taken her to tell the tale, Andy hadn't once interrupted. "Let me get this straight," he said now. "According to you, the bottom line is that Irene Petworth Cramer is really Amanda Kent."

"Yes," Lili said.

"And the real, the original Irene, is Loyola Perez?"

"Also yes."

"And Loy is your mother?"

Lili shrugged. "You can put it that way. Loy gave birth to me, arranged some financing, then apparently washed her hands of motherhood. I was a major inconvenience, a threat to her glamorous life."

"Don't forget she was crossing Diego Parilles Mendoza," Andy said. "That would make most people nervous."

Lili shook her head. "Don't defend her, it doesn't matter. She's not my mother in the real sense, Irene is. I have to call her that, I can't start saying Amanda at this late date."

He suspected she was kidding herself, that Loy mattered enormously, but this wasn't the time to say so. "Okay. For now let's leave it at that."

"Would you like some tea?"

"Yes, please."

Lili went into the tiny blue and white kitchen. Andy watched her fill a kettle and reach over her head for cups and saucers. "Why four?" he asked.

"Irene is in New York. She flew in from Florida yesterday morning. We had . . . a long talk. She and Loy are due here any minute. They want to see you."

He put his head in his hands. "Bloody hell, what a hornet's nest. Where's Irene staying?"

"At a small hotel downtown. Loy offered to put her up and I suggested she stay here. Irene preferred a hotel."

"Lili, are you sure they're telling the truth about these switched identities? Charlotte said—"

Lili raised her hand in a forestalling gesture. "Wait. Don't tell me yet. They'll be here any minute. They'll want to hear too. You'll only have to go through it all again."

Loy arrived first. Lili was startled that Peter was with her. "I insisted on coming," he said, offering the terse explanation as he shook Andy's hand and kissed Lili's cheek.

Peter was visibly holding himself in check, and he seemed angry. Loy was unnaturally quiet and reserved. She settled into one of the big easy chairs while Peter brought a straightback from the dining area and pushed it into position close to Loy's side. He moved stiffly, every gesture seemed an exaggerated exercise in control. Then he took Loy's hand and gave her a long look of unmasked love and concern, and for a moment Lili saw the warm, affectionate Peter she knew so well.

He knows, Lili thought. Loy's told Peter the story. What did he think? What could anyone think of a tale so macabre, so bizarre? And why was there so much repressed anger when he looked at Lili? No, she amended as she watched him, it's not me he's angry at, it's Andy.

Andy was the threat. Peter must know that Andy Mendoza had been searching fifteen years for Amanda Kent and Irene Petworth. He'd finally found them, and he could blow their elaborate masquerade out of the water with his typewriter. Which would mean what? Lili asked herself. A murder trial forty-three years after the event? When, Lili wondered, did the statute of limitations expire in Britain? Was there a statute of limitation on murder? Did it matter? Wouldn't the scandal and notoriety be enough to destroy a number of lives, including hers? The venomous expression on Peter's face when he looked at Andy told her Peter was asking himself the same questions.

Andy ignored the waves of hostility coming from Peter. He was standing behind Lili's chair, lightly stroking the nape of her neck. "You okay?" he murmured.

"I'm fine."

For Lili, Andy's touch was comfort beyond words. He wouldn't deliberately throw them to the wolves, she thought. But no one knew better than she that he had his own demons to exorcise, the weight of his own emotional baggage to lug around. She put her hand over his, pressed it.

The silence between the three grew oppressive. Peter cleared his throat. "I got the marketing reports we asked for this afternoon," he said to Lili. "The test surveys of your name recognition in the Midwest and the West were very encouraging."

"That's good. I'll be eager to see them." She tried to remember the details of the deal they were discussing with the manufacturing company that made cookware and came up empty. Her thoughts wouldn't focus.

The bell rang.

"That will be my mother," Lili said as she stood up and went to the door.

It was the first time Andy had met Irene. He studied her openly.

According to Lili, this was Amanda Kent, the woman who had haunted him all these years. She was a nice-looking blond lady on the wrong side of sixty. If he met her in the supermarket, he wouldn't look twice. Okay, he'd long ago learned that murderers are not signed with the mark of Cain. He glanced at Loy and his doubts were reinforced— her stunning beauty, the fact that she didn't appear anywhere near sixty-five—Loy made the story almost impossible to believe.

Irene was given a chair, a cup of tea. She murmured her thanks and seemed to retreat into a world of her own. Her face was blank.

She's out to lunch, Lili thought with a touch of exasperation. Irene was running true to form, but it was too late for her to retreat into her shell. Lili looked pleadingly at Andy. When Loy first suggested this meeting, Lili had understood that its purpose was to neutralize the threat of Andy's written words; now she didn't know how to begin.

Andy understood Lili's silent message. He started to speak, but Loy interrupted him.

"Perhaps we'd best get started," she said. "First, I've told Peter everything." She glanced at him, smiled softly. Peter smiled back. The intimate exchange lasted only a few seconds, but there was in it a quality Lili recognized as new, as acknowledgment of Peter's love that Loy had denied him until now. Lili had no time to analyze the meaning of that sea change. Loy was speaking again. "I presume Lili has put you in the picture, Andy?"

"She's told me the story you told her," Andy confirmed.

"And now you're wondering how two women could be so stupid, make such a shamble of their lives?" Loy asked quietly.

"Something of the sort."

Loy held Peter's hand and seemed to speak as much to him as to Andy. "I can't explain in any satisfactory way. All I can tell you is that when one is doing something, however exotic, it makes sense. Only later does it begin to look insane. By then it's too late."

Listening to Loy speaking again in that voice which only two days earlier told her the story that had destroyed all her illusions, Lili couldn't sit still. She got up, mumbling something about getting more tea.

In the kitchen she caught herself considering making sandwiches and a bubble of hysterical laughter rose in her throat. The eternal female: No matter what the crisis, offer food. She could hear Andy speaking in the living room. He was questioning Loy. Lili choked back the panicky giggles and listened.

"Do you honestly believe that Diego has never known about Lili? Aren't you underestimating him?"

Lili heard Irene moan softly. It was a pathetic sound. She moved to the doorway of the kitchen, holding the teapot she'd just refilled, and waited for Loy's response.

"He does now." Loy's voice was raw with bitterness. "After all my efforts, all these years, now Diego knows."

Lili gasped. The teapot crashed to the floor and shattered.

Andy jumped to his feet and went to her.

Lili pushed him away. "He knows?" she demanded shrilly. "Are you saying that this . . . this international thug knows he's my father?"

"Yes," Loy admitted. "He wormed it out of me when I went to Spain to get more money for LPL."

Andy tried to lead Lili back to her chair, but she stood where she was, ignoring the shards of the china teapot around her feet. For once her anger wasn't fire, it was ice. She knew now what was meant by an emotion that chilled the blood. "You told him?" she asked, her voice edged with the frost of despair and disbelief. "You told him?"

Loy leaned forward, her whole body pleading for forgiveness. "Lili, please darling . . . I'm begging you to try to understand. There seemed so few options. I had to—"

Lili held up her hands as if to push away Loy's words, her explanations. She turned to Irene. Silent tears ran down her mother's cheeks, made little rivulets in the perfect makeup. It was the first time Lili had ever seen Irene cry. "Did you know this? Did Loy tell you that she'd spilled the beans to my— To Diego?"

Irene sniffled once, then nodded. "Loy called me from Madrid when she was there in April. She felt she had to tell me. We didn't know what Diego might do, you see. He's so unpredictable. So hard."

Lili was white-faced, and she began to tremble. She thought she might crumple, simply fall into little pieces.

Andy grabbed her to him roughly. She felt like a rag doll, seemed to have no control of her arms or her legs. If he were not holding her, she would have fallen. "He knows," she whispered against Andy's chest. "He's known for weeks. But—"

"Forget it," he whispered urgently, his words meant for Lili alone. "The bastard's not worth your anguish. Please, darling, come sit down."

Lili allowed herself to be led to a chair. Andy perched on the arm, his body protectively close to hers but his eyes on Loy.

Anguish had ravished her beautiful face. The skin seemed to be drawn mask-tight over the delicate bones. It looked fragile, like porcelain that would splinter at a touch. In spite of himself, Andy felt sorry for Loy, but he wouldn't relent. For Lili's sake he couldn't. "Look," he began.

Peter had been gazing at Loy; now he turned to Andy. "Shut up. You've said enough."

Andy wouldn't back off. Lili was his first concern and he recognized what she had to know, though she hadn't the strength to phrase the question. "Not quite enough yet," he told Peter quietly. "Loy has to tell us what Diego said when she told him about Lili."

Peter started to rise. Loy put a restraining hand on his arm. "You promised," she murmured. "I don't mind telling, though it won't give Lili much comfort." Peter sat down again. "Diego said he'd deal with it later, in his own way," Loy said flatly.

A strange wounded-animal sound issued from Lili's throat. Andy tightened his arm around her shoulders. "Why are you so sure it was news to Diego that he had a daughter?" he demanded. "Years ago, when Lili first started looking for Harry Cramer and I was helping her, Diego asked my brother Mark to warn me off. Why would he do that if he didn't know about Lili?"

"The warning had nothing to do with Diego," Loy said. "He approached Mark because I asked him to. Remember, Lili wrote to Irene. When she heard you were looking for Harry Cramer, she called me. I prevailed on Diego to intervene, but I never told him why."

"And he didn't guess?" Andy sounded unconvinced.

Loy shook her head. "He did it for me," she repeated. "Until I told him the story of Lili's birth and what had happened in Paris, Diego had no idea who Cramer was."

"You told him when you went to Spain," Lili said dully. "That was a couple of months ago. Why, after you'd kept silent for so many years?"

Peter exploded. "That's enough! Jesus, Lili, can't you see what you're putting her through? You've got one pound of flesh, do you have to hack off another?"

"Please, stop shouting," Loy begged. "Lili has a right to know. More than anything, I want her to understand."

She stretched out her hands again in supplication. "Don't you remember, Lili darling? He'd tried to cut off my funds. After I left Diego in 'seventy-one he set up a trust for me. He'd always been generous, but suddenly he wouldn't let me invade the capital. Jeremy Crandall kept him informed of all my activities. I'd always known that. Santiago Cortez, the Venezuelan poet, is another of Diego's spies. Diego needs to feel in control, but he'd never before interfered with anything I did. Now he had. And I so wanted you to have a business of your own, to be free of that awful Dan Kerry, to have a wonderful partner like Peter. I wanted all that to happen for you. I'd never been able to do anything, then suddenly I had this opportunity. Diego was trying to spoil it."

"You said he wormed it out of you. How?" Lili demanded. There was no sympathy for Loy evident in her tone.

On their separate sides of the living room both Peter and Andy drew back. The movement was barely perceptible, a matter of an inch or two, but each man had somehow recognized that the pain they were witnessing was not theirs to share or comfort. In this instance love gave them no rights. Lili and Loy owned their own agony, the crime and the punishment belonged to them. The combat was between these two women linked by nature.

Irene was part of it too, Andy thought. Why was she saying so little? He looked at her. Irene was staring at the ceiling. The wild emotions loose around them seemed not to touch her. Her detachment was chilling. Andy shuddered.

Loy was still trying to explain. "When I went to Madrid, I spoke to a number of people, old friends. They told me Diego had mellowed. But when I asked them to lend me money, they backed off. Everyone was afraid to cross him."

"Small wonder," Andy said under his breath.

Loy glanced at him, then looked back at Lili. "I even tried to talk to Manuel; we'd always been close. But he'd been ill. Susan said—"

Andy bent his head and murmured in Lili's ear, "Manuel's head of the house, sort of the reigning monarch. His wife died a few years ago. Susan is English. She lives in Córdoba at the palace. These days she looks after Manuel."

Loy waited for him to finish the quick explanation, then continued. "Susan said it was a very bad time to bother Manuel with problems. He's over eighty. He'd had a long bout with a virus. In the end there was nothing I could do but go to Diego himself. Don't you see?" she begged, leaning toward Lili once more. "I wanted so much to make everything perfect for you. It seemed worth any risk."

"Did it?" Lili asked coldly. Andy could actually see the tension in her shoulders, the rigidity in her neck. "Then what happened?"

"We met at Diego's lodge in San Domingo de la Cruz. He wanted—" Loy broke off, looked quickly at Peter, then began again. "That's not important. What matters is that in the end the only chance I had of getting the money was to explain that it was for you, Lili, and that it was wicked of him to refuse because you were his daughter."

"But he didn't give it to you," Lili said.

"No, he didn't. He said I was disturbing a situation that had been stable for many years. That I was making waves. That he wanted me to stop."

"Waves about me," Lili said bitterly. "He wanted you to forget about me and he intended to do the same. I didn't matter a damn."

Loy leaned back and closed her eyes, exhausted by all the talk and emotion. "It really wasn't about you, though I know that's not what you want to hear. Diego saw an opportunity to punish me for lying to him years ago, then leaving him. He pounced. He's not a forgiving man."

Lili buried her face in her hands, struggling with bewilderment, the terrible sense of betrayal. Loy, the woman for whom she'd had so much affection, had deposited her in Fielding and virtually ignored her for thirty years. And the man who was her father, about whom she had nursed so

many fantasies, was alive and well and living in Madrid—
and thoroughly disinterested in his daughter's existence. "I'm
certainly being force-fed the facts of life," she whispered.

"I didn't want you to know any of this, ever," Loy said
wearily. "A choice had been made years before. It seemed
best to stick to it."

Loy's hands were clenched in her lap and she stared at them
as if there might be some solace or at least comprehension in
the long, slim fingers, the white knuckles, the tracery of thin
blue veins. "This is all my fault. I made a terrible mistake
in trying to get to know you after I met Peter. Irene warned
me—"

The mention of her name reminded them of the presence
of the third woman. As one they turned to Irene. She was
slumped in her chair. Her chin sagged, making the flesh of
her neck collapse into little creases and folds. Her shoulders
were hunched forward and the angular bones stood out. Some
of the pins which held her updo in place had dropped out.
The ash-blond hair usually so controlled hung loose around
her face. In the past few minutes Irene had become an old
woman, worn out and used up.

"Irene?" Loy murmured. The word questioned the other
woman's existence.

"Mother," Lili said.

Irene did not respond to either of them.

Lili was afraid. There was something uncanny and terrible in this apparent disintegration. "Mother," she repeated,
urgently now, "are you all right?"

Irene seemed not to have heard.

Lili leaned across the small space between them and took
Irene's hand. It was cold and lifeless. The fear in her grew,
blotting out the other feelings she'd been struggling with
throughout the evening. Whatever had happened, whatever
any of them had done or omitted to do, this was her mother,
the woman who had raised her. She searched desperately for
a way to get through to her.

"Mother, last night when we met at Loy's, when we talked
about Harry Cramer and everything that had happened, do you
remember telling me—" Lili broke off. Irene's gray eyes had
focused on her now, but they looked at Lili with no trace of

recognition. "Mother," Lili repeated, a rising note of panic creeping into her voice, "don't you remember saying you sometimes still thought about Charlotte?"

"Charlotte," Irene whispered. "Charlotte."

Lili was on her knees beside Irene's chair now, grasping both her hands, trying to chafe some warmth back into them. "That's right, Charlotte Mendoza. Andy saw her a few days ago. He can tell you how she is."

"Charlotte," Irene repeated. "Charlotte." She kept saying the name over and over. "Charlotte, Charlotte, Charlotte . . ." It was an invocation—half blessing, half curse.

Lili tried another tack. The words welled up from deep inside her, unplanned, but what she desperately wanted to say. "Mother, I understand. About you and Loy, I mean. I don't blame you for what happened. You mustn't think that. I know you always tried to do the best you could for me."

Once more Irene ignored Lili's words. The woman who spoke was no one Lili knew. "Charlotte didn't know where I'd gone," she whispered. "I was so careful, so clever."

A thin stream of laughter akin to a cackle punctuated the words. Lili wanted to stem the flow, but she couldn't. Irene went on as if her daughter were not there, as if none of them was there. The audience she addressed was composed of ghosts.

"Charlotte always thought she was so smart, but she never found out I'd changed my name and returned to America. Then Charlotte lost her mind, so she couldn't have done anything anyway." Again that brittle, mirthless laugh spiraled to the ceiling and echoed in the small room. "Charlotte lost her marbles," Irene pronounced triumphantly. "I always told her she would and she did."

Loy's indrawn breath was audible. "Don't," she murmured. "Please, Amanda, don't."

Loy had not called her old friend that in forty years, now she alone had recognized the spirit risen from the grave and given it a name.

Someone Lili had never met was imprisoned behind her mother's face. Amanda Kent had returned. She was crowding out Irene, crowding out today, forcing them all back to a different time and a different place. "Mother,"

Lili begged, "please come back. I need you. Don't go away now."

Suddenly Irene looked at Lili, really looked at her. There was a hint of recognition in the gray eyes, a flicker of struggle.

"I need you, Mother," Lili repeated. She had not realized she was crying until she felt Irene's trembling fingers brush away her tears.

The blond head moved slightly, settled itself in a different way. They all saw it happen. It was as if a blind were drawn, a curtain pulled across a window. The façade so long maintained slipped back into place. "Of course I'm not going anywhere, Lili darling, what a silly thing to say," Irene's voice was normal, her own.

She patted Lili's cheek and her hand was steady, the flesh warm and alive. "Goodness, I'm a mess," she murmured, lifting the hair that had come loose and pinning it firmly in place. Now no shadowy intruder lurked behind her eyes. "Were we talking about poor Charlotte?" She turned to Andy. "Lili tells me you've seen her. How is she?"

Andy let out a breath he had not realized he'd been holding. There were rustles of movement from the others as the tension dissipated. Lili got off her knees and returned to her seat. "Tell her," she urged Andy. "Tell us all about Charlotte."

"Are you sure I should?" he asked, nodding briefly in Irene's direction.

"Yes, I am," Lili said after she'd looked again at her mother, and darted a quick confirming glance at Loy and at Peter. "Let's get it over with."

"I think Charlotte's peaceful in her own way," Andy began. "Most of the time she has no idea where she is or what's happening. She's confused and disjointed, but I think she's content."

"You did say she's at Westlake?" Irene asked. It was obvious that she was making a simple inquiry, a request for information about an old friend. She seemed unaware that a moment earlier she had terrified them. And except that once, for no apparent reason, she leaned forward and patted Lili's hand, she did not acknowledge her daughter's absolution.

"Yes, Charlotte's at Westlake," Andy said. "Mark's done everything he could to make her comfortable. Most of the time she's kept in her room with nurses round the clock. They say any excitement upsets her. The doctors call it premature senility. It set in before she was fifty, but went only so far and stopped. It hasn't got any worse for years now. She's on hold."

"Did your brother know why you wanted to speak to her?" Loy asked.

"I didn't see him. Mark was in London with Manuel and my cousin Susan. Manuel's much better, by the way. Perhaps you know, he likes to go to the theater and do the shops."

Loy nodded. "I know. Manuel loves England." A small smile hovered around her mouth.

"I skipped London and went directly to Grasmere," Andy continued. "Told Mark I wanted a rest, a few days in the country. When I got to Westlake I talked the nurse into letting me meet Charlotte in the garden."

He rose restlessly, went to the window, and stood with his back to it. "Charlotte seemed quite happy to talk to me, though I doubt she knew who I was. I think she was glad to chat with someone besides her nurses. She rattled on and on. Most of it didn't make any sense. Until—"

Andy paused, looking from one to the other. The three women were watching him eagerly. Only Peter still seemed angry and tense. Andy's eyes sought Lili's.

"Go ahead," she urged. "The genie's out of the bottle. We can't put it back."

"Okay. As I said, we chatted. Eventually, I showed Charlotte the photograph that had been taken in Málaga in 1939. At first I thought she didn't recognize it, then she started laughing. 'That's the day Amanda and I ran away,' she said."

He glanced at Irene. She was watching him with interest, but there was no alarm in her face. He might have been telling a story about something that had nothing to do with her.

"I asked her why the picture didn't look like Amanda," Andy continued, still watching Irene. "She didn't answer at first, but later, when I thought she'd forgotten all about it, Charlotte suddenly whispered, 'She had plastic surgery.

That's how she got to be Loyola Perez too. You mustn't tell, it's a secret.' "

Unconsciously, Andy had mimicked his cousin. He sounded exactly like an old woman whose mind was shattered, whose thoughts were captive birds beating their wings against the bars of an unbreakable cage. "Apparently the two 'shes' weren't the same," he added. "I assumed they were, but I was wrong."

For long moments none of them spoke, then Lili whispered, "How sad."

"Charlotte's paid for all her sins," Irene said, dabbing her eyes with a handkerchief she produced from the handbag at her feet.

Lili noted that the gesture and the posture belonged entirely to the Irene she knew. Amanda had gone back to wherever she'd come from.

"We've all paid," Loy said softly.

Peter leaned toward her. "Let's go. You're exhausted. We've talked enough; there's nothing more to say."

"There is one thing," Loy added. "The original purpose of this meeting." She looked at Andy. "All these years you've wanted to solve the mystery, and now you have. You know everything. Are you going to write about it?"

He took a pipe from his pocket and began tamping tobacco into the bowl. "As far as the book is concerned, I'll do whatever Lili wants. I don't know how any of you could have imagined it would be otherwise. About the rest, I know who's who"—his gaze held Loy's—"I'm not sure I know exactly what's what. Except that where the Mendozas are concerned, there are always wheels within wheels."

Loy looked at him, acknowledged with a small movement of her head that what he'd said was true, and stood up. Peter rose when she did and so did Irene.

Lili couldn't bear the thought of her mother returning to a solitary hotel room. "Stay here," she suggested. "Please, you shouldn't be alone."

Irene glanced around the tiny apartment. "That's very sweet, darling, but you don't have enough room."

"I have plenty of room," Loy said. "Don't be so stubborn, Irene. Come home with me."

It must have been the habit of years that had made Irene refuse that offer when it was first made after she arrived from Florida. Her voice betrayed her real desires when she asked, "Do you think I dare? Is it wise?"

Loy sighed. "There's nothing more to protect, Irene. It's perfectly safe for you to stay with me."

"Very well, I'd like that, if you're sure."

It was midnight when Lili closed the door behind Irene and Loy and Peter. She went to the kitchen and began sweeping up the mess made by the shattered teapot.

For a few seconds Andy stood and watched her, unsure how to proceed, how to say all the things that needed saying now that they were alone. Then he pried the dustpan and brush from her fingers. "I'll do that."

Lili made a half-hearted protest, before she relinquished the tools and leaned against the kitchen counter. He saw that she was crying again, but felt somehow compelled to go on disposing of the evidence of her earlier fraught emotions. "Diego's not worth your tears," he said, an angry overtone in his voice.

Lili wiped her eyes. "You're right." She sounded tremulous at first, then there was a hint of her customary spirit, her usual feistiness. "The hell with him. I've managed without a father all these years, I don't need one now."

She went back to the living room, began tidying with purposeful movements, but stopped in the midst of plumping a pillow and sank into one of the big teal-blue chairs.

Andy dumped the broken crockery in the bin, put the dustpan and brush away, and stood in the doorway looking at her. He longed to put his arms around her, but he decided he mustn't, not yet. He had to make her face what she felt, bring it into the open. "You really don't want to say the hell with Diego, do you?" he asked.

"What's the point of anything else?" Lili began, making an apparent effort to speak firmly. Then she stopped. "There is a point," she said. "At least for me. I want to *know*."

"What do you want to know?"

She didn't reply, and he took a step toward her, close enough to put his hands on her shoulders. "Tell me, Lili," Andy begged. "Tell me and tell yourself. What do you want to know?"

"Who I am!" she shouted through the tears that had started once more. "Where I come from! I don't want to be simply a piece of . . . flotsam. Something to be thrown away like that damned broken teapot."

"You're not. That's crazy." He took her face in his hands, making her look at him. "You're the woman I love. You're Lili."

"That you love me is wonderful," she whispered. "But it's not enough."

Andy's arms dropped to his sides. "That puts me in my place, doesn't it?"

Lili jumped up. "No! Don't say that. It isn't true. I need you. But this is different." She began pacing.

"It's so crazy. So complicated. How am I ever going to sort it out, Andy? Where am I going to find me? Everything's been cut away. One thing after another has been destroyed." Her voice had grown hoarse with sobbing and shouting. "First it was my house and you said bricks and mortar weren't really important and I tried to believe you. But now all my anchors have drifted out to sea."

Andy crossed the room and picked her up, lifting her into his arms and pressing her body close to his, wanting to share his strength with her, his certitudes. It flashed through his mind that all his history, the place in the universe that had been created for him by ancestors with identifiable names and characters both good and evil, were also Lili's. He had always protested that he hated his family and their schemes, but he knew they had marked him. Whether he liked it or not, he was a Mendoza. And so was she.

He carried her into the bedroom, lay her on the bed. Lili curled up in a ball, but Andy was determined not to allow her to shut him out. He lay down beside her, murmured her name over and over, stroked her hair, her spine, kissed the back of her neck. Finally he realized she'd fallen asleep and he got up long enough to find a quilt and cover them both.

Andy didn't know what time it was when he sensed that he was alone in the bed. "Lili," he called into the dark. "Where are you?"

He heard her respond from the bathroom and a few seconds later she was beside him, smelling of soap and fresh lemons and wearing a nightdress and a robe. "I had to get out of those clothes," she murmured. "I'm sorry I woke you."

"It's okay." He pulled her down on the bed and stroked her hair. It was damp. It felt like wet silk to his touch. "Better?" he asked.

"A little. Calmer anyway. I keep thinking about my mother. I mean, Irene."

"I know who you mean."

"Do you think she'll be all right? Will it happen again? Do you think she's going to keep relapsing into her old persona?"

"No, I don't. I think it was seeing you so miserable that triggered it. She's had a lot of practice at maintaining her alias. And from everything you've told me, the way she manages it is to deny any emotion. That was damned hard to do here tonight, so she broke. But it probably won't happen again."

Lili moved closer to him, adjusting her body to the familiar contours and crevices of his. "Andy, I've been thinking, since I'm really a Mendoza, we must be cousins."

"You're not going to worry about that, are you? If you want, I'll check the genealogy charts. We're probably seventh cousins thrice removed. It doesn't make any difference."

"No, of course it doesn't." She propped herself on her elbow so she could see his face in the first light of dawn coming through the unshaded window. "Andy, I want to meet them."

"Who?"

"The Mendozas."

"Do you mean Diego?" he asked. This was the thing he most feared, that Lili would force a confrontation with Diego and be brutally rejected. He'd give anything he possessed to spare her that.

"Eventually perhaps," Lili admitted. "For openers, I was thinking of the English Mendozas."

He pulled her down so he could nuzzle her neck, inhale her scent. "I've been thinking the same thing," he admitted. "I've always kept you apart from them because of the way I feel about my family. But they're your family too. You're definitely not rootless or anchorless, or whatever you were saying. You have very long roots indeed, my darling. We both do."

"I need to see them," Lili said. "At least I need to see one branch of the tree."

"Yes," he agreed. "I think you do."

Lili bit her lip, thought for a moment, then picked up the telephone and punched in some numbers. "It's me, Peter," she said a few seconds later. "Yes, I'm fine. . . . Look, I don't really want to hear how she feels. . . . That's not what I'm calling about. Could you manage without me for a week?"

Lili looked at Andy. He held up two fingers. "Listen, Peter, it might be two weeks. . . . Okay, I can do that."

When she hung up she said, "He wants two more articles in the bank just in case. I can get them ready in a few days if you'll help me put them in writer-style English."

"Sure, glad to. What about your show?"

"That's easier," Lili said while she punched more numbers into the telephone. "Dan Kerry can get them to do a few more reruns. It's summertime, the silly season, as you say in London, no one will know the difference."

❧ 23 ❧

London, Westlake,
and New York: 1981

At Heathrow Lili and Andy had to separate to go through passport control—British subjects and fellow Europeans to the right, all others straight ahead. They met again in the baggage area, claimed their luggage, and followed a porter into a chilly and damp early July morning.

Andy had arranged for an attendant at the garage where he stored his car to bring it to the airport. Lili half expected the old Morris Oxford, but these days Andy drove a massive Bentley. She could see her face in the polished blue depths of every immaculately tended inch.

"A bit much, isn't it?" he asked sheepishly. "I bought it after the debacle with Fiona, to cheer me up because I'd been such an ass and married the absolutely wrong woman. Besides, blue always reminded me of you."

Lili smiled and didn't comment. During the four days since the meeting with Loy and Peter and Irene in her apartment, she had been distant and preoccupied. Andy wanted to believe it was because of the business pressures involved in arranging for two weeks away from New York, but he knew better.

It was close to ten when they drove into the heavy web of traffic surrounding the airport, but well before noon the powerful car was moving swiftly along the motorway, cutting a swathe through the industrial heart of England as it headed north. A couple of times Andy asked if she wanted to stop for something to eat; each time Lili shook her head and they went on. By two the scenery was gentling, becoming less prosaic and mercantile. Lili began noting billboards that told her she was heading for the Lake District, the place for a perfect holiday.

Soon after four they arrived in Grasmere, a Hollywood-dream English village of mellowed stone cottages and old-fashioned pubs. The village was dominated by Grasmere Lake, which managed even in the dull sunless afternoon to wear its picture prettiness as a halo of light. Lili could not make herself behave like a tourist, though she tried for Andy's sake. He made a few attempts to point out the local sights, but heard her forced responses and lapsed into the silence that had characterized the journey.

They drove through the town, keeping parallel to the lake until Andy turned up a dirt track. Lili saw a sign pointing north that said DUNMAIL RAISE. "One of the high fells," Andy explained. "A local beauty spot." He swung the Bentley in the opposite direction onto yet a smaller track and slowed to accommodate the inferior road.

For a time they followed a high stone wall, then they arrived at a massive pair of wrought iron gates, standing open. There was a porter's lodge, but it seemed deserted. Andy turned up the drive, then stopped. "I'd better shut those gates. I expect they were left open for us."

He had one foot out the door of the car when an elderly man in work pants and a plaid woolen shirt emerged from a stand of birch on the right and came toward them.

"No need, Mr. Andrew," the man called. "I'll take care of it. Sorry not to have been on duty when you arrived. Flossie whelped last night, six pups and she had a bad time of it. I'm taking these three into the house for Alice to look after."

He had reached the car by this time and he held out a basket for their inspection. Inside were three tiny balls of amber-colored fur. The pups' eyes were not yet open and their outsize ears were pasted to their heads, still damp with birth.

Andy turned to Lili. "This is Jason Durant, our game warden. Flossie's a golden retriever." He touched the pups with a gentle finger. "Her great-great-grandmother was my pet when I was a kid," he said before introducing Lili as a special friend from America. A few seconds later they drove on, leaving Durant to close the gates behind them.

The road, too substantial to be called a driveway, was blacktopped and in perfect condition. It was bordered on both sides by a forest of silver birch and oak and walnut.

"Mixed hardwoods are a specialty of the estate," Andy commented, trying desperately to ease Lili's tension. "They're almost a threatened species. Everyone plants quick-growing conifers. Mark made an enormous effort to save our elms. It didn't work, they're all gone, but he's replanting with a new strain that—"

Lili's silence was a soft smothering blanket between them.

"You're not terribly interested in the flora and fauna, are you?" he asked.

"Not right now," she admitted. "I'm sorry, I—"

"No need to apologize. I understand."

Lili touched his arm in a fleeting display of warmth, then drew back. "I can't help it," she murmured. "It all seems so unreal to me. This place, even you in this setting. I can't feel any connection to . . . to anything."

"Give it time, love." He wondered if he should warn her about the overwhelming magnificence of the mansion they were approaching, then reminded himself that this was Lili Cramer, who had made a career of houses, the woman with whom he'd once visited what seemed like all the stately homes in England.

As if she read his thoughts, Lili asked, "The house is Tudor, isn't it? I seem to remember you saying so."

"Yes. Built in 1507, two years before Henry VIII came to the throne. No one had lived in it for a hundred years when old Joe Mendoza bought it cheap in 1825."

They'd been driving for more than five minutes since entering the gates. "When do we get there?" Lili asked. "This is the longest approach road I've ever seen."

"It's not far now. Look over there." Andy pointed left. "You can see the roofline above the trees."

Lili looked and saw a mass of towers and turrets looming black against the pewter sky, rising like surreal sentinels from the mist and fog.

•　　•　　•

Andy opened the unlocked door and ushered Lili into a vast lobby. An elaborately decorated cupola rose high above them and the curves of an exquisitely graceful double staircase formed embracing arms on either side.

An elderly woman in a black dress and a white apron rushed to meet them, a smile nearly splitting her face. "Good afternoon, Mr. Andrew. Nice to see you again so soon, if I might say. They told us you was coming. The family's in the conservatory, sir. I was asked to give you this soon as you arrived."

"Thank you, Imelda." Andy took the note the maid offered and read it quickly.

"It's from my cousin Susan." His voice almost echoed in the seemingly limitless space. "She and Manuel arrived from London this morning. Mark told her we were coming."

He stopped reading and glanced at his watch, then at Lili. She was staring at the lush colors of the murals above her head. "Everyone's at tea," Andy said. "We're to join them if we wish. Susan says they'll understand if we don't. And she suggests we use the Rothschild suite."

"Sounds impressive," Lili said.

"What do you want to do? Plunge in and meet them at their most English, having tea in the conservatory?" He saw her slight shiver. "Look, you don't have to. We can go upstairs and get some rest. There's plenty of time."

"That might be better," Lili whispered.

"Okay." He turned to the maid. "We're going to sneak away upstairs and get changed before we say hello. Is the Rothschild Suite ready?"

" 'Course it is, Mr. Andrew. I'll get Frank to bring up your bags."

Andy gave her the keys to the car, then took Lili's hand and led her up the stairs.

The suite was composed of two bedrooms, a sitting room, and a huge bathroom. Lili paused in the doorway of the bathroom, surveying the mahogany-paneled walls decorated with framed hunting scenes, the gilded furniture, and the marble tub in the center. "I could fit my whole apartment in here," she said, taking a step forward to examine brass taps in the shape of dolphins, each engraved with the letter R.

"The suite was completely redone for Baron de Rothschild when he came to stay in 1870," Andy explained. "He was a friend of the family."

"Naturally." Lili ran her fingers over the upswept tail of one of the dolphins and added, "My house in Fielding was built in 1870. That's the year Sam and Amanda Kent got married."

Andy found her voice unnerving. It was distant, seemed to come from far away. He remembered how she'd been when he made love to her the night before they left New York, as if she were acting, as if the real Lili had disappeared and left this mannequin in her place. "Listen," he said, "would you prefer your own bedroom? There are two. I'll understand if you'd rather be alone."

"Like when we went up to Great Barrington?" she asked. "The day I found out my house was gone."

"Lili—" he began

Suddenly she turned and cut off his words by flinging herself at him. Lili wrapped her arms around his neck and clung with all her strength. "Andy, what's happening to me? I don't know who I am anymore."

"I know who you are," he insisted, holding her close, grateful that the dam seemed to have burst, but terrified lest she be swept away in the flood it unleashed. The only thing he could find to say was what he'd said before; he knew no comfort other than the truth. "You're my adorable love. You're the only woman I've ever wanted. Don't shut me out. Please, darling, don't go off to some private world of your own and leave me behind."

"I won't," she whispered. "I don't want to." She tipped her head back so she could see him, and traced the familiar, beloved planes of his angular face with her finger. "Andrew Mendoza, I love you," she said softly.

Incredibly, despite the long years since she had recognized that basic fact of her existence, this was the first time she had spoken the words. In the old days she had not dared to say them, because she knew he did not want her to. Since he'd come back into her life she had not been sure she wanted to.

Now they seemed the single certainty in a shifting, unsteady universe.

"I love you so damned much," she said fiercely. "That's the only thing I'm sure of anymore."

Lili pressed her face to his chest. She inhaled the laundry scent of his white shirt, the faintly damp odor of the tweed sport coat he still wore, the slightly musky smell of his skin, a little sour because neither of them had showered for close to twenty-four hours. She moved yet closer, straining to join her body with his, rejoicing in the uniqueness that was Andrew Mendoza, the man she loved and the man who loved her.

"Say you'll marry me," Andy pleaded, the words spoken against her shining hair. "Let's jettison the past, all the ghosts. We've waited such a long time, Lili darling. Taken so many wrong turnings."

Again Lili tipped back her head and looked at him. Behind his glasses the tiger eyes were gazing at her with so much love and longing and commitment she knew she could never doubt him again. "Yes," she said. "Yes."

Andy pressed his mouth to hers, kissed her for a long time, then carried her to an immense canopied bed. He lay her down gently, and moved to a pair of casement windows with small leaded panes. When he threw them wide, the mingled scents of the garden rose strong in the damp air. "Is it too cold for you?" he asked.

"No. It's lovely." She sat up and looked out at the vista he had unveiled.

Early evening had finally seen the mist burned away by the sun. Warm yellow light suffused the sky, and shafts of pink and gold picked out the jewel-green tops of the rounded tree-less mountains called fells. Lili could see only the horizon, but she could identify by their perfume the carnations and pinks and roses that doubtless bloomed beneath the window.

Andy returned to her side. He began undressing her, kissing each inch of flesh he exposed. Lili kept whispering his name.

They made love with the same sense of awe and discovery they had shared all those years earlier beneath the calico quilt in Prince's Mews, but with more awareness, more knowing. Little cries of need and pleasure and sometimes of triumph saw the day end and the night come, and sleeping and waking happened in waves that established a rhythm of their own unrelated to the passage of ordinary time, or the life of the world that waited for them beyond the bedroom door.

In the morning Lili accompanied Andy downstairs, slightly embarrassed not to have appeared for dinner the night before. "Don't fuss," Andy said. "They won't. One thing this family is very good at is being discreet when required."

Unlike yesterday, this morning was glorious—all the things an English summer day should be but seldom was. Breakfast was served in a dining room adjoining a sunlit terrace. The light danced on covered silver dishes on the sideboard and a butler asked if Miss Cramer would prefer sausages or kidneys or kippers, and did scrambled eggs suit or would she like them boiled?

For the first time in days Lili was hungry. She ate sausages and toast and marmalade, but she skipped the eggs. It was glamorous and straight out of a book, but eggs that had been kept warm in a chafing dish weren't really worth eating.

A nice-looking woman joined them. She was small and slim and neatly made. Her short curly hair was darker than Andy's and had a lot of gray she didn't bother to hide. Lili thought she must be Mark's wife, but Andy introduced her as his all-time-favorite cousin, Susan. "This is Lili," he told her. "The love of my life."

"Hello, Lili. Andy has spoken of you often. Welcome. I hope you're comfortable." Susan's smile was warm and genuine.

"Very comfortable, thank you," Lili said. "It's a glorious house."

Susan made a face. "Andy and I could tell you a bit about that."

"We were united in hating it years ago," Andy said. "But Lili is an expert on houses. If she says it's glorious, it must be."

They chatted about the house for a few moments, then Susan went away and they were alone again. Neither Andy's

brother nor his cousin Manuel appeared. "One thing about
having two hundred and forty rooms," Andy explained, "is
that everyone can go about his business without seeing anyone
else. As advertised, they're being discreet and giving you time
to rest and recover. We can join them for lunch if you like. Or
wait until dinner."

"But it's very rude of me not to meet my hostess," Lili
protested.

"You have," he said. "The bloom is off for Mark and his
wife. They're almost never in residence at the same time.
Since Susan is here, she naturally assumes the role as lady
of the manor."

"Okay," she agreed. "Can we walk in the grounds,
then?"

"For as long as you like," Andy said. "It would take a
month to hike the perimeter."

"I wasn't thinking of hiking. More like a geriatric stroll."

He laughed heartily at the small joke because he was
overjoyed that she sounded so much more like herself, and
led her into the gardens.

Susan had lunch with them, making apologies for Manuel,
who was feeling tired and had elected to have a tray in his
room. Mark, it seemed, had gone into Grasmere on some
local business. Afterward Lili and Andy's jet lag caught up
with them and they went upstairs and took a long nap. For
Lili, at least, it lasted through the cocktail hour. She woke
as Andy returned to her side and said it was time to dress
for dinner.

By the time she and Andy came into the dining room
the others were seated. The two men rose immediately.
"This must be Lili," the younger of the pair said. "I'm
Mark Mendoza, Andy's brother. Welcome to Westlake."
Lili murmured a reply, Susan indicated a place to the right
of the distinguished-looking older man.

"My cousin, whom we call Tío Manuel," Andy said. The
man bowed. Lili held out her hand and he took it and lifted
it to an inch or so beneath his lips. "Tío Manuel's mother was
English; he understands nearly everything but speaks only a

little," Andy explained. "Don't worry, Susan will translate for you."

The other woman was on Lili's left. Andy took a place at the far end of a table that seemed at least a mile long.

It was Susan who kept the small talk going during the soup and the fish, then Lili turned to the elderly Spaniard. "Do you come to England often, Don Manuel?"

He didn't answer and she thought he hadn't understood. She started to repeat the question, but he interrupted her with a flow of rapid Spanish, his rheumy old eyes fixed at a point between her breasts.

"Tío Manuel is asking about your pendant, Lili," Susan said.

Lili was wearing a simple white silk caftan. Gleaming against her breast was the triangle of gold with the Hebrew inscription. She glanced down at it, then looked up to the face of the old man beside her. "Please tell him it's something I found," Lili said quietly. "Tell him that if he likes, I'll explain where and how after dinner."

Mark took a small blue velvet box from his desk and opened it. "Here are the other three pieces."

Lili had her bit of gold in her hand and she leaned over and fitted it into the empty space on the satin lining. It filled the gap, creating a half-moon.

They were in Mark's study. There was coffee and brandy and Manuel was smoking a cigar. He was seated a few feet away and he craned his neck, gazed for a moment at the velvet box, then reached inside his shirt and withdrew yet another piece of gold. This one was larger, an entire semi-circle in its own right, and had a hole punched at one end through which was threaded a leather thong. When Manuel held it in position against the four other parts, the circle was complete.

"The lettering matches up perfectly," Andy said. "You don't have to know the Hebrew characters to see that."

" 'If I forget thee, O Jerusalem,' " Susan quoted softly, " 'let my right hand forget her cunning.' "

"Do you know the rest of it?" Mark asked.

Susan shook her head.

The sixth Baron Westlake looked out the window at an elegant garden where white and silver plants clustered around a stone birdbath. The tableau shimmered in the moonlight. For a moment the garden seemed to absorb Mark, then he turned to Lili. " 'By the waters of Babylon where we sat down, how we wept when we remembered Sion,' " he quoted softly.

"That's been made into a popular song!" Lili said, surprised. "I didn't know it was a psalm."

"Yes, I know the song," Mark said. "But they left out the tough parts. There was nothing sentimental about the ancient world." He watched Lili as he went on. "The last verse says, 'Babylon, pitiless queen, blessed be the man who deals out to thee the measure thou hast dealt to us; blessed be the man who will catch up thy children, and dash them against the rocks.' "

The words echoed in a room suddenly silent. Lili's mouth was dry. The Mendoza way—he who is not with me is against me, vengeance upon all my enemies. Exactly as Andy had always said.

Manuel reached forward and reclaimed his half of the pendant, breaking the circle. Lili hesitated, then retrieved the sliver that belonged to her. She sensed Mark and Manuel looking at each other, sending silent messages, but she did not acknowledge either man as she once more slipped the gold chain around her neck. She knew, too, that Andy was watching her, but she didn't meet his gaze.

It was Susan who broke the tension, pointing to the three pieces of gold still on Mark's desk. "Why is it so small? The plaque has to have been much larger if it made the mark that's on the wall in the room in the old wing of the *palacio*."

"Because this isn't the plaque," Mark explained. "That disappeared ages ago. The pendant arrived in England in the sixteenth century with the first Mendoza to come here, Ramón, who organized the sherry trade. He brought it from Córdoba. In one piece, incidentally. It was Robert the Turncoat who divided it a couple of hundred years later. He was an Englishman, but head of the house in Spain," he added in an aside to Lili. "It was Robert who broke the pendant in two and gave half to his son, who would be the Spanish patriarch after him, and half to his English nephew, my great-great-grandfather, Joseph Mendoza."

"How did the English half get divided?" Andy asked. "And how in God's name did a quarter of it finish up in a tiny little town in the northeastern United States?"

"It's a fairly straightforward story," Mark said. "Joseph had twin brothers fifteen years younger than he was, Cecil and Roger. Sometime around 1835 he sent Roger to New York with a piece of the pendant, some capital, and instructions to open an American branch of the Bank of Mendoza. Joseph also had three sons, James, Norman, and Henry. They each got a third of the portion of the pendant that remained."

Mark gestured to the pieces of gold on his desk. "What we're looking at are those three bits. But Roger disappeared down a black hole. No one knows what happened to him. And until this moment"—he glanced at Lili—"no one's known where to find the missing fourth piece."

"Didn't Joseph look for his younger brother?" Susan asked. "It's a very un-Mendoza thing to do, simply lose a member of the family." She glanced at Lili when she said that.

It was the first indication Lili had that the others—or at least Susan—knew of her parentage. Andy must have found an opportunity to tell them. While she slept this afternoon perhaps.

"We don't usually do that," Mark agreed. He, too, looked pointedly at Lili. "If we know they exist."

Mark was smiling and Lili had to acknowledge it as a kind smile. She managed to smile back. It gave her an odd feeling, a sense of being accepted, somehow baptized, which she told herself was sentimental nonsense, but which was nonetheless real.

"As for Roger and Joseph," Mark continued, "there's a lot that's unclear about the period. Either, unlike most of our ancestors, Joseph didn't keep a diary, or it's gone missing. In any event, it isn't in the library here or the one in London. So Joseph may have looked for his brother, he may even have found him, but we don't know a damned thing about it."

"That still leaves the mystery of how something belonging to Roger Mendoza finished up in Lili's house in Fielding, Massachusetts," Andy said.

"It does indeed," Mark agreed. "Lili, please tell me again exactly where you found it."

"Behind a painting in my house, supposedly a Constable. In fact, it's a fake, though I didn't know that until a few years ago. Anyway, when I was thirteen I wanted to see what the wallpaper looked like behind the painting and I took it down. This was wedged into the rear of the frame."

"In an envelope with a message on it," Andy added. "Lili showed it to me years ago. We couldn't read all of it, but what was decipherable said, 'Córdoba, Spain, the house of M-something.' Mendoza, presumably."

Manuel had been sitting very still, watching all of them. Occasionally the English had become too quick for him and Susan had murmured a quiet translation. Suddenly he stood up. *"Necesita explicárselo a ella."* The old man sounded deeply agitated.

"Tío Manuel says you must explain to her," Susan said.

"Explain what?" Andy asked.

Mark seemed to shake his head, as if warning off his cousin, but the impression was fleeting. It was Manuel's son Roberto who these days ran the Spanish business operations, but Manuel remained head of the house and in many ways the old rules still applied. The old man began to speak, pausing every few moments for Susan to translate.

"Tío Manuel says the pendant is a *letra accreedor*. I guess what we'd call a due bill. He says it was made by a thirteenth-century jeweler for Benhaj Mendoza, who was then head of the house."

Susan stopped speaking and listened to more of Manuel's story. It was not one she'd known previously and she had to question him a couple of times to be sure she understood. When their murmured dialogue ended, she resumed the explanation.

"In 1391 all Andalusia was ablaze with anti-Semitism. One night a man secretly warned Benhaj of an impending riot in Córdoba and Benhaj went into hiding with his wife and his sons. The next day two thousand Jews were slaughtered and left to rot in the streets. The entire *juderia* was burned to the ground, including most of our house, but the family had survived. Benhaj gave the man who had warned him the pendant as a promise that at any time he could claim aid from the House of Mendoza."

Manuel spoke again and Susan listened, then translated. "More than a century later one of the man's descendants presented the pendant and claimed his reward. He was a vintner and he became a partner in the Mendoza sherry business. By that time the Jews had been formally expelled from Spain and the family were Catholics, except for Ramón, who had reconverted to Judaism. If he stayed in Córdoba, they'd all have to face the Inquisition, so Ramón's father helped him get to England. He gave Ramón the pendant to take with him. It was to be a mark of the link between the two branches of the family, a claim on the Cordobéses that would always be honored."

Manuel cleared his throat. The story was finished, but he had more to say. Once again Susan listened to the old man's murmur, finally she turned from him to the others. "Tío Manuel says because Lili is in possession of this thing, she, too, has a claim on the family. It must be satisfied— and she must return her bit of the pendant. He says it must be made whole."

Mark waved a dismissive hand. "For God's sake, times are different now. Look, Susan, tell him in Spanish that—"

Manuel had understood the younger man's words. "*!Es una vergüenza!*"

"He says it's a disgrace," Susan said. "The House of Mendoza never defaults."

Mark turned to Lili with an apologetic shrug. "My dear, I'm sorry. We are still very old-fashioned and feudal, as you can see. Is there anything we can do for you or give you that would make you willing to give up your piece of the pendant? I hesitate to mention money, but if you were willing to set a price, of course we—"

"It isn't money I need, Mark," Lili said softly. She felt Andy staring at her, but she kept her eyes on his brother. "I get the feeling you all know about me," she said.

There was a moment's embarrassed silence.

"Darling, you don't have to ex—" Andy began.

"I know I needn't explain," Lili interrupted. "But let me be very American for a moment. Lay the cards on the table.

I'm a bastard. Apparently you know who my parents were, and that I was farmed out in infancy."

She fingered the pendant around her neck, held it so the lamplight made it glitter. "But this is an intriguing link, isn't it? It makes the circle complete in more ways than one. That seems to be what I need most at the moment, links. So I'll tell you what, you find out what happened to Roger Mendoza and how this little treasure ended up in Fielding and tell me about it. Then I'll give it back."

❦ 24 ❦

New York, Grasmere,
and London: 1981

New York was unrelentingly sunny and hot. Loy minded it more than usual, perhaps because Lili and Andy had left for London two days earlier, and she couldn't shake a sense of impending catastrophe, of a sword about to fall.

"Lili will be all right," Irene said, understanding the source of Loy's anxiety. "I'm sure she will. I think going to England to meet Andy's family was a sensible idea. It will help her adjust."

"Perhaps," Loy said fretfully.

"You're nervous as a cat," Irene said. "There's no need. Everything will be fine. You'll see. If Diego were going to do something, he'd have done it by now."

"We can't be sure of that. I keep thinking about what we haven't told Lili," Loy added in a very low voice.

"Don't think about it," Irene said firmly. "Forget it. You must." There was no trace of the lapse she had suffered that terrible night in Lili's apartment. When she shook her head she was the woman she had become, the self she had invented. "That's the one thing nobody knows but you and me. We mustn't ever tell."

Loy opened her mouth as if to speak, then closed it again. This was the final burden, the truth she could not share even with her Siamese twin, her alter ego. Irene was wrong, it wasn't true that no one else knew. Diego knew.

Loy had told him years before. If she had not, he wouldn't have permitted the final trip to the Swiss plastic surgeon, the one that created the masks behind which both she and Irene now hid. Diego had never once mentioned it, never threatened her with his secret knowledge, never so much as referred to it in forty-three years—but Loy knew he remembered it well.

"Yes, Irene," Loy said, hiding her distress as she'd hidden it so well for so long, "I'm sure you're right."

A few minutes later she pleaded a headache and went up to her sitting room. Standing a moment, staring out the window at Tenth Street—dusty and deserted in the metallic glare of the late afternoon sun—she made up her mind.

Loy sat at her desk and began writing. Her pen moved swiftly over the page; it was as if she were purging herself, as if the black ink were some foul poison she was expelling from her system. An hour later she'd finished. She folded the five sheets, put them in an envelope and sealed it, then she felt a bit better.

There was a light tap on the door. When she called "Come in," Loy expected Irene. It was Peter who came to her side and kissed her.

Loy pressed her face to his in a gesture that for a moment was fierce in its need and naked desire, then she smothered the blaze that threatened to erupt. Her smile of welcome was warm but restrained.

"How are you doing?" Peter asked, studying her.

"I'm fine. I'd be better if I heard from Lili, but I expect that won't happen."

"Probably not," he agreed. "Look, I know how you feel, but it's Lili's problem now. She has to work it out in her own way."

"Yes. I wish that weren't true, but I know it is."

Peter had obviously come from the office. He loosened his tie and undid the top button of his shirt. "It's hot as hell in here. Something wrong with the air-conditioning?"

"I hadn't noticed," Loy admitted. "But you're right. There must be something wrong."

Peter took off his suitcoat, threw it over the back of a chair, and went to the window and started fiddling with the air conditioner. Five minutes later he gave up with a snort of disgust. "Nothing simple. It's beyond the abilities of the Fowler home repair service."

He lit a cigarette, watching her over the flame. "Look, you may as well know, I'm planning to move in as soon as Irene goes back to Florida, and I think we should get this place centrally air-conditioned. It's a lot more comfortable and reliable. We'll like that when we're old."

Loy's gun-metal eyes were sad, her tone subdued. "Peter darling, I am old. You have to face facts. I'm going to be sixty-five my next birthday."

His chin jutted out. "So?"

"So you are fifteen years younger. It's insane."

"Where is it written that loving somebody is insane?"

"Lots of places, Peter. Lots of places. In the whole history of the human race."

He stubbed out the cigarette and dropped to his knees beside her. Loy ran her fingers through his thick brown hair. Everything she was thinking was evident on her face.

"Tell me the truth," he said, "if it were the other way round, if I were the older one, it wouldn't seem quite so unthinkable, would it?"

She smiled. "No, not quite. It would still raise eyebrows, but it's not unheard of."

"Exactly," he said as he stood up and pulled a chair close to hers. "And I'll tell you why the man has to be older. It's an ancient taboo based on the need to reproduce the race."

He was sitting across from her now, commanding her full attention. Peter was pitching an idea—which was exactly what he'd come to do this afternoon.

"Think about it," he said. "Men don't have an identifiable cut-off point for fertility. As long as the woman is capable of bearing children, people accept May and December marriages. I don't think the race is in danger of extinction because we won't reproduce, do you? Besides," he added with a grin, "it will give me exquisite pleasure to be Lili's stepfather. Think of what a weapon it will be against her smart mouth."

Loy giggled, then grew serious. "You have been thinking about this, haven't you? I don't mean only with your heart, with your head as well."

"I've thought of damned little else," he admitted. "When I first learned your real age, I was shocked, I'm not denying that. But I thought about how I felt, how much I love you, and nothing else mattered. Marry me, my darling Loy. Please marry me."

She shook her head. "No. I've thought about it too. And I can't marry you. I just can't."

"Why the hell not? Loy, do you love me?"

"Yes," she admitted, her voice suddenly very low. "Yes, my dearest, I do."

"Then it's settled," he said triumphantly, reaching forward to draw her into his arms. Loy ducked away. Peter pulled back, stung and instantly wary.

She fingered the envelope on her desk, the one containing the pages she'd written before he arrived. "No, it doesn't settle it. I've seen too much, my love, been through too much. I can't commit myself in the way a marriage demands. Quite apart from the absurd difference in our ages, I need . . ." She hesitated. "I need distance."

"Even from me?"

"Yes, even from you."

That gave him pause, and he didn't answer immediately. "Are you saying you want me out of your life?" he asked after a few seconds, unable to keep the hurt and pain from his voice.

"No," Loy whispered. "That's what I should say. It's what you deserve. But I'm too selfish. I'll understand if you go, but I cannot say I want you to."

"I'm not going. I've been searching all my adult life for something special. Why else would I still be a bachelor? Finally I've found what I was looking for. Don't expect me to walk away from it."

"Peter, I won't go on forever. I'll start to show my age, fall apart, get awful diseases. Maybe get senile like poor old Charlotte Mendoza. Then what?"

"Maybe I'll get hit by a car tomorrow," he countered. "I

could become a paraplegic. Or maybe I'll get cancer, or go blind, or any of the other thousand things that 'flesh is heir to,' as they say. Then what?"

"Then I'd go on loving you and taking care of you as long as I could, but the odds aren't the same, darling."

"Okay, I accept that. The thing *you* have to accept is that at the moment we're both healthy and we're in love. Let's grab what happiness we can, Loy. It isn't distributed even-handedly, in case you haven't noticed."

"I've noticed." She picked up the envelope. "I want you to do something for me."

"Anything in my power," he promised instantly.

"Take this letter. Don't read it now, put it away. If something happens to me, or if you come to hate being tied to me, read it then. It will give you—" She broke off, unsure how to express her thoughts. "It will provide you with an escape route of sorts. A sop for your conscience, should you ever need it."

"If we both live to be a hundred and fifty, I could never hate you," he said solemnly.

Loy didn't reply. She still held out the envelope. After a few seconds he took it and put it in his pocket.

"Aren't you curious?" she asked.

"A little I suppose. Not enough to make it number one on the agenda. I doubt it ever will be. Your secret communiqué seems like a red herring to me. What about us? What do you want to do?"

Loy leaned forward and put her hands on either side of his face. "I want to go on as we are for the moment," she said. "But the contract is renegotiable, Peter. At any time, by either of us. Agreed?"

"Agreed," he said. "And I'm still going to start acting like Lili's stepfather."

"I can't wait to see that."

Their kiss tasted of laughter.

Susan opened the door of Charlotte's room without knocking. "Good morning," she told the nurse. "I've come to visit my cousin."

The woman eyed Susan warily. "She's not supposed to get upset. Having visitors upsets her."

"Nonsense, I'm not a stranger." Susan looked around the sitting room. The nurse had made it her own. Her knitting was on the sofa, her magazines were spread across the tables. "Where is my cousin?" Susan asked.

"Miss Mendoza is in her bedroom, which she seems to prefer."

The nurse was heavyset and slow-moving. She'd risen when Susan came in; now her large white oxfords seemed rooted to the floor. They were chalky with many polishings and the uniform was so stiffly starched it could surely stand on its own.

"In her room," Susan repeated brusquely, pushing past the other woman. "I'll see her there, then. Only for a few minutes." She was across the room and through the door before the nurse could react.

Susan closed the bedroom door behind her and looked for a key. There was none. Logical. They wouldn't want Charlotte locking herself in.

Her cousin was seventy-one, seventeen years older than Susan herself, but Charlotte looked ancient. Her hair was yellow-white and thin, her face a web of wrinkles. Susan felt a wave of pity. This was a far different woman than she remembered. Why didn't the damned nurse put a rinse in her hair so it wouldn't be that awful color? And set it occasionally?

She crossed to where Charlotte sat beside the window. "Hello, darling, it's me, Susan." She bent over and adjusted the blanket that covered bony knees.

At first Charlotte didn't seem to hear. Susan wondered if she was deaf. She spoke more loudly. "Charlotte, you remember me, don't you?"

The lined face turned to her, one trembling hand reached out and touched Susan's hair. "Of course I do. It's your birthday, isn't it? You're fifteen today."

Susan took a deep breath. "Yes, that's right. We had a special luncheon for my birthday. All the things I like best. A joint of lamb and creamed potatoes and sherry trifle."

"And the savory was prawns on toast. It's usually sardines, but it was prawns today because it's your birthday."

"And you've invited me to your room to see your treasures. You did ask me, didn't you, Charlotte?"

"I don't remember. I guess I did. Would you like to see them now?"

"Oh, yes, please."

Charlotte started to rise. Susan put out a restraining hand. "Tell me where they are, I'll get them. You're tired. It's been a busy day."

"Tired. Yes. The beads are in that drawer there, the one in the dressing table."

Susan went to the oblong table with its marquetry top and skirt of broderie anglaise. The drawer was empty. God, how awful. Why would they take away her beads? "They're not here, darling." She returned to her cousin's side. "Did you put them somewhere else? In a hiding place perhaps?"

"A hiding place." Charlotte spoke the words in a flat monotone. Suddenly she emitted a harsh, cackling sound. It took Susan some seconds to recognize it as laughter. "Nobody knows about my hiding place."

Once more Charlotte turned her face to Susan's. For a few seconds the pale eyes were sparkling and alive, as if the old Charlotte were peeking from behind a veil. "I'm a sapphist, you know. I will not deny it. The whole damned family simply has to accept facts. Are you going to grow up to be a sapphist, Susan?"

"I don't think so, but I think you've every right to be if you choose. Do you have letters in your hiding place, Charlotte? From women who have been your lovers, perhaps?"

The eyes clouded over. "I'm not telling."

"But you did say you would show me your treasures. Tell me where your hiding place is, darling, so I can find the beads. Remember, you promised and it's my birthday."

Charlotte didn't answer. She turned her face away and stared out the window at the rose gardens and at the glass houses where long ago a wildly expensive rose hybridizing program had given the world a yellow climber known as Cecil's Folly. Susan followed the older woman's glance. "Cousin Cecil made the rose gardens, didn't he, Charlotte? In 1839."

The answer came rapidly, in swift, matter-of-fact tones.

"No, he started them in 1840. Nobody but me ever gets the history right in this family."

"Yes, you're the expert. What about Cecil's older brother, Joseph? Did he keep a diary, Charlotte?"

"Of course. All the Mendozas kept diaries. I've been working with it."

Susan tried not to show her excitement or her nervousness. She'd been in here nearly ten minutes, and the starched harridan in the sitting room was likely to burst in at any second and break the mood. She took Charlotte's hands in her own, willing the real woman to return through the fog of unknowing. "Please, darling, can't I look in your hiding place? So I can see the beads, and maybe have a peek at Joseph's diary?"

Charlotte's fingers fluttered, for the space of a single breath her grip became firm and purposeful. "Very well, since it's your birthday. The panel over the fireplace opens if you push it."

This wing of the house was Queen Anne, added in the late sixteen hundreds, well before the Mendoza occupancy. The fireplace was small and elegant, surrounded by woodwork painted a soft color somewhere between white and palest rose. Susan crossed the room and ran her fingers along the simple marble mantel. Above it were two rows of oval panels outlined in delicate molding. She applied pressure to each in turn. Nothing happened.

"Which panel, Charlotte? Where do I push?"

There was no reply. The fog once more enveloped the woman sitting by the window.

Susan heard noises from the sitting room. The nurse must be coming. Quickly she ran an exploratory finger along each bit of molding. When she reached the end of the first row she found the hidden catch. When she released it the panel dropped forward on a chain and four shallow shelves were revealed.

There were half a dozen boxes—some leather, some china, some painted silk—and three leather-bound, gilt-edged books. Susan removed the books and put them aside, then she opened one of the boxes. "Look, darling! Here are your beads."

Ropes of malachite and jade and carved ebony, and a dark

red stone Susan took to be garnet were crammed into the boxes. Susan tipped handfuls of them into her cousin's lap. Charlotte made that cackling noise again, and ran the beads through her gnarled fingers. "My pretties. I haven't seen them in such a long time."

The nurse opened the door. "Excuse me, ma'am, but I really think—" She stopped speaking when she saw what her patient was doing. "Blow me! Are those the beads she's always asking for? We never could find them. Her ladyship keeps buying new ones for Miss Charlotte, but she always makes us take them away."

"Yes, well, these are the ones she wants. There are more boxes full in that cupboard behind the paneling. It's a bit of a trick opening, you have to release a catch behind the molding."

Susan gathered up the gilt-edged volumes and went to her cousin and kissed her cheek. "I'll be going now, darling. Thank you for my birthday treat."

Charlotte didn't acknowledge Susan's good-bye. She was busy playing with the beads, hanging three and four strings of them around her neck at the same time.

"It's Joseph's diary all right," Susan told Lili and Andy the next day.

It was a little after eleven. Breakfast had finished a couple of hours earlier, then Mark had ushered Lili into his study and questioned her.

"I'll need as much information as you can give me if I'm going to solve your mystery, Lili," he explained.

"I'll tell you what I know, but none of it is likely to shed any light on the connection between my house and your family."

"It's still where we have to begin," Mark insisted.

So Lili had described Fielding and her old house, and how Amanda Manning had come from New York to marry Sam Kent in 1870—and what she knew of the way they had lived, the secrets she had gleaned from the home they had left behind.

"It sounds like you really loved that old place," Mark said when Lili stopped speaking. "Who lives there now?"

"No one, it doesn't exist. My mother sold the house in 1971.

A few months ago it was torn down to make room for a new development. Fielding's become a fashionable suburb." She had not quite been able to disguise the catch in her voice.

"There's a lot of that happening here as well," Mark commiserated. "A damned shame. It doesn't seem like progress to me."

Lili stood up. She couldn't bear to sit there discussing the folly of modern development with a man who probably funded a large measure of it. "I'm afraid that's all I can tell you."

Mark rose as well. "It's really a great deal, you know," he said as he accompanied her to the door. "We had no way to trace Roger Mendoza before, but now you've given us a definite lead. Knowing the name Manning may make it fairly straightforward. There are a number of agencies who do this kind of work. I'll have my people in New York get on to it immediately."

That would probably be Jeremy Crandall's next job, Lili thought. All she said was that she was looking forward to hearing whatever they might discover.

"You'll be the first to know," Mark promised. Then he paused in the act of opening the study door. "May I say something else?"

"Yes, certainly."

"Andy tells me you and he are to be married. I'd like to offer my best wishes, and say how pleased I am to welcome you to the family. I mean in this more . . . shall we say, regular way."

Lili didn't acknowledge the reference to her bastard status. Mark had not meant the remark unkindly. "Thank you," she said. "I love Andy very much, I'm sure we'll be happy." And with that she'd fled. "There are always wheels within wheels among the Mendozas," Andy had said, and he'd been right.

Now she was in the morning room with Andy and Susan, drinking coffee from a delicate porcelain cup, ignoring the rain outside the windows, and looking at the books Susan had identified as Joseph Mendoza's diaries.

"Charlotte was working with them years ago, before she became ill. Pages of her notes were folded inside."

Susan spread the papers on the table. She found it hard to

believe that the firm, clear handwriting had flowed from the fingers that now trembled in the Queen Anne bedroom, but unquestionably it had. "It seems Charlotte was tying Joseph's references to other documents she'd been studying at the British Museum," Susan continued. "She was filling in data about the sixteenth century and how Ramón Mendoza first established himself in the East End."

Andy studied the pages of notes, the researcher in him intrigued. "It's good, careful work, all the references cited with page numbers and book titles."

"Why did Charlotte hide the diary?" Lili asked.

"I don't really think she did," Susan explained. "I think she simply kept whatever she was using in her room, often in the cupboard behind the fireplace. She came and went from here a great deal. When she left for Paris with Irene, she probably simply forgot to put the diaries back in the library. By the time she returned, her mind was going."

"Okay," Lili said, "what does it tell you about the pendant?"

Susan frowned. Unlike Manuel and Mark, she felt no pressure to get back Lili's piece of the old treasure, but she liked the American woman. And she empathized with Lili's distress over the way her natural parents had treated her. Susan simply wanted to fill in some of the blanks, perhaps make Lili feel better, and satisfy her own curiosity.

"Not much, I'm afraid. Joseph does mention having the pendant cut and sending one piece to New York with his brother Roger. He goes on for two paragraphs about something else—a letter from Sofía that he says he'll send to America with Roger as well."

"What letter?" Andy asked.

Susan shrugged. "I've no idea. Anyway, Roger didn't want to go. He didn't want anything to do with the business, he wanted to be an artist. 'Damned nonsense,' Joseph calls it."

There was a discreet tap on the door and the butler came in to announce that Miss Cramer had a telephone call. Lili followed him out of the room; five minutes later she returned. "That was Irene," she told Andy. "Calling from Loy's house. They wanted to know how I am. The end of the world must be imminent if Irene Petworth Cramer calls long distance to ask if I'm all right."

Susan gasped, then covered her mouth with her hand as if she wanted to take the small sound back. It was too late, both Andy and Lili were staring at her. "You did say Irene Petworth?" Susan murmured in tones of disbelief.

"Irene Petworth Cramer," Lili amended. "My mother. At least the woman who raised me, the one I always thought was my mother. Loy Perez arranged for her to adopt me a few days after I was born."

Andy turned to Susan. "You know about Irene's connection to Swanning Park, don't you? I always suspected you did. You were in on it when my father was running around sweeping everything under the rug after the murder."

Susan hesitated, then sighed. "I suppose there's no point in denying it now. But you can hardly say I was 'in on it.' I was eleven years old when Amanda Preston-Wilde shot her husband. The only thing I knew was that Uncle Ian said we weren't supposed to talk about it if any newspaper types came snooping. Especially we weren't supposed to mention Irene Petworth, Amanda's secretary."

"Why did you stick with that story years later? When I asked you, it was 1971. For all you knew, Irene was dead and gone."

Susan shook her head. "Not likely. She was very young when it happened. And I remembered what I'd overheard. Irene was an innocent victim. Charlotte and Amanda were the cause of the trouble. I did believe Amanda was dead. I still think she killed herself after she murdered Emery. You said Charlotte was mad, so that left only Irene. If she was worth protecting in 'thirty-nine, then she was worth it in 'seventy-one."

"Bloody hell," Andy muttered. "When I think of what you could have saved me . . ."

"Don't look at me like that," Susan protested. "I did try to put you in the picture that Christmas in Córdoba. Don't you remember that I brought up Charlotte's name?"

"I guess I do. Vaguely. But at the time I didn't make the connection."

Susan closed the book on the table. "Well, that wasn't my fault. And now it's your turn to answer a question. What does all this have to do with Loy Perez?"

"Have you met Loy?" Andy asked, carefully keeping his voice neutral.

"Certainly. Everyone knew about her and Diego." Susan busied herself with the diaries and avoided looking at Lili. "And Loy sometimes came to Córdoba to see Tío Manuel. They'd worked together during the war. Loy was a real heroine. Manuel's told me some incredible stories."

Andy and Lili looked at each other. It was the name Irene that had startled Susan. She knew nothing of who Loy was, nothing about switched identities. Their eyes telegraphed the same message of silence.

Susan was busy with her own thoughts. "But how does Loy know Irene? Oh, I see," she said, making the connection. "Loy must have known her if it was Irene she gave her child to when—" She broke off. "I'm sorry, I'm making a mess of this. It must be painful for you, Lili."

"I'll survive," Lili assured her. "I've had a lot of practice."

❧ 25 ❧

It took the wheels of the Mendoza machine four days to grind out the information Mark had requested. Except that a Sunday intervened, they would have managed it in three.

The first Lili knew of their success was after dinner on Wednesday evening.

"I've arranged for coffee and brandy in the Long Gallery," Mark said. "I've quite a story to tell, and that seems an appropriate setting."

The Long Gallery ran the entire length of the second floor of the east wing. One of its walls was lined with windows that looked out on gardens and parkland, the others were filled with portraits of Mendoza ancestors. Andy had brought Lili there the previous afternoon. They had, in fact, noted a few cleft chins very like hers among the numerous forebears, though Andy admitted he'd never before seen the resemblance.

The gallery looked entirely different by lamplight than it had by day. The portraits receded into the shadows and the living dominated the dead.

"I told Davis we'd look after ourselves," Mark said, explaining the absence of the butler. "Here we are, everything's arranged."

The refreshments had been left on a wheeled cart placed by a group of chairs. Lili settled herself in one of them, adjusting the folds of the red silk trousers she was wearing with a many-colored Moroccan tunic. "You look fantastic,"

Andy murmured in her ear as he sat down beside her. "It requires all my self-control not to ravish you right here."

"You'll be known as Andrew the Rapist when you get your picture on the wall behind us," she whispered back.

Mark offered Lili a brandy, pouring it from a bottle with a picture of a Gypsy on the label. "Is that supposed to be Sofía?" Lili asked, taking the crystal snifter of dark amber liquid.

Mark glanced at the bottle. "I doubt it's a likeness of La Gitanita, but it must have been inspired by her. It was Sofía's husband Robert who began shipping sherry to England in marked bottles. Before him it came only in casks. From specific sherries to identified brandies was a short step."

Lili waited until the others had been served and Manuel was smoking the daily cigar his doctors permitted. Then she murmured "Cheers," along with the rest and sipped the potent brandy. Her eyes never left Mark's face. He looked a little smug. Unconsciously, she fingered the pendant around her neck and Mark saw her and smiled a knowing smile, and Lili realized what she'd been doing and dropped her hand.

"Shall we begin?" Mark asked.

No one bothered to reply.

He took a wad of folded sheets from the inside pocket of his dinner jacket. "This came in late this afternoon. By the way, it was sent via a remarkable new technology in which, as luck would have it, the Mendoza Venture Capital Fund has a more than modest interest. They're calling it facsimile mail, though I don't doubt it will soon be simply fax."

He held up one of the sheets for their inspection. The paper was thin and shiny. "Uses the telephone wires to send what is in effect an instant photocopy. Similar things have been around for some time, but this one's going to be cheap enough for everyone to buy. I predict it'll soon be as ubiquitous as the telephone."

"Mark," Susan murmured, casting a sympathetic glance in Lili's direction, "stop rubbing your hands over the profits and get to the point."

"Yes, of course. Well, it seems there was a Roger Manning living in New York from—" He paused, put on his glasses, and glanced at the papers he held. "At least from 1840, when he married, to 1882, when he died. He was an amateur artist and owned a small shop that sold art supplies. In an area known as Murray Hill." He looked questioningly at Lili.

"The East Side of Manhattan," she supplied. "In the Thirties."

Andy turned to her. "Something's suddenly occurred to me. Do we know if Amanda Manning Kent's father was named Roger?"

Lili shook her head. "I have no idea what his name was. I never had any reason to try to find out."

Mark cleared his throat. He was still looking at his papers when he said, "In 1846 Roger Manning registered the birth of his fourth child, a daughter born to himself and his wife, Rebecca. The child's name is given as Amanda."

"Bingo!" Andy exulted.

"And don't forget," Susan said, "according to Joseph's diary, his brother Roger was unhappy about being sent to America because he wanted to be an artist." She turned to Mark. "You said this Roger Manning was an amateur painter, didn't you?"

"So I did. And I, too, have had a look at Joseph's diary. There are a couple of entries that confirm that Roger had no head for business. Joseph says his brother made poor investments and lost all the money he'd been given to establish an American branch of the bank."

"Yes," Susan agreed. "Joseph sent additional funds, but when Roger lost them as well, Joseph apparently washed his hands of him. According to the diary, he never heard from Roger again."

"I'll give you odds Roger Mendoza changed his name to Manning," Andy said. "He must have wanted to be free of the family, since he'd botched things in America. So Roger Manning was really Roger Mendoza, and the father of the Amanda who lived in the house where Lili was raised, where she found her piece of the pendant."

He turned and took Lili's hand. "Looks like Mark's answered your question, darling."

"Yes, he's kept his side of the bargain." Lili freed her hand from Andy's and slipped the chain holding the sliver of gold over her head.

"Wait a moment," Mark said. "I can do a bit better. There's a remarkable amount of information in here." He gestured with the wad of paper. "It seems our people put no fewer than fifteen researchers to work after I made my request. One of them found papers and a journal belonging to Amanda Manning Kent at the New-York Historical Society."

Lili caught her breath. "I don't believe it. Amanda's papers? Things she wrote herself?"

Mark nodded.

"I never knew . . . All those years I daydreamed about her and I didn't know I could have found out so much more. I wonder why they didn't have Amanda's things in the library in Fielding."

"Apparently she returned to New York. When she died, some niece or nephew probably gathered all her things and handed them over to the Historical Society. It's not unusual, you know. Masses of private papers are dealt with in exactly the same way. They stay unread and untouched unless a researcher happens to investigate. Amanda lived an unremarkable life. No one was likely to care about her. Except us. I think—" Mark broke off. "Look, the best way to explain is to read you the whole report."

He paused a moment, then began.

New York and Fielding: 1841–1910

A few years after he arrived in New York, Roger Mendoza married Rebecca Shulman. In England, Roger's brother Joseph had converted to Christianity and joined the Church of England. Roger was not devout, but he thought of himself as a Jew. His bride was also Jewish, but it was she who suggested that since neither of them had any interest in religion, they should stop identifying themselves as Jews.

Roger, in fact, blamed his failure to succeed in business on the prejudice he'd met in New York. "It won't matter what religion we claim," he told Rebecca. "Americans think of Mendoza as a Jewish name."

"We'll change it, then," Rebecca declared. "Why don't we call ourselves Manning? And you should stop trying to be what you're not, Roger. Forget your family in Europe, let's go off and live our own lives in our own way."

A few months later Mr. and Mrs. Roger Manning left the fashionable downtown world where they were known and moved to the less affluent neighborhood of Thirty-third Street and Madison Avenue.

It was Roger who had the notion of opening an art supply store. He scraped together the last of the capital he'd been given by Joseph, and opened a small shop on Broadway, where he sold canvases and brushes and paints. This venture provided a modest but adequate income, and between 1841 and 1846 Rebecca and Roger produced four children, the youngest of whom, and the only girl, was called Amanda.

In 1870, when Samuel Kent brought her to Fielding as his second wife, Amanda Manning Kent was twenty-four. Until Sam came along, she had feared she would be an old maid. Amanda knew what had made it so difficult for her to find a husband. Despite the careful maneuverings of her parents, rumors persisted that there was Semitic blood in the Manning ancestry.

Amanda grew up knowing that this hateful suspicion was in fact true. She knew her parents had been born Jews, though this unpleasant fact was never discussed outside the most intimate family circle. More important, Amanda had always understood that her greatest responsibility was to marry discreetly. She must catch a husband who wouldn't bother to examine her pedigree too closely.

When her father chanced to meet Sam Kent and subsequently invited him to dinner, Amanda divined at once Roger's intention. She kept her eyes demurely cast down throughout the meal, but she knew that though he was more than twenty-five years older than she, the man from Massachusetts was smitten by her. The next day she asked her mother about the stranger.

"Seems he has plenty of money," Rebecca said pointedly. "And your father says he's well thought of. His wife died nearly five years past and his two daughters are married and out of the house." She sighed loudly. "Poor man recently built himself a mansion near Boston. What good's an empty mansion, I'd like to know?"

Amanda decided instantly to marry Samuel Kent, and it proved easy to do. Sam was as willing to pursue as she was to be caught.

By the time Samuel and Amanda had been married five years, she'd produced three children, two girls, followed by the joy of Samuel's life, a son whom they named Thomas. Amanda kept her secret from her children as she had kept it from her husband. Neither Thomas nor his sisters were ever told of their Jewish ancestry. Amanda had determined that the heritage was now far enough in the past to be buried once and for all.

Samuel Kent lived to the age of eighty-eight and died a happy old man in 1908. He left reasonable bequests to his daughters by his first and second wives, all of whom were now married, and to Amanda; but the bulk of his fortune and his house on Woods Road with all its contents went to Thomas, who was then thirty-three and a bachelor.

"You've become a man of considerable wealth and property," Amanda told her son soon after Samuel's death. "It's time you married."

Thomas had been managing his father's business interests for ten years. He knew to the penny exactly what he'd inherited, and that his mother's assessment was accurate. But he quite enjoyed his bachelor life and his small flat on Beacon Hill in Boston. It suited him to return to Fielding only on weekends, while Amanda continued to run the house. "We'll see," he said. "There's plenty of time."

Amanda had no intention of being used in this manner. A year after Sam's death she announced that she intended to return to New York to live with a widowed sister-in-law. She would wait another twelve months. If her son did not provide a mistress for the house in that time, it would simply have to be shut up. Thomas Kent bowed to necessity. Ten months later he married Jane Shilton of Dedham.

Shortly after the wedding, when Amanda was packing for her return to New York, she found herself thinking again of the decision she'd made when she was young. Perhaps she should tell her son and her new daughter-in-law the secret of their Jewish connections. The idea agitated her for some days, then she dismissed it. Even the now-diluted Semitic blood would be a source of embarrassment to Thomas and Jane, particularly in this small New England town. Jane might accuse Thomas of marrying her under false pretenses.

Amanda decided she must say nothing, but she would make a record of the facts as she knew them, the stories her parents' had whispered in the house on Thirty-third Street. Perhaps someday long after she was dead it would be read, and in that unknowable future, better understood.

That decision was some comfort, yet Amanda remained troubled. Despite how carefully her dead husband had disposed of his wealth, there remained another legacy, one that was solely in her gift. On her wedding day Amanda Manning's father had given into her keeping something remarkable.

"You are leaving my home, my dear, and I can no longer answer for your happiness," Roger Manning had said solemnly. "I'm giving you a painting by the English artist Constable, which is in its way very special and may someday prove of great interest. And this as well."

Roger had pressed a small, hard object into Amanda's palm. "If ever you're in great need, if you've exhausted every avenue of assistance you can think of, take this to Córdoba in Spain, and present it to the head of the House of Mendoza. No explanations will be required, mere possession will be enough. I promise, you'll be given whatever help you need, no matter what it may be."

The young bride was puzzled more by the advice than the object which she'd not yet examined. "Papa, if I were in such trouble as you suggest, how would I get to Spain?"

"That you must solve for yourself. But do it, child. Believe me, I'm not overstating the case. This is the most precious thing I own. In years gone by it has been passed from father to son, but I have never been one to believe that because things have been done a certain way they must never change. Your brothers are men who can look after themselves. As a woman, you are in greater need of protection. That is why I've decided you should have this treasure."

Amanda had slipped the token into her drawstring bag. "Thank you, Papa," she whispered as they shared a good-bye embrace. "I'll take good care of it, I promise."

Not until later, alone for a few moments in the cabin of the ferry carrying her to Boston, was Amanda able to examine the small piece of gold her father had given her. There appeared to be writing along the edge, but the alphabet was unfamiliar to her and she had no idea what it said. Amanda put the thing away, and filed its existence and her father's strange advice in the back of her mind—to be recalled if ever the need arose.

As it happened, it did not. No great trouble plagued Amanda's life, nothing sent her on the extraordinary journey her father had described. Certainly she never discussed the token with Sam. To do so would have meant she must explain the odious past. Only dire extremity would have made her do that, and fortunately there was no such circumstance. By the time Sam was dead and Thomas was married, Amanda had nearly forgotten the existence of the little piece of gold. Then she found it among the jewelry she was packing to take to New York, and realized she had not quite discharged all her responsibilities.

On the night before the last day of her tenure as chatelaine of the house on Woods Road, Amanda opened her jewel box and retrieved the little twist of tissue paper in which the piece of gold was wrapped. For long moments she held it in her hand and considered anew her decision to say nothing to her son about his secret heritage. No, she decided at last, she was right, she would not change her mind. But she would do something else that might possibly matter someday.

After midnight while all the household slept, Amanda crept down to the parlor in the dark. She was sure no one had heard her, but still she locked the door, and though electricity had recently been installed, she lit only a single candle. Then she brought one of the red velvet chairs to the fireplace and climbed up on it and took down the other gift her father had given her, the Constable. The frame was gilt and the picture was almost too heavy for Amanda to manage, but eventually, with much effort, she got it to the floor.

The struggle had made her terribly warm and she had to pause. She went to the door and listened, fearful that she'd been noisier than she thought, but there was no sound in the house. Then, working as swiftly as she could, Amanda turned the painting facedown on the carpet. As she'd hoped, there was a slight space where the frame met the canvas.

The gold token was in the pocket of her nightdress, in a sealed envelope. On the flap she had written the words, "Córdoba, Spain. The House of Mendoza." Amanda saw that the last word had smudged, but she had no writing materials with her and she did not dare leave the front parlor and risk waking Thomas or Jane. She folded the envelope as tightly as she could and kept folding until it was a very small package. This she wedged into the shallow crevice between the gilded wood and the canvas. Then, calling on all her strength, summoning it from reserves she did not know she possessed, Amanda lifted the picture, climbed back on the chair, and hung it in place.

She was satisfied. As best she could she had kept faith with both the past and the future. The rest was in the hands of God, or fate, or whatever it was that ruled men's destinies and wove the intricate tapestry that ordered life.

Mark stopped reading. No one spoke. He folded the papers and lay them on the table beside him. "I'll have a copy made for you tomorrow, Lili," he promised.

"Thank you," she said quietly. "In the meantime, you'd better have this." Leaning forward, she gave Mark her sliver of gold.

"Está bien," Manuel murmured. "Gracias, mi niña, tu también has guardado la fe."

"Tío Manuel says you, too, have kept faith," Andy translated as he slipped his arm around her shoulders. "And I wonder if you'll allow me to replace one piece of jewelry with another?"

"Andy, there's no need. The pendant belongs here with the rest of—"

He pressed a finger over her lips. "Quiet, woman, you're spoiling my big moment. It's not tit for tat. This is different." Andy reached into his pocket. "I was going to buy something new, but I remembered this and asked Mark if I could have it and he agreed. It belonged to Bess Mendoza, my four times great-grandmother." He took her hand and slipped a ring on her finger.

Lili looked down and saw a large dark red ruby winking from an elaborate setting of silver filigree. "Darling, it's exquisite," she whispered. "I hardly know what to say."

"Say you're not going to go back on your word. Right here, in front of witnesses. Say you'll marry me at the first possible opportunity."

Lili looked up. Her smile was pure sunshine. "I will. I solemnly swear it. Right here in front of witnesses."

Mark and Susan and Manuel broke into loud cheers of "*¡Ole!*" and "Hear, hear!" followed by a round of applause.

Andy got to his feet, pulling Lili up beside him, and cupped his hands to his mouth. "Oyez, oyez!" he shouted at the top of his voice. "All you ancient Mendozas with your beady eyes and your endless secrets, you lot up on the walls, did you get that? The most beautiful, wonderful woman in the world is going to marry me, so I can't be such a black sheep after all." Then he grabbed Lili and kissed her.

She heard the sound of a popping cork. Evidently Mark had known, and prepared. He produced a silver ice bucket and a bottle of champagne from where it had been hidden in the shadows of the gallery. "Don't wake all the ghosts," he admonished his brother. "This is French champagne, not Spanish cava. They may send down thunderbolts."

But they drank the entire bottle of Dom Pérignon '66 with absolutely no sound made by the portraits on the wall.

For Lili most of the next day passed in a golden haze of contentment. She loved Andy, he loved her, they were going to spend the rest of their lives together. Most of the questions that had plagued her life had been answered, the others she would simply forget. There remained burdens, scars, but she resolved not to think about them; she would not allow them to spoil her happiness.

Then, as it had so often before, the past came up and hit her in the face.

It was Susan who brought the news. She found Lili and

Andy in the Long Gallery a little after five. They were standing before the portrait of Bess Mendoza, who had died in 1807. The picture showed Bess in her prime, seated in a high-backed Jacobean chair, wearing a sumptuous gown of jewel-green velvet. "Look," Andy said before Susan could speak. "She's wearing the ring. You can just make it out against the folds of her skirt."

Susan looked. "Yes, I'm sure you're right. That's the ruby. Bess was rather an acquisitive type, always had to have the newest thing. There's some wonderful late-eighteenth-century solid silver cutlery that she commissioned. I'm going to suggest to Mark that you two should have it as a wedding present. I—" She broke off. "Oh, God, I was forgetting what I came up here to say."

"Which is?" Andy finally noticed how pale she was, how distressed she looked. "C'mon, Susan, spit it out and get it over with."

"It's Diego," Susan said. "He's here."

Lili gasped, then looked around wildly as if she thought Diego Parilles Mendoza was soon to come charging into the Long Gallery.

"Here?" Andy demanded disbelievingly. "Why the hell has he come here?"

"He hasn't said," Susan admitted. "I imagine it's to see Lili."

Andy grimaced. "Not his style. Diego sits like the spider in the middle of the web and summons the flies to him. He—"

"I'm no fly," Lili interrupted, her voice quiet and only a slight catch in her throat betraying her emotions. "Has he asked for me?"

Susan couldn't meet her eyes. "No, he hasn't. He arrived unannounced half an hour ago and now he and Manuel and Mark are having tea. As far as I know, Diego hasn't explained anything. I'm only making assumptions, but I did want to warn you."

"Thanks," Andy said.

"Does he come here often like this?" Lili asked.

"I don't think so," Susan said. "It's never happened when I've been here. He doesn't even come to Córdoba much. As Andy said, Diego tends to summon people to him."

Andy turned to Lili, took both her hands in his. "Well, do you want to go down and beard the lion when he's not in his own den? Walk right in and let him say whatever he's come here to say?"

She could tell from his tone of voice that it was what he wanted her to do. Lili didn't think she could manage it. She shook her head. "I need a little time to get used to the idea." *He's here!* a voice in her head was shouting. *He's come to see me! He does care. . . .* Another voice kept warning her to be careful, to hope for nothing so she would not be disappointed yet again.

"We'll be having drinks in the library at seven-thirty," Susan said. "Why not leave it until then?"

Lili nodded gratefully.

She dressed carefully, took enormous pains with her hair and her makeup. When she finally came out of the bathroom, Andy was waiting for her. He could read on her face everything that she felt.

"You look stunning," he said. "I was afraid you were going to wear black."

"I'm not in mourning for him or anyone else," Lili said defiantly. She'd chosen a dress of pale blue crepe de Chine with a short skirt that ended above her knees in a tumble of layered ruffles. Six months ago, in another life, Loy had found it on sale and insisted Lili buy it. Lili didn't want to think about that. "Let's go," she said.

They were the last to arrive for the predinner ritual of drinks in the library. Mark and Manuel and Susan were standing by the fireplace talking. Another man stood with them, but somehow slightly apart. When Andy and Lili walked in, he turned and stared. The conversation petered out, smothered by the tension no one could deny.

Lili walked forward into the silence, each step seeming to her as if it covered a yawning chasm that somehow widened rather than narrowed. But finally she was standing in front of her father.

He spoke first, swiftly, as if he did not intend to allow anyone to go through the charade of introductions. "So this is Liliane," Diego said in his flawless, unaccented English.

She felt Andy move closer to her side and take her hand, but she continued to look only at Diego. "Lili," she corrected him, wondering even as she did why it was so important.

"Very well, Lili," Diego agreed. "And you are to marry Andy?"

"That's right."

"Good, I approve."

Lili was speechless. Did he imagine that she cared anything for his approval, his belated blessing? She looked at his eyes, the same hazel as her own, and the cleft in his chin. She tried to find a hint of caring in his face, but Diego wore a mask of indifference.

Manuel's glance shifted from Diego to Lili. He waited— as they all waited—for Diego to say something meaningful, to acknowledge his daughter. Nothing happened.

Mark cleared his throat. "Let's go in to dinner, shall we?"

The small group moved forward en masse, playing out their appointed roles as if nothing unusual were happening. Mark indicated that Diego must sit at his right, Andy placed himself beside Lili. The food was pleasant, the others attempted to make conversation. Mark managed to engage Diego in an involved discussion of some obscure point in international banking regulations. Susan and Manuel and even Andy offered an occasional comment.

Only Lili was silent.

She heard their voices as from a distance, a background hum almost drowned out by the cacophony of voices in her head. Her ears were ringing. She felt dizzy. Once Andy leaned toward her and murmured, "Steady."

"I'm all right," she whispered.

But she wasn't. She was struggling to keep from sinking into the morass of despair that threatened to engulf her. Beneath the cover of the lace tablecloth Lili pressed her hands into fists, digging her nails into her palms so the pain would focus her, keep her aware of her own existence.

Damn him! She wasn't going to give Diego the satisfaction
of passing out or making a scene. She took a deep breath
and turned and said something to Susan about the age of the
lovely crystal chandeliers.

"They're French," Susan said, recognizing the great effort
Lili was making and wanting desperately to help her. "The
story is that Charles Mendoza, who was the third Baron
Westlake, took them in payment of a gambling debt. Charles
was a very sober type, an upstanding solid citizen until he was
nearly fifty. Then he suddenly became addicted to playing
high-stakes card games. They had to ease him out of the
business before—"

Suddenly Diego turned his gaze on the two women. "Stories," he said scornfully. "In this family we are all addicted
to the old stories."

"It's our history, Diego," Susan insisted. "Our birth-
right."

"Maybe our curse," Diego said acidly.

"You don't approve of telling the old tales?" Mark
asked.

Diego sighed. "Maybe I do. I'm not certain." He cast a
sideways glance at Lili. "What I do know is that this probing
of the past can be painful. You can never be sure what hidden
betrayals you'll find, or how you'll feel about them."

Lili opened her mouth to respond. She wanted to say that
the betrayal had not been hers, but before she could form the
words, Diego turned aside in a gesture so abrupt and pointed,
it was as if he'd told her to shut up.

The meal continued. They kept trying to pretend it was
perfectly natural for Diego to have come to Westlake, that
it was not extraordinary for him to sit at dinner with the
daughter he'd never before seen and act as if she were not
there. Lili couldn't stop herself from staring at him, but Diego
carefully avoided meeting her gaze.

Think about him, Lili told herself. Analyze him. Look at
him like he's simply another human being. That's what he
was, a man like any other, not some mythic creature out
of her past. That person—the man she'd dreamed of for
years, the man she had once imagined loving her before
she was born and putting money aside to provide for her

college education—did not exist. She'd made him up; now she would unmake him.

Diego did not look younger than his seventy-one years, but the good looks of his youth had left an aura. It was impossible to see him and not understand why Loy Perez had once found him irresistible. Of course, that was it! In a moment of revelation Lili understood why Diego had wanted to see her.

Loy was the key. It was Loy who interested Diego, not Lili. He'd come to verify the facts, to prove the truth of what Loy had told him a few months earlier in Spain. Lili wasn't important, that she was his daughter was almost immaterial. What mattered was that she was living proof that once in their many years together Loy had lied to him. Lili was some kind of exhibit, evidence for old grudges, old loves and hates.

Lili looked at him, at his profile because he still refused to turn his face to her, and she knew she was right—and something inside her, some little flower of hope that had been born a few hours ago, started to wilt and die.

The butler was removing the crystal bowls that had held fresh raspberries and cream when a young maid came to the door. Mark and Susan looked at her expectantly, but the servant stayed where she was and simply nodded to Diego. He inclined his head in what was obviously a prearranged signal, and the maid went away as silently as she'd come. They looked expectantly at Diego. He waited a moment, then spoke.

"Mark, you must forgive me for imposing on your hospitality, but I have taken the liberty of inviting another guest," he said. "She has arrived."

Before Mark could respond, Loy walked in.

❧ 26 ❧

London and Bethlehem,
Connecticut: 1982

All the men rose when Loy came into the dining room, but Manuel was the first to greet her. He went to her side and kissed both her cheeks. "I do not know why you have come," he murmured in Spanish, "but it is always a joy to see you, *mi niña*."

He turned to Mark. "You have met Loyola Perez?"

Mark inclined his head in a small formal bow. "I have."

Loy's customary poise seemed to have deserted her. She sounded distraught. "Please forgive me for walking in like this. I have no business intruding on your home and your family, but Diego insisted. He said—"

"Yes, I understand," Mark interrupted. "Please sit down. Have you eaten? Can we offer you something?"

"Nothing, thank you." Loy slipped gratefully into a vacant chair. No one thought it accidental that she chose the one beside Lili.

Lili couldn't look at her, instead she looked down at her clenched hands.

Diego cleared his throat. "Mark, once more I must beg your indulgence. If you will excuse us, I believe it imperative that Loy and I be given some time alone with our daughter."

Lili's head jerked up. At last he had put the truth into words. Did he expect her to jump up and throw her arms around him? It was too little far too late, and except for that first involuntary reaction, she made no sign that she'd heard his belated declaration.

Mark had sat down when Loy did, now he stood, as did Manuel and Susan. They left the dining room, but Andy stayed where he was. "If it concerns Lili, it concerns me." His words were edged with unconcealed belligerence. "I'm not going unless she wants me to."

"Stay, please," Lili murmured.

Diego shrugged. "As you wish," he conceded as he went to the sideboard and poured a sherry for Loy. He hadn't asked her what she wanted. He didn't have to. Diego knew, as he knew everything else about her. *"Toma, querida,"* he said quietly, handing her the drink.

Loy smiled her thanks, overlapped her hands around the fragile little glass, and took a long sip before she spoke. When she did, she addressed herself only to Lili. "I'm here because Diego thinks we must explain to you."

"More explanations?" Lili asked bitterly. "Hasn't there been enough said? I know damned well there's been more than enough done."

Loy pulled back as if Lili had slapped her.

Andy looked at Diego, expecting him to explode in anger, but the older man looked intent, not angry.

"Lili," Diego said, "listen to me." He leaned forward, willing Lili to look at him. Finally, she did.

"For the past two hours, since we first set eyes on each other, you have been waiting for me to say something. To indicate in some way that I appreciate your pain, that I recognize my role in it. But I cannot, because no one can ever truly understand another's pain. I hope you can accept that truth. I hope you can forgive me for the fact that like everyone else, I am its prisoner."

"You're asking me to forgive you?" Lili whispered.

"Yes, I am. Not because I deserve it, but because you need it. Forgiveness is not so important for me—or even for Loy," he said softly. "It is vital for you. The Mendozas are good at hating. And we always extract our vengeance. But we pay a high price for it. I do not wish to pay that price, neither does your mother. We—"

"That's something you have to understand," Lili interrupted, her voice fierce with passion. "You're not my father and she's not my mother, not in any way that matters."

"I know that," Loy said urgently. "I don't expect anything else, but what Diego says is true. Hatred is toxic. It gets into the blood and poisons everything."

Lili dropped her head, clenched and unclenched her hands. She seemed to be fighting some terrible interior battle and when finally she spoke, her words came slowly, hesitantly, the result of thoughts as yet half formed.

"I've been trying to work it out for days. What I feel. Why I don't hate you. I certainly couldn't be bothered to hate him." She jerked her head in Diego's direction. "But I don't know if I can forgive. Some of it I think I understand. You lived in a world where you were accustomed to taking charge, to making things come out as you wanted them to. Of course, suddenly finding yourself pregnant was an impossible situation. I understand that. I can even understand that you decided to give me away. At first I didn't, but the more I've thought about it, the more I've come to understand that it must have seemed like the only answer. You had to choose between me and the man you loved." Lili's eyes flicked toward Andy, then back to Loy. "In your position I think I'd have made the same choice. But—" She stopped, the words seeming to shrivel in her mouth.

Diego and Andy had become almost invisible. They had withdrawn, were hiding themselves in the room's deep shadows. What was happening here was between the two women, and both men recognized that fact.

"But what?" Loy demanded, reaching out her hands in that gesture of supplication she seemed to have used so often in recent weeks. "There's something more. Tell me. Please, Lili, I'm begging you. Don't let there be more things unsaid between us."

"Irene," Lili whispered. "Irene." The name burned her tongue, made her throat feel raw. She was shaking. "Irene is what I cannot understand."

Lili looked beyond Loy into space. It was as if she were trying to stare into the past, to see it and make it real. "It's terrible to say this," she whispered. "I'm betraying the woman I truly think of as my mother. But don't you see? It turned out fine. Irene was a good mother to me in all the ways that matter most. I have nothing to blame you for, but how could you know it would be like that?"

Despite the enormous effort she was making, Lili's voice began to rise, to grow shrill with emotions wrenched from the essence of herself. "Given the history you and she shared, how in God's name could you trust Irene to raise your child? If you cared anything at all about me, how could you do it?"

Loy's head hung forward. Her shaking shoulders betrayed the fact that she was weeping, though she made no sound. It was Diego who stepped forward and put his hand beneath her chin and tipped her face back and wiped her cheeks with his handkerchief. "Don't cry," he whispered. "Tell her. She has to know if there's ever going to be any peace in her heart or in yours."

England: 1939

On the seventh of April, on the afternoon of Good Friday, a single ray of sunlight glimmered on the sodden earth of a rainswept garden in Sussex. And before she went inside, Lady Swanning heard the first cuckoo of spring.

The house was hushed and still, as she expected. In the gun room she quickly found what she wanted, a Mauser that Emery had appropriated from a German officer in the Great War. The night before, while Emery slept, Amanda had taken the key to the sixteenth-century Jacobean cabinet where he kept his ammunition. It had been quite simple. Simple, too, to load the small snub-nosed pistol and hide it in the pocket of her tweed jacket.

Amanda returned to the long corridor, her footsteps making no sound on the Oriental carpet. Moments later she stood before the study door and looked at her watch. It was two forty-five.

Amanda was exactly on time. She smiled, then went in. Emery stood with his back to her, staring out the tall French doors that led to a walled rose garden. His broad back blotted out much of the gray light. "Damned rain's starting again," he said without turning around.

"Yes."

Amanda took the pistol from her pocket and thumbed off the safety catch. It made only the tiniest sound.

"Well, nothing for it, we have to go."

"No," she said quietly. "I don't think so. Not today."

"Don't be silly. There's no way we can—" Emery turned, an expression of annoyance on his face. Then he saw the gun. "What are you doing with that?"

She didn't answer. It seemed to her unnecessary since her intention must be obvious.

Emery and Amanda stared at each other. An ormolu clock on his cherrywood writing table ticked away the seconds. "Well," Emery said finally, "shoot if you mean to. Otherwise we'd best leave for church."

Amanda's small white hand tightened on the butt of the pistol. She felt her index finger move a fraction, but she did not pull the trigger. "It's your own fault," she whispered. "I have to kill you because you've been such a fool."

He managed a small shrug, even the beginnings of a smile. "Being a fool is not a capital offense. Besides, I don't consider that I have been. Now, will you please give me that? Safer for both of us, I think." He extended his hand.

Amanda looked from her husband to the gun. A shadow passed in front of the French doors. One of them opened. Amanda gasped.

Emery turned. "Irene, thank God! Will you please help me convince Amanda she's being very silly—and putting herself at great risk, not to mention me."

He hadn't moved from behind the writing table. Irene skirted him, her gaze never leaving his face.

Something like fear was born behind his eyes. "Irene," he murmured again. "Irene."

She reached Amanda's side. Without looking at her friend, Irene stretched out her hand. "Give me the gun."

Amanda handed it to her. "Are you going to—"

Her words were cut off by the sound of two shots.

Emery's body twisted with the impact of the bullets. The

Mauser was very small, but at such close range it had power enough to spin him halfway around. He fell not over the table but facedown on the floor.

Irene held the smoking pistol in front of her and didn't move. Amanda's body jerked and recoiled, as if she, too, had been shot. Sobbing, she collapsed at Irene's feet. "I couldn't. Oh, Irene, I simply couldn't."

"I thought that might happen. That's why I waited in the rose garden. Get up. You've got to get hold of yourself, Amanda. I'm going to leave and you have to act as if you've just discovered the body."

For a moment Amanda stared up at her oldest, her dearest friend. For a moment she clutched at the escape offered, then she shook her head. "No, I won't be able to do that either. They'll question me and I'll fall apart. I'll implicate myself as well as you and Charlotte."

She stood up and straightened her jacket, smoothed her hair. Two minutes had passed since the shots were fired. There was very little time left. Amanda grabbed the Mauser from Irene's hand. "Get out of here. Go back to your room where you were supposed to be."

Irene hesitated. She heard the steps of the servants coming from belowstairs. A second went by. Two. Amanda stared at her and Irene stared back. The hurrying footsteps grew louder. Irene opened the door and slipped into the shadowed corridor.

For the length of one deep breath Amanda looked at the dead body of her husband. Then she ran past him and let herself out the French doors and sped along the damp garden paths to where she knew Charlotte was waiting.

"That really is everything," Loy said softly. "Now you know it all."

The telling had calmed her. She spoke now in clear low tones that made her words more terrible. "I, not his wife, shot Emery Preston-Wilde. Amanda couldn't do it in the end. There's always been a wide streak of gentleness in her, of kindness. She knew he was a Nazi and prepared to be a traitor to his country. She knew what those things would cost her personally, but she couldn't be the one to mete out his punishment. I could."

Lili started to speak. Loy shook her head. "Wait, let me finish. That's the difference between Amanda—Irene now—and me. It always has been. She's basically good. When she could have simply screamed and summoned aid and accused me of murder, she didn't. Instead, she disappeared with Charlotte. All the blame immediately fastened on her and I wasn't so much as suspected. When she wanted to become Irene Petworth, I couldn't refuse. I owed it to her. Amanda had every right to my identity, as the person presumed innocent, because she was innocent."

"And the right to the child," Andy said softly, coming forward to stand behind Lili, his hands lightly on her shoulders.

"That too," Loy agreed. "But not merely for her own sake, for Lili's." She turned back to her daughter, to the only judgment that mattered.

"You must understand, you must. I gave you to Irene because I knew it was right, not because I didn't want you. Whatever it looks like now, Irene was good underneath, deep inside where it matters. I'm not, not in that way. She deserved you and I deserved the pain of giving you up—but more than that, you deserved not to have a murderess as a mother."

Loy stopped speaking. Everything had been said; now she waited for Lili, judge and jury, to pass sentence.

Shadows began to gather beyond the large windows as the long English day finally succumbed to night. Somewhere a bird began to sing. Loy had risen. She stood absolutely still, the strength of will which had shaped and determined her life an armor that both sustained and imprisoned her.

Lili was trembling, Andy could feel her body quiver beneath his fingertips. She glanced up at him, lightly brushed one of his hands with one of hers, then shook off his protective touch. "Loy," she whispered, rising and taking a step forward. "Loy."

The older woman tried to see in the half light the face of the child she'd abandoned, to read there forgiveness or the ultimate rejection of revulsion.

"Loy," Lili said again. She took another step, and finally they were in each other's arms, cheeks pressed close, tears mingling.

They stayed so for a long few moments, then broke apart. Each of them knew the past could not be undone. They were friends, not mother and daughter. Loy had paid for her crime, would go on paying for it. Her only child was not hers and never could be. That unique and extraordinary bond Loy had herself severed and it was irreparable—but they could cherish each other, and they could understand. It was enough. More than enough.

Diego cleared his throat. Lili turned to him, reminded of his presence. "One last question," she said. "When Charlotte brought Amanda to you, they told you Amanda had shot her husband. When did you find out what had really happened?"

"When Amanda proposed her great deception, the switching of their identities, I thought she was insane. I wouldn't let the woman I loved give her face to someone else. That's when Irene—Loy—told me the truth."

The past had surrendered all its mysteries. There was nothing more to puzzle about, only the future to meet.

The room was quite dark now. Diego switched on a small lamp, making a circle of warm yellow light that embraced the four of them. "Listen to me," he said, his eyes on Lili's tear-stained face, his power and dynamism vibrating in every word.

"I gave you life by accident, as it were, and it's too late for me to become a father to you. But I have something to give you now. I discussed this earlier with Manuel and Mark. They both agree that you should have it."

Diego took from his pocket the blue velvet box Lili had last seen in Mark's study. "You know what this is," he said. "It's a uniquely Mendoza thing which fathers have given to their children for generations."

He snapped open the hinged cover and lifted the pendant from its satin cushion. Since Lili had seen it last, the pendant had been made whole. When Diego slipped the chain over her head, a full circle of gold gleamed softly against her breast.

Diego reached for Andy's hand, put it in Lili's, pressed the two of them together. "Be happy, both of you. Never forget what this pendant means or how it came to exist, but don't get bogged down in the ashes of the Mendoza past. Don't be afraid of it either. Used properly, the past can make you strong. You need strength to survive"—he glanced at Loy— "but most of all you need love."

On the following Sunday morning Lili and Andy boarded a Pan Am flight to New York. Loy had left two days earlier. "I thought she might stay with Diego," Andy said.

Lili shook her head. "No. He wanted her to. He never wanted her to leave in the first place, but Loy decided to go back to Peter. She told me they had reached an understanding."

"Lucky Peter," Andy said, taking her hand. "Lucky me."

The flight was long, but pleasant and comfortable. Andy had decreed that they go first class. "You'll have to get used to being a rich man's wife," he'd told Lili in mock seriousness. He switched to his Bogart imitation, "Stick with me, baby, first class all the way."

It was early afternoon when they landed at Kennedy. "Hang on a bit," Andy said when they'd reclaimed their luggage. "I've arranged for a car, have to pick it up."

"Why a car?" Lili asked. "We only need a cab to get to the city."

"That's not where we're going."

And he'd explain no more, not until two hours later, when they arrived at the little town of Bethlehem, Connecticut. "What do you think?" he asked, driving slowly so she could observe and make a judgment.

"A nice town," Lili said approvingly, looking at the single main street, the old-fashioned shops, the inn, the lovely Federalist houses flanking the village green. "But what are we doing here?"

Instead of answering, he said, "It's a lot like Fielding, isn't it?"

"Yes, it is. Andy, have you found a house here? That country place you told me you were looking for?"

"Yes, and please don't say anything until you see it."

He had a map and he studied it, then drove a mile out of town, on to a wooded back road, and turned up a driveway marked by a bright red rural mailbox. "I bought the place sight unseen because it sounded perfect. But if you don't like it, the agent promises it can be sold again."

The house was a style known as Dutch Colonial, heir to the same heritage that had informed Samuel Kent's Fielding property. This one wasn't dark and shingled but covered in white clapboard. The shutters were green.

Andy clapped his hand to his forehead. "I screwed up. I remember now, you said your house had blue shutters. We can paint them, I'd have had it done before if I hadn't forgotten. There's a screened porch out back. I'm told there's also wisteria, but that it's past flowering now."

"It's too late in the summer for wisteria," Lili confirmed.

He recognized how subdued her reaction was, but he didn't try to force enthusiasm. "Come inside," he urged. "I've got another little surprise."

Andy unlocked the house and they walked through empty, echoing rooms, saying nothing until he identified one closed door from a note pinned to his map, and opened it with a flourish. He had revealed a large square room crammed with furniture. Lili stood and stared.

Her eight chairs were there, and the table that matched them. Next to it was the scrubbed pine table that had been in the Fielding kitchen. A dozen pieces of cranberry glass were on the windowsill, and a large assortment of familiar flow-blue china was spread on one of the tables. She recognized a scarlet velvet sofa from the old parlor in a far corner, and one of the marble-topped tables that had stood beside it.

There were numerous boxes as well. Lili lifted the lid of one of them and found it full of linens she knew had once been in the cedar-lined drawers. She turned to Andy and stared at him, speechless with amazement.

"I know it's not a tenth of what you lost," he said, "but it's all we've been able to find so far. I started the hunt after you bought the chairs. I went to see the guy who'd sold them to you and told him what I wanted. I made him, as they say, an offer he couldn't refuse. He's been very diligent. I expect he'll come up with more. At least I hope he will," he added in a low voice.

"Oh, Andy," she murmured. "Oh, my darling."

It was all she could manage, but the emotion choking Lili was not nostalgia. Her joy was not based on things, however beautiful. What filled her heart was a recognition of the love that had inspired this wildly extravagant, almost irrational treasure hunt. "Oh, Andy," she repeated.

He put his arms around her. "It's not Fielding, not the old Kent place, but will it do?"

Lili clung to him, her happiness fierce in its completeness, its totality. Finally the beating of her heart subsided and she could move far enough away from him to look up into his beloved face. "Tell me something," she said. "The absolute honest truth. Do *you* want to live here in the country?"

"I want you to be happy. I want to make that ache inside you go away, fill that place that's been hollow since you saw the hole in the ground up in Fielding."

She spoke slowly, knowing how important it was that he understand. "The ache is gone," she said. "And there's nothing empty inside me. Everything is filled." She made a wide gesture with her arm. "Not because of this, however wonderful it is. Because of everything I've learned. Because of what happened in Grasmere. Because I know what my roots really are. Most of all because of you, because we love each other."

"You're sure?" he asked. "Lili, are you really sure?"

"I'm sure. Andy, you told me to be myself, not to worry about suddenly finding out I was a Mendoza. This past week I've been able to take that in, digest it, make it mine. But you have to as well. All your life you've been driven by this love-hate thing with your family. No more. Not for either of us. You're Andy and I'm Lili—and together we're something more."

He pressed her to him, their bodies swaying to the rhythm of their combined heartbeats. When at last they broke apart, he said, "All the same, we have to have someplace to live."

"Yes," she agreed. "We do. Why not something fabulous in the city? Maybe a loft downtown near my office. I could do something terrific with space like that. This old furniture would look great."

"To me that sounds super," he said. "I love city living. But by definition it seems to imply a kind of impermanence, not like sinking deep country roots. What about your sense of place?"

"I've figured out what it really is," Lili said softly. "It's a place in my heart. I carry it with me, darling. And as long as you're in it, and I'm in it, then it's the place I want to be."

৵ Epilogue ৵

New York and Córdoba: 1984

The restorer was a renowned expert. Lili and Andy were in his shop on lower Broadway looking for perhaps the last time at the phony Constable that had hung over the fireplace in Fielding, then in Irene's house in Florida, and most recently in Lili and Andy's apartment on West Sixteenth Street. Now it was to be destroyed.

"Can you get the paint off the canvas?" Andy asked.

The other man laughed. "Sure, with something like this so could any amateur. All you have to do is pour on the chemicals and let it dissolve. I presume you know this is a crude copy. Mind telling me why you want to bother?"

"It has suddenly occurred to us that it's been painted over something important." Lili said.

For three years they'd been wondering about the yet unexplained entry in Joseph Mendoza's diary. He'd said he was sending Sofía's letter to America with his brother Roger. They had solved the mystery of what happened to Roger, but not the one about the letter. Now they hoped they would.

The restorer nodded. "Do you think there's another painting underneath?"

"No," Andy explained. "A letter or a document of some kind."

"Written when?"

"Between 1810 and 1820."

The other man made a careful note. "Any idea where it originated?"

"Córdoba in Spain," Andy said. "Is that important?"

"If you want the letter to come out whole and intact, it's vital. I make the right guess about the kind of ink your document's written in and we win, otherwise we lose." He looked at Andy and Lili. "Look, you do understand I can't make any guarantees? And when I'm done, your painting won't exist anymore."

Andy looked at Lili.

She nodded. "Yes, we understand."

The restorer hefted the heavy painting and held it to the light. "Weighs a ton. But it looks like fairly conventional nineteenth-century backing. Could be that the artist glued whatever he wanted to cover onto a piece of canvas and painted over it."

"That's what we think," Andy said.

"Right. Well, check back with me in a few hours. Maybe I'll have some answers for you."

They returned to the shop at three P.M. The restorer greeted them with a broad grin. "Here's your letter. It was glued to the canvas. The artist covered it with a layer of gesso, a kind of plaster of Paris, added another layer of canvas, and did his little picture on top of that. That's why the thing was so damned heavy, but it made getting the letter back a piece of cake."

"Roger was careful," Lili said thoughtfully.

"And obvious," Andy added. "I'll bet that's why he made it such a patent fake, why he signed it Constable. Roger Mendoza, aka Manning, *intended* his picture to raise questions. He meant it to be guessed that there was something underneath."

"Only he didn't allow for the ignorance of a small town like Fielding," Lili said. "Or what philistines the Kents were or—"

"Look," the restorer interrupted, "I have other work to do. Do you want the frame?"

Lili said she did and it was wrapped for her. Andy wrote a check. Then they were on the street, holding Sofía's letter. It wasn't in an envelope, it was simply two sheets of paper held together with a small gold-topped pin.

"Can you read it?" Lili demanded.

Andy ran his eye over the large, flowing script. The ink had faded, but it was still clear. The problem was that it was written in old and formal Spanish.

"Not quickly," he admitted. "There's a coffee shop across the street. Let's go over there and sit down with this thing."

They ordered cappuccino and Andy let his grow cold as he stared at the first page of the document. "It's not so much a letter as a testament, dated July 1835."

Slowly and with difficulty he began translating the stiff, formal Spanish. " 'I, Sofía Valon, the widow of Robert Mendoza, she whom they call La Gitanita, wish to declare that I'm a Jew. I send this to you, esteemed Cousin Joseph, because the Inquisition yet lives here in Spain, and before he died I promised my beloved husband I would remain cautious for the sake of the family.

" 'I was born a Jew in France but my life brought me to Spain and, as the Mendozas did three hundred years ago, I forgot my heritage. May the God of our fathers, of Abraham and Isaac, forgive us all, and may He accept my vow that I will make us Jews once more. All that the Mendozas possess will someday be again at the service of our people . . . ' "

Andy paused and looked at Lili.

"Incredible," she murmured.

"Makes it obvious why old Joe wanted the thing out of his house. In 1835 he was a newly minted Christian. He didn't have the *cojones* to destroy Sofía's testament, too much a Mendoza for that, but he sure as hell didn't want it around. Sending it to America a couple of years later with the feckless Roger must have seemed a perfect solution. He probably figured his younger brother would lose it, or get rid of it somehow, without involving Joseph directly in the betrayal of Sofía's trust."

"Is that all she says?" Lili leaned over to examine the words, the enormous ruby winking on her finger as she ran it over the page. It was terribly frustrating to understand nothing of what she saw. "Is that everything?

That Sofía's a Jew and vows to make the family Jews again?"

"No, there's more. She speaks of a cave of secret treasure."

"I don't believe it!" Lili was thunderstruck. "It's a fairy tale. A treasure cave? Come on."

Andy pursed his lips. "Part of me doesn't believe it either. But with the Mendozas, it may be possible. Susan told me years ago that there was a legend about a cache of things hidden somewhere in Córdoba."

"Could we find it?" Lili was almost dancing with excitement, a child suddenly transported into a fantasy made real.

Andy turned to the second page and looked up at Lili and grinned. "We can find it. Sofía's left us a map."

Lili arrived in Spain at a few minutes past eleven on a July morning, a hundred and forty-nine years after La Gitanita had penned her testament. One thing at least was unchanged: As it had in Sofía's day, the ocher land of Andalusia lay still and silent in the grip of fearsome heat.

"The golden land beneath the golden sun," Andy murmured as they got off the plane. "The poets don't mention the humidity."

A short time later Lili saw for the first time the unadorned white exterior walls of the Mendoza Palace in Córdoba. The austere façade did not prepare her for the moment of glory when the massive front doors of the Patio del Recibo were opened.

The walls of the courtyard were decorated with mosaics created by Mudejar artisans in the fifteenth century. Where the sunlight touched them it splintered into prisms of vibrant green and blue and red. Here and there trickles of lacy shade rippled off the branches of a chestnut tree like water dripping from a fountain. Beneath Lili's feet the ancient cobbles glowed as with some interior fire, a polish tread out of their depths by the footsteps of countless generations.

"It's a different world," Lili whispered. "It's magic."

•   •   •

The orange trees and reflecting pool in the Patio de los Naranjos moderated the heat. Andy and Lili and Susan sat in the shade, speaking quietly while they waited for Manuel.

"It occurs to me that Sofía did what she promised to do," Lili said. "If the Mendozas gave millions to fight the Nazis, Sofía really did put the family wealth at the service of the Jewish people."

"We did," Susan said. "And some, like Manuel, gave more than money. But it wasn't until Beth Mendoza, Manuel's mother, that the family here returned to Judaism. The Cordobés Mendozas remained Catholic for a century after Sofía wrote her testament."

"But they're Jewish now?" Lili asked.

"I suppose you're asking that old question," Andy said thoughtfully. "What is a Jew? Most of the Mendozas in Spain or England wouldn't be acceptable to any rabbi. What has happened is that the family has . . . I guess you might say 'come out of the closet.' The Jewish past has been acknowledged and admitted. Some, like Tío Manuel, are genuinely religious in one way or another. The others aren't hiding anymore."

Manuel arrived before they could speculate further. The old man walked slowly toward them, looking at the watch he wore on a chain at his waist. "It is time. Please, come with me."

They followed Manuel's tall figure, moved at his measured pace, through myriad paths and gardens to the Patio de la Reja. Andy explained that it was named for the heavy wrought iron gate that covered a shallow declivity in an outcropping of stone.

Three men in work clothes were already there; they had pickaxes and chisels and two wheelbarrows. When Manuel appeared, the men quickly took off their straw hats and waited for the signal to proceed.

Manuel nodded to them, then turned to Lili. "Everything is now prepared," he said in his labored English. "If that paper you found is truly *el último testamento de* La Gitanita, here we will find her treasure."

Speaking English obviously taxed him. He returned to

Spanish, pausing every few sentences so Andy or Susan could translate. "According to the legend, this was the ancient strong room. The Mendozas are supposed to have kept their gold here. Later they opened the first bank in Córdoba, eventually many banks. But that is enough talk. It is time to do."

Manuel took a key from his watch chain and opened the huge padlock that hung on the *reja* and removed it. Then he motioned the workmen forward and they opened the gate, slowly swinging it wide. In seconds the whole of the small grotto was revealed. There was nothing inside but dust and cobwebs.

Manuel said something and the workers went into the shallow cave and began scraping the rear wall. A few moments later one of them came back to the watchers and spoke in fast guttural Spanish. Susan supplied a running translation.

The mason was rubbing the dust he had removed from the wall between his fingers. He held out his hand. "It is, I think, sand and horse dung and lime. A coating of this mixture has been spread over the back of the cave to make it look old, Don Manuel. But underneath is mortar and cut stone. You can see for yourself."

Manuel stepped into the cave and examined the spot the man indicated. Behind what looked like natural rock there was a strata of a different color. He turned and gazed at Susan and Lili and Andy, then spoke to the masons. "Break through."

Gold, they had assumed—but what they found was a treasure infinitely more precious. They discovered a history made tangible, a record of the past that made Lili weep.

Sofía's cave was an extension of the small space behind the *reja*. In it were wonderful, incredible things, all carefully packed away in wooden kegs and barrels covered with oiled cloth. Explanations were murmured as each new treasure was unwrapped.

They found a gold seder plate and the jeweled cup reserved
for Elijah, both accouterments of the Passover service. They
found silver decorations that had once graced Torah scrolls;
silken *tallithim,* the fringed shawls Jewish men wore at prayer;
a tiny lace cap to fit an infant, worked with the Hebrew character that stood for life; a ceremonial candelabra, a menorah,
in twisted silver encrusted with turquoises, and another in
gold with garnets. They found the silent witness to a heritage
denied, sometimes despised, assembled in secret by men and
women who had kept faith in the only manner they dared.
Eventually, they found the plaque.

The two-foot-long brass rectangle was by itself in a wooden
box at the rear of the cave, wrapped in a *tallith.* Manuel
reclaimed the prayer shawl first, folding it carefully and
reverently placing it with the others. Only then did he bring
the plaque forward and hold it up to the light.

They brought the plaque to what had been a dining room, and
was now one of many small parlors, simpler and more austere
than the rooms Lili had so far glimpsed. The only decoration
was a frieze of mosaic acanthus leaves around the tops of
the walls. Her trained eye examined the muted earth tones
and the primitive design. It was unlike the Mudejar designs
she'd seen elsewhere. This was earlier work, perhaps ancient.
Susan's words confirmed the impression.

"We're in the oldest part of the palace," she explained.
"The only corner that has survived the various burnings and
sackings of the *juderia.* This is supposed to be the one room
remaining of the original structure, so it's never been touched
or redecorated. Look, you can see the mark on the wall.
According to the legend, that's where the plaque used to
hang."

Manuel and Andy carried the rectangle of brass to the
place Susan had indicated. Lili held her breath while the
two men lifted it into place. There were holes in each of
the plaque's four corners. They lined up exactly with the
four ancient nail holes in the stuccoed wall. The brass was
dulled by the tarnish of centuries, but the deeply graven
words were entirely legible.

"Im eshkachech Yeroshalayim," Manuel intoned, his body swaying slightly as he prayed in the ancient way. *"Tishkach y'mini, tidbak l'shoni."* If I forget thee, O Jerusalem, may my right hand forget her cunning.

"We've come full circle," Andy murmured.

"We've come home," Lili said, taking his hand. "We've kept faith with Sofía and the others and we've come home."

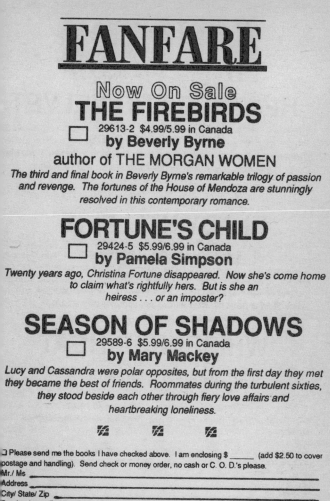

FANFARE

On Sale in MAY

HEATHER AND VELVET

☐ 29407-5 $4.99/5.99 in Canada

by Teresa Medeiros

She was an innocent lass who haunted a highwayman's dreams
"A terrific tale full of larger-than-life characters and
thrilling romance."
--Amanda Quick, <u>New York Times</u> bestselling author

LADY HELLFIRE

29678-7 $4.99/5.99 in Canada

☐ **by Suzanne Robinson**

author of LADY GALLANT

A rakehell English lord . . . A brazen Yankee heiress . . .
And a passion that would set their hearts aflame . . .
"Excellent reading." --<u>Rendezvous</u>

WHISPERED HEAT

29608-6 $4.99/5.99 in Canada

☐ **by Anna Eberhardt**

A sizzling contemporary romance.
"Sensual . . . sexy . . . a treat to read."
--Sandra Brown, <u>New York Times</u> bestselling author